PRAISE

"... a most cunningly crafted tale—a perfect read for trains, planes and automobiles... or even for your armchair."

– Madison Smartt Bell
Author of *All Souls' Rising*

"From the first story ... I knew I was in for an enjoyable ride. Goodman is a keen, compassionate and refreshingly un-ironic observer of the human condition. In *Tracks*, [he] skillfully weaves stories of chance encounters, lost opportunities and new beginnings into a tight, colorful, breathtaking tapestry which he says is a train ride, but seems an awful lot like life."

– Bathsheba Monk
Author of *Nude Walker*

"Eric D. Goodman's novel-in-stories, *Tracks,* allows the reader to journey with his characters in their moving and transforming destinies. Sincere and empathetic, Goodman delivers. These intertwined stories are melodious and brim with soulful compassion."

– Victoria Patterson
Author of *Drift*

"Who among us hasn't sat on a train and played at reading the minds of strangers? In this way, *Tracks* is a voyeuristic fantasy fulfilled. But here's the real surprise: Once you have mental telepathy, it's hard to call anyone a stranger anymore."

– Aaron Henkin
Baltimore's NPR station, WYPR

"... an absolute delight. The beautifully-written stories of strangers riding the same train will hypnotically pull you in and captivate you to the very end."

– Jessica Anya Blau

Author of *Drinking Closer to Home*

"Goodman limns the lives of his characters—all travelers on the same train—with a light and sensitive touch, yet he manages to delve deep, right to their very hearts. By turns comic and poignant, these pilgrims are united in one significant way: they all seek to make sense of life's unpredictable journey."

– Yona Zeldis McDonough

Author of *Breaking the Bank*

"...[A] wonderful debut."

– Mary Beth Keane

Author of *The Walking People*

"A terrific use of the novel-in-stories as form."

– Rebecca Barry

Author of *Later, at the Bar*

"... insightful, engaging and, in so many ways, truly moving."

– Toby Devens

Author of *My Favorite Midlife Crisis (Yet)*

"... an unforgettable journey that cuts deep furrows in both the inner and the outer landscape."

– Patry Francis
Author of *The Liar's Diary*

"... a refreshing narrative presented through deep reflections and vivid imagery that will propel readers into a page-turning adventure."

– D.L. Wilson
Author of *Unholy Grail*

"Goodman's alternating harsh and tender stories travel the spectrum of human emotion, and his care for his characters is evident from the first page to the last. By the end, we have not only lived through every character, but we are every character."

– Jen Michalski
Author of *Close Encounters*

"In the best literary tradition of *The Decameron*, *The Canterbury Tales*, and *Spoon River Anthology*, Goodman's novel-in-stories reveals the rich textures and patterns in the tapestry of human experience. *Tracks* is elemental storytelling."

– D.R. Belz
Author of *White Asparagus*

"... entertaining and thought-provoking."

– Pat Valdata
Author of *Inherent Vice*

"... a tour-de-force ... If one of the goals of great fiction is to set forth into new fictional territory, *Tracks* is that. And then some."

– Nathan Leslie
Author of *Believers*

"... reminds us of the richness of train travel."

– Gregg A. Wilhelm
Executive Director
CityLit Project, Baltimore

"Eric D. Goodman is a virtuoso."

– Nancy Greene
Author of *Portraits in the Dark*

"... a rollicking ride from Baltimore to Chicago with a passenger list of colorful characters ... well worth the price of the ticket!"

– Charles Rammelkamp
Author of *The Secretkeepers*

Tracks

A Novel in
Stories

Eric D.
Goodman

Tracks

An Atticus Trade Paperback Original

Atticus Books LLC
3766 Howard Avenue, Suite 202
Kensington MD 20895
http://atticusbooksonline.com

Copyright © 2011 by Eric D. Goodman. All rights reserved.

Printed in the United States of America. No part of this book may be used or reproduced in any manner whatsoever without written permission of the publisher except in the case of brief quotations embodied in critical articles and reviews.

This is a work of fiction. Names, characters, places, and incidents either are the product of the author's imagination or are used fictitiously. Any resemblance to actual persons, living or dead, events, or locales is entirely coincidental.

Excerpts from *Tracks*, in this or a slightly altered form, have previously appeared in *Scribble Magazine, JMWW Anthology 2, Slow Trains, Coloquio, Freshly Squeezed: A Write Here Write Now Anthology,* and *To Be Read Aloud*. Readings of some stories, abridged, have been broadcast on National Public Radio's Baltimore station, WYPR 88.1 FM.

For more information about *Tracks: A Novel in Stories*, please visit www.TracksNovel.com

ISBN-13: 978-0-9845105-7-3
ISBN-10: 0-9845105-7-5

Typeset in Scala
Cover design by Jamie Keenan

For the friends and family who have encouraged me along this exciting, sometimes treacherous line of track. You thought I could, you thought I could—and I thank you for that.

The train is empty now. Quiet. But once those doors open, it'll be a whole different story. Business people and vacationers and all sorts of travelers will stampede aboard these empty hulls and fill them with life. Every crowd is different, but somehow they're all the same. I've been working on the train since the company started, way back in the seventies—I'll probably be working the line as long as I live. So I know all about the passengers being alike and different at the same time.

There's something about a train that moves people. Harry Truman once said, "You get a real feeling of this country and the people in it when you are on a train." The President got at something there, but I'm not sure he really understood it the way I do. He rode the rails, but I live on them. My best friends are lonely travelers. I'm no scholar, philosopher, or whistle-stop politician—just a conductor who likes to talk to people. But I know a thing or two about the sort of person who takes a train.

The train has a way of transforming a person. Sometimes passengers become aware of things they didn't know before boarding. Something about the stillness on a moving train, being around people and alone at the same time. They're neither here nor there—in transition. That frees them up to do things or say things they might not ordinarily do or say.

Well, it's time. These empty cars won't be quiet much longer.

Contents

Prewitt's Plans	1
Reset	20
Futures	43
Live Cargo	65
The Silences	89
Freedom	102
One Last Hit	126
Reunion	139
A Good Beer Needs a Good Stein	159
Mountain of Sand	178
Cold Bars	199
The Deed's Doorstep	223
Seconds	235
Idle Chatter	259
She's Gone	272
New Course	292
Late Lunch	302
Acknowledgements	315
About the Author	316

Prewitt's Plans

Prewitt stood facing the closed doors of the train; he was the first in line at Baltimore's Penn Station. Dozens of passengers swarmed behind him, but even in his stillness he remained at the front of activity. To them, he knew he was just another aging businessman, too antiquated to matter. The younger ticket holders wanted to take his place, to pass him by, but Prewitt wouldn't have it. He'd planned ahead and arrived early, earning his position. He'd been here before the others had even awakened. The crowd hummed anxiously, but Prewitt remained calm as he waited with his back to them.

The train doors opened. Prewitt knew the mob behind would trample right over him if he didn't proceed immediately, so he stepped onto the train.

"C'mon! Let's move it!" A kid in a business suit nudged him with an elbow. The boy's brow furrowed, disturbing the barbell piercing it. All around Prewitt, young professionals yapped on cell phones, typed text messages, and read emails as they pushed impatiently onto the train. They reminded him of the young people who'd infested his workplace. *They can send me to a conference if they want, but they won't kick me out of the job without a fight.* The pierced boy tackled him again and Prewitt responded by slowing his pace along the aisle of the train.

Prewitt knew his unhurried stride annoyed some of the restless ticket holders in the back, but he took no more time than was fair for a seasoned businessman. He hadn't come early and stood in line for the fun of it. Planning ahead earned him a position in front. He wasn't the type to demand respect, but the sense that it was his due hovered about his modest nature.

"Times have changed," Prewitt said under his breath as it was nearly knocked out of him by another aggressive passenger—a girl with wires sprouting from her ears and an oversized purse pressing into him. When Prewitt was young, people didn't act this way. People had respect for one another instead of contempt. There was a time when you could say *hello* to those you met on a train or at the office and they'd actually hear you and care enough to return your greeting. Now, everyone was in a rush and no one had time to pay attention to their surroundings. It irritated Prewitt, turned him red in the face and made his heart beat a little too fast. Even in the narrow aisle of the train, hurried people pushed ahead of him, their purses and briefcases nearly knocking him into the empty seats beside him.

Prewitt no longer flew when he could avoid it, not since September 11. Airports seemed more trouble than they were worth. His company allowed him to travel in style; he had a sleeper car. He'd once traveled across the country in the seat of a train, but now his back couldn't tolerate it. As he walked along the center aisle, he felt connected to the passengers even as he detached himself with silence. Some of them were commuters, he could tell, and would get off in DC. Others would ride on to distant destinations. Prewitt found his compartment and escaped their frenzy.

Prewitt was particular. That is, he was a detail-oriented person. His daily planner was his compass; hardly an hour of his workday went by without consulting its pages—if not for guidance, then for reassurance and comfort. His planner, in its rich brown leather binder, rested on his lap once he'd settled into his compartment.

A satchel full of clothes, toiletries, and paperwork rested at his feet. Although he traveled light, he was already winded from the grueling grind down the aisle. A bit disoriented, he tried to regain his steady breathing pattern. Prewitt's planner kept his details in order and helped calm him.

Some details he didn't keep in his planner: he was closing in on sixty-five, a practical man who loved his wife, daughter, family, and friends. His ashen hair was cut short and side-parted in the traditional business fashion. Today he wore slate-colored pants and a matching tweed jacket. At the office he normally wore a white shirt and solid tie; today, however, he went with an open collar and a blue button-down. He wore ironed boxers. His wife, Anna, always ironed his underwear to sterilize it; she carried on her mother's tradition from the old world. Prewitt was neatly groomed and well tailored— his wife saw to that.

The whistle blew, but the train remained still. Prewitt peeked at the Swiss watch on his wrist, the silver face catching the sun from his window. It was time to go. Amtrak wasn't known for its timeliness. Even according to the company's own statistics, the trains were often late. So Prewitt did not expect to arrive in Chicago on time, and thus had scheduled himself to arrive earlier than necessary. Still, to be five minutes late before even beginning the trip did not sit well with him or his planner. Before returning his wrist to his lap, his body jerked as the train snorted, creaked, and inched forward.

Once the train had put itself steadily in motion and Prewitt was certain they were on their way, he unzipped the rim of his binder and opened his daily planner: a Franklin-Covey two-page-per-day, the original green-on-white design. Prewitt had seen the recent catalogs with the more fancy designs—flowers, seasons, jokes, cartoons, tips on being a better person or a more efficient executive—but he found those frills distracting and unnecessary. The purpose of a planner was to map the course of one's life and to make a record of it. He had no need for the pretty packaging. Prewitt opened the pages to yesterday's date so he could close everything out. The planner vibrated in his lap with the train's movement.

Pack for conference. Check. *Call daughter.* Check. *Spend time with wife.* Check. *Go to bank/handle accounts.* No, he hadn't accomplished that. He drew an arrow and carried the task over to next week. This week wouldn't do, since he'd be at the conference. Next Wednesday would be the best day. He added the task to the few items already on next Wednesday's to-do list.

Though it had never been urgent, he considered it important to put his secret savings account in both their names, in case anything should happen to him. When he'd opened the account decades ago, he'd kept it from Anna, knowing she would find an excuse to spend it. Now that they were getting older, it was time to start sharing the wealth instead of accumulating it.

He felt a nervous fluttering in his chest and took a slow, deep breath to calm it. Already he was exhausted. Poring over the things to do created tension in his neck and shoulders. He wanted to rest, but it was too early.

Now, for today. Prewitt turned the page. Some users would write today off as a useless travel day. Not Prewitt. Time was a valuable resource, he knew, and one had to use the gift of time to do the things that were important but not urgent. Even train time was important, if only for the planning itself.

Importance above urgency, he reminded himself. What Franklin-Covey referred to as "quadrant-two living." He looked at the tasks on his list. *Memorize people to meet.* Yes, there were a handful of people he needed to rub elbows with at the conference; he'd be sure to write a list and commit them to memory. *Stock considerations.* Yes, he had his portfolio pie charts and numbers with him and needed to do some serious thinking: buy more, sell everything, keep as-is? He couldn't take the risks he'd once taken, so he was leaning toward selling them, paying off the mortgage, and putting the bulk of their savings in Euros. He would certainly do some serious thinking about that today. He returned to his list.

Retirement. He looked at the word and then closed his eyes. It ran around in his head like an electric train set around the Christmas tree from his childhood. *Well, that's the biggie, isn't it?* One word, black ink boxed in green. He'd toyed with the idea of retirement for so long that it seemed a plaything, something not quite real.

He looked up from his planner and peered out the window. The urban landscape greeted him: office buildings surrounded by trees, the trees planted by the very companies that had cleared the original foliage, back when raping the land hadn't mattered to mainstream America.

Prewitt was one of those old trees. He knew the young management would gladly cut him away were it not for age-discrimination laws. They remained polite to him—the references to clearing the dead wood were subtle—but the message was there. "Is it autumn already?" and "I wish I was eligible to retire! I'd be out of here in a heartbeat!" and "So, what're you going to do when you're free of these workplace shackles?"

Prewitt had not reached full retirement age for Social Security, but he had thirty-five years in and his pension checks were ripe for the picking. His plan had been to hold on until sixty-seven, at which time he could get a slightly higher pension check to go along with his full Social Security payments. Financially, it was the practical thing to do. But he didn't need his planner to remind him the most important things in life could not be found at the bank.

Prewitt looked out the window at the boulders and trees decorating a distant mountain. He never questioned the big rocks, the most important things in life. Yet he realized, looking back through the years, that he'd given far too much time to work and not enough to those he cared about. In the big picture, family always came first. Day-to-day, family was at the bottom of the list.

Retirement would remedy that. Like a cradle, the gentle rocking of the train eased him and made him want to nap.

Looking away from the window, he returned his attention to the planner in his lap. He wrote a list on the right side, on the page for notes. *Cons: reduced Social Security; reduction in pension; two years less salary; fewer contributions to 401k.* He looked at the list and realized these were all financial matters. He began a new column. *Pros: freedom; more time with Anna, Suzy, family, friends; time to read good books, see movies; time for theater, opera, symphony; time to meditate, relax, pray, travel. Move closer to Suzy.*

Anna had nearly broken down when their daughter and her husband moved away. Rusty had found the career of a lifetime working for a British company in Russia.

"Suzy, you can't do this!" Anna had a way of blowing things out of proportion. "You can't go live on the other side of the Iron Curtain! It'll kill your father!"

"Now Anna," Prewitt had said in his calming voice. "Those days are gone. It's fine over there. Besides, this isn't about me or us. They have their lives to live."

"Lives without us?"

"Mom, we're not leaving you," Suzy had assured her. "We're only an email away."

Anna threw up her hands. "An email! Not even a phone call!" She frowned at Prewitt. "I don't know how you're taking this sitting down! You're going to let her go?"

"Why don't you sit down?" Prewitt suggested, reaching up and placing his soothing hand on her forearm. "It's not the end of the world."

"It's the *other* end of the world!"

"Mom!"

Prewitt tossed a gentle look to Suzy that told her not to worry, that everything was fine, that it was just Anna's temperament and they both knew it would pass. But the truth was Prewitt wished

Suzy would stay. He wished his daughter was innocent again, sitting in her room and playing with her dolls. Back then, he'd spent more time focused on her future than her present. Now that she was attached to another man and in another country, he wished he could re-plan the past.

They were right to go. But it had been five years, and Anna and Prewitt had managed to visit them only once. It was a long trip. Without the trappings of a career, Prewitt figured they could actually get a seasonal apartment outside Moscow, live near their daughter, and help raise their grandchildren and watch them grow.

"If you'd invested in gold and diamonds instead of Internet stocks, we'd have been retired years ago," Anna had griped while driving him to the train station.

"I've always admired your perfect hindsight," he responded.

She laughed. "If hindsight meant anything, would I be wearing these glasses? I'd have perfect vision." She handed him his own pair of reading glasses from the compartment between their seats. "Better attach these to your head so you don't forget them."

Anna had once joked that without his planner to remind him of things, he may already be diagnosed with Alzheimer's. He'd played along, asking her who she thought she was talking to him like that and then consulting his planner to remember. But sometimes he wondered if there wasn't some truth to her words.

"Be safe," she'd said after they pecked one another goodbye. He left her in the car and entered Baltimore's Penn Station.

Now, in his compartment, Prewitt unpacked the bag of food Anna had prepared for him. He ate a sandwich, a bran muffin, and an apple. His bottle of decaffeinated tea reminded him to take his blood pressure and heart pills; last year, the suggestion he switch to decaf came with his new prescriptions. He'd felt safe enough when he only depended on his planner. Depending on medications and diet made him uneasy. He took some paperwork from his satchel and began to work between gazes out the window.

He could imagine his co-workers laughing about him now. "The old man took a ream of paperwork with him on the train! He can't give it a rest!" Of course, Prewitt knew his work ethic was something from the past. How many times had he walked by the team leader's cubicle on his way to the bathroom during his designated fifteen minute break only to find the kid playing a video game or looking at lewd women on MySpace? It was sickening how lazy most workers were today. Even his manager was a loafer, doing as little as possible, just enough to get by.

Once they were in West Virginia, Prewitt needed to stretch. He left his bag in his room but carried his planner at his side like a schoolboy's textbook. He imagined meeting someone exciting in the lounge and inviting her back to his sleeper car, but he knew he could never do a thing like that. He and Anna were more likely to play matchmaker than mate taker.

Once, at an office Christmas party, the guest of a young co-worker mistook him—the oldest person there—for the boss. She asked for a private tour of the office.

"I don't think that would be appropriate."

She batted her long-lashed eyes. "I'm really interested. Please?"

He'd submitted, and took her into the dimly-lit corridors of cubicles. Once they were beyond view of the hearty party, she'd advanced, planting a kiss. Her tongue was exploring his mouth before he could ascertain what was happening. He pulled away. "I'm sorry, but this isn't right. I'm a married man."

Of course, the story she told her boyfriend after the party was that he'd made a pass at her. He was the butt of jokes for the entire first week of the new year. "Trying to put in some overtime, dirty old man?" and "Looking to firm out your job duties?" and "What happened, did your wife slip some Viagra in your coffee?" Prewitt knew it would be worse for the girl than it was for him if he told the truth. She'd become engaged to the guy. He simply said that nothing had happened, and left it at that.

Arriving in the lounge car, Prewitt discovered that the train didn't carry his favorite beer, Baltica, one suggested by Rusty during their visit to Russia. Some of Baltimore's liquor stores carried it, but on the train he settled for an American beer—crisp and refreshing—and took a seat in the lounge.

Early afternoon had arrived, and already the lounge had filled. Passengers came and went, restless in general seating or lonely in their compartments. An attractive woman sauntered by and Prewitt looked at the tempting tattoo on her lower back, revealed between her tiny blouse and low-cut jeans. Prewitt remembered a time when that space was considered private. The elaborate design spread from one hip to another and resembled an open planner, covering the area above her bottom. Involuntarily, he felt his heart race and forced himself to look away.

An older woman—too old to be traveling alone—drank a screwdriver and took deep breaths, the fear upon her face melting as the drink soaked in. There were young people in the lounge car too. A couple—probably teenagers—sat silently together, the love between them as clear as the bottled water they drank. They reminded him of the first years with Anna, when every day had been exciting and new. Another woman, seated in the corner, seemed to have lost love; her teary eyes read over what looked like an old love letter on fine stationery.

At the back of the car sat a man—a boy, really—in an army uniform, a distressed look pressed on his face. An older couple sat together, sipping iced tea. They looked German, or their parents must have been, their features chiseled and angular. It occurred to Prewitt that, fifty years ago, the young man in the army uniform might have openly killed these two, or people like them. Now he'd probably kill Iraqis instead.

Prewitt stopped people-watching and focused on his question. *Retirement.* He may have allowed the consideration to slip away had it not been written there on his task list, the pros and cons balancing on the opposite page.

Already, he missed his wife, just as he missed his daughter who resided on the other side of the world. It wasn't a painful want—he knew he'd return to his wife in a matter of days and that he'd see his daughter again in another year. The missing came as a slight, repetitive itch in need of scratching.

Anna hadn't been thrilled about this business trip when she found out last week. "Another conference?" she'd asked with annoyance. "Do you have to go?"

"Yes," Prewitt had said. "It's my job. What can I do?"

"You can quit and live by *our* schedule instead of theirs!"

"Another year and you'll have me all to yourself, Anna."

"You'll kick the bucket before you drum up the courage to retire."

"Then the suitors will line up at the door to take my place."

"Oh, Prew."

He hadn't been able to tell whether she was angry or sorry.

There had been a lady at the office in her eighties who worked until the day she died. Bessie had a husband and grown children. "But there's no way I could spend all day, every day with that bunch," she'd said with a cheery cackle. "It's not that I love my job and don't want to leave it. It's that I love my family too much to spend every blinking minute with them. It'd drive us all to our graves."

At her graveside, after the funeral service, Prewitt met the broken widower and grown, weeping children. They seemed to regret Bessie's decision. They'd have been happy to have her to themselves for a few years.

The effects of the beer amplified the train's movement. He knew he shouldn't have a second, but he felt like it, so he did. Prewitt caught himself staring out the window at the trees. He'd been through the area in spring, when the trees had been green and lush. Now their colors had changed, were changing still. Some excited red and innocent yellow, others calm orange and decrepit brown. Some were naked already. For the others, the leaves were numbered. They would all be bare soon, buried beneath a blanket of snow.

The moving locomotive allowed no time to focus on any individual tree. Like the pages of his life, the scenery passed too quickly to fully grasp. He turned from the window and from the strangers around him. He refocused on his plans.

Another item on his task list for today's considerations: *Twenty-fifth*. Next month, Prewitt and Anna would celebrate their anniversary. He wanted to plan something special, take her out for a nice dinner and possibly a show. He'd have to see what was going on in Baltimore that evening at the Lyric, Hippodrome, or Meyerhoff.

It seemed strange, but Prewitt imagined they were likely to have another twenty-five years together after he retired. He didn't expect it, but they did need to be prepared. People were living longer than ever; many now lived to be more than a hundred. *It's not a stretch to hope for the nineties.*

Prewitt looked up and imagined another life stacked on top of the one he'd already lived. With a little planning, the final act could be even better.

That made Prewitt think of a Paul Simon lyric; Anna had tuned the car radio to the song when she drove him to the station. *The thought that life can be better is woven indelibly into our hearts and our brains ... like a train in the distance.* He sighed and wished he was still in the car with his Anna. He longed for his daughter to be in the back seat. How he'd love to hear Suzy ask over and over again, "Are we there yet?"

Across from Prewitt, a young man scribbled in a spiral notebook with a stubby pencil—the scribblings of a poet or inventor, Prewitt guessed. A stocky man in a brown leather jacket sat with a cup of coffee and fidgeted with an unlit cigarette as he watched a gentleman with silver hair reading note cards. Prewitt generally liked people, but he didn't care for the silver-haired man. This gleaming reader in his gray suit and silver tie reminded him of his company's new management. The man didn't look lazy, like many young workers, but he probably didn't know what real work was. He emanated a smug pride that said *I know more than you, I have more than you, and I'm a better person for it.* The guy might as well have had a star tattooed on his belly. People like this had themselves fooled. The man may have been richer and smarter, but he certainly wasn't better. Prewitt looked back at the working-class man in the leather jacket. That guy probably had a work ethic.

The intricate tattoo lured Prewitt's gaze again as the slender woman passed by and left the lounge. From this angle, the design looked more like the shadow of a vulture than a planner, with wings spreading from hip to hip.

"You like to get away, don't you?" his wife had said a few days ago. "To get a vacation from me?"

He knew that she knew better. He wanted to be away from the spoiled brats at his office, not his wife. Now, on the train, he realized his fault, but at the time, her words had touched a nerve already exposed at work. "Sure, Anna," he'd said with an irritated sigh. "It's easier to have affairs away, in other cities. Fewer complications." It sometimes seemed easier to mock her irrational gripes than to manage them.

Anna had played along. "Then I'll have to let the FedEx man know it's time to deliver another package," she'd said calmly. In recent years, theirs was an unspoken love. It lived in the silent moments between them.

What's happened to us? The answer came to him as soon as the question formed in his mind. *We know one another so well, we can read each other's thoughts before they're spoken.*

Prewitt decided that, as soon as he got back home from Chicago, he would tell her all the things she already knew but hadn't heard in far too long. He opened to the day he was scheduled to return and wrote *Heart-to-heart with Anna.*

A few seats away, a young woman—probably about Suzy's age—talked with an older man—probably his own age—about her boyfriend. She exuded generation X nonchalance as she told the stranger how she'd sacrificed her fiancé to pursue a career in Chicago, as though it were an honorable thing to dump someone for a professional prospect.

The older man, in a light blue blazer and red tie, raised a dull, yellow mixed drink to her white wine. "You made the right choice," the man said. "In my experience, long-lasting relationships never last long." The two laughed. Prewitt knew a con artist when he saw one. He usually didn't meddle, but he had an urge to enter this conversation, to ward off the wolf. Remaining in his seat, he broke in.

"They do if you want them to."

"Huh?" the man turned to face him. The young lady looked as well.

"My Anna and I have been married twenty-five years," Prewitt said. The two looked at each other, then back to him. "Happily," he added.

"That's great," the young woman said. "Congratulations."

Prewitt saw that he needed to clarify his meaning. "I mention it because I overheard you talking about your boyfriend."

"Oh, Craig," she dismissed. "He's history."

Prewitt smiled. "Of course, I don't know the details. But think about it. You may live to regret it."

"You think?" she asked. "I mean, I invited him to come with me. He wouldn't."

The man between them excused himself to get another drink.

Prewitt smiled gently. "Just consider carefully what you're planning. You might be making the right choice, depending on who this guy is that you left behind. But at the end of the line, success is measured in love, not money—in people, not position."

She laughed. "Yeah, but you don't know Craig."

"Just remember, an ideal relationship is based on compromise." Prewitt smiled. "Consider your plans carefully."

As she finished her wine, she seemed to be absorbing his advice as well. "Thanks. I will." She smiled at Prewitt, then slipped away.

The train jerked around a bend. Prewitt wondered why he'd been compelled to tell this young woman to put family above finance. The impulse to counter bad advice had been hard to resist.

The last time Suzy had asked for his advice, they were at a Mongolian barbeque in Moscow. As she and Rusty told Prewitt and Anna about their adventures finding an apartment in the world's most expensive city, Prewitt half-listened, distracted by the bill to come, tallying the costs of their entrees and converting rubles to dollars in his head.

"So should we get the dacha, Dad?"

Startled, Prewitt stopped calculating the tip for the bill they'd not yet received and refocused on Suzy's inquisitive expression. She and Rusty sat across the table with red and black lanterns casting an otherworldly glow upon them.

"What's that again?"

"The weekend cottage. Should we get it? We could show you if you weren't headed back so soon. It's two hours away by train, but the kids need a garden to run around in on weekends."

"If you can afford it, I think it's a good idea," Prewitt had said without taking the proper time to examine the pros and cons. Why was it that he planned so hard to make moments like that one, but when he got to them, he wasn't fully there, already planning the next one?

Time slipped away; late afternoon inched into twilight—late enough for whisky. Since the train was in Kentucky now, traveling alongside the Ohio River, Prewitt ordered a Jim Beam Kentucky Bourbon.

A loud voice carried across the lounge. "You know why this line's called the Cardinal?" The train conductor in full uniform—blue cap and all—made conversation with the couple Prewitt had taken to be German. Fritz and Mary, he overheard. They spoke without accents.

"Why?" asked Fritz.

The conductor smiled. "Well, I'll tell you why. It's named for the official bird of every single state and territory it travels through!" He spoke with excitement, as though delivering the punch line to a complicated joke. "Washington DC, Virginia, West Virginia, Kentucky, Ohio, Indiana, and Illinois! Official bird's the cardinal, every last one of 'em!"

Glad I'm from Baltimore. Prewitt laughed to himself. *At least the oriole's original.*

"We're traveling in the same direction as the old B&O line," the Amtrak employee said with a cheerful smile. The conductor knew how to mingle. He must have been in his early seventies, probably ready to retire himself. "The B&O went from Baltimore through Ohio to Chicago. Just like the Cardinal."

Prewitt considered. *Six states and a territory weren't enough; had to go and name a train after the bird too.* When creativity ran dry, they just retried what had already been done. Movie remakes, sequels to books by authors long dead, taking an old television show or comedy skit that was lackluster the first time and pumping it into a full feature—people were too lazy for originality. *Better to retire than to keep trying and failing miserably.*

The conductor wiped his bald head with a red handkerchief. He returned the cloth to his back pocket and the cap to his head. "Yes sir, I can remember when Amtrak was just getting started, back in the seventies. Less'n two hundred trains, just over three hundred destinations. I was one of the first few hundred employees."

"Wow," Mary said.

"Now we've got five hundred trains and we cover most states—twenty-two thousand miles of track with just as many employees. And I was one of the first!"

"That's really something," Fritz said.

"When I started working this line, I never expected to be here almost forty years later. Lord, no. I figured I'd work a few years and get out as soon as I could rub two nickels together." The crow's feet around his eyes danced as he laughed. "Of course, a nickel bought a lot more back then."

"That's true," Mary said. "Can't buy much with pocket change these days."

"Nope, not at today's prices," the conductor agreed. "Why, I remember when you could buy a hamburger and fries for a nickel." He caught Prewitt watching them, latched onto his gaze and held it. It seemed the conductor was trying to direct him in. Prewitt broke away and looked down to his planner. He found the conversation interesting enough to listen to, but he didn't want to have to contribute. He felt overburdened already.

"Are you looking forward to retirement soon?" Fritz asked.

The old man in the Amtrak uniform laughed an empty, sad laugh that made Prewitt look back up from his planner. "Oh, you know. You spend your life doing something for so long, spend your time talking about retiring with your co-workers and thinking about it like it's the reward at the other end of a tunnel. Then, when the time comes, what's there to retire for? I'm doing what I do, what I've always done, what I like to do. Working the line."

He smiled to soften his words, to allow himself to say what he felt like saying, wanted to say, needed to say to anyone who cared enough to ask. "Not much good for family life, working on a train. Gone from home most of the time. The train became my home. Never got married. Couldn't find anyone who'd put up with me being gone all the time. Guess you could say that marriage, for me, was swept away by the steel breeze. So the time comes to retire, and what do you retire to? Leave the life you know and love just to go and be alone?" His audience fidgeted uncomfortably. The conductor shook free of his tangent. "Well, I hope you enjoy the ride as much as I do," he said cheerily. But as Prewitt watched the old man leave, their eyes met again just long enough for Prewitt to recognize regret in them.

Prewitt returned to his private room. Back in seclusion, he thought about the old conductor, an original Amtrak man. He wondered whether Amtrak had tried to push him off the train, into retirement. Prewitt found himself hoping they wouldn't, because they needed to keep him on, for his own sake. Besides, wasn't a working retirement the most cost-effective sort of plan from a company's point of view?

Prewitt knew he was fortunate. Work was work; family was life. As he looked at the countless tasks in his planner, he realized work had put an enormous tax on him and his family. He turned to the day he was scheduled to return to work after the conference and wrote one word on the daily task list: *Retire*.

Not that he would forget, but writing it down helped make it real. An abstract *retire* floating in the back of his mind like smoke from a train's stack was not concrete; the key was to pin the task down, make it precise. *Some say the devil's in the details; deliverance is there too.*

Prewitt looked through the pages of his planner. Decorating his calendar with events had become an event in itself. In fact, on busy days, he even scheduled an hour in his planner for planning.

Tension built in his neck as he became overwhelmed by all of these countless tasks that never seemed to end. He came across one that lightened his mood: *Heart to heart with Anna.* He took a deep breath and looked out his window at the landscape speeding by. *Why wait?*

His cell phone was for emergencies only, but he decided to use it now. He dialed home, only to hear his own voice coming back to him on their answering machine.

"Anna?" he asked as though he expected her to respond. "I'm still on the train, but I ... just wanted to see how you were doing."

He paused. "I miss you, Anna." The machine beeped and cut him off. He hadn't said what he'd called to say, so he pressed the redial button. "Anna, it's me again. Call me when you get this. I love you." Again he paused, hoping to hear his words echoed in her voice. After the machine beeped once more, he hung up. Reflexively, he took up his pen and began to check off the task. Then he laughed at the absurdity of considering such a thing "done."

He looked at his watch. It was early, but he wanted to rest. He placed his planner on the table, open to this day. Most of the tasks were checked off, some were not. He wondered if they'd ever all be checked off. *Not as long as I live. Planning's just a part of life. There'll always be more to do than time to do it. Otherwise, what's the point?*

He thought about that for a moment. "What *is* the point?" he asked his planner as it looked up at him from the table. He imagined the twelve volumes of planner pages back in his office, the heavy binders overtaking an entire shelf. Retirement sounded like the best plan he'd come up with in years. He decided to do more than plan it. He would go into the office next week and tell them he quit. "And I won't even write it down!"

The idea emboldened him. He looked at the open book on his bedside table as though he expected it to object, but it just lay there. "Maybe I don't even need you anymore. Not if I'm retiring." He lifted his planner and realized just how enormous and heavy it was, filled with all its nagging lists. "What does a retired man need with a taskmaster anyway?"

Trembling with excitement, Prewitt broke the posted rules and opened the window to his compartment. He half expected an alarm to go off or for the train to screech to a halt. The wind blew his ashen hair and the pages of his planner fluttered violently. He hurled the planner out and then lunged forward to close the window, as though the planner might fight to get back in.

"There!" he said of his spontaneous act. He let out a heavy lungful of breath and plunked down to his bunk. "It's done."

Prewitt continued—for the time being—to proceed in the wrong direction, toward Chicago. He decided that as soon as he got to the Windy City, he'd change the date of his return ticket and go back to Baltimore early.

Out of habit, Prewitt reached for his planner to make a note of the change. His chest tightened. He fidgeted with his thick hands and stared at the speeding scenery outside. Standing up to his planner had felt good. Now, he indelibly wished he could sit down with it. He'd cut away a vital organ.

Everybody loves the sound of a train in the distance.

Prewitt looked at his watch. If the train was anywhere near its scheduled timetable, there would be a stop in half an hour. He would get off, exchange his return ticket for the next train available, and return home to Anna straightaway.

His heart pounded and his breath was heavy with excitement, but Prewitt assured himself that he was headed in the right direction, that for the first time in his life, he had his priorities in order.

Reset

Gene Silverman eased back into his seat to enjoy the ride. He rode the rails so often, sometimes he felt as though his heartbeat had reset to the rhythm of the train. The cars were different, the destinations varied, but the similarities were stronger than the differences.

A window seat was the best kind to have. A seat on a train without the window view was like a virgin martini: what was the point? There was more to drinking than taste, more to travel than destination. There was the ride, and that was the better part of it.

Gene peered out the window. Oaks and maples waved to him in autumn hues. A pair of squirrels circled up a trunk, packing away acorns. The scenery outside his window had become an old friend. It was relaxing, attractive—but less so when seen through the countless miles of dust and grime shading the train's window. The dirt looked better on the ground where it belonged.

"Morning," the conductor said, breaking Gene's train of thought. "Ticket please?"

"Yep, right here." Gene took the ticket from his briefcase and handed it up to the man, who was riding the movements of the train like a seasoned pro. The uniform was what people saw first, Gene realized. He had learned—out of necessity—to look beyond packaging to see the person hidden inside. This guy looked like a career man, pushing seventy, skin as dark and coarse as the grime on the train's windows. A decent blue-collar man all the way. The conductor's aged eyes glanced at Gene's chrome briefcase on the empty seat.

"There's a lounge car up front." He handed back the punched ticket and placed a paper marker in the slot above the seat. "In case you need an office with a view."

Gene smiled. "Maybe later." For now, the view from here was just fine. He looked back out the window to see a stretch of garbage-littered field. In the distance, dilapidated warehouses with soot-covered stacks stubbornly held their places. He wondered what sort of hideout a place like that would make, should he ever need one.

A woman strolled down the train's open aisle and pulled his attention back inside. He admired the striking tattoo coloring her lower back. He longed to see beyond the area revealed between her short shirt and low-cut jeans. He figured she'd make a fine prostitute. He knew all about prostitutes. He knew their comforts as well as their profits, knew how to work them, how to enjoy them, how to make money with them and spend money on them. He knew prostitutes as well as he knew gambling, as well as he knew drugs. In part because he enjoyed them, but primarily because it was his business to know them.

For most, it was the other way around: pleasure first or pleasure only. But Gene had learned to partake in the pleasures he profiteered. That is, he came to the vices first as a way to make money, then learned to enjoy them. Of course, he'd done his time in the field before making money in it. But at the climax of his criminal career, *money* had flowed.

Now his money didn't come from the prostitutes, drugs, or gambling as it once had. It came from his knowledge of the vices, from his expertise. Now, he made his money as an activist and speaker.

Gene took a legal pad out of his briefcase. Paper-clipped to the pad were the notes he'd used at his last speaking engagement, the same ones he planned to use at the next. The nation was filled with small groups of citizens who wanted to see these vices legalized, and they wanted it enough to pay his lecturing fees. These interested parties paid for his travel, lodgings, and expenses. They offered him a comfortable life and a good amount to sock away for an early retirement.

He stared at his notes, not really seeing them. He considered his absurd resumé with a laugh, a resumé he'd never actually print out; it existed only in his head: *Gene Silverman. Education: Bachelor's in Computer Science. Employment: Head Geek of Hardware Helpers, mafia IT man, identity thief, political activist, and speaker. Areas of expertise: computers, information technology, organized crime, Internet fraud, drug trafficking, gambling, and prostitution profiteering. References: Available at your own risk.*

The train screeched around a bend, the rhythm changing from that of a rocking cradle to a jarring vibration. Startled, Gene shot to his feet and looked around. The passengers sat in their seats, reading, chatting, watching their DVD players, playing solitaire on their laptops. A couple of guys—one of them apparently dim-witted—even played Uno with a real deck of cards. Gene chuckled and sat back down. The sharp turn got him every time.

Each stretch of track had its own sound, its own feel, and he'd become familiar with them all, like favorite songs from a play list. On the other hand, every set of passengers gave the train new life. In Gene's experience, although the movements and courses of the locomotives were alike, no two trains had the same essence.

Gene peered around the car. Trains were safe. Finding nothing out of the ordinary, he pushed back his seat to relax for a moment. He remained content in his seat, but he knew that contentment didn't last. Always on the move, he wasn't prone to fall into the comfort of a place—that was dangerous. The seat he now occupied served its purpose, but in a few hours he would be done with it and it would be time to move on.

Gene's speaking engagement in DC had gone well. It was the closest he'd ever come to returning home to Baltimore for a public event. He'd been away from the old fraternity longer than he'd been in it. With ten years between him and his old life, he was no longer consumed by his fear of being followed. Caution remained a habit, but he'd learned to ease his way back into public life, had fallen into his current position, and felt relatively safe making public appearances.

He towered over the lectern and waited for the applause to subside. "It's about choice," he declared. "As long as you're not hurting anyone, there's no reason you shouldn't be able to do what you want to do with your lives! It's time to keep *their* legislation out of *our* leisure!"

Much of the crowd loved him, hung on his words. Of course, most of them were here in this private clubhouse because they agreed with what he had to say, because they'd paid him to say it. This was his core audience: the people who wanted to legalize the vices that caused more problems as illegalities than they would as legal pastimes. Only a fraction of the crowd consisted of the curious and the invited guests, people who weren't completely on board. The rest were all his.

Gene put up his hands to stop the applause—must have been close to a hundred there—and spoke with the fervor of a southern preacher on revival Sunday. "And that, my friends, is why we must fight to legalize gambling, recreational drugs, and prostitution on a national scale," he called out. "Partaking in or avoiding these activities is a matter of choice, and that choice should be left to the individual. Making them a crime does not stop people from doing what they're going to do. It only costs the taxpayers money in enforcement—money better spent putting more cops on the streets to protect the citizens of our great nation from *real* criminals, money that could be used for treatment and therapy for those who have real problems. Criminalizing the casual use by those in control is not the answer. Treating those who have no control over their vices—be it alcohol, drugs, sex, gambling, or cigarettes—is far more effective."

Gene greeted the cheers of agreement with a subtle smile. He thrived on the energy of such groups, and if he let his true feelings show, he'd beam. But Gene knew how to look professional, political even. He maintained a youthful energy, still hanging on to his thirties. He knew when people looked at him on stage, they didn't see age; they saw the youthful, timeless features of a news anchor or junior senator, the wisdom of a leader who could bring attention to their ignored cause and get it on the national agenda. In his deep gray, three-piece suit, silver tie, and crisp white shirt, he represented fresh energy. He smiled and put his hands up so they'd let him conclude.

"I urge you all to take action, to make our opinions heard! Talk to your community leaders. Write, call, and visit your senators, congressional representatives, even the President, to let them know what you think and how strongly you feel about it. With your help, with our combined efforts, we can make this happen! You can give this movement the momentum it needs to succeed!"

Gene also knew what most winning politicians knew: that the key to winning a crowd was to remain vague. It was hard to agree with *Legalize Cocaine Now*. But who could argue with *It's About Choice*?

"When it comes down to it, my friends, it's about choice," Gene said. "*You* should decide what's best for you—not the government."

There had been more people at the start. They'd stayed with him during his talk about legalizing gambling on a national scale. He'd lost a few when he started talking about medicinal marijuana, and he'd lost a few more when the subject of decriminalizing recreational drug use came up. But a dozen or more people walked out when the subject of prostitution had arisen. He scanned over the remaining crowd and opened the floor to questions.

"I can understand marijuana," a man called out. "But what about the hard stuff? Do you really advocate recreational use of cocaine and heroin?"

"I advocate the *legalization* of it," Gene answered without faltering. "I'll tell you why: because it's your choice. If you're not hurting anyone else, if you want to fool around with a dangerous substance yourself, that's your choice. You, sir, should not be dragged from your home, from your family, and put into jail because you decide to try a line of coke, because you've always wondered what it was like. Or because you already know, and you like it. It's your choice."

"But it's highly addictive," a woman yelled out.

"Yes. So are cigarettes. So is alcohol. And food, for that matter." He eyed the dissenter, a chunky woman who could use a little cocaine, in his estimation, to speed up her metabolism. "People have problems with coke, legal or not, just as people have problems with sweets, fast food, cigarettes, and liquor. Spending money on jailing people with these problems does not solve the problem. Offering treatment does. Next question?"

A young woman spoke next. "You said legalizing prostitution would make it safer. That don't seem right. Legalizing it would make it more popular, and that would cause more diseases to spread. What about that?" As Gene watched her, he figured she was probably a prostitute in fear of losing out on the high wage illegality offered.

"Well, dear, prostitution isn't exactly safe now. If it were legal, it could be institutionalized. Prostitutes could undergo regular testing to ensure they're safe, for their own health and the health of the customers. So while you're probably right—that making it legal would make it more popular—it would also cut back on the spread of venereal diseases and HIV infection."

"And it'd be cheaper!" cheered a young man with enthusiasm. Laughter fluttered from the crowd.

"Actually," Gene contradicted him, "I don't think we'd see a significant reduction or inflation in prices; I think the prostitutes and pimps would get less money per trick, but there'd be greater volume. Plus, the government would surely tax the service as heavily as they do gasoline and cigarettes, and that would make up any difference in the market adjustments, as far as the customer is concerned."

A young man spoke out. "My grandmother goes out of state to the casinos every couple months and blows the better part of her Social Security check on slot machines. Making it legal everywhere is just opening it up to people with gambling problems."

"Again, treatment is the answer, not making the activity illegal. You said it yourself: your grandmother finds a way, even when it's not legal where she lives. Those with the problems have the problems either way; making it legal allows everyone to enjoy the choice without the judgment of the government."

"What makes you such an expert?" a man asked.

A steely smile crossed Gene's face. "Experience, my friend. I worked at the hive, pimped the prostitutes, rigged the gambling rackets, dealt the drugs. I know because I was *there*. And I know that everyone who wants it gets it anyway; there's no reason for the inconvenience and expense of making it a crime."

A sultry-looking woman toward the front of the crowd caught his eye and offered a question of her own. "So does your endorsement of legalized prostitution mean you have a thing for prostitutes? Or need one for the evening?"

"Not necessarily," he said with a gentler smile. "But we can discuss it further at the reception." This seduced a hum of laughter from the audience. "Thanks, everyone! And remember, pleasure is not a crime!" He left them cheering this mantra—*pleasure is not a crime!*—as he stepped down from the podium and waded into the comfortable pool of supporters. Gene was charged by such events, but the excitement was laced with paranoia. As he eyed the crowd, he always half-expected to see someone with a gun pointed at his head. The feeling of a president or pope. The plight of a person who'd abandoned the underworld.

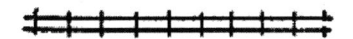

Gene used to be Eugene, before he changed his name from Eugene Beckett to Gene Silverman. Where Gene Silverman was wise, handsome, respected and could hold an audience as easily as he could hold the smoke of a joint in his lungs, Eugene Beckett had been an insecure nerd who manipulated a keyboard more easily than a woman's body. Computers were Eugene's thing—he knew them inside and out, could make them purr, make them put out and do for him whatever he wanted. After graduating with a degree in Computer Science, he took a job with *Hardware Helpers* as a geek on patrol. He enjoyed the life of an on-call computer fixer, driving to businesses and homes to troubleshoot their computers.

Eugene would probably still be repairing computers today had his co-worker, Andy, not asked him if he'd like to make a little extra cash. Andy was moving out of state for a nine-to-five programming job.

"Extra money? Who wouldn't?" Eugene had said.

Andy grinned. "Even if it means helping a guy who doesn't exactly abide by the letter of the law?"

Eugene looked at Andy, confused. "I guess so. Bad money's good enough for me—as long as it's not dangerous." Andy told him to expect a call in the next few weeks.

The call came when Eugene was on duty, as though it were just another routine service call. The inner-city rowhouse looked like any other. Eugene knew Fells Point as the party central he never visited, where blue and white collars merged with college students and tourists, all of them seeking beer and wine, dancing and dates, everyone in search of a time so good that more of them would end in pain than pleasure—a hangover, an overdose, or a regrettable bed partner who appeared considerably uglier in the sobering sunlight than in the two a.m. drunken crescent of a moon.

Eugene knocked nervously on the Wolfe Street door, just a stone's throw from the excitement of the pubs and clubs along Broadway. Even then, Eugene recognized his mandated greeting as uncool. "Hi. Your Hardware Helper is here."

The heavy man at the door looked thirty years his senior, not yet an old man. "Yeah, c'mon in." No pleasantries, just business. "You Andy's friend?" Eugene said that he was. Cigar in hand, the man led Eugene up the stairs and into one of three bedrooms, where the smoke in the air was thick enough to spoon out. Eugene saw the computer desk in the smog. The bedroom had been converted into a home office, but this was no home. "You can keep secrets, can't you, whiz kid?"

"Sure I can," Eugene said.

"Good. 'Cause if anything here ends up on the street, I'll have to cut your puny, key-pecking fingers off." The man was hard to read: Eugene laughed at the joke but the man did not. "No kidding," he said seriously. "You come highly recommended, so I'm gonna trust you. But if anything you see on this computer or in this house makes its way out ... you ain't using a keyboard no more."

Eugene's hands began to tremble and he wondered if he'd made the right decision in coming here. "I'll keep quiet," he assured the man.

It was hard to peg the man. He wasn't black or white, but something in between. Appeared to have some Italian blood, a spill-over from bordering Little Italy. He spit out a cloud of smoke. "I depend on the computer more than I should. Now I'm getting screwed for it. Can't find my stuff. Everything's corrupted. I need you to find my stuff."

"Uh, what kind of stuff?"

A frustrated breath of smoke came out before any words. "Well, you're the whiz, aren't you? You know, stuff! Files, documents, things like that. Whatever the hell's stored in this box. Can you find it?"

"I can do that," Eugene assured him. He sat at the computer and began pecking at the keyboard. He noticed, as he began his work, three other men in the hall, men who were younger, fitter, more muscle than fat.

"Good. Get to work. Stay put—no snooping around."

Eugene's nerves calmed when the man left the room. The mystery was easier to solve with the space cleared. He worked best when left alone with the machine. There was an intimacy between Eugene and any PC he encountered. Some people got along with dogs, some men could charm women, but Eugene found his comfort with computers. This one contained Microsoft Money files, he ascertained. Some Word documents and old Word Perfect files, a few Excel documents and Access databases. Eugene found the backup files in a matter of minutes. He went through them to make sure the information was still intact. As he did, a strange smell emerged from the closed door of the next room—stronger than the harsh cigar. It was a smell Eugene had caught wind of a number of times in college, but one he had never celebrated himself: marijuana. He kept a formulated concentration on his face in case someone from behind one of the two closed doors came out and detected his discomfort.

His worry intensified as he read through the files. They were accounts all right. The Girls: Amber, Angel, Bambi, Barbie, Candy, Cutesy...each woman had her own revenues and expenses. He even found a list of male prostitutes. Then the drug database: accounts for marijuana, cocaine, hash, heroin...and the pills: Adipex, Darvocet, Percocet, Percodan, Tylenol-Threes, Valium. There were the names of suppliers, the costs, and what they sold for on the street. The income was multitudes more than the expense. And there was the in-house gambling: the booking, lending of money, collection of debt and interest, the cost of ... taking care of deadbeats. And a list of men who could do the job: Charlie, Erich, Frankie, Gustav...more than Eugene wanted to see.

The man who'd led him to the office came through one of the doors, still in conversation with the others in the room. "I'm done," the big guy said to the men in the smoke. "You finish 'er up." He closed the door, then opened the door to the third room, the one across from the office, and yelled in. "What are you girls doing? Stop powdering your noses. Time to get to work." Eugene saw four women in scanty outfits, white powder in sharp lines on the glass table between them. He quickly looked back at the computer screen and hid his discomfort before the man turned back in his direction and entered the office. "An' how 'bout you, whiz kid? Got anything?"

"Got everything," Eugene bragged. "I think I've found it all."

The big man looked down over his shoulder. "Well I'll be damned. You're good, kid." He took a wad of money from his pocket, held together by a gold clip. "How much I owe you?"

"You owe Hardware Helpers..." Eugene looked at his order book. "One hundred thirty nine dollars and fifty eight cents, tax included."

The man huffed out a laugh. "Here, whiz kid." He peeled off a few hundreds. "A little extra for your fast work. And because you know how to keep your trap shut."

Eugene's eyes widened. "Wow! Thanks, man!"

"Boss," he corrected. "I'm the Boss around here." He walked Eugene back to the front door. "I ain't much good with a computer. You're even better than that Andy kid. When I need something, I'll call you."

"I'll be here, sir."

"And remember, not a word to anyone. If I find out you spilled the beans to your parents or bragged to your friends or some piece of ass, you'll be sorry. And believe me, I find out everything."

Eugene swallowed. "Consider me password protected." The Boss nodded, opened the door, and let him out. As Eugene sputtered away in his beat-up Chevy Cavalier, he questioned whether it was worth the money, getting involved with such shady operations.

Two weeks later, the Boss called, and the lure of easy money put Eugene on the job. Then the Boss called again in another week. In time, he was calling Eugene regularly, sometimes just to key in account information, more secretarial than IT. "You like workin' here?" the Boss asked.

"Yeah," Eugene answered enthusiastically, his previous leeriness lost in the financial windfall he'd seen in *keep the trap shut* bonuses. "You're my best client."

"Why don't you lose the loser shirt and work for me? I'll pay you twice what those jokers do, plus a little extra for good work. All under the table, tax free. Whaddya say?"

Eugene said yes.

Getting in with the mafia was like getting involved with any person or group: it was not a deliberate plan made or a visualized goal reached. It just happened by a stroke of luck, good or bad. He fell into it like an addiction. From computer geek to IT man for the mob.

The mob? Eugene questioned just what the mafia was these days. There were still the big guys, the kind that people thought of after reading a Mario Puzo novel or watching a Scorsese film. But Eugene suspected the majority of organized crime was just barely organized, held together with the help of normal people like himself. This mini-mob was more like a fraternity, really, a small club of about thirty people—forty, tops. There was the Boss. There were the ones who ran the games. There were the dealers who peddled the drugs in the streets. And the prostitutes, male and female, who loitered along East Baltimore Street near the X-rated movie houses and sex stores.

There were other members in the frat, like the bookies and the hit men. Of course, the Boss was a relatively humane person who never had anyone whacked. Fingers had been severed, but mostly it was beatings and threats, slashed tires and sugar-filled gas tanks. Violence was kept to a minimum. It wasn't like the movies at all. Just a bunch of guys making a decent living.

Eugene was employed full time, but there wasn't full-time work to do. He lounged in the house most workdays and remained on call around the clock. The leisure time of his position taught Eugene how to relax. It felt good to belong to a secret society. As the days strung into years, he learned to enjoy pot, pills, and prostitutes. In all things—work, drugs, sex, and basic social skills—Eugene's competence flourished during his years working in the Fells Point rowhouse. And the things he learned were more valuable, more tangible, and more pleasing than anything to come from his four years of college.

Eugene worked for the Boss for seven years. By his third year, he partook regularly of the drugs and whores. The freelancers were like strands of hair, far too many to get to know. He made more effort to know the prostitutes and their unique qualities—Charlotte's pierced nipple, JoJo's pierced navel, the barbell in Tamika's talented tongue, Samantha's glowing-white teeth, Cyn's red pubes, Vera's webbed feet. He learned to love each one in the same way he learned to love the easiness of a marijuana high, the energy of a diet pill, and the cloudy consolation of valium. By his fifth year, there was no question that he was a different man with new appetites. He'd acquired ambition. Once, he'd been happy with acceptance; now he hungered for admiration.

Of all the things he knew, he still knew computers best. He could only take so many drugs and screw so many whores in a day's time, so he surfed the net and began to hack into other systems, developing his online proficiency. One day, he realized his expertise could amount to something worthy of respect.

"Hey, check this out," he called as the Boss entered the room, cigar in hand.

"What'cha got?"

"A way to make a killing," Eugene said, sitting before the computer.

The Boss came around to stand behind him. He looked over Eugene's shoulder at the screen full of incomprehensible code. "How's that?"

Eugene swiveled around in his chair and faced the Boss. The man sat his bulk on the dark pine desk and flicked a clump of ash into Eugene's coffee cup. "I've been thinking," Eugene began, a grin on his face. "We could make this computer work for us. Make some money."

"I'm listening."

"When was the last time you checked your email?"

The Boss scoffed. "I don't check my email. I pay you to do that. Do I even get email?"

"Not yours personally—I check the *business's* email." Eugene reconsidered his approach. *Doesn't even have his own email account? Talk about computer illiterate!* He restarted. "Okay, here's the idea: email scams are big. You send out a mass mailing, doesn't cost a thing—like sending an offer to a million people. You make up some story, make them think that by giving their account info we're going to deposit some money for them. Make it look like the email came from another country, from someone important, from a broker with a big firm, from Wall Street. Whatever."

"Can you do that?"

Eugene smiled more coolly than he'd once known how to do. "It's a computer. I can do anything I want with it."

"Sure, whiz kid."

"Anyway, say we get a one-percent response. But we get the account numbers and routing numbers from that one percent—we got their cash, everything in their accounts. And that's just the beginning. Send out another email that looks like it's coming from some big company—Wal Mart, Pier One, Target, Disney—and sell something dirt cheap. Maybe a set of a dozen Disney flicks for 20 bucks or something. So you're gonna get a big response. I could hack into Disney's website and even get the emails to do a targeted mailing."

"Tried that before, kid. There ain't enough money in pirated movies."

"No, no, there won't even *be* any movies. We get their credit card info—everything we need—then we rack up the charges. People have a hell of a lot more in credit allowances than they do in their bank accounts. So we max out their cash advances—in moderate increments so the credit card companies don't get suspicious—and get a shit-load of money!"

"I like it, kid. Can they trace it back to us?"

"I won't let them," Eugene said. "I'll cover our tracks, mislead them. Hell, I'll make it look like an executive at Disney orchestrated the whole damn thing!"

"I love it!" The Boss laughed and flicked more ash into Eugene's cup. He reached into his jacket pocket and pulled out another cigar, already cut. "Here. Tell me more."

Eugene took the cigar, placed it under his nose and sniffed it from end to end. More than the spicy fragrance invited him. In his four years of working for the Boss, he'd never been offered one of his Cubans. "Nice." He lit up. The taste was better than cigarettes, better than pot. It was strong but smooth and left a tingling sensation on his lips. He coughed a bit, but quickly took another toke to show it was a fluke, that he could smoke a stogie with the best of them. He was one of the gang.

"That's just the email part of it—then there's the Internet scams we could do. Hack right into other systems and get the same sort of info: bank account information, credit card info, stock and bond funds. Especially with all those day traders out on the web."

"Aren't most of those websites secure?"

"Secure?" Eugene laughed as he blew out smoke, but some of it got caught in his throat and made him hack. He regained his composure. "Nothing is so secure that it can't be hacked into. I hear the word *secure* and I think *puzzle*. It can be figured out."

"Well, get to figuring, kid. We'll see what you can do. And here's a little incentive: you make this happen, you keep ten percent of whatever you can pull."

"Thanks, Boss."

A month later, it was the Boss who was thanking Eugene, with an entire humidor full of Havanas and a bundle of bonus money on top of his commission. Just as a matter of style, Eugene had offered the *Gangster DVD Collection*, a list of popular mobster and street films. They'd already 'sold' two hundred sets, amounting to more than a hundred credit cards that pulled in close to a quarter million dollars. Then there were the emails congratulating winners and asking for account info, promising to fill them with deposits, then sucking them dry a week later.

What made Eugene feel good about these lucrative exploits was that they were, he rationalized, moral crimes. On the surface, these were crimes against people. But the multi-billion-dollar companies were the ones who paid. Most of it would be written off by the banks and credit card companies. The people being scammed would have their inconveniences, to be sure, and would lose their credit ratings. But the bulk of the monetary losses weighed on the companies to whom it was but a coin in the vault.

In the months that followed, Eugene earned hundreds of thousands of dollars in commission, gifts of cigars, cream-of-the-crop call girls, gold chains, Rolexes, and diamond-studded rings. He traded his tucked in, discount-store polo shirts for cool, untucked, Egyptian cotton button-downs. He threw out his generic sneakers for top-of-the-line Italian loafers. He no longer worried about his ten-year-old Chevy breaking down because his new Corvette was serviced regularly. He ditched his apartment full of roommates and rented a furnished condo with a harbor view. He learned to live without his credit cards and paid cash for everything. His only bank accounts were offshore, invisible.

Eugene had all the things he wanted. But he earned more than that. He earned the respect of the Boss and the organization. That was something he had never been able to command before and an asset he was thrilled to possess.

As his email and Internet scams continued, Eugene began obtaining Social Security numbers, dates of birth, mothers' maiden names, and other information to begin applying for credit cards in other people's names, then maxing out those cards. He had men go dumpster diving at industrial parks and near government offices and financial institutions. Now and then, one of his hoods would score a garbage bag full of unshredded documents, and Gene would pay some lout to do the grunt work, to fill out applications. He threw bones to the men who helped him help the Boss, like fine cigars out of his stash, bricks of weed for their personal use, and money.

Two years after his sales pitch to the Boss, his computer and identity crimes were bringing in almost as much money as drugs, gambling, or prostitution. He'd become one of the most important members of their little frat. Then it began to get dangerous.

The seat on the train had been comfortable, but it had served its purpose. Unable to stay in one place for long, Gene decided to take a walk. The passengers in the car sat in their seats, sleeping, reading, talking, eating. He gripped the luggage compartment above his seat and secured his footing. It always took several minutes of walking before he had the rhythm down; in the same way, he knew that when he returned to stable ground, there would be moments of disorientation during which he would still feel the movements of the train.

He exited the passenger car and entered another, his chrome briefcase in his left hand, a silver ring on his finger. What was it about silver that attracted him? Silver was more alluring than gold, more beautiful than bronze or any jewel. It had been easy to change his name to Silverman, simple to be the negative to the usual middle-age photo, coloring his once-brown hair. His new hair, face, body, personality and name assured that no one from the old days could peg him. Besides, if the Boss had sent professionals to look for him, they would have found him years ago.

There had been a stop recently—somewhere in Virginia?—and the conductor was making his rounds to validate new passengers. Gene began to squeeze past him in the narrow corridor, but the conductor seemed to want conversation to go with their dance.

"So, what are you, a preacher?" he asked, looking at the briefcase in one hand and the yellow legal pad of notes in the other.

Gene laughed. "Hardly." But he understood where the question came from. In some ways, preachers, politicians, and public speakers all had the same confident look of authority. They all knew how to bury their fear and uncertainty and cover it with a shiny veneer. They were tin men. "Just a speaker," he answered.

The conductor put a hand on Gene's arm and drew close, as though to reveal a secret. "Well now, if you have a speech to write, there's no place more inspiring than the window view in the lounge car. Picture window to America."

Gene nodded, brushed politely past the blue collar, and walked on. He entered the lounge car and found it half full already. Many of the seats were taken by families and individuals who stared out into the tree-studded landscape. Some of them talked, others plugged their ears with buds and headphones. A few people read books.

Gene took a seat toward the middle of the car and looked out. In the distance, he saw a black Lincoln idling in front of an office building. *A nice way to travel, if you want to make yourself a target.* He was certain chauffeurs talked.

Life in the mob had become good for him, but then it got risky. When he started, identity theft was still a relatively unknown crime, not the sort of thing people talked about. But by the end of his time with the Boss, it was a hot topic, one of the most serious crimes in the nation. So serious, in fact, that the government had really begun to crack down on it. The Federal Trade Commission, Social Security Administration, Federal Bureau of Investigation, and the local police had caught on and were working together; they'd already arrested several identity thieves in the area. It was no longer a safe crime of stealth; everyone was watching. The enormous growth of the identity theft industry was its downfall. His downfall.

The trouble hit home when he got a call at his apartment. "Is this Eugene Beckett?" the voice had asked.

"Who's calling?"

"We'd like to meet with you. Talk."

Eugene could hear the shuffling of paper, the clicking of keyboards, the ringing of office telephones. These were g-men. "Send me an email."

"Can't do that. We're offering you a deal. Do you want to meet before we change our minds?"

Confused, Eugene hung up. Just the week before, a story had broken all over the morning papers and evening newscasts about a woman who'd racked up a million dollars in merchandise by stealing people's identities. It had become a familiar story.

They had his name. They had his number. They had his address. They knew. It got to where he couldn't leave the Boss's rowhouse office or his own apartment without seeing a dozen potential undercovers waiting to pounce. He just couldn't take it. Now, years later, he realized he'd have been better off to stay with the Boss. But looking back was only useful when you were looking behind you, for someone ready to attack.

There was no way of telling the Boss he wanted out. No way to avoid the disappointment, the protest. He wasn't just a computer repairman any longer. The Boss had grown accustomed to Eugene and his enterprise. They were tight, almost family. The Boss wouldn't let him go. So Eugene got out the best way he could think of: he simply left, unannounced. He upgraded the organization's computers so they practically ran themselves. He transferred all of his money to an off-shore account the Boss didn't know about. Then he packed his bags, chucked his Corvette, stuffed his possessions in a less obvious, five-year-old SAAB hatchback, and skipped town. He spent more time looking in the rearview mirror than at the road in front of him. Sometimes he wished he'd met with the feds and made a deal.

He'd gotten out because he didn't want to always feel like a fed or cop was ready to drag him in. But these days, he lived with the fear that one of the Boss's men would drag him out.

In the lounge car, the view beyond the glass wall had become a blur. It was a nice sight, but he didn't feel comfortable with his back to the open aisle of the car. He stood and decided to get a drink.

He ordered a cup of hot tea and took a seat at a table, so he could see all around him. He looked about and saw no one of concern. The conductor was chatting up one of the other passengers, his cap in hand, revealing his dark, bald head. Gene turned and glanced out the window. The hills of Virginia were beautiful. Or were they already in West Virginia? It didn't matter; it was just there to be seen, to be enjoyed, passed by.

His next speaking engagement was in Chicago. He'd ridden back and forth on the silver rails so many times, he'd begun to consider the bus. Traveling back and forth was enough to make a person restless. Or, in his case, it was a way to occupy a restless person.

He clicked the latches of his chrome case and opened it, then took out some additional note cards. It would be essentially the same speech. He anticipated the same questions and objections. He was prepared, but it didn't hurt to look them over again, to personalize the talk. Just a habit, better than a vice.

The train came upon a bumpy stretch of track, so Gene found it hard to read his notes. He looked back outside.

As soon as he left the Boss, he left town. Out of Baltimore, in Cleveland, he'd gone to a salon and had his hair changed from brown to sterling silver. He'd gone to the mall and gotten contacts to replace his glasses. He'd had his face reconstructed, and the fat from his pot belly sucked out as simply as he'd sucked so much money from oversized businesses. He changed his name, bought a laptop and printer and generated himself a fake identification with the name Gene Silverman, the Social Security number of someone long deceased, and became a new person. A year later, he went to a specialist in Chicago and changed his eye contacts to steely blue. Appearing older, cooler, and harder boosted his sense of security. It was like trying on a tin suit.

Gene watched as men and women entered and exited the lounge car at random. A young man in an army uniform strode into the lounge. Gene wasn't a fan of uniforms, but this confused-looking young man was nothing to fear. Gene watched him get his beer and stop to talk to an old lady who looked like she was on her way to a nursing home. A moment later, the odd couple separated. Gene turned back to the door, sensing another person there.

The man who came in was sturdy, a guy who wore his excess pounds in a way that made him look tough, well-rounded. He was a gruff character, a rugged, leather jacket of bomber-pilot brown draped over him. Gene watched the man, who himself looked casually at each person in the room.

Their eyes met, and Gene turned away from the man's stare. He looked back a moment later and watched the man order a cup of black coffee. He didn't bother to remove his jacket, fitted over his black tee-shirt like a second skin. The man had a cigarette tucked behind his ear. He got comfortable in his seat, sipped his coffee and looked around the lounge.

A people watcher, Gene observed. Gene had learned to become a sociologist as well. It was important to see every person for their potential: what harm they could cause or what purpose they could serve. At the moment, in the lounge car, he saw neither use nor harm in anyone here. He returned to his notes, not really seeing the blur of yellow paper and blue ink in front of his eyes as the train shook them on his lap.

He'd worked a few white-collar jobs after getting out, doing IT work, but it was just for something to do. He had more than a million stashed away, interest compounding, and could survive a long time on that. After a couple years had passed and he realized the Boss wasn't after him, he decided to ease back into the world. He left Cleveland and began to travel the rails. It was safer, he figured, to take the train. *Who in the mafia takes the train?* The train was the safest way to pass from place to place undetected.

He'd attended a grass-roots roundtable discussion advertised in the paper in San Francisco. The subject was the legalization of marijuana. Gene had gone to listen, interested in the subject. After all, he'd been involved with marijuana, professionally and personally, for years. To his surprise, he found that he had a lot to say at the roundtable discussion, and expressed strong opinions. The others listened and offered him their respect, their support. They rallied around his expertise. When contributions began coming in and people wanted to hear him speak, he couldn't help but get lured in. It was a fun life, traveling around and talking to fired-up crowds about controversial issues. It wasn't like he was a national figure; his fame was only within the circle, mostly college kids looking for something to start fire in their bellies, or hippies who'd never graduated to yuppies. They met in cornfields and private clubs, basements and warehouses.

Gene had learned to reboot a computer early in life, and he'd reset his own identity more than once. *Resetting your course in life is as easy as upgrading a computer. You just have to know the code.*

Gene didn't plan on resetting his life anytime soon, pleased with his current software. He looked around instinctively once again, then eased back in his seat. Nothing had ever happened to him on a train. But, ever cautious, he knew it wasn't the end of the line just yet. With every train ride he took, he felt that much further from his old life. Gene had found a new fraternity. But he would never forget his years working for the Boss, despite his certainty that the Boss had all but forgotten him.

Futures

Walking on a train isn't free and open, like walking on a sidewalk or in a building. Nor is it stiff and uncomfortable, like walking on an airplane. There's a steady, rhythmic comfort to strolling leisurely down the aisle, balancing hands on the heads of seats as you go. Christi's direction was clear, but her destination was not. She was in no hurry to get there, wherever "there" was.

In Baltimore, Christi walked all the time, along the Inner Harbor from Federal Hill to Fells Point and back again. When she got to Chicago, she looked forward to a stroll along Lake Shore Drive and a walk down the Magnificent Mile. But for now, the aisle of the passenger train would have to do. She'd already gone all the way to the caboose and was now headed back to her seat.

When her secretary, Jen, had offered to book her flight, Christi had quickly insisted on the train. She needed to ease slowly from one impressionistic place to another. Dashing from Baltimore to Chicago on a plane was like jumping into a too-hot bath. This was a big transition, even if it turned out to be temporary. She'd been submerged in Baltimore yet tethered to Chicago all her life. It took time to drift from one reality to another.

She found her seat and fell into it. Beyond her window, the autumn trees swept by. A man, barely her senior, caught her attention as he passed down the aisle from behind. He carried a spiral notebook in one hand and the yellow stub of a pencil in the other. She admired his physique until he took his seat next to another woman. Christi preferred to look at men, but she turned back to her window and watched a collection of leaves in the distance separate from a branch in a gust of wind. She considered the future. Winter would be here soon. She wondered where she'd be living when the first snowfall came. She wondered who would be living with Craig.

Christi found herself distracted again by the scenery inside the train, which was a relief as it allowed her a momentary escape from the decision at hand. A young man in uniform—army—caught her eye and strode by without giving her a glance. But she looked him over thoroughly as he walked along the center aisle, imagined him holding her in his strong embrace. *Wouldn't work; military guys are too authoritative.* The soldier walked through the door, leaving her passenger car for another.

Since Craig had become a thing of the past, Christi caught herself checking out good-looking men more often, the way she might consider a future job prospect. The scenery outside the window didn't distract her, perhaps because the ever-changing view mimicked her thoughts as she imagined the infinite answers to her problem. The trees, the hills, the rolling farmland—it was like background music from a CD so familiar that she could hear it even when it wasn't there; sometimes the tracks played and she didn't even notice it. Right now, she was around track seven, around the middle of her journey, houses spotting the distant hillsides. She didn't have to make a decision right now. Only consider it. Should she remain on course, living contently in Baltimore, and try to patch things up with Craig? Or should she take on the challenges of Chicago, letting the tracks ahead carry her into unknown places?

She cringed at the sound of the shrill voice behind her. The young couple was at it again. "*Say* something," the girl insisted.

Christi heard the boy's paperback slap his leg. "What do you want me to say?"

"Why don't you tell me you love me?" the girl pleaded. "Like you used to?"

He sighed. "I love you." His words sounded forced.

The girl seemed to pick up on it. "It's not the same when I have to tell you to say it."

"Can't win for losing," the boy griped. "You just asked me to say it, I said it, and now you're upset because I said it! What the hell do you want? Do you even know?"

Christi did her best to tune out the youngsters as she shifted in her seat, but sometimes it was difficult to silence something that sounded so familiar, like a scene from her own broken relationship she'd rather forget.

Christi moved into the aisle again, this time walking in the direction of the engine. She felt a set of eyes upon her, checking her out just as she had checked out the army guy. At twenty-nine, she still had the look. *I move my caboose as well as any train.* She smiled at the comparison. *Craig doesn't know how good he had it.*

She exited the car and entered another, continuing her leisurely stroll. A balding man—too old—offered her a smile. She smiled back but moved along. She put Craig out of her mind; she had no time for dwelling in the past. She had a future to consider. Or rather, two.

Back in Baltimore, Craig had been a real asshole about things. He was a year older than Christi, but sometimes acted like he was her father. He'd been a nice guy at first, but then she'd gotten to know him. Oh, he knew how to draw a person in, how to charm with flattery. But once taken in—once he knew he had her—he struck with his bossiness, with his stubbornness, with an aggression so startling that Christi didn't even bother telling anyone about it, knowing that anyone who knew him at arm's length wouldn't believe her if she did.

But then again, doesn't everyone nit-pick the faults of people they love? She realized that many breakups were caused by impossibly inflated expectations.

One evening, Christi and Craig were waiting for their dinner to be served at Red Brick Station, a beer pub and restaurant northeast of the city. Craig lived in Federal Hill where it was more expensive, but as an attorney, he could afford it. Red Brick was a place they both liked for its beer, burgers, and steak. She'd turned him onto the place; it was a spot she'd once frequented with her parents when she was still living with them in their Rodgers Forge rowhouse. She'd been old enough to drink the beer but not yet old enough to live on her own. Now she had a good job, her own apartment in the Forge, and the confidence to go solo, to live wherever and however she pleased.

Craig cringed the first time she'd suggested a restaurant on The Avenue, one of those fabricated "old town square" places, a glorified strip mall across the street from White Marsh Mall, in view of the city's only IKEA. She never told him that her plates and coffee mugs had come from the chain he so detested. But she'd convinced him to give the suburban restaurant a try, dangling the microbrews as bait she knew he'd take.

"Not as good as Ryleigh's or Oliver's," Craig said as they waited for their steaks, "but pretty damn delicious." Red Brick had become a weekly staple for them on nights when he stayed at her place. He'd tried all of their regular house beers; Daily Crisis IPA was his favorite. She usually went to him, where the action was, in the Federal Hill area or downtown. Suggesting Red Brick was her way of reestablishing some independence, of testing him to see whether he would meet her halfway and do things she wanted to do.

"More roomy than Ryleigh's or the Wharf Rat," Christi defended. "And better food."

"But the beer," Craig insisted like a true connoisseur. "The beer steers the meal."

"Beer without food is like a man without a woman," Christi teased. "You need substance."

After a moment of quiet sipping, Craig cleared his throat. "Listen, Christi," he said in his lawyer's voice, demanding attention. He was already on his second beer; she was only halfway through her first. "We've been an item for what, seven months now?"

"Nine," she corrected.

"So I think it's about time." He pulled out a small jewelry box of blue velvet.

"No way!" Her heart pounded and she began to feel dizzy, the way she felt sometimes when she had to make a presentation before the executive board. "No way!" She took the box in her hands and looked up at Craig's smiling face.

"Go on," he said.

She opened the box to find . . . a key. The look of overwhelmed joy she'd planned melted away and became confusion instead.

"It's a key to my place," he burst out. "I think it's time you move in with me!"

Disappointment lingered, to be sure, but relief came too. She appreciated the gesture, but found his approach arrogant: the setup, the fall, and his assumption that he'd offered her some great gift, like shelter for a stray dog. "Craig, I don't know. I've got my own place. I like my place."

"Christi, come on! We're talking Federal Hill here!" Federal Hill was, after all, the place where young professionals played, if not always where they lived. Craig's neighbors were all doctors, lawyers, landlords, realtors, or executives, none of them over forty. Sitting there in the restaurant, Craig outlined the pros of living together in Federal Hill. His apartment on William Street was a hop to dozens of their favorite pubs, restaurants, and hangouts—and a crawl back. They were just a block from Cross Street Market, and the harbor was only a five-minute stroll away. By the time their New York strips arrived, neighbored by baked potatoes, he'd convinced her.

"I'll have to break my lease," she said. "That'll cost me my security deposit—a month's rent."

"Then as an added gift," he offered, "you don't have to chip in the first month. After that, you only have to pay half the rent. Not much more than you're paying way out here."

"That's right," she said, realizing what she hadn't considered before. "We'll have to get practical. Groceries, households, utilities, cable, rent—straight down the middle?"

"I don't know about that." He grinned. "I mean, I can put in a little extra. I'll have you in my bed every night. I'm sure you can make up the difference."

Christi paused, her steak knife in hand; she had a sudden urge to use it. She sliced through the medium-well strip of meat. "Funny," she said, her tone making clear that it wasn't. His sense of humor had been one of the qualities she'd fallen in love with — that, and his hot, GQ look. *It'll be a test. We'll see if we're really compatible.* She chewed.

"Way I see it," Craig said, mouth full, "this is better than getting hitched." He took a hearty gulp of ale, his mouth still working at the meat. "All the benefits, none of the drawbacks." When the waitress came, he clinked his empty glass with his fork. Christi continued to nurse her first beer.

Christi moved along the train, once in a while spotting a young man with a cute face or an older man with a look of respectable distinction. There were women and children seated on the train too, but her eyes honed in on the men. So many choices seated before her, each smiling at her with charm and promise. *But don't they all look like that at first? With their put-on manners and made-up appearances? Then, you let them get comfortable with you and they reveal who they really are.* She wondered whether Craig's proposition that she live with him had been nothing more than a calculated act of convenience—a woman in bed every night and someone to pay half the bills.

Part of her still wished Craig was coming with her to Chicago. She wasn't exactly a stranger to the city, but she'd never been alone. Christi had been twelve, still an impressionable child, when her parents took her to spend the summer with Grandma in Chicago. They'd gone to the Windy City for brief visits since before she could remember, but that summer, Christi got to know Grandma—and Chicago—intimately. Grandma had taken her to the Art Institute, where they'd spent a heavenly day admiring the paintings, her favorite being Seurat's *A Sunday on La Grande Jatte.*

At the end of another passenger car, Christi stopped, closed her eyes, and saw the beautiful picture again: gentlemen in top hats and canes, women with their parasols, children playing, boats upon the water. As a grade-schooler, she believed such a place existed, a place with such gentlemen, where she could be a sophisticated lady and go for a Sunday walk in the park. She'd always imagined the place in that picture was somewhere in Chicago.

Christi opened her eyes and continued strolling down the aisle. Sometimes she felt she belonged in Chicago as surely as the Seurat belonged in the city's Art Institute. Other times she considered the city just one small dot on the canvas of her life, her true home being Baltimore.

Her company's headquarters were in Chicago, and this one-month assignment was meant to be a test-run for her and for the company. She was one of the young superstar executives in the Baltimore office, so it was natural for her to be at the top of their list.

Moving to Chicago would mean a promotion to Senior Associate under one of the four vice presidents of the company. She would be the second person to reach such status within the company at such a young age; the first—Mr. Ubukata—had made vice president at age thirty-one. He was a child among the other top brass, all of them in their sixties and crowned with silver hair.

She would need the raise if she was going to get an apartment near the office. She'd found a place online. Presidential Towers was nearby and offered everything one could want right within the base of the towers: restaurants, bars, a grocery store, copy center, jewelry store, even a health club. But if she was going to live in the big playground of Chicago, she wanted to get out and play. She wanted somewhere close enough to work, but also close to Lake Shore Drive, where she could stroll to Navy Pier, walk along the beach, feel the water of Lake Michigan. She wanted to amble through the city, enjoy its architecture, touch the Chicago Picasso. And there was Grant Park with its beautiful Buckingham Fountain, where she'd left her pennies during her last visit with Grandma.

"You'll be coming back here," Grandma had said after watching her throw in the penny.

"Really? Why?"

"When you drop a penny in a fountain, that means you'll be coming back."

Christi did return to visit Grandma, but she looked different in the funeral home, like wax. Chicago looked the same; it felt like Grandma. But Baltimore felt like everything else.

Christi never actually believed she would move to Chicago. But life had its unexpected bends. *Who'd have expected me to become so successful so fast? From sales rep to senior associate in five years!*

There were several women in senior associate positions, but none in the vice president slots; she hoped to be the first. If Ubukata could manage it by thirty-one, certainly she could get there too. Ubukata was an intelligent man, but she had more than smarts. She had the looks and charm she needed and knew how to strut with confidence.

With each step along the train, Christi grew more certain that she was headed in the right direction, leaving Craig in Baltimore and finding her future in Chicago. She began to walk more freely, strolling along without the help of every other headrest. She anticipated the twists and turns of the train as she went forward.

Her sure footing was an illusion. The train shot around a curve and she tumbled off her feet, landing in the lap of an older man. She scrambled to get a grip on something and ended up grasping his arms, their faces inches apart.

The man grinned. "Nice to meet you."

"Sorry," she said, struggling to lift herself out of his lap.

"Are you headed for the lounge?"

Christi regained her footing. "No. Just for a walk." As she strolled away, she could feel his experienced eyes running along her backside. *Yes,* she thought as she walked on. *I've still got it.* There were men in Chicago, better than Craig. It was a big city.

Baltimore was known as many things: The City That Reads, The City That Believes. Benches along the streets referred to Baltimore as Charm City and The Greatest City in America. But to Christi, who was born and raised due north of Baltimore in the tight-knit community of Rodgers Forge, Baltimore was simply her home and harbor.

Christi's family lived only half an hour's drive from the Inner Harbor, so they went often. As a child, she'd enjoyed the playground atop Federal Hill, and when she became too old for the swings, she enjoyed the view of the harbor from the same location, beneath the giant flag and beside the cannon, watching the people walk along the promenade from the same place Americans had watched for British ships in 1812.

In the humid days of summer, descending from the hill into the harbor was like sinking into a familiar hot tub. People flowed around her, currents in both directions. Children's laughter accompanied the carousel's cheerful music. Volleyball games took place in the same arena that saw ice-skating in the winters, not far from the giant mast that paid tribute to the goodwill ship lost at sea, the *Pride of Baltimore*. Street musicians played guitars and pan flutes, saxophones and drums, and entertainers rode unicycles, juggled flames and knives, told jokes, and performed magic. Artists painted and chalked the edges of the boardwalk. Water taxis blew their horns, leaving port only to be replaced by others within minutes, a steady cycle that took people from the Inner Harbor to Fort McHenry, Fells Point, and more than a dozen harbor-side destinations. The *USS Constellation* sounded its cannon, and the *Clipper City* and dinner cruise ships beckoned. The twin-pyramid points of the National Aquarium towered above. Then, on to Little Italy, home of Vaccaro's, the best place for dessert. And from Little Italy it was just a skip to Fells Point with its many pubs.

Places touched Christi more than people. Places were reliable. They didn't change overnight or move or die, as people did. Craig and her parents were important, but a warm comfort spilled over her when she thought of her favorite places. When she thought of her parents, she thought of her house, her neighborhood, the Baltimore Zoo and the B&O Museum. When she thought of her grandmother, she thought of Chicago and all the places they'd visited together that windy summer. When she thought of Craig, she thought of their favorite restaurants and pubs.

Christi had never timed the walk from Federal Hill to Fells Point. That would be hard to do since she stopped to enjoy the sights, not the least of which was the Chesapeake Bay itself, filled with sailboats, tall ships, paddle boats, and dragon-shaped boats for the kids.

"Let's take a taxi," Craig insisted one beautiful Saturday afternoon.

"I want to walk." Christi needed time to think, time to prepare for her news of the evening. She'd already told her parents she was going to Chicago; she'd apprehensively saved the closest person for last.

Craig followed along, annoyed to be passing the water-taxi stop. "It'll take us an hour to get to Fells Point! We're gonna pay for a day pass to get back home anyway; let's take advantage of it now."

"I want to walk home too." They were going to hit the pubs of Fells Point after dinner in Little Italy. *Should I tell him at dinner, or over drinks?*

"That'll take an hour and a half! In the dark!"

She continued looking straight ahead as they walked along the harbor, facing the Hard Rock Cafe's giant guitar on the smokestacks above the Barnes & Noble bookstore. "There'll be plenty of light. It's a full moon tonight."

"We'll be drunk; you want to stumble home?"

"You'll be drunk," she corrected. "It's a beautiful walk."

He huffed, then grinned. "You might be walking home alone." But she knew he wouldn't let her do that.

Craig could be moody, but that wasn't who he was. It was only a sliver of him—even if it was the sliver that sometimes seemed to splinter her. There was the better part of their time together— his protective hold, his romantic words, the spark between them as they held hands and went for an evening stroll. A hundred places in Baltimore reminded her of Craig. She imagined Craig overshadowing Grandma in her mind as they visited the sites in Chicago. At dinner, Craig toasted to their night ahead. Christi couldn't wait to break the news.

After dinner, they strolled to Fells Point and he suggested they go to the cigar lounge on the second floor of Max's. She admitted it was a handsome room: dark wood, attractive posters, leatherback chairs. But there was more to a place than the look of it.

"I feel like we're in a giant ash tray." Christi waved her hand between them. "A nice ashtray, but an ashtray."

Craig responded by blowing a puff of cigar smoke above them. It hovered there like a dark cloud. He drank a German dopplebock. She sipped a Degroens, one of the local brews.

"I wish you wouldn't smoke those awful things," she said.

"You don't want me smoking in the apartment and I give you that! Let me have one here. Better than cigarettes."

"A bullet to the arm's better than a bullet to the head. Want me to get a gun?"

He laughed. "Just once a week, baby. No harm in that. Beer's not good for you either."

"Not when you guzzle it the way you do." She continued to sip her third brew of the night. He'd lost count after five.

More than cigar smoke made Christi uneasy. Tonight it was her turn to demand his attention. "Listen, Craig, I need to talk to you about something."

He took the cigar from his mouth and flicked off the ash, then casually checked the red-hot end. "What?"

"I got the best news at work! An opportunity I can't pass up."

Craig's blank gaze showed that he wasn't sure whether this was good news or bad, for him. "Really?"

"Next month, I'm going to Chicago!" She watched his face register the news. "It's temporary," she added before he could speak, wanting to reassure him that she wasn't leaving him. "One month." Then, thinking better of it and wanting to be honest about the whole thing, she admitted, "But if it works out, it could turn into a permanent position." She watched him. "A promotion."

He puffed his cigar.

"Senior Associate."

He blew smoke in her face, as though to cloud out the news.

"It'd be a great opportunity for you to take a couple weeks off, have an all-expense-paid vacation in Chicago. Why don't you join me?"

Craig masked his feelings with a practiced lawyer face. But his eyes reddened, and it didn't seem to be from the smoke in the room. "Chicago, huh?"

"Yes! Isn't it great? The Windy City!"

"Windy, but not very charming." Through the gruffness, it sounded like he was on the verge of tears.

"Okay, so it's not Charm City. But I like Chicago."

"I can't take off on such short notice." He spoke more to the cigar than to her. "I've got the fraudulent futures case."

"The what?"

"You know, the broker who scammed those novice investors, selling them futures that didn't exist? I'm defending him."

"You're defending that sleaze?"

"Got the assignment this week." He hardened; now his eyes were more defensive than sad. "I've got to."

"I thought you were going to argue for a better assignment."

Craig shrugged his shoulders; they looked too heavy for him. "I take what I'm given." It was as though he was giving up, on work and on her.

Smoke enveloped them; it was easy to drift in the fog. After a moment, Christi suggested, "Maybe you could just come for a long weekend."

"Maybe," he said, offering nothing. "When are you going?"

"In three weeks."

He nodded. "So I guess I'll need to find a new roommate."

"What?" Her eyes widened with shock. "Craig, don't be crazy! I'm not moving out! You come to Chicago with me, try it out. If you hate it that much, I can come back here."

"You know better than that," he said. "They'll want to keep you. You won't pass up a promotion, Miss Upward Mobility."

"What's that supposed to mean?" She took a gulp of beer.

"You're always looking to move up."

She slammed down her pint. "It's called ambition! Something a lazy-ass like you wouldn't understand!"

"Ambition?" He scoffed. "Hell, that's why you moved in with me! Miss Working Girl leaves suburbia to live with Mr. Attorney on the hill."

Christi leaned into the table. "*You* asked *me* to move in, like it was some sort of great gift or something! I was happy where I was! You're the one who wanted it, hon!"

The cigar was beyond smoking, but he continued to puff on the blunt. She watched him grimace as the harsh smoke stung his lips and tongue. "I thought we both wanted it," he said.

She walked home alone that night; Craig took a taxi. He *was* decent enough to ask her to get in with him, but that wasn't enough. He was supposed to toast her success, to celebrate by seduction. He was supposed to revel in the adventure they would have, taking the train to Chicago where they had the opportunity to start a new life. Instead, he'd left her in the moonlit harbor to walk home alone.

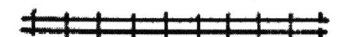

So she was headed for the lounge car after all. That's where her walk along the moving train took her. Beer reminded her of Craig, so she had a chardonnay instead. She strolled across the lounge and sat in one of the vacant seats. She glanced at those around her—a woman with a tattoo on her back, an older couple drinking beer and iced tea, an old man writing in his daily planner, a woman about her age crying over a piece of paper—and then Christi looked directly out the window at the autumn trees, their leaves blown to the ground, expelled from their branches.

She'd been evicted, more or less. She'd been in love with Craig, felt comfortable with him, actually believed he might be the man she would marry one day. The future she envisioned with him turned out to be a fraudulent one. *So why didn't I cry?*

By the time Christi had decided to indulge herself with a second chardonnay, the annoying young couple she'd left her seat to avoid stood at the other end of the lounge. She watched them from her seat, far enough away not to hear them. They'd made up, apparently, sporting goofy, puppy-love smiles between sips of bottled water. Christi looked away and took a swallow of chardonnay.

Some women remained in abusive relationships for years before wising up. Others never found the wisdom to move on. Christi knew Craig wasn't perfect, but he was never abusive either. She wasn't naïve enough to believe in fairy tales and happy endings. She'd settled for Craig, figured that even with his faults, he was as good as it got. Good enough. But now she wasn't so sure. She hoped this temporary exile would help her sort things out.

She was excited by the promise Chicago held, but wasn't sure she wanted to pick up and move her entire life to a new city in the middle of the country. She longed to stroll along Lake Shore Drive and feel the lake's cool breeze. But that would mean giving up the Inner Harbor. She imagined exhilarating Sundays spent in the Chicago Institute of Art, but that would mean giving up the American Visionary Arts Museum downtown and the Smithsonian in DC. She could see herself walking down the Magnificent Mile, but did the Magnificent Mile hold a candle to the National Mall and all of the capitol's monuments? She longed for a fresh start, but her best memories were anchored in Baltimore. Many of them with Craig.

Christi knew Craig would take her back. All she had to do was call him up, tell him she changed her mind, decided on him over her career. Maybe they still had a future.

Her things were back at her parents' place. She would always have her parents to visit during holidays and vacations. *Well, not always, but for a long while yet.* She'd have all of her friends, and business trips to the Baltimore office, to be sure, for weeks at a time during the course of a year. Living in Chicago wouldn't mean cutting the lines to Baltimore.

Out of the corner of her eye, she saw the uniform again. She turned and looked, saw the soldier there, sitting and sipping a beer. The young man had a concerned look pinned to his face, like a medal he'd rather not have. *There are wars going on,* Christi thought. *He's got real problems to worry about.*

She knew her decision probably wasn't as difficult as the soldier's, but it was hers, and it was real. *How did that Tracy Chapman song go?* The track of a familiar CD played in her head. *You've got to make a decision: leave tonight or live and die this way.*

Christi looked out the window, the landscape progressing from eastern to mid-western. She wanted Baltimore and Chicago—Craig and a career—to fit neatly together like the cars through which she'd just walked. She needed to decide which future to take, and abandon one for the other, just as Craig had abandoned her—or she had abandoned him for her ambition.

As she sat, sipping her chardonnay, *he* walked in—the man whose lap she'd fallen into. He waved and smiled as he waited for a drink. Once he had his mixed drink in hand, he walked over. "Thought you were walking."

"I was," Christi said. "This is where I ended up."

He took a seat beside her. "Guess you never know where you'll end up."

"Nope." Christi didn't particularly want to talk with this man. But she did feel like talking things out. "You can end up doing one thing for years and not see the opportunities lining up until they're right in front of you."

The man nodded and took a gulp of his yellow-orange cocktail. He thrust his hand in her direction. "Name's Murdock."

She took his hand and gave her name.

"Christi," he repeated. "Nice name. Got a boyfriend waiting in Chicago?"

"Baltimore," she replied reflexively. "Well, not anymore, I guess. We broke up."

"No kidding?"

"We were practically engaged—lived together over a year. But then I got this opportunity in Chicago." She sipped her wine, a story filling her mind and covering her sense of loss. "So I dumped the bastard."

Murdock lifted his glass to salute her. "You made the right choice." They clanked glasses. "In my experience, long-lasting relationships never last long."

She laughed. But as she sipped her drink, she hoped he had it wrong.

The man with the planner, a few seats over, joined their conversation. "They do if you want them to."

"Huh?" Murdock asked as he and Christi turned toward the stranger.

"My Anna and I have been married twenty-five years," the ashen-haired man said. The planner in his lap looked like a Bible with its rich leather cover. "Happily," he added.

"That's great," Christi said. She preferred this man's advice to what Murdock had to sell. "Congratulations."

The planner man elaborated. "I mention it because I overheard you talking about your boyfriend."

"Oh, Craig," Christi sighed. "He's history."

Murdock looked down at his worn shoes, seeming uninterested in a conversation he wasn't controlling. The older man talked over

Murdock's head. "Of course, I don't know the details. But think about it. You may live to regret it."

"You think?" she asked. "I mean, I invited him to come along. He wouldn't."

Murdock excused himself to get another drink. This kinder man had no obvious agenda other than to offer advice. He told her his name was Prewitt. "Just consider carefully what you're planning. You might be making the right choice, depending on who this guy is you left behind. But at the end of the line, success is measured in love, not money—in people, not position."

"Yeah." Christi shifted in her seat. "But you don't know Craig."

"Just remember, an ideal relationship is based on compromise." Prewitt smiled gently. "Consider your plans carefully."

Christi looked at him and then peered into her wine as though it would answer the question for her. It didn't, so she drank it down. She looked back at the ashen-haired man. "Thanks. I will." She slipped out of the lounge and made her way slowly down the aisles of passenger cars.

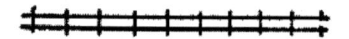

Christi knew a person couldn't walk forever. Sometimes you had to settle down and rest. She'd been sitting in her passenger seat for hours now, looking at the orientation package from company headquarters and enjoying the scenery—inside and out. So many potentially interesting places and people passed by.

Her head raced. She imagined herself with a Prewitt-aged Craig, giving up on her promotion and returning to him in Baltimore. Booting out whatever floozy he'd found to split his rent, letting him know she'd given up her ambition to be with him. She imagined their elegant wedding, their honeymoon on some exotic island, settling into a house somewhere between the city and the suburbs. She imagined living the stress-free life of a sales associate, enjoying restaurant dinners seasoned by Craig's stories of each sleaze he defended, the two of them laughing at the money made in helping the rich get away with murder. She could see herself with Craig, taking an anniversary vacation, telling another passenger on the train that they'd been married happily for twenty-five years, that relationships could last if you worked hard at it.

And what a lot of hard work it would be. Even as Christi imagined a life with Craig, she knew it wasn't really what she wanted. Sure, she needed someone to love, wanted someone to share her life with, but when she allowed rational thought to trample over her feelings, she knew that Craig wasn't the right man for her. Or was she expecting too much in a man?

The lovebirds behind her were at it again.

"What are you thinking?" the boy asked.

"You know," The girl teased.

"I love you too," he said.

This was worse than when they'd been arguing. She plunked the open orientation booklet on the empty seat beside her and began another walk. She headed toward the lounge car.

She passed the place where she'd fallen into Murdock's lap earlier. The seat was empty now, which probably meant she'd see him in the lounge. She'd have to find a place to sit where he couldn't creep in beside her. All she really wanted was to be alone right now. If she *had* to talk to someone, she'd rather it be the nice old man with the planner—Prewitt.

She exited one car for another, and sure enough, there was Prewitt, walking toward her. There was something different about him, as though a part of him were missing. He looked worried, confused, upset. "Hi," she greeted as they met toward the front of the passenger car.

"Hello," he returned. He took a deep breath and regained his composure. "Have you given some thought to your boyfriend back home?"

"I have," she said. "And I decided you're right. A healthy relationship should last."

"Good," Prewitt said. "Then you'll be going back?"

"No." Christi let out a little laugh. "Craig and I would never last that long. But you made me realize I need to find a better man. One I can grow old with."

Prewitt nodded and smiled. He opened his mouth to say something more, but his cell phone rang and interrupted him. He looked at the phone's screen. "My manager," he said in an excited tone. "Excuse me." He stepped toward the front of the car, holding onto the railing next to the doorway with one hand and placing the phone to his ear with the other. Christi wasn't sure whether to stand and wait, or walk past him, through the doorway. She had an awkward feeling she should stay, as though their conversation hadn't finished. She longed for another breath of his wisdom to validate her decision.

"Yes," he said to the phone. "No, not off the top of my head... no, I don't have it with me. I'll look. Yes. I'll call you back..."

When he disconnected and slipped the phone back in his pocket, he seemed to have forgotten she was there. He grasped the handrail with both hands, pressed his forehead against the wall, and breathed heavily.

Christi stepped gingerly toward him. "Are you all right?"

Startled, Prewitt pushed away from the doorway and turned to face her. He took a deep breath and opened his mouth to respond. A shocked look jolted across his face.

"Oh my God!" Christi cried, standing directly in front of him. He seemed to want to say something, his eyes pleading as he clenched at his chest, but he found no time for words as he gasped for air.

She knew what this was. "A heart attack!" she yelled. His wide eyes called for her, one hand at his chest, the other reaching out. She tried to hold him up, but he tumbled into her and his weight was too much. They both fell to the floor in the open aisle.

"Help!" she called from the floor, Prewitt gasping beside her. A murmur hummed throughout the car, the confused passengers watching, some standing, others remaining in their seats. Christi got on her knees and managed to turn Prewitt over to his back. She yelled again. "He's having a heart attack! Is there a doctor, nurse, anyone?" The confused noise swelled to a roar, but no one answered the call directly. Christi knelt over Prewitt. She ripped open his shirt and began pumping his chest with her hands, struggling to remember how it went. *Pump, then breathe? No, clear his mouth first! Turn his head? Pump hard—don't be afraid to break his ribs!*

"Is there trouble here?" asked a man's voice. Christi looked up to see the conductor approaching from the far end of the car. "What seems to be the problem?"

"Heart attack!" Christi cried out.

"Lord have mercy!" He darted back the way he came. "Any medics on board?" He left the car on a mission.

Prewitt's open eyes stared up at Christi, but no life remained in them. She didn't give up, pressing her lips against his, pumping his gray-haired chest.

Paramedics rushed into the car and asked everyone—including Christi—to clear the aisle. The conductor kept a respectful distance at the back of the car. Other passengers sat in their seats and stared in fascination, as though they'd scored front-row tickets to some morose, sold-out show. The paramedics worked on him for nearly ten minutes before placing his body on a stretcher. "The next stop is in fifteen minutes," one of the paramedics said for the unwanted audience to hear. "An ambulance is waiting."

Christi went to Prewitt's side and looked into his exhausted face. He appeared more in pain than at peace. *No one should be alone when they die.* She took his heavy hand—still warm—and held it between hers until the paramedics asked her to step aside so they could get him in position to rush off the train as soon as they arrived at the station.

They didn't cover his body as they hurried him off the train, but Christi knew he was dead. She remembered how happy he had seemed earlier when he'd talked about his wife and their twenty-five years together. Christi imagined his wife, how it would feel to have a large part of one's self cut away.

If Christi went to the lounge car now, she'd probably be forced to tell the story a dozen times over, about how she'd tried to save this dying man and failed. She went to her seat. The boy in the seat behind her read his paperback of Poe while the girl leaned on him, her eyes closed and a peaceful expression on her face. They looked like purity itself—the kind that could last a lifetime. The kind she imagined Prewitt and Anna possessed. The kind she and Craig could never achieve. Christi sat, took a deep breath, and stared out the window.

She couldn't wait to get to Chicago now. She still missed Craig more than she blamed him, but that wasn't enough to wrap a life around. He'd been more of a stepping stone than a soul mate.

Christi shut her eyes and saw Prewitt. It was time to choose a direction and start walking. She had more faith in Chicago than she did in Craig. Chicago was bigger than any one man and the opportunities were infinite.

Live Cargo

Helen's childhood was so mingled with misery, she hadn't known there was any other kind. Arriving in America did not eliminate the ache, but it tempered past sufferings with new contentment. Over the decades, she'd grown accustomed to her tender husband, their cozy home and quiet neighborhood, their yard and friends to tend. She'd come to know a peaceful life. Now, at seventy-nine, she'd met up with misery again.

The train glided steadily along the iron tracks. The movement unsettled Helen as she struggled to get comfortable in her seat and searched for escape through the view outside her window. Even that made her dizzy, the nearby trees and bushes blurring as they sped by. She tried to focus and drive the ghosts from her mind—ghosts not easily evicted in any environment, but especially on a train. It was a bumpy ride, regardless of how easy the Amtrak brochures claimed it to be.

At least it's easier this time. This was the second leg of her trip, her return home to Chicago after her visit to DC and the terrors she'd forced herself to face there—although no terror matched that of a train, to her mind. She'd avoided trains all her adult life. The journey was worse than the destination. Trains were the transports of more than people and cargo—the two being one and the same. She knew trains as the veins of an oppressive system and in their engines pulsed the bloodlust of the oppressors, the eliminators, those who turned flesh to ash. Hers were charred memories from another lifetime, yet never far away.

She looked out the window and longed to be on the other side. The nearby foliage had passed and now a more distant view drifted slowly by. *Things always seem slower from a distance.* The scattered American houses reminded her of the hillside cottages in Poland. But the black smoke emitted by the chimneys made her squirm inside her wrinkled skin. Blackness had seeped from the smokestacks of the crematory ovens too.

She turned away from the window. She took deep breaths, looking blankly at the seat in front of her, trying to clear her mind of the images—charred piles of bodies, blackened flesh clinging to faces like the burnt skin of overcooked marshmallows. It was important to face one's fears, and she had done so by taking this trip to DC and back again. You couldn't let the terrors of the past haunt you forever. Helen had looked her mind's phantoms straight in the eye. When she did, the spirits dissipated into the air like smoke, leaving her, if only for the moment. The return home wasn't nearly as difficult. But it wasn't easy.

Maybe a walk would relax me. A drink in the lounge car. She would consider a cigarette—they'd always been dependable for soothing stress—but she'd given up smoking decades ago. Cigarettes reminded her too much of Germans. Germans reminded her of Nazis, and of German citizens who'd done nothing to save her people, some going so far as to encourage the Nazis. Her breath became short again. *A walk. A drink.*

She entered the lounge car. In the seats, side-by-side, she spotted the malefactors. She'd learned early in life to recognize the hard features of Germanic heritage. This man was obviously German, or of German descent, and the mere sight of him (associated with her feelings about being on this train) caused her to step back and lean against the open doorway. He was drinking a beer as his companion sipped iced tea. The man and woman appeared content, at ease, comfortable. Too comfortable, to Helen's mind. These were the ones—scoundrels like these—who'd allowed it to happen, who'd allowed two-thirds of European Jews to be eliminated with the ease and normalcy of pest control. Swallowing their beer the way they swallowed the lies and viciousness Hitler fed them. Stirring their tea as they should have been stirring the humanity within themselves to stand up and end the violence, the torture, the death. She turned away. She knew better—these people where too young to have had anything to do with it. But the pain was ever present and she needed someone to pin it on. *A drink.*

She ordered a screwdriver and took a gulp. The cold liquid warmed her. She'd taken up screwdrivers because her husband used to drink Polish potato vodka and she couldn't tolerate it straight. The bright juice made the vodka's harshness bearable. She'd become good at finding ways to make harsh things bearable.

She walked the floor instead of taking a seat; her own movement masked that of the train and she imagined she stood on stable ground. But when she sat, there was no denying the motion: where she was, how it felt, what it reminded her of, what she'd managed for decades to close out and now cursed herself for conjuring. Crammed into the cattle car like slabs of meat, so tight together she could barely breathe the fetid air, wanting to get off the train but dreading the destination, fearful of what fate awaited on the other side of the door.

Next to her, a young couple whispered sweet nothings to one another. Normally, she would smile at such a lovely sight, but not here, confined within the hull of the car. She lost her balance as new passengers materialized in her mind's eye—the people in the forced labor camp, Plaszow. Extended families who'd been together a lifetime, who'd loved one another, and who'd given up the will to live, hoping for nothing more than to be allowed to die together. They'd been torn apart, never to see one another again, separated into hordes of men and women, then into old and young, then into the usable and the disposable. They'd not been allowed to die together, but they had been allowed to die. They'd been made to die.

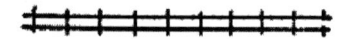

Washington DC was as impressive as she'd remembered it. Years ago, Helen had visited the capital with her husband, Moshe. Their visit by car had been more than twenty years ago; his death had been four. Their immigration to the United States had been almost sixty. Back then, when they'd been welcomed to America's harbor, Helen was going on her nineteenth birthday, although there had been a time when she seriously doubted she'd see her ninth.

Now she stood with her memories at the nucleus of freedom, the heart of the liberated life she knew and loved. This heart, the nation's capital and all it represented, would live on, though she knew her time would come before another visit.

Helen was fit for a woman going on eighty. As she toured DC, she hailed no taxis and used the metro sparingly. She moseyed from one sight to another, noting that even from afar, as she made her way by foot, she could enjoy the majestic sights of the monuments and buildings.

Her first stop was the Capitol building. She'd waited in line and taken the tour of the interior, though she remained most impressed with the elaborate exterior. Up close or from afar, in daylight or darkness, it was a spectacular sight, this glowing yarmulke of a dome crowning the white building, a beacon of hope and peace.

Helen took the elevator to the top of the Washington Monument and enjoyed the view. She could see Washington DC and beyond, into Virginia and Maryland. She would visit Maryland during this trip.

There were the fine memorials—Lincoln, Jefferson, Roosevelt—and, of course, the Smithsonian. The National Gallery of Art was her favorite. Then there were the sights she'd come all this way to see, the ones she didn't expect to enjoy, but intended to force herself through. Her friend in Chicago, Rebecca, had recently visited them and told her to be prepared. Helen didn't look forward to the visits, but she owed it to *them*—to those who had fought for her release and those who had died because the allied forces had aligned too late. These attractions hadn't been here when she and Moshe had come to DC.

She visited the National World War II Memorial. She slowly orbited the outside ring, carefully reading each state's pillar. Then, she hovered inside it. When she spotted a pigeon's droppings on one of the pillars, she sighed. She wanted to tell someone about it, to instruct the caretakers to take care of the disgrace. But she looked around and found no one to tell. So she took her own handkerchief, spit in it, and worked away the crust—brown, orange, red, black, and white. The stain reminded her of blood and flesh crushed on stone.

After cleaning the mess as best she could and dropping her handkerchief into a nearby garbage can, she remained for another hour before deciding it was time to move on. The war monument hadn't been easy. But the Holocaust Museum would prove excruciating. She resolved to visit the monument in Baltimore first to prepare herself, as Rebecca had recommended.

Happiness was never the norm, even after arriving in America. But it was possible, and it came in brief moments. Still, memory lingered and the suffering survived in their daily conversation.

Helen remembered vividly when Moshe had learned about the plans for a National Holocaust Memorial Museum. He considered it a necessity, a national treasure for America as well as for the Jewish people. "It needs to be remembered," he'd said.

Helen hadn't been so sure. "We need to remember good times, not bad. Isn't there already enough suffering? We can't forget, won't forget. Why make ourselves live through the piercing details again?"

"Remembering the bad times prevents their return."

"Remembering the bad times *is* their return."

There had been a lot of good times between Helen and Moshe. They'd not had kids, something Helen regretted in old age. But it had seemed right, back then, not to have them. How could they bring innocent children into the world? America offered security, yes, but so had Poland, before the wrong people came into power. So Helen and Moshe had found happiness in other things—gardening, good books and movies, cooking, and traveling. They'd adopted the neighborhood children with pastries and pies on school-day afternoons. They'd cultivated the best friends anyone could hope for. And above all, they'd found contentment in one another.

After the museum had opened, Moshe had insisted they visit. "It's an obligation," he said. "We have to go. Not just to support the cause, but to pay tribute to our parents and families and friends. We owe it to everyone who wasn't as lucky as us."

"Lucky? I don't want to relive the pain," Helen told him.

"We must." Moshe was determined.

But not as determined as his bad health. Before they got around to making plans, his heart arrhythmia had confined him to bed. Even as he lay dying, he insisted she make the pilgrimage. "If for no other reason, Helen, do it for me. You have to go in my place. And when you're there, light a candle for my parents, and yours. It'll bring you a new peace."

Helen didn't want to go, but how could she deny her beloved's dying wish? It took her four years to build the courage to go through with it. She was healthy, but not fit enough to fly, according to her doctor, and certainly not fit enough to drive the distance herself. Most of her friends were her age, or worked and couldn't take off. Helen could read the signs. She'd avoided trains all her adult life, had always been afraid of them like a child fears a monster in the closet. But monsters in closets only existed in childrens' minds. The monsters hiding on the trains of Helen's memory were real.

Nonetheless, she had to face them.

Boarding the train was one of the most difficult things Helen had done since coming to America. It wasn't hard in the same way that burying her husband was, but it was no less demanding. Her heart pumped faster, blood pounding in her neck, her wrists, even her eyes. Her hands shook, her steps fell unsteadily, and nausea nudged her insides. When she'd been a child, she'd gotten used to the trains; they were just a part of a larger, doomed world, no worse than being in the ghetto, better than the destinations to which trains often transported live cargo. But in her old age, she didn't have the fearlessness that helped her survive her troubled youth. In America, she'd grown accustomed to the comforts that came with freedom. When she boarded the Amtrak Cardinal, she remembered that familiar childhood sense, unsure whether she would survive the trip, not certain she wanted to.

As she walked down the center aisle, everything blurred around her, even though the train remained motionless at the station. Lightheaded, she felt the urge to lie down, but there were others behind her waiting to find their seats. She walked on, not sure about where she was or what she was seeing. She stopped in her tracks for a moment, supporting herself on the headrest of a chair, then breathed deeply, trying to calm her nerves. She knew she was in the twenty-first century on a commercial passenger train, but she couldn't clear her mind of the sensation of being on the Nazi transport. The untreated wood, barbed wire, a box car with no seating, no toilet, no water, no food, no escape. The grumbling that came when she held up the crowd was the same sound that had come from her adult companions years ago, in that other life.

"Ma'am, are you all right?" The question came from a suited gentleman behind her. He was not the sort of person one would expect to see in a Nazi transport for Jews, nor was his question in the tone a Nazi would use. He grounded her in the present.

"Yes, thank you," she said. "Just a little short of breath." She proceeded and took a seat, allowing the other passengers to find their own. As the people trudged by, she saw the dirty, sweaty, broken Jews herded in. She closed her eyes to escape it, but the images became clearer when reality was blocked out. When the engine came to life, the whistle blew and the train began to move forward, ever so slowly, then faster and faster, she was not a passenger on the Amtrak Cardinal, but a filthy sub-human on a nameless cargo transport.

"Ticket," the conductor demanded. When the man touched her shoulder and she turned to see his uniform, she gasped. His black skin and old age made no difference to her—he was a Nazi for sure, weeding her out as one of the useless ones, one who could not produce work, one who needed to be eliminated. The Amtrak uniform looked nothing like military garb, but just being a uniformed man of authority was enough. "Miss, I just need to see your ticket."

"Oh, of course," she said, relieved. "I'm sorry." She gave him her ticket.

"Thank you, ma'am." He returned her ticket and placed a paper in the slot above her seat, marking her final destination. "You just relax and enjoy the ride, ma'am." He offered a smile and moved on to the next passenger.

Deep beneath the ground—far deeper than a grave—Helen sat and waited for the metro. She would take the metro to DC's Union

Station where she could board a MARC train to Baltimore. She heard the rumbling of a metro coming from the other side and going in the wrong direction as she continued to sit on a cool, stone bench and look at the wall beyond the empty tracks.

Her eyes focused on an ugly blotch before her on the wall. The gray-white cement of the underground station had distorted in one spot, transformed to a nasty crust—brown, orange, red, black, and white.

"Would you look at that?" a man standing nearby said to his companion.

"It's seepage," said the other. "They ought to do something about it."

The metro came and carried her to Union Station. From there, she took the commuter train to Penn Station. In Baltimore, she visited the monument and sculpture that had left such an impression on Rebecca.

Helen cringed at the horridly beautiful sculpture. A massive flame filled out by the bodies of holocaust victims—starved, broken, naked. Their skeletal bodies epitomized agony. The overwhelming flame offered these figures the only means of escape from their suffering. George Santayana's words haunted the base of Joseph Sheppard's sculpture: *Those who do not remember the past are destined to repeat it.*

Helen didn't want to stare into the flames of the sculpture, into the hollow faces and naked rib cages, but she found that she couldn't turn away. After several moments, she wrenched herself away from the sculpture and visited the memorial's triangular walkway.

What Rebecca hadn't mentioned when describing the memorial to Helen were the colossal concrete blocks made to resemble European trains during the war, or the metal grates in the center, made to look like crowded box cars, or the steel wedges at each end, representing cowcatchers that may just as well have been Jewcatchers. Or the lamp posts, right out of a yesteryear train station. Rebecca hadn't warned Helen of the vintage railroad tracks from 1940, meshed into the monument. Grass grew sporadically within the tracks, giving the eerie railway an abandoned look—as forsaken as they'd felt during the Nazi oppression. *People knew what was going on. They had to have known.* Helen went to the old rails, touched one of them. *Why didn't they help us sooner? Mama could've come with us.*

One concrete block bore these words from Holocaust survivor Primo Levi:

BOTH SIDES OF THE TRACK
ROWS OF RED AND WHITE LIGHTS APPEARED AS FAR AS THE EYE COULD SEE ...
... WITH THE RHYTHM OF THE WHEELS, WITH EVERY HUMAN SOUND NOW SILENCED,
WE AWAITED WHAT WAS TO HAPPEN.

Helen retreated from the concrete trains and the lamp posts, backing away from the train stations of her youth. The vision was blurred behind her tears as she backed away and bumped into something hard behind her. She turned and found herself face to hollow face with a Holocaust victim soon to be saved by fire. Helen cried. She knew she had to return to the train station, to get back to the metro and back to her hotel in DC. She didn't want to be near this cement train or inside the real one that would transport her. She just wanted to close her eyes and await what was to happen.

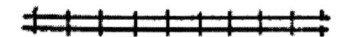

As a child, Helen learned early on to associate most things in life with danger, fear and sorrow. The train that arrived in camp one day loomed dark, like most things for as long as she could remember, and its very sight frightened her. But her fear did not stop her from proceeding toward it along with the rest of the skeletal crowd. She'd learned instinctively that you couldn't let fear stop you. If you showed your fear, you got yourself killed. She'd seen the warm blood and bits of skull on the cold cement wall, had watched her resistant friends shot dead. Fear was a fine alternative to death.

Helen was thirteen the day the train came for her and Mama. She hadn't seen her father in days, not since the men had been shipped off. Only women remained, and some of the children, like her. She knew her mother was somewhere in the crowd, but she'd lost her. There wasn't time to cry; bullets kept the mass moving. A man in uniform grabbed Helen by the arm and swung her up into the boxcar like a sack of potatoes. *They'd be more careful with potatoes.*

There were no seats on the train. Untreated wood held together by black metal and bolts made up these box cars. There were small openings at the ends of the car, but she couldn't get to one of them; they'd already been taken by the more aggressive passengers. Dull light came in through the barbed-wire openings, but it did little to brighten the place. They were packed in, standing one against another, no room to roam. There was no seating, no toilet, no water, no food, no escape.

"Mama? Mama!" Helen called out. There must have been close to a hundred women on the car, but not one of them was her mother. There were other cars; she would see Mama once they reached their destination. Wherever that was. The Germans didn't tell cargo anything.

Sweat poured from her forehead. She was so hot, even with her hair cut short by the dull German shears days ago. It had been warm outside, but inside the car an unbearable humidity bore down on them. Helen's armpits dripped, but not hers alone. Before the train even started its voyage, the room filled with the awful stench of body odor, a familiar backdrop they'd all grown to tolerate.

The train took off into the unknown. A girl younger than Helen began begging for water, but there was none to give. After some minutes of listening to the child whine, an older woman offered her a smooth stone. "Put this in your mouth," she said. "On the center of your tongue. It will help." The stone would make its rounds in the hours and days to come. When it was Helen's turn, she sucked the stone dry with no regard for the disease some of her predecessors certainly carried.

What little food they'd eaten before their trip had its own path to take. The woman next to Helen could hold it no longer, and she managed to lower her trousers and squat in her place. The woman's putrid smell added a new layer to the stench already filling the sticky air.

After hours of shifting from leg to leg, following the motion of the train, Helen could stand it no longer. She edged her way through the pudding of sweaty flesh until she reached a corner, only to find it covered in human waste. She quickly backed away from the buzzing flies and headed for another corner. More of the same. She conceded and followed the example of the woman who had squatted next to her. Nobody flinched. It was nothing, really. The shit wouldn't kill them, and dignity was something excreted long ago.

The next day, when she could stand no longer, Helen found a place along the wall and leaned against it. She wanted to lie down, but the urine and defecation prohibited it where flesh did not. There were those who did lie in it, but they were the weak, the old, the dead.

"Ouch!" A splinter of wood slid into her arm and broke off. She worked at it for a while, and then decided to let it go. It stung, but it didn't show. She feared if she worked it too much, it would become red and bloody—just the sort of open sore to make her appear unhealthy, unfit to live. Just the thing to earn more than a splinter in her flesh.

Urine, waste, and vomit decorated the floor. She'd become thirsty. She looked for the woman with the stone. Helen found the woman on her back, soaking in the floor's warm sludge. The woman's eyes were open and did not blink, but the train's motion gave her life. Helen searched the old woman and found the stone on the floor next to her, between the fingers of her dead hand. She shook off the stone, dried it on her own soiled clothes, and put it in her mouth. Within a few minutes, she had sucked away the unpleasant taste.

Coming from the cover of the Smithsonian Museum of American History, Helen turned left onto 14th Street, the Washington Monument towering beside her. She passed over Independence Avenue and found herself standing directly in front of the place she had come to visit, the place that would imprison her for the better part of the day.

The United States Holocaust Memorial Museum bore down on her with its heaviness—blood-red brick, dull cement and granite, glass cased in metal bars. The building throbbed with the dread that defined the Holocaust.

The unfinished, industrial feel lingered inside too. Helen passed through the guard station and shuffled into the lobby. Overwhelmed and confused, she sat on a cold stone bench and recouped her breath. She didn't know where to begin or what to do. She decided to pace herself and begin with something easy. She opened the door to the Children's exhibit.

Remember the Children: Daniel's Story may have been for children, but it was not kid's stuff. She was pulled along by the story of this Jewish child growing up in Nazi Germany. Surrounded by children and their parents, tears ran down Helen's face as Daniel explained separation from his mother, exile to a ghetto, shipment to a camp. Helen knew Daniel. She was Daniel.

By the time she'd escaped the children's exhibit, her legs were weak and she needed to sit. She didn't have time to make it to a bench. She got down on hands and knees and sat on the lobby floor.

"Ma'am, are you feeling all right?" a security guard asked.

Helen quickly dried her eyes. "I'll survive."

"Do you need help?"

"No." There was no antidote for her ailment. She forced herself up and ordered her ticket to the permanent exhibition.

The ticket was large and weightier than she had expected. She dropped it more than once as she carried it across the lobby to the black, metal elevator. A young museum worker handed her a miniature passport.

"What's this?" she asked.

"Each visitor gets to travel through the exhibit with a real person who lived through the Holocaust," the worker explained. "That makes the experience more personal."

"Oh." Helen looked at the passport, half expecting to see someone she knew.

The elevator door opened and Helen boarded along with the other visitors. Helen didn't block out the disrespectful jokes and snickers exchanged between some of the younger visitors, or the inappropriate flirting and groping. These modern Americanisms helped remind her that she was not really here in this, that it was just a display. But she read anger in the rigid face of the old man across the elevator.

A young girl giggled and pointed to her exhibit passport. "Look, I'm an old man," she giggled. "Mr. Rood."

"Guess that makes me a fag," her companion said.

"Yuck!" the girl said.

"Don't be Rood!" The boy grabbed her in a playful embrace.

The old man grew red in the face. "Zhis iz not Diznee-land!" he hissed through a heavy Slavic accent. The kids quieted, but did not respond. Helen couldn't tell whether the elevator was taking them up or down. It opened on a dark, somber room. The young ones snickered as they darted out of the elevator.

Helen took a deep breath and exited. She shuffled through the displays, captioned pictures, and short films. Along with exhibits, photographs and bits of information, theaters offered glimpses of different aspects of the Holocaust and the treatment of Jews throughout history.

So the kid's exhibit *had* been child's play. It was all relative, after all. These three floors of pain carried her in excruciating detail through the 1930s and 1940s, through the rise of Nazi Germany and the fall of Europe's Jewish citizenry.

Some television screens were blocked off at about five feet up, so only mature visitors could view them, and only if they chose. Helen didn't want to, but she felt obligated to look. She dropped her passport as she watched the clips of medical experiments done on living men, women, and children. Had she eaten lunch, she certainly would have been sick. She recovered her passport and went to sit and rest in a peaceful-looking hall of glass. But inside the hall, devoid of exhibits, she heard the piped voices of survivors telling their horrid stories. She stood and left, only to be faced once again with visual terrors.

There were piles of discarded shoes within the exhibit. Bags of shaven hair. Gates and relics from camps. But what most troubled her in the exhibit was the bridge in her path: a wooden box car just like the one she remembered from her childhood. Untreated, rough wood planks, barbed wire on small slits-for-windows. She boarded the car and was drawn to one of the two windows, instinctively seeking an escape. She was shocked by the car's cleanliness; it was devoid of the stench she remembered, cleared of the dead bodies she'd carried with her all these years.

A crowd of young people boarded the bridge and began tromping back and forth.

"Wow!" said one.

"Cool!" cheered another.

"Is this for real?" asked a third.

"This doesn't look so bad," chimed a teenager.

Suddenly, Helen found herself yelling at the boy. "It *was* so bad! You can't imagine how real this is!" Her excitement tapered into a quiet sadness. "It *was* so bad, and worse, even." She slumped into the corner of the car.

"Sorry," the teenager said. The group exited the car on the other side and proceeded on, but Helen remained in her corner.

How could they know? How could they understand? Even with all of this to show them, to teach them. These kids hadn't forgotten—they'd never known. Everyone wanted them to *remember the Holocaust*. How could you make a person remember something they never knew to begin with?

The Nazi train seemed to go on and on forever. The heat and humidity had risen; the stench swelled from the waste at their feet. The conditions worsened as they traveled along the iron tracks, unsure of their destination. But their tolerance remained steadfast. Still no food, no water, no opportunity to rest. Some of them had already given up hope, their corpses lining the floor.

What to hope for? Helen had found a place at an opening and looked out at the landscape. Cottages scattered the land—comforting safe havens, pictures from a storybook too fantastic to be real, memories made sweeter by distance, surely not as good as they seemed. *Are we better off here, in this train, or at our destination?*

In Helen's experience, nothing ever got better. Not since the Nazis had taken their lives from them. First, their home had been taken. They'd been forced into a ghetto, to share a room with other families. Then they were driven out of the ghetto, caged in a labor camp where men and women were separated, where families could no longer be together, where they watched their friends and loved ones tortured and killed for things as trivial as coughing out of turn, sometimes for no reason at all.

"This is intolerable," grumbled a middle-aged woman in the Nazi transport car. She'd wiped herself with her hand after a bowel movement and rinsed it in the floor's steaming residue. "They treat cattle better than this!"

"This is not so bad," said a younger woman. "At least guns aren't at our heads. They're not screaming orders at us. We're being left in peace here."

"Peace? Peace, you call this?"

Peace. Helen searched her memory for its meaning. She sucked desperately at the air from the barbed-wired opening, still looking at the black smoke coming from the chimneys. *At least Mama will be there.* She didn't know whether she'd see her father at their destination. And she knew she wouldn't see her grandparents again. They'd both been shot more than a year ago, right in front of her. They were just the right age for wise grandparents, for sharing the lessons of life taught by time. But they were too old for the hard labor the Nazis had in mind.

No, this isn't worse than where we're headed. She looked away from the window, back toward the darkened car and the shadowy people within it. *This may be as bright as it ever gets for us.* She tried to keep her mind from wandering ahead to the end of the line, to whatever worsened condition awaited them there. It always got worse, from shoveling shit to standing in it. She looked back outside and was startled at the sight. "It's snowing."

"What?" asked a woman. "It can't be snowing! In this heat?"

"Look," Helen said.

The woman came to Helen's side and peered out. "She's right. But how?"

Several others went to the opening, pushing Helen's face into the wire as they did. "That's not snow," said one, fear in her narrowing eyes. "That's ash." A hush fell over them.

"The war," another woman said. "They must be burning casualties."

"Yes, of course." But the woman's tone said something different. *At least Mama will be there.*

The train stopped abruptly, sending Helen and a number of others to the floor, face into the sludge. She threw up, then struggled to regain her feet.

They heard the gunshots, could even hear the bodies falling. *This is it, then.* For a long time they stood in the car, craving the relief of release but not wanting the doors to open, not wanting to face the Nazis with their guns. *God, let me see Mama just one more time.* When the door slid open, soldiers stood there with guns pointed at them. But they were not Nazis, and their weapons lifted away at the sight of the passengers.

"You are free," announced a young soldier, not much older than Helen. He wore a Soviet Army uniform. The Jews in the car swarmed out; the Russian soldier retreated quickly, the stench overtaking him. Helen shared the same desire as all her companions: she wanted to reach out and embrace this man, this hero. But Helen and the rest of the train's waste-drenched cargo had become the sub-human zombies the Nazis made them out to be. They fell out of the box car, wallowing in their own filth, barely alive, broken.

Helen went from car to car, looked into every face of the crowd, calling out, "Mama, Mama!" But she never found her. Mama wasn't there. Helen had seen a lot of Jews shot dead during the loading of the train. Mama would've looked for her before agreeing to board. There was little doubt her mother was back at the labor camp on the ground, her skull crushed against concrete, and that she, like Helen's father, like Helen's grandparents, like everyone from both her childhoods, would never be seen again.

In the Holocaust Museum, Helen remained in the corner of the train car, remembering the Nazi transport of her childhood, remembering Mama, remembering the Russian liberators. She was left alone for several minutes after the group of youngsters left. Someone boarded. She looked up and saw the old man from the elevator. He caught sight of her and stepped slowly her way. "May I assist you?"

"No," Helen said and offered a forced smile.

He didn't smile back. "I vemember zhese trains too."

She placed his accent. "I was liberated by Russians. From a train like this one."

"I vas liberated by Am-air-ee-ka."

"You're Jewish?"

"No. I vas Russian Army. Captured by Germans. After German camp I vas called traitor and put in Russian verk camp. So after I get out, I come to Am-air-ee-ka."

Helen nodded. The Russian offered his arm and helped her up. She stood next to him. "Thanks," she said.

"Zhese kids don't know."

"They can't know," Helen said. She understood. But that hadn't stopped her tears. The Russian shed no tears from his rigid eyes. His bitter face said that he would never understand such kids.

Helen and the Russian proceeded through the exhibit. Neither was bound to the other, yet they remained within view of one another, as though for comfort.

She'd seen the awful clips of atrocities before, of bodies and skulls in ovens, of walking skeletons, liberated but disoriented. She'd lived the scenes herself. But she hadn't seen these clips before: bodies being dragged by conquered Nazis to mass graves, not-so-innocent bystanders from nearby communities forced to bear witness to the atrocities they allowed by not standing up against the Nazis, bulldozers pushing the decaying corpses.

The three dense layers of the exhibit ended with a large movie screen showing survivors telling their stories. Helen rested in one row, the Russian in another. She wanted to take comfort from these stories of survival, but they were too laden with tears. The stories brought to mind her own experience and reminded her that it was not unique. There were too many stories like hers, like these. As she retreated to the relative comfort of the lobby, the free literature reminded her that such stories continued in places like the Darfur region of Sudan, places like Chechnya and Rwanda. Her story was her own, yet it was only one raped, tortured, murdered, charred remnant in a million, waiting to be bulldozed into a pit of indifference and forgotten a generation later.

The Russian exited the exhibit shortly after she did. Spotting her seated on a bench, he nodded and broke into what must have been a smile for his stone face. As he left the museum, she thought of the Russian soldier who had liberated her from the train all those years ago. She had the urge to thank him, to thank *someone* for her freedom. Had this old man in the museum not been captured by the Germans and encamped himself, he very well could have been the soldier who set her free. She left the museum and searched for him, but he was no longer in view.

Helen walked along 14th Street all the way to Independence, then backtracked and stood again before the oppressive building of brick, metal and glass. It had already been a long day, but she felt herself being drawn back inside the museum. She wondered how she could be lured by something that brought such pain.

She made her way to the Hall of Remembrance. Distracted by the Russian, she'd almost forgotten. Solemn silence held the hall together. She slowly rounded the circular room, taking in the glow of the *ner tamid,* or eternal flame, and the rows of memorial candles. She lit candles of her own, for Mama, Papa, and Moshe's parents. *May their memories be a blessing.* Her heavy breath echoed as she shuffled out.

On her way to the exit, Helen came upon a display of old photographs. These were happier pictures, shots of Holocaust survivors in better years, long after liberation. It offered the happy ending she needed, reminding her that there were others like her, others who had come through the misery and found joy again. People and couples and groups stood before homes and monuments, in vast fields and lively cities. Survivors lived on. Captions read *Belarus* and *Ukraine, France* and *America.* One photograph caught her eye and wouldn't let go.

"It's her!" She couldn't believe it. She moved closer, squinting with hope. A group of women stood on the coast of the Baltic Sea in Lithuania. There was no mistaking her. Helen's eyes welled, but the photograph remained clear. It was Mama—only older—with a group of friends. She must have been ten years older than the last time Helen had seen her. Helen laughed through her tears. "Mama!" Of course she'd have died of old age by now, but still, joy flooded Helen. She imagined the full, content life her mother must have lived. Not joy and happiness exactly, but certainly Mama had tasted contentment again, had lived again. Mama had survived. Helen felt blessed. She thanked God. Moshe had been right to make her come. On the other side of misery, closure waited.

Helen couldn't believe how quickly the years had raced by, once freedom had been granted by the Russians and secured in America. She looked outside the lounge's window, bound for Chicago. Trees and bushes lined the tracks in the foreground, blurring into one mass of green, brown, and red. The rapid movement did little to steady her queasiness. She refocused on the train's interior.

A woman stood from her seat in the lounge car and walked toward the attendant. Helen watched the woman in her low-rider jeans and high-cut shirt. She had a barbell in her navel. The woman's back turned into view as she ordered a drink. Helen almost dropped her screwdriver at the sight—a tattoo branded her lower back. Helen remembered her own tattoo, the tattoos marking every prisoner in camp, marking them as property. They were known by their numbers, not by their names.

A bald man complimented her tattoo enthusiastically as he pointed and laughed. The tattooed woman ignored the grinning man and walked to another part of the lounge.

"Look, she got old!" the bald man said, pointing directly at Helen. The pointing finger, as well as the comment, startled her.

His companion, a larger, older man, hushed him. Helen realized as she watched the unguarded emotion in the bald man's face that he was slow, and she tried to dismiss the words. But she couldn't. *Yes, I was permitted to grow old.* She remembered when the train doors had opened to a Russian soldier liberating them and how the subtle difference in uniform had been all the difference in the world.

A man in uniform entered the lounge car now. This wasn't the uniform of an Amtrak worker; this young man wore military garb. The very sight, along with the movement of the train, disoriented Helen. She'd seen plenty of military men over the years, but the last time she'd seen one on a train was from a time she wished she could forget. She allowed herself to fall into an empty chair. She gasped for breath, her heart pounding harder, deeper, faster, racing ahead of the train's rhythm. The soldier marched her way, armed with a beer. She saw his face clearly, the Nazi who'd shot her grandfather. The uniformed man who'd murdered her grandmother. She'd never considered they were the same Nazi—*this* Nazi. She saw the menace come toward her, the Nazi who had beaten her with the butt of his gun, the soldier who had pushed her down into a pile of dead bodies when she cried at the sight of them, the one who'd stripped her of her clothes and then spit on her for not being developed enough. And the one who'd thrown her on a train like a sack of potatoes. She saw the soldiers—dozens of them—who'd brought misery worse than death for so many years. They all had this same face now.

"Hey," the soldier said gently. "You okay?"

Helen downed the rest of her screwdriver. She looked up at the young man, not much older than she'd been back on the Nazi transport. She came to her senses and realized this was a U.S. soldier. "Yes," she managed. "I'm fine."

"Enjoying the ride?"

"Not really." Her breath came hard, but less so with each word. "I don't much care for trains."

"Me neither," he sighed. "Sometimes trains can be difficult." He took a sip of his beer. "Depending on where they're taking you."

Helen looked deep into his rigid face and realized it harbored none of the Nazi hatred she so feared. She recognized the heroism of the Russian soldier who'd freed her.

He looked past Helen for a moment as though scoping out the area, then returned his gaze to hers. "Sure you're okay?"

"Thank you," Helen said. "I mean, for what you're doing. For your service."

"Oh." The soldier's face grew heavy. "Thanks."

"The world needs more good men," Helen said. "It was men like you who saved me from the Nazis."

"Thanks, Ma'am." The soldier nodded. He passed her and took a seat near a window. He sipped his beer and peered longingly outside, as though he too yearned for an escape. This young man had his own demons to dominate, his own wars to fight. Real, physical wars. Helen was relieved to see him, content that there were still people fighting the evil forces of the world.

She stood and found her composure. She walked out of the lounge car and headed back to her passenger car. The floor was dry, there were facilities, food and drink, and she had a seat.

Sometimes trains are difficult... depending on where they're taking you, he'd said, as though he'd been sent to her. *This train's taking me to the comfort of home.*

Helen returned to her seat. The memories lingered—they'd always be a part of her, the foundation of her life. The train still made her uncomfortable, but Moshe had been right to make her visit. She found herself imagining Mama's unknown life, pictured her with her girlfriends on the beach in Lithuania. She considered how much weight had been lifted by one feather-light photograph. One grainy, old, black and white image had made all the difference in the world.

She looked out her window and tried to see the world as it existed now, not then. Houses and barns speckled the pastoral landscape. The phantoms haunted her, probably always would. The motion of the train stirred them. But Helen stared right back into their smoky depths. Mama's picture reaffirmed what she already knew: happiness was not the norm, but on the other side of misery, contentment waited.

The Silences

They were young, this couple seated on the train. Too young, their friends back home had teased them, to be riding an old-fashioned locomotive. But they'd boarded anyway, and here they sat, side by side, caught in the quiet of the passenger car during one of those rare moments when no one was speaking. The sound of the train's movement met their ears like a lullaby, a soothing soundtrack to the window's serene scenery.

Malcolm and Tina were the same age: nineteen years old, just out of high school. She'd loved him for as long as she could remember, first as a friend, then as a soulmate. Malcolm worked as a dishwasher at Red Brick Station; Tina was a sandwich artist at Subway. They both had futures ahead of them, they knew, but their individual lives came second to their life together. They considered themselves two halves of a stable whole. They'd been a steady couple for years, ever since they transitioned from middle school to high school, and if they were sure of anything, they were sure of their love for one another.

That's why they weren't in any rush to get into college. There'd be plenty of time for that in the years to come. They knew where to place their value: in one another. It was more important to get married, have children, and devote themselves to one another and their family, than to chase all the education, wealth and worldly success they could possibly procure.

"Too many people place too much importance on glamour, wealth and success," Tina had said early in their relationship, before they'd even graduated tenth grade, before they'd even seen one another in full.

"You got that right," Malcolm had been quick to agree, his gray eyes sparkling. "If people put the kind of effort into their families that they put into their careers and making money and getting successful, we'd live in a better world."

"Right," she'd said. They used to spend their after-school hours by the neighborhood pond. The surrounding green was punctuated by aesthetically placed stones and perfectly positioned trees. The tree without a bench underneath it was their favorite place—*their* place. Others could have their benches; Malcolm and Tina preferred to sit side-by-side beneath the tree in the fresh grass, his arm around her, cuddling in the shade and watching the sun reflect off the water. They smiled contentedly and watched the ducks try to catch the reflecting sunlight, dipping their heads in the water, their tail feathers rising in the air. "It would be a better place. More... old-fashioned."

Their parents and friends often teased them for being old souls in a new world. Malcolm and Tina just laughed it off. They listened to swing, show tunes, classical music, and jazz. He could name all of Glenn Miller's songs, but not one artist on the current pop charts. She'd seen every episode of *Gilligan's Island,* but not one segment of *Survivor.* Others teased them for their old ways, but Tina was sure unspoken admiration was at the heart of their jibes.

On the train, Tina glanced at Malcolm, his copper hair reflecting the sun. He'd be a shift supervisor in another year; then they could afford to move out of their parents' homes, get married, and start their life as one. She'd get the perfect wedding gown; it would be snow white, even though he'd taken her virginity when he gave his to her. "It'll be a storybook wedding," he'd promised, describing the horse-drawn carriage that would sweep them from the chapel to the swinging reception with big-band music. It sounded wonderful.

It was quiet now, on the train. Too quiet, for Tina's taste. Sometimes it seemed they had everything they needed in the having of one another. But now, she needed more. She needed his words, his attention. Malcolm was in the center of one of his silent spells again. She hated it when he fell into silence, and he seemed to do it more and more often the more comfortable he got in their relationship. She wanted him to say something romantic now. Something about how her radiant smile made his heart as light as her feathery hair, or the how the sound of her voice made his soul sing. She probed for the poetry of their past. It had been his idea, after all, to take the train. He'd said the plane was in too much of a hurry and that a train was nice and slow, that they'd have lots of time together, side-by-side. "Railroads are romantic," he'd said.

Tina looked at the man of her life: young, handsome, and at her side, his gray eyes reading a paperback of Poe's collected works. He'd been reading it for an hour straight, not sending so much as a word her way. While Malcolm read, Tina alternated between watching the scenery outside the window—young trees intermixed with old—and looking at him. Finally, Malcolm caught her staring. "What?"

Tina's longing eyes begged as eagerly as her voice. "Say something."

He slapped his paperback down, resting it open on his leg. "What do you want me to say?"

"Why don't you tell me you love me? Like you used to?"

He sighed. "I love you." The words and the annoyance in his voice did not match.

Annoyance infected her voice as well. "It's not the same when I have to tell you to say it."

"Can't win for losing," Malcolm griped. "I mean, you just asked me to say it, I said it, and now you're upset because I said it! What the hell do you want? Do you even know?"

Tina noticed the woman shifting in the seat in front of them. The lady peeked back at them, then quickly faced forward. Under the sound of the woman's sigh, Tina lowered her voice, not wanting to disturb the passengers around them with the personal problems between her and Malcolm. "I just want you to notice me!"

"Notice you?" Malcolm's voice didn't lower to meet hers. "You're right next to me—you're a part of me! How can I not notice you? It's like not noticing my left hand or right foot!"

"So you're comparing me to your right foot?" Tina couldn't help but turn up the volume herself. "Nice."

"Tina." Malcolm emitted a deep sigh. "You know what I mean."

The lady sitting in front of them continued to shift uncomfortably. She was probably ten or fifteen years older than them. The woman stood from her seat and walked the aisle of the moving train, riding its rhythm. Tina watched her, embarrassed to have driven away this quiet neighbor with their argument. This wasn't the first time the woman had gotten up for a walk. Tina looked back at Malcolm to find him watching the woman as she strutted; his eyes glided down the curvature of her back, onto her rounded behind, down her long, denim-hugged legs. *She knows how to move,* Malcolm's captivated gaze was saying—although he never would—as he admired the woman's slow, leisurely stroll.

"She's nice looking, for a thirty-something," Tina said softly.

"What? Oh, I was just staring off into space," he said.

"Yes, I saw the space you were staring off into."

Malcolm put on his devilishly embarrassed grin. "Cheer up, Honey! Of course I love you. Can't I read a little without having to say it?"

"I just want to spend some time with you, Mal. That's why we're here, isn't it?"

"All right," Malcolm said. "What do you want to talk about?"

"I don't know. Anything."

He held up his paperback. "How about Edgar Allen Poe?"

"Never...never mind," Tina said. She was no Poe fan. She gave Malcolm a look as distressed as the writer's prose. "Just go back to your reading."

He smiled and pecked her blushing cheek. "I'll just finish this story," he said. "Then we'll talk."

Tina smiled compliantly. She watched him return to his book, and she turned back to the window. They were somewhere along the border of Ohio and Kentucky, and she could see the Ohio River flowing outside. Leaves from nearby trees descended from their secure places and fell toward the water. Like little kayaks, the leaves floated along the Ohio. Some had run one onto the other, connected. They traveled together, the pairs becoming wholes. But most drifted alone down the cold autumn river. Only the lucky ones traveled in pairs.

Tina remembered a time when it had been all she could do to get a word in when Malcolm was talking. He'd spoken about everything under the sun and some things beyond it. Their early conversations had revolved around school subjects and teachers, then went on to movies and books. When puberty hit, the conversations grew awkward for a while, but they leveled out into romantic proclamations and private poetry recitals, Malcolm declaring his love for her. Tina found it difficult to ignore his words or decline his kisses. But then, she never really tried to.

Like their first few dates, their first intimate relations had been more awkward than satisfying. But since those early days, they'd landscaped one another's bodies and now knew the lay of the land. He didn't need the rhythm of a train to arouse her.

As their relationship flourished, their conversation shriveled. Tina guessed he was less out to impress and more comfortable with her, and that made him less ambitious in his speech. Or perhaps he'd already said everything he had to say, exhausted all of the subject matters he'd mastered. She wondered whether there was anything he knew or thought that he'd not already told her. There was no question of his love for her. But she didn't want to be the comfortable old brown shoe for his right foot. She needed to be lifted from the place to which she sometimes dragged herself down.

Sitting alone on the train—Malcolm being submerged in the world of Poe—Tina worried about the route they were traveling. She had a clear vision of their future as husband and wife. There would be the exquisite wedding, the magical honeymoon, the excitement of children. But she wondered what they would be left with when the rearing of children was behind them, when the conversations of a busy life were abandoned.

They would sit in the living room of their cottage, just the two of them. He'd have his newspaper or a book open in his hands. She'd be watching a program on television or looking through an album of photos, remembering better times, wishing photos had audio clips, snippets of Malcolm's words, of the conversations that had made her fall in love with him. Sounds from before the silence. *Who is this person beside me?* she would wonder. *And why won't he say anything? Why won't he talk to me?* Tina would cook dinner and Malcolm would eat it. They would look at each other, perhaps he would grunt, "Mmm. Good, Honey." And then, back to the activity or inactivity that kept them from talking.

Tina imagined that in that far-off future she would have to break the ice sometimes. She would look at her husband of thirty years and see him in his recliner with the newspaper, working the crossword in his mind. "What are you thinking?"

He'd look up, startled by her voice. "What, Honey?"

She'd smile at him. She'd still be pretty and fit, attractive, still able to get his attention. "What are you thinking about?"

Malcolm would continue to look at her, puzzled by the question. "Nothing." He'd return to his crossword, hiding his face behind it.

"No, really," she'd persist because she'd need his words, the words of their youth, the ones she'd fallen in love with. "You've got to be thinking about something. What?"

This time he'd keep his face hidden behind the newspaper. "A seven letter word akin to love," he'd answer. Or he'd begin talking about a book he was reading that she never would.

Tina would put it to him directly. "Do you think we could talk?"

He'd squirm. "I'm working on this right now."

"After you're done with the paper," she'd say, tightening her grip. "Can we talk then?"

"Well, sure. Sure we can."

But the newspaper would take longer to read that day. He never looked at coupons or the *Taste* sections, but Tina imagined he would that day. Finally, he would finish, only the entirety of the stock listings unread, and he would depend on Tina to guide their exploration of once-familiar territory.

Tina would fall silent. She wouldn't know what to say when the opportunity to say it came, not any more than Malcolm would. After a lifetime together, after retiring from their jobs and sending their children out into the world to establish their own lines of communication with loved ones, there would be nothing left for Malcolm and Tina to talk about. Once you've said everything, what more was there to say? And so, in their uncomfortable silence, Malcolm would pick up a book and Tina would find yet another photo album to revisit, another silent set of images from the days when there was enough romance to keep the dialogue going.

The train continued alongside the Ohio River. Malcolm put the paperback of Poe on his lap and turned to Tina. "So what're you thinking?"

Tina turned from the window view. "Huh?"

"What're you thinking about? You're in a dream."

She smiled, seeing the book out of his hands. "About you," she said. "About us."

"That's what I like to hear." Sincere happiness resided on his face. "Let's go get something to drink." Tina agreed, and the two of them walked hand-in-hand from one passenger car to another until they hit the crowded lounge car.

The woman from the seat in front of them was here in the lounge, drinking a glass of white wine. It appeared she had come here to think, not to talk. Others engaged in friendly conversation: a woman with a huge tattoo on her lower back flirted with a younger man; an old couple talked about their grown kids as they sipped beer and iced tea; a man in a military uniform comforted a confused-looking old woman. But many passengers sat silently: an older man jotted in his planner like he was in a race against time; a silver-haired guy read note cards; a big man in a leather jacket played with an unlit cigarette as he looked around the room.

A sad lady with a dragonfly broach on her breast caught Tina's attention. The woman seemed to be trying to mend a broken heart with an old love poem on antique paper, crying over the words or what they represented. Tina hoped that wasn't how she would turn out: a forty-something crying over her memory of Malcolm's words.

Early in their relationship, they'd promised one another that there would be no secrets. Tina had remained true to her word, until recently. She hadn't told Malcolm about her daydreams of their quiet future. She hadn't told him that such visions had driven her to seek out alternatives. That she'd setup an email account just to correspond with her friend from high school, Katie, who'd moved to New York after graduating. Katie waited tables while her agent tried to find her work as a model. Before leaving, Katie had encouraged Tina to join her and Tina had refused; it wasn't part of her plans with Malcolm. But recently, Malcolm's silences had made her question the depth of his devotion, the intensity of his love, the stability of their future.

Tina had begun using the hours that Malcolm was at work to investigate the idea of moving to New York City on her own. She'd even called an apartment tower and inquired about rates and availability. The lady on the phone had gone over the details of several apartments she had open, stressing the unlimited opportunities waiting in the Big Apple. "Want me to reserve one for you? We can do the application over the phone."

Tina's heart raced at the idea. She had to swallow down a lump in her throat before answering. "I'll call back," she said, and hung up. But she never did. The Big Apple seemed a forbidden fruit, and she couldn't bear the thought of taking a bite without sharing it with Malcolm. Just thinking about it made her feel ill.

Forgetting the idea of an alternate life wasn't as easy as hanging up the phone. Tina thought about life alone in the big city often. That wasn't her desire—she needed Malcolm—but she didn't want to end up living with his silence instead of him. All she needed was his love, his words, his assurance. She wished he'd offer her something now.

"Coke?" Malcolm asked.

"Bottled water's fine."

Malcolm got their drinks and found a corner with two empty chairs. They uncapped their bottles and drank. Malcolm broke the silence. "So what exactly were you thinking about us?"

"Oh, your favorite subject," she joked. "I was thinking about how much I need you."

Malcolm looked around, embarrassed. "Aw, we don't have to get into that right now."

"Well, you know it's true. I love you."

"Of course I know," he said softly. "You too."

Silence slithered back between them. Then he asked, "What do you want to do first? When we get there? Tickets to the Bears? Or hit the Field Museum?"

"What about Sally and Bo?" Visiting them had been the pretense for their visit to Chicago. Sally and Bo were friends from high school who had graduated a year earlier and moved to Chicago to attend the American Academy of Art. "They'll be at the station when we get there; they may have something to say about our schedule."

Malcolm took a drink of his water. "Yeah, but they'll want to do what we want," he said. "They live there; we're only visiting."

"Don't worry," she said. "We'll see the Bears in action, we'll get to see the dinosaurs at the Field Museum. They'll take us to Hard Rock and Jordan's restaurant."

Malcolm smiled at the activity their week promised. "And that place with the deep-dish pizza they're always talking about...Giordano's." He laughed. "Tina, we're gonna have a great time together."

Tina bent forward and kissed him. As they parted, leaning back in their seats, each took a drink of water. They looked out the window at the passing hills. Their silence lasted a couple minutes, but it seemed unbearably long to Tina. "I hate the silences," she whispered.

"What?"

She met his eyes, then looked at the little bit of water left in her bottle. "The silences. I hate it when we don't have anything to say."

Malcolm looked at her as she averted her eyes. Her soft blonde hair swept along her shoulders. "I love them," he said.

Annoyance crept back into her voice. "Whatever."

"Really, I do," he said. "They're comfortable, the silences. We don't have to be yapping all the time. We can be comfortable just being together, without saying a thing."

Tina thought it over. "I guess so. I just hate it when we run out of things to say."

"We're not running out of things to say," Malcolm protested. "We're finding easier ways to say what we have to say." Registering her puzzled look, he elaborated. "We know each other so well, we can say things without really saying them. I know you really want a Coke by the way you keep measuring how much water you have left, like you're fulfilling a requirement first. You told me without saying a thing. You want something with flavor, but you're trying to do the healthy thing and get your daily allotment of water in."

Tina grinned. "I guess that's true." She wanted to look at the bottom-dwelling water in her bottle again, but self-consciously refrained.

"The way I see it, the fact that we have these silences just proves how comfortable we are together, how we're made for each other. Your left hand doesn't have to talk to your right foot. We don't always have to be chatting to be into one another."

She smiled and gave him a purposeful look. "Then you're not bored with me? You didn't stop saying you love me because you stopped loving me?"

"Of course not, and you know it. It's just that when a couple is as tight as we are—practically one person—we don't have to keep saying it. It's like breathing, or our heartbeats. It's automatic. We just know. It's there, in you, in me, in the speaking and the silences."

She took his hand in hers and looked him in the eyes. "It's still nice to hear it once in a while."

"All right, all right. I love you, Tina." This time he didn't look around to see who might have heard. "Now, how about a Coke?"

As they walked back to their seats, they passed the old Amtrak conductor. "You kids enjoying the ride?" He'd already chatted with them earlier, in the lounge car. He may have been the only person she'd met who talked as much as Malcolm, when Malcolm was in the mood to talk.

"We sure are," Tina said, her arm around Malcolm's waist. "Thanks for asking."

The old man chuckled. "It's sure nice to see young'uns who appreciate the train." He tipped his cap and walked on. Tina and Malcolm took their seats.

"He seems like a happy guy," Malcolm said.

"He's lonely," Tina said.

"Lonely? He was all smiles."

"He's friendly, but he's lonely. You can see it in his eyes and the way he has to talk to everyone."

Malcolm grinned. "See? You know what I'm talking about better than I do."

Tina smiled back. "Maybe I just needed you to tell me what I already knew but hadn't figured out."

They were close now, somewhere west of Indianapolis. According to the map, after the next stop the train would bend to the right and proceed north to Chicago. Tina looked forward to a fun week with Malcolm, Sally, and Bo. As anxious as she was to get off the train, she even looked forward to returning to it for their ride back to Baltimore together. Tina had a definite vision of her future with Malcolm.

In that distant future, Malcolm would be reclining in his favorite chair and Tina would be on the sofa. It would be quiet in their living room, with their children all raised and sent out to make tracks of their own in the world. Retirement would keep Malcolm and Tina together most of the time, enjoying each other's conversation, each other's presence, each other's silence.

When Malcolm finished the newspaper, he would look over to the sofa, over to Tina. She would return his gaze, no words between them, and pat the open space beside her. He would stand, strut over, and take his place by her side. They would look together at the photo album and remember good times together. There would be no need for audio clips—they would provide their own live commentary. They would talk about those times, remind each other of feelings conjured by the pictures. They would talk, and then not talk. They would kiss and make love and make more good times. Then they'd enjoy the silence.

Tina decided that when she got home she would delete her secret email account. Katie could have her modeling career in New York City. Tina had all that she wanted in her life with Malcolm.

Back in their seats, she looked out the train's window at the autumn trees once again. Leaves came down like sporadic droplets from branches after a hard rain. Once in a while, two leaves remained connected at the stems, falling as one.

Freedom

Joe watched the American landscape pass by as the train chugged along the tracks. It was comforting, this picturesque view, as he rode home to visit his parents. It would be a good visit, a happy reunion. He needed a happy reunion. The rolling farmland fell behind a forest of oaks and elms.

Joe thought of McMurphey, his buddy back in Afghanistan. McMurphey could have told him with certainty whether he'd made the right decision regarding Bi'nh and the war. Joe wished he could see things as clearly as his old friend had. McMurphey had a way of summing things up simply. "We're fighting for freedom," he'd once said in the dusty heat of a late Afghan afternoon.

"Regular heroes," Joe said.

Manning, their friend and agitator, laughed as he wiped sweat from his forehead and flung it to the dry sand at their feet. "Whether we're heroes or henchmen depends on who's doing the introductions."

McMurphey flicked his cigarette butt into an ash can. "Ain't no question about it. We're willing to go into harm's way for democracy, willing to kill for justice, willing to die for freedom. Way I see it, that makes us heroes."

"You got it," Joe agreed. "That's why I'm here."

Manning scoffed. "Shit, man. Not me! I'm here 'cause I signed on the dotted line to get college money—back when I thought we were a peaceful nation."

McMurphey lit another cigarette. "That's how you got in, but *this* is where you are. We're fighting the good fight, boys. Doing our part to restore order out of chaos, to fix this half-assed world."

That's how Joe had seen it too, along with many of his brothers-in-arms. They'd come to the understanding through training and first-hand experience. When they'd been together in the blistering desert heat, Joe had stood behind McMurphey in shared convictions. But now, as Joe leaned his head against the cool window of the train and watched one Rockwell landscape pass into another, he questioned his mission. Not that it mattered what he, as an individual, thought.

Joe's time as a free man was passing by quickly, his days of roaming the country and visiting loved ones vanishing into the cool autumn air like the train's black smoke. Time passed quickly, but uncertainty lingered. *Am I a free man or just the government's property?* The term *human resource* took on a new meaning since he'd joined up.

His girlfriend, Bi'nh, had planted the seed. When he got his pass for one month's R and R, Bi'nh had been his first priority. They were supposed to have a happy reunion. She was to feed his stomach with her spicy Vietnamese food, his desire with her slim, golden body and his ego with her patriotic admiration.

He got his all-you-can-eat buffet, and he got more love during that week than he could manage. But still his ego hungered. Bi'nh was not as generous in praising his heroism as she was in sharing her food and flesh. He just didn't know how to take her.

Outside the window, farm houses and barns speckled the pastoral landscape. A sturdy flagpole towered in front of one modest home. The stars and stripes waved confidently in the wind, and it was all Joe could do to keep from saluting. There'd be time enough for such formalities in a couple weeks.

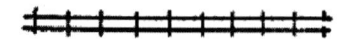

Poor Xing Wu, brainwashed. Joe missed his old roommate. They'd spent two years in college together, each earning an Associate Degree in Business Administration. Wu was an exchange student from China, and he was the first foreigner Joe had gotten to know as a true friend. Joe had met people from other nations before, but he'd never befriended one the way he did Wu.

Joe did not aspire to become a businessman. He just wanted to make a difference in the world, one way or another. It had turned out that the business degree was the easiest to acquire with the courses he had under his belt.

Things were different for Wu. His employer had studied in America and felt that, even in their communist society, it was good for a businessman to be exposed to the capitalist way of thinking. Their communist government was permitting more capitalistic practices than ever. Thus, Wu was granted two years to study business in America, complete with salary.

The value of the Chinese currency, the Yuan Renminbi, was pegged to the U.S. dollar, so Wu's salary never fluctuated. That wasn't the case, Wu told Joe, with many of the exchange students who were here with stipends and salaries. Wu considered it his good fortune. In more cases than not, fluctuations were in favor of the dollar, not the exchange student.

So here was Joe, placed by the college administration in tight quarters with a Chinese man. *They seemed like tight quarters at the time; that was before the military.*

At first, Joe was reluctant to become familiar with this strange man, this foreigner. But Wu turned out to be one of the friendliest people he'd met, even if he was from a communist country. When Wu got his first monthly deposit, he invited Joe out to the local pub. He insisted on Chinese beer and Joe insisted on American. They compromised and each drank the other's beer.

Joe knocked back the beer and asked about communism. "You'd think China would've gone the way of the Soviet Union by now."

Wu sipped his, smacking his palate as though searching for the taste. "Capitalists like to sell water and call it beer. The businessman tries to get rich at the expense of the people. In China, everyone's equal." Joe started to disagree, but Wu hastily added, "Equally poor."

Joe laughed out loud and his eyes regained their easy glee. He had a hearty gulp of the Tsingtao, slowly acquiring the taste. "See, we've got potential here in America. Capitalism allows anyone to work hard and make it big. Everyone's got a chance."

"It is the American Dream." Wu smiled, still unsatisfied with this king of beers. "But it is a nightmare for most people. Only rich people have good dreams. In China, everyone gets the chance to work hard. But nobody has false dreams."

"False dreams?" Joe asked. "Whoa, Wu! So you really like communism better than the American way?"

"It does not matter what we like better. We have what we are given."

As the classes got more difficult for Joe, they seemed to get simpler for Wu. It was convenient to have the campus super-brain nearby to copy from when the assignments got tough. Sometimes Wu even offered to do Joe's assignments for him, stimulated by the opportunity to learn more through the experience of doing. Compared to his schedule back home, Wu had a lot of free time on his hands, and he could only stomach so many American beers.

The tall ship carried Joe and Bi'nh out of the harbor, into the waters of their first date. It had been Wu's idea for Joe to take Bi'nh on a two-hour cruise for their first date. Wu had met Bi'nh at a meeting of the International Club. They'd hit it off from the start, despite their differences—Wu was interested in the common man, while Bi'nh was more interested in the environment that common men recklessly used up.

When Wu had asked whether he could buy her a Tsingtao, she'd said she preferred Bud. He'd smiled. "You'd get along with Joe." Wu was more interested in getting along with American women anyway, while in America.

Joe and Bi'nh stood on the deck of the tall ship. The crew rushed around them, manipulating the ropes and heaving sails, sending invitation to the wind. In contrast to the sounds of a crew hard at work, the carousel's music from the harbor made its rounds in the salty air, complimented by the songs of street musicians on the boardwalk, playing steel drums and pan flutes.

The two stood together and watched the waves of activity around them. As the crew continued to lumber to and fro on the wooden deck, Joe and Bi'nh watched the cityscape behind the Baltimore harbor drift further away. When the sounds of the Inner Harbor had faded, leaving those of splashing water and surrounding conversations, Joe searched for some conversation of his own.

"This is great!" he said, realizing after he had said it that he shouldn't compliment his own suggestion for a first date.

Bi'nh took in a deep breath of the sea air as she leaned her arms on the edge of the ship, overlooking the water. "Yeah, I love the water." She smiled. "And it sure beats one of those cheesy indoor dinner cruises."

Joe mentally scratched what had been his idea for a second date. The sandal fit, though, that she'd prefer natural sailing to the excess of a motorized dinner cruise. Bi'nh was an environmental science major, a real tree-hugger. But she was a *hot* tree-hugger, golden skin on a thin frame, black hair that flowed like velvet beyond her shoulders. He wanted to touch it as the sea breeze lightly salted it. Standing beside her, he did.

Bi'nh smiled when Joe took her blowing hair in his hand and followed the lines to her face. "Isn't it beautiful?" she asked. Her hair *was* beautiful. But as she turned from him to look at the setting sun, he realized what she'd meant.

"Oh." He folded his arms in front of him and leaned on the edge beside her, facing the sun. "Yeah. This is great." The wind was cool, but the sun warmed their faces. Her skin shared the sun's golden hue—and was equally as warm, he suspected. He reached out to her.

She *was* warm. She allowed herself to be taken under his outstretched arm and cuddled against his chest. The horizon was still red-orange, but the wind grew cooler and stronger. He shielded her from the chill, his lips pressed lightly against the neat part in her hair. Their warmth swelled as the sun penetrated the wet horizon.

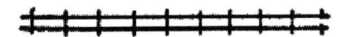

After graduation, the three separated—Joe returned home to Chicago, Bi'nh moved just outside Baltimore to Towson University, and Wu returned to China—but they kept in touch.

The day he left, Joe held Bi'nh's hands in his as he faced her. "How are we going to do this?"

She looked up into his eyes. "Long-distance relationships are hard, but better than the alternative. Love transcends distance."

Joe took her in his arms. "That's easy to say now. We can still touch and see each other. But tonight, when we can't, it's the distance I'll notice."

"It's only about a day by train," she reminded him. "It's not like you're moving to China."

But Wu had. There were the occasional phone calls between Joe and Wu, but it was email that kept their friendship alive. Joe filled in his friend on the changes in his own life, his decision not to go back to college, to join the Army instead as a way to make a difference in the world. *To win the world over to capitalism,* he'd joked.

A few months later, Wu sent an email to Joe explaining that he'd made a big decision too: he'd followed Joe's lead and joined the Chinese Navy. It was his way to counteract the overbearing capitalistic influence of the world's bully. *Touché,* Wu had written, accompanied by a smiley face.

Joe's decision to join the armed forces didn't come immediately after he, Wu, and Bi'nh had relocated. A more tragic event pushed him into the role of soldier.

For Joe, it took time for the devastation of that awful day to seep in. He sat at his computer, entering figures into a database at the office where he temped. Marge, the chatty woman in the cube next to his, had a habit of reading the hot Internet headlines out loud. She was the office herald, alleviating Joe of the need to read the news himself. On this particular morning, she stood up to bellow out a big one. "My Lord! An airplane's just hit the World Trade Center in New York!"

Joe finished the set of figures he was keying in before pausing to let the news register. "Wow, that's pretty bad." It was bad news in the way that a lot of news was bad: an airplane has been hijacked or has crashed; young children have been taken hostage and are being killed; several teenagers in a rural town have been murdered in another school shooting; a weather disaster has taken countless lives; an ethnic cleansing campaign has been reported in Africa or some far off country no one pays any attention to. Joe sighed and went back to his work.

Before he'd filled his screen, Marge was shuffling up and down the cubicle aisles announcing that a second plane had collided with the other tower. Then he knew it was not just more bad news, not just another terrible accident. Hysteria broke out in the office when the Pentagon was struck. Eventually, everyone was sent home early because no one knew how this day would end.

On the car radio, as a fourth plane crashed in Pennsylvania, the devastation sounded even worse. But when he got home and saw his mom—stunned—on the floor in front of the television, he fixed his eyes on the screen's images for the first time and saw the unimaginable for himself: people jumping from the high, flaming windows, the towers crumbling into rubbish heaps of flesh, stone and glass. The more he heard, the more he saw, the worse it seemed. And for the first time in as long as he could remember, he was not ashamed of the tears that streamed down his face.

Wu called to offer his condolences. "Everyone here in China thinks this is terrible. Almost like it happened to us. Hard to believe. We are with you, my friend."

Joe called Bi'nh in Baltimore.

"It's terrible, Joe!" she cried. "I mean, I'm okay, don't worry. But it's terrible! It's not far, you know, the Pentagon, only an hour away. Right in my backyard! And the towers! God, Joe, I wish you were here! What's this world coming to? Where's it going?"

Joe didn't know where the world was headed, but he knew where *he* was going. His slightly-over-minimum-wage assignment through the temp service wasn't important to him; Bi'nh was. He took a train the very next day from Chicago to Baltimore. He wasn't about to fly if he didn't have to. He spent a week with her, crying with her, holding her, his lips pressed against the part in her silky black hair as she nestled against his chest.

In the hours before his train was to take him back home to Chicago, Bi'nh held him in the privacy of her apartment. "Thanks so much for coming." She was the first person to offer a genuinely happy smile in days, and it was a welcome sight. "I love you, Joe."

He kissed her deeply, hugged her tightly, her golden cheek against his chest. For a long time they stood there, interlocked. Already he could taste the pain of missing her. "I love you too, Bi'nh."

Joe's original decision had been to quit college only temporarily after getting his two-year degree. Then he would work for a year or two, make a little money, and go back to finish up his bachelor's degree. But that all seemed insignificant as he held Bi'nh in the wake of September 11.

Shortly after his visit with Bi'nh, Joe joined the army. By the time he made it through basic training, the air strikes had ceased and the war in Afghanistan was over. That was just fine with him; he would rather be a peacekeeper than an aggressor.

When Joe finally arrived in Afghanistan, it was not what he had expected. The nation, in the aftermath of America's attack, was barren. The Taliban had been conquered, but the civilians of war-stricken cities and villages suffered. Joe and his brothers-in-arms kept the peace and watched over the efforts to rebuild.

His outfit never stayed long in one place. It was just as well not to get to know these people, not to make friends. Some approached the American soldiers with smiling faces, respect, praise, and gratitude. They came with flowers, gifts, and heartfelt thanks for freeing them. But there were others too, and although the laughter and happiness of the friendly citizens were emotionally satisfying, the bullets and bombs of Afghanis who were resentful of the armed guests were more than dissatisfying; they were deadly.

One evening, as Joe and his fellow soldier Manning slept, they were awakened by the sound of gunfire. A small group of Afghanis stood along the border of their camp. "Go home!" they demanded ferociously. "Americans go home!" Joe and Manning jumped up, guns in hand, only to realize that McMurphey already had the situation under control.

McMurphey held his gun on the leader of the three protesters. "Get out of here before things get ugly," McMurphey demanded.

"You get out!" their leader retaliated. They held their primitive guns at their sides. "Afghanistan is not your state—it is ours!"

McMurphey lowered his gun. "Go on home to your families," he said. Joe watched as a few other on-duty soldiers came to stand at McMurphey's side. But the primitive weapons of the enemy came back up and McMurphey had to put them down. Fire erupted. The four American soldiers, with their superior marksmanship and weaponry, easily took care of the Afghani rebels. When the fireworks ended, three bodies lay lifeless on the earth. McMurphey looked around and spotted Joe and Manning. "Since you guys are up," he said, "we could use some help."

During his first two months of peacekeeping, Joe had seen three friends fall and two others injured. *Usually the stats are the other way around—more injuries than casualties.* But there were a lot of contradictions, when he stopped to dwell on it. He was a peacekeeper, but he fought and killed. He was a liberator, but he seemed to oppress the natives of this land. The war was over, but the battles waged on.

Sure, there are the ungrateful protesters, the rebels who want to take Afghanistan back to where it used to be, Joe wrote in an email to his parents. *But for every one of them, there's a nice old lady who thanks me, a young man who's shaved his beard for the first time, a beautiful woman who finally knows the feeling of the sun on her bare face and arms while in public. Not everyone wants us here, but we're restoring freedom to these people. We're really helping them. I just saw a new school finished this week. We're providing emergency food, shelter, and medical attention. We're installing basics, like electricity and water.*

We're building roads and medical clinics and improving security. We're building their nation into something better than it was before. And most importantly, we're giving them democracy.

Later, as Joe walked through the crumbled town near camp, his convictions were affirmed. A young man, cleanly shaven, walked hand in hand with an alluring young woman, her smooth skin being caressed by both the sun and her man's gentle hand. Joe watched as the couple stopped and faced one another. They kissed deeply, stirring him as he stared enviously. *This is why I'm here.* It was also why he longed to be back in Baltimore.

The clunky laptop from Joe's college days went with him to Afghanistan, a symbol of his time with Bi'nh and Wu. It was his most valued possession, his one piece of evidence that a normal world still existed. During leisure time, he would log on and visit the world he longed for: he read the headlines on the news websites and imagined Marge bellowing them out; he visited the gossip pages to gain some feeling of life outside the hard, uniformed men and women around him; and most importantly, he emailed his friends and family—especially Bi'nh and Wu.

You should not be in Afghanistan, Wu wrote in an email, his tone more militaristic than ever before. The Chinese Navy was rubbing off on him, Joe thought; Wu was submerged in Chinese military thought as deeply as he was submerged beneath the ocean in the submarine he crewed. *It was wrong to attack the entire nation to find one man and his band. It is the American way: bomb the disposables and think only of self.*

Joe constructed his response. *The Taliban ran this country before we liberated the Afghani people. They did not cooperate with us. We gave them a choice, and they chose for us to strike. They harbored terrorists and were on the side of our enemy.*

Wu retorted. *These words are shit from mad cow. It is the American way, or no way, to your mind. And when anyone disagrees with you, you destroy them. You disagree with me, so maybe you should cut my throat or throw bombs at my country?*

Of course not, Joe typed back. *You're not harboring terrorists. We don't attack those we disagree with, just those who help wage war against us.* Joe considered, then continued typing. *We're here to liberate the world from violent militants.*

Wu's emails grew increasingly aggressive. *You are the violent militants! You demolished a nation to prove your might to a few religious men, and still didn't find the man you were looking for!*

Joe responded instantly. *Over 3,000 people died and the terrorists are going to attack again! Can't you get that? We've got to strike back. I'm fighting for justice, for democracy, to protect the world from terrorism!*

Wu's retort shocked Joe more than anything he'd seen in Afghanistan. *Joe, you and your people are naïve. Since joining the Chinese Navy, I've learned much. The Chinese military knows the truth. Al Qaeda had nothing to do with attacks on America. Bin Laden claimed responsibility, but he was not the mastermind. It was your own people. Your government arranged the attacks as a way to justify war and stimulate the American economy. And it won't stop with Afghanistan.*

Joe was aghast. *That's wack, Wu! That's crazy talk! I'm fighting for freedom!*

Wu remained steadfast. *No, you are not fighting for freedom, you are fighting for politicians. They knew war would stimulate an ailing economy. They took a calculated risk. They attacked their own to achieve war, support from their people and popularity as strong leaders. I have lost my appreciation for America. We are enemies.*

Joe became ill at the thought of losing a friend to such rot. *Whoa, Wu! Lighten up!* But Joe had received his final email from his old college buddy. Xing Wu had gone under, surrounded by more than frigid waters; he was surrounded by Chinese sailors, officers, and propaganda.

Even when the United States attacked Iraq months later, Joe knew Wu's conspiracy theory was unfounded. But it was eerie. Wu had predicted the United States would not stop with Afghanistan, and it hadn't. With Afghanistan still crumbling around him, Joe felt uneasy that his nation was beginning to wage another war.

McMurphey wasn't going to vote. He, Joe and Manning sat together in the scorching noon-day sun after lunch. Joe came straight out and asked his buddies what their plans were, knowing the absentee ballots were on their way.

McMurphey answered simply enough. "I ain't got the right to vote. I don't know the issues well enough."

Manning blew out a cloud of cigarette smoke. "Shit, man, you're out here saying we're fighting for people's rights and you won't even give yourself the right to vote?"

Manning's smoke to McMurphey was like blood to a shark. He lit his own cigarette. "That's right. How can I vote in one of the most important elections of my lifetime?"

"With conviction," Manning answered.

Joe said, "I plan to vote, but I haven't decided who for yet. I mean, the bickering back and forth between Bush and Kerry isn't enough to base my vote on. And the liberal press is owned by the conservative businesses, so who're you gonna believe?"

Manning smoked his cigarette down to the filter. "Well you gotta vote, one way or another. We're all out here killing and dying for our nation's agenda. We've earned the right to help define it."

McMurphey's cigarette butt followed Manning's into the ash can. "Doesn't matter whether we vote or who for anyway. We're doing our jobs. That's what matters in the end."

Manning drank warm water from his bottle. "There you go again."

Joe took the middle road. "I guess it's important to vote, but no matter who wins, we'll still be here awhile." He looked to McMurphey for support. "Doing our part."

Manning fixed his gaze on Joe. "Maybe *we're* doing our part, but is our government?"

Joe peered at him. "Look, I can't answer for the government. We've all got to answer for ourselves."

Manning laughed loudly. "Man, they got you both brainwashed."

McMurphey smiled. "We're all influenced by something. Might as well be on the right side."

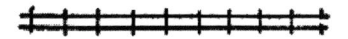

The tank fired, hitting the building; the dried mud crumbled and a cloud of dust surrounded the enemy. Fire came at them from the other side of the ruins.

Joe leaned around his own intact wall—the remains of a building that had been bombed months ago—and returned fire. McMurphey followed him.

"More of 'em than we thought," McMurphey said, both of them back behind the wall. They took turns, the seven of them, ducking behind the wall, then peeking out to fire back.

"Least we've got cover," Joe said. Last time, their cover had been blown out by an Afghani with a rocket-propelled grenade.

Joe's turn again. Bullets whizzed around him, some so close he could feel them. *Imagination,* he figured as he fired back. Then he stopped, confused. Was it possible, what he was seeing? Not just men, but women and children? They continued firing at him, but he didn't return it.

"What's up?" Manning asked. "Get outta' the way!" He pulled Joe back behind the wall and took his place.

"What happened?" McMurphey demanded, getting ready to take Manning's place.

"There aren't more men than we thought," Joe said. "They're women and children!"

"Aww shit!" McMurphey nearly dropped his M-16. "Well, they're trying to kill us, aren't they?"

"They sure as hell ain't trying to make love," Manning said.

The American tank fired again.

McMurphey crept back to the edge of the wall and began to fire. Joe looked down the length of the wall; two more soldiers took turns firing from the right edge. A medic worked frantically to save another man in their squad who twitched on the ground.

"Almost got 'em," McMurphey said. "Get over here, Joe!"

Joe hesitated, the sight seared into his mind: a woman not much older than his own Bi'nh, knowing she would be killed, picking up a gun and fighting the Americans anyway. Beside her, an old woman, as old as his grandmother. And the kids. *What are they, thirteen? Twelve? Maybe younger?* There must have been twenty of them pouring out of the crumbled building.

"Fuck it!" Manning yelled, taking Joe's place and firing. But he underestimated the women and children. Blood spurted in a line across his chest. He fell back, screaming. The medic sprinted over to him.

Joe stood above Manning and fired. They were a blur to him now; he didn't see the faces of the women or the children, just their shadowy silhouettes in the dusty air beyond the crumbled ruins that had once been their homes and neighborhood, their schools and places of worship. Manning had taken his place; Joe owed him.

One woman remained, the bodies of children twitching at her feet. He could see her face now, or imagined he could. She was beautiful, innocent, driven to something she shouldn't have been forced to endure. Joe would just as soon love her as kill her, but she was trying to end his life. He fired at the same moment as the tank. By the time the dust settled, she already had. Her body lay still on the ground. Joe wasn't sure whether he or the tank's fire had killed her. His head dull, his entire body hollowed by battle, he wasn't sure it made a difference.

Behind their wall, two men were dead, five still alive. Manning was among the dead, and it was Joe's fault. No one would say it, but Joe knew. A dust cloud of guilt surrounded him. He inhaled the dust and coughed, choking on it. At least McMurphey was still alive. His best friend, Xing Wu's replacement. They'd have a smoke and a beer back at the base.

Joe stood behind McMurphey, who kicked down the door with the full force of his muscular leg and military boot. The door fell open and the four American soldiers stormed the home, M-16s at the ready.

"Sayed Hamid!" McMurphey yelled forcefully above the commotion. "Where's Sayed Hamid?"

"Sayed Hamid!" Joe repeated in an equally authoritative voice. They were here, in this private Afghani home, under the authority of the United States Government.

"No, no!" A middle-aged woman in traditional garb huddled over her three children. All four soldiers stood above the family, their rifles raised to the sky but ready to aim at a moment's notice.

"Ma'am, we need to know where he is. Where is Sayed Hamid?"

"No, no!" she repeated in her limited English.

"We've got reason to believe he's involved with plotting a local uprising," McMurphey said. "We've got to find him before he gets himself killed or endangers us."

"No know," she said, and this time Joe perceived her meaning. McMurphey and the others still heard the uncooperative "No, no."

"All right, then," McMurphey said. "Guess we'll have to take them into custody." Joe lifted the squatting woman to her feet, and then her three children: one a teenager, the others younger. McMurphey cuffed them. All the while, the other two men held their guns on the rebellious Afghanis. "We'll get an interpreter and get some info out of 'em."

Suddenly, gunfire sprayed in from another room. One soldier was down. The other three turned and fired, killing the man who'd attacked them. McMurphey lay gurgling in his own blood. The woman screamed and the children cried, but Joe didn't hear them until the gunfire ceased. Sayed Hamid—father and husband to this family—was dead. So was McMurphey. Their mission was accomplished, and now Joe was in charge.

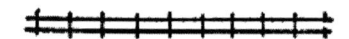

When he returned to the states, Joe's first destination was Bi'nh. Her emails had been loving and supportive, but it wasn't enough. He needed her in the flesh, the touch of her golden skin and black hair, the scent and look of her.

She met him at Penn Station in downtown Baltimore. He spotted her first—understandable, he figured, since he was one of hundreds coming off the train. She was a gleaming bit of jade in a garden of stones. "Bi'nh!"

"Joe!" Her distant look focused on him, brightened, and she ran toward him. He dropped his bag to take her in. "I'm *so* glad you're back!" she said. "It's good to have you here, safe."

She drove them to her studio apartment in Towson, half an hour from the train station. He watched her as she drove. This was surreal, being back in her life, a different life. "Got a new car," he noted.

"It's a Prius." She beamed. "A hybrid."

"Weird." He laughed. "Like, electric?"

"Hybrid. Gas *and* electric. Gets fifty miles to the gallon in the city."

"That's good, with these prices."

"Yeah, I know." She sighed. "You'd think they'd lower the prices, with us owning Iraq and all."

Joe laughed, not because he thought it was funny. He didn't care about the car or gas prices or Iraq--he cared about her. She wove through traffic along Charles Street, dodging pedestrians and skirting past slower-moving cars. At a traffic light, she turned to eye him. Her serious driving face melted into one of carefree warmth. She kissed him until an SUV behind them honked.

He watched her all the way to the parking lot, saying very little. She yanked the parking brake and looked at him again, smiling. "We're here."

She unlocked her apartment door, but before she could step inside, he took her in his arms again. She yelped as he lifted her and carried her across the threshold.

After they made love, Bi'nh donned a silk robe and went to work in the kitchen. Joe lay on the bed and watched her work. The familiar scent of Vietnamese cooking soon filled the small apartment.

She'd gone all out. Dinner began with *chan chau*, a hot, sour fish soup. Her fragrant rice—she called it *com*—was an expected staple, but he'd never tried her *bahn tom*, crusty shrimp pastries. After Bi'nh, seafood was the next thing he missed most about home. And, of course, Xing Wu.

"I told you Wu joined the Chinese Navy..."

"Yes," she said, her mouth full of spicy vegetables. "You emailed me."

"Poor guy's been brainwashed."

She shrugged. "That happens. Most people tend to conform to those they hang around with."

"I guess...but to believe our president attacked his own people to bring on a war? That's plain stupid."

"To *us* it sounds stupid," she said. "Our government would probably say slavery was a stupid idea, now, or Indian massacres. The Holocaust, to most Germans, is wrong in hindsight, but it's easy to go along with the crowd. It's easy to get convinced when everyone around you believes."

"I guess."

They washed the dishes together. It was nice to do something domestic with the woman he loved. To live such an uncomplicated life—school, cooking, dishes—appealed to him. They sat on the loveseat with Sam Adams in glasses, James Galway blowing traditional Japanese music through a flute on the stereo. He felt her through her silk covering until she took his roaming hand in hers.

"Tell me about it."

"About what?"

She searched his eyes. "It must be terrible over there."

"Oh, that." He lost his mood, slouching back on the soft cushion and grasping for words.

She scanned his face for signs of emotion. "War is bad enough, but to know you're fighting an unjust war..." she probed.

Emotions came, but not those she expected. "What?" he asked. "Oh, not you too!"

"No, I'm not with Wu. His story's a little far-fetched. But it *is* obvious that our government is using September 11 as an excuse to wage unnecessary war."

"Bullshit!" Joe sat up. "I'm fighting a war against terrorism! I'm fighting for the freedom of these people! We're liberating them!"

"Joe, I know you're doing what you have to do as a soldier. But these wars are not being fought for the right reasons. There's no connection between Saddam Hussein and Osama bin Laden or September 11. All made up. And no weapons of mass destruction have been found."

"Bullshit!" Joe's autopilot response fired. "There *are* weapons of mass destruction and we'll find them! And there's proof of communication between Saddam and Osama."

"Sure." Bi'nh laughed. "They're probably in a cave right now, playing poker, smoking cigars."

Joe smirked, but the tension remained. "It's all part of the war on terrorism, to keep us safe, to keep the world safe." He took a drink. "There's evidence they communicated."

"Maybe they did," Bi'nh allowed. "Dan Rather talked with Saddam too—he did it right on national TV. But we're not going to war with CBS, are we?"

"What about all the bad things Saddam's done to his people? All the atrocities?"

"What about worse atrocities we ignore—Rwanda, Sudan?"

"We're fighting for democracy," Joe said. "Spreading democracy—that's what this is all about."

Bi'nh sipped her beer. "Joe, if we really believed in democracy," she began in a careful voice, "wouldn't we bow to the wishes of the United Nations? 'You're either with us or against us' is not democracy—it's bullying the rest of the world into doing it our way. On a world scale, it's tyranny. Democracy would be giving all nations an equal vote in the matter. We like to claim democracy as our goal, but we don't give a damn about democracy, not really. America's not fighting for freedom. America's fighting for what it's always fought for—its own interests. Maintaining its place as the superpower over the rest of the world. Inside, America may be a democracy. But really, we're the tyrants, over the rest of the world; we believe in a global dictatorship."

Joe gulped his beer to the end. "Doing what the UN wants instead of fighting for what's right?" He stood, carried his empty glass to the kitchen area, and refilled it. "I'm afraid I can't agree with that. The UN can growl, but they don't have any bite. You can't just threaten a country to 'disarm or else' and then not bring down the hammer when it doesn't."

"Just because we've got the might doesn't mean we should ignore the rest of the world!" Intensity rose in Bi'nh's voice along with its pitch. "We have a responsibility to practice the democracy we preach on a world scale—not to just pretend we're the leaders of the world and go it alone."

Joe came back to the loveseat, though it felt more like a war zone. "We *are* the leaders of the world, and we've got to do what's right."

"Don't you think every nation wants to do what's right? The difference is our definition. For America, it's always been might is right—well, once the colonies were freed from the might of the British."

Joe took a drink of his fresh beer. They sat in silence for a moment, the tension settling slowly, like dust after a desert battle.

Joe tried to keep his voice calm, but there was an edge to it. "Bi'nh, I was there. I know what I'm talking about. You get your information second-hand, from the news, or third-hand, from friends who saw the news. I was there. Sure, there's bad stuff. But there's good stuff too. New schools, new medical facilities, new roads; there's food, water, and shelter for the people who need it. We're building them back up to something better than they were."

"You see the details but not the big picture," Bi'nh said. "This'll be another Vietnam, you know. Fighting for our precious democracy at the cost of another nation."

"Hey, my dad fought in Vietnam! Watched his friends die, just like me! My dad put it all on the line for your country!"

"*My* country?" She slammed her glass down on the end table. "I'm an American!"

"You know what I mean. Your people. My dad fought for their freedom!"

She took a deep breath. Her voice had begun to quiver. "Joe, I respect your dad and everyone who fights for their country. I really do. But just because the soldiers are honorable doesn't mean the politicians sending them to fight are."

She was a convincing debater in her thin, silk robe. Joe didn't agree with her. But looking at her excited movement, her expressive face, her waving hands, the crunching of her toes into the carpet, he found her quite agreeable. "Maybe we should liberate ourselves from this subject," he forced, along with a smile.

Hers came naturally. She allowed her hands to be taken into his and the tension melted away. "Good idea," she agreed.

Joe grinned suggestively. "Maybe America should occupy Vietnam again?"

She frowned at him the way she might frown at a mischievous child. "Let's stop talking about war and start thinking about love."

He knew she meant it in a broader sense, on a global scale. But it registered as an intimate suggestion. For the moment, her love washed the residue of war from his thick skin.

Even with all the people around him on the train, Joe was alone. Memories of Wu, McMurphey, Manning, and Bi'nh echoed in his mind the way the train echoed when it passed through a dark tunnel. There had been the good parts to the visit: holding her, loving her, her face nestled against his chest, his lips on the warm part in her silky black hair. Still, something had died between them during this visit as surely as his friends had died at his side in Afghanistan.

At the station, she'd invited him to stay with her and not go back to war. Joe held her at arm's length and looked her squarely in the eyes. "I have to go."

"No," Bi'nh insisted. "You don't. You can go AWOL. You'd be morally justified. You can stay with me and forget all the nonsense over there."

"Bi'nh, I'm enlisted. I'm a soldier. I don't have a choice. And even if I did, I'd go. I believe in what I'm doing."

Bi'nh's face contorted. "You mean you'd go to war instead of staying with me, even if you were free?"

"I don't mean it that way! But, I mean, somebody's got to fight this battle."

Bi'nh pulled away. "I never thought you'd turn out this way. You used to be gentle and kind. What have they done to you? To make you actually *want* to kill people and destroy nations?"

Joe tried to wrap his arms back around her, but she wouldn't be captured. "I'll come back," he promised. "As soon as I get back, you'll be my first stop."

"No." Her golden face hardened. "Stay with me now. Or don't come back at all. If you go back over there and hang around soldiers all the time, you'll change even more than you have. The next time I see you, I won't recognize you. I couldn't bear that." The train's whistle blew. "Stay with me."

"I can't," Joe said. And he stepped onto the train. He found his window seat and looked out to her, waving. But she didn't wave back.

Finality filled her teary eyes and it tore at his heart as the train proceeded and left her alone at Penn Station. When he left her for the war, he chose it over her, over them. Nothing in the war was quite as painful as this. As the train carried him away, he wished they'd never talked about the war. He didn't mind fighting in it as much as talking about it. Talk could be destructive.

The train slowed to stop at a station, and he looked into the distance. Outside his window, Joe saw an American flag, tattered, mutilated, on the ground. There, in the middle of the street, it fluttered like a hit animal, road kill not yet dead, struggling to get up.

Most people tend to conform to those they hang around with. Bi'nh hadn't been talking about Xing Wu, Joe realized now, for the first time. His friend had been submerged in Chinese military propaganda, yes, but Joe had been just as deeply buried in the dust of American military dogma.

The tattered flag continued to flutter outside the window, as black as it was red, white or blue, crossed with as many rips as stripes.

In the dust of war, visualizing Bi'nh in his arms had given him something focus on. He tried to imagine what would take her place. This fallen flag?

The train's conductor interrupted his thoughts. "Getting a little R and R?" Joe answered by giving the old man his ticket to punch, but the conductor didn't leave it at that. "Some days can be hard work, but I'll bet it's easier to wear my uniform than the one you've got on."

Joe looked at the blue Amtrak uniform. "I guess so."

The conductor gave back the punched ticket and placed a marker in the slot above Joe's seat. "No guesses about it: you deserve this rest. Have a good time."

"Is there a café on this train?"

"There sure is," he answered cheerily. "The lounge car is directly ahead, three cars up."

"Thanks," he said, without emotion. Civilians didn't understand. Joe didn't understand himself. Maybe a drink would clear things up.

First his parents in Chicago, then Iraq. Mom and Dad would be proud to see him step off the train in uniform. Then he would return to a war-stricken land, to the job of being a peacekeeper who fought, a liberator of people who didn't want his brand of liberation. The injured and the orphaned would all be waiting for him, along with those who appreciated American efforts. Maybe he'd have to help put down a rebellion. Perhaps he'd be shot at by women and children. Beautiful women like the one he or the tank had killed, who, in a different situation, he could have loved instead of killed.

Joe clung to the idea even as it dissipated into the cool autumn air, smoke from the train's smokestack: he fought for freedom. But the belief was leaving him just as he'd left Bi'nh at the station. Just as he'd chosen America's war over Bi'nh's love. It was an elusive freedom for which Joe fought, a freedom he could not claim as his own.

One Last Hit

Charlie hovered at the back of the train's passenger car, watching the people in their seats. There was one person in particular Charlie wanted to keep his eye on: Gene Silverman. Silverman was an easy man to keep in sight; the whiz kid stood tall above the crowd with his crown of silver hair. Charlie walked past him and found his own seat, but continued to scan the car as a pretense for keeping his eye on his target.

Charlie considered himself an observer by nature, so tuned in to those around him that he studied them even when he wasn't thinking about it. *By habit, not by nature,* he corrected himself. *After all, what is a person's nature if not an internalized skill or habit?* People-watching was a necessary skill in Charlie's line of work, one he'd been forced to learn. Now, it had become second nature.

He had until Chicago to do the job. He needed to keep Silverman in sight for the bulk of the trip. He'd wait until the rural flatlands of Indiana to confront him.

With the train flowing steadily along—*choo-ka, choo-ka, choo-ka*—and with most of the passengers settled in for the long ride ahead, Charlie once again leaned forward and peeked around at all the people he didn't care about in order to steal a glance at the one he did. Silverman sat with a yellow pad of paper open on his lap. Charlie stood and walked past him, returning to the back of the car. He took a pack of non-filtered Basics from the pocket of his brown leather jacket and flicked his wrist until one of the cigarettes popped up. He took it into his lips, returned the package to his pocket and got out his gold Zippo. With a practiced, one-handed motion, he sparked fire.

An old man seemed to appear out of nowhere. "Hold it, Mister." He wore a uniform with the *Amtrak* name and insignia on the blazer. "I'm afraid there's no smoking on the train."

"No smoking?" Charlie's voice was as rough as his appearance: purposeful, intense, demanding. "You mean to tell me I can't even have a cigarette here in back?"

"Afraid not," the old man said. "Company policy. Now, you can get off and smoke at the stations on the platforms if you'd like. But not on the train. We're a smoke-free train."

"Ain't that something," Charlie griped. He put the cigarette back in the pack and walked slowly to his seat. Moments later, he peered back again. Silverman still stared at his yellow pad with blank eyes, seeming not to read it. *He ain't going nowhere. If he does, I'll see him pass.* Charlie sank back into the undersized chair. He could allow himself to rest, but he couldn't go to sleep. He had to stay alert. When he got this job done, that would be it. He'd be out. It would be enough for him to retire on. *I can't screw this one up.*

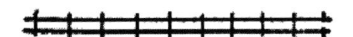

Before sending Charlie after Silverman, the Boss had filled him in. To say that the Boss had *all but forgotten* Eugene Beckett (aka Gene Silverman) was true enough; that is, he had not forgotten his former employee at all. It was as big a surprise as the Boss had ever received, when he realized the whiz kid wasn't coming back—a bigger surprise than when the kid had set up their entire new enterprise of identity theft and Internet crimes. Eugene had screwed him in the ass by taking off without training a replacement. Eugene Beckett needed to be taken care of.

On the other hand, the Boss owed a lot to the kid, not the least of which was gratitude. A replacement could be found. The Boss couldn't manage the online bookkeeping or the accounts, but the prostitutes, drug dealing, and gambling racket still brought in the dough. It took a few weeks, but the Boss had made some calls, screened some people, and found someone who could take over the kid's duties. Eugene had set them up with a great business and doubled their income with little to no increased expense. Was that something to punish, especially considering that the kid decided to leave all future profits to him?

No. If anything, Eugene Beckett deserved royalties. That's why the Boss had let it go. Water under the bridge. The Boss had practically forgotten the kid... until years later when the little bastard resurfaced with talk about legalizing the illegal activities that had made him who he was. Silverman needed to be silenced; before the Boss realized Silverman and Beckett were one and the same, he put some spies on the job to dig up Silverman's story.

The Boss often described surprises as unexpected gifts received without occasion: a string of pearls for the skillful girls who'd known how to make him feel good; the extra wad of bills to the dealer who'd managed to move a briefcase full of coke the night before the cops were to raid the buyer's crack-house; the home theater for the nice cop who'd tipped them off. These were good surprises.

But there were surprises the Boss did not like: finding out one of his prostitutes had AIDS and, desperate for money, didn't tell him, turning tricks until she had infected several loyal customers; catching one of his men pinching from the drugs he was supposed to be selling and stealing from the money he was getting for what he sold; the whiz kid leaving him—and to top it off, the surprise that the asshole trying to undermine his livelihood was the same kid who'd helped build it up. Gene Silverman was Eugene Beckett, his spies informed him. Whatever name the little prick went by, it was time to knock him off. So the Boss called Charlie.

Charlie got the call in the summer, when the Boss knew he was in town to visit his teenage son. Charlie had split with his woman, but he still spent a week or so with her and the kid every few months, for the boy's sake. While Charlie was in Baltimore, the Boss invited him to his restaurant in Little Italy. It was an invitation he couldn't refuse.

Charlie said goodbye to his boy and then checked into the Hotel Monaco; it was his way of keeping his family and his profession in separate compartments. He whet his whistle at the hotel's B&O bar, then hailed a cab and went to Little Italy.

The meal was good, but he hardly enjoyed it, anticipating what the Boss wanted. Charlie wasn't a regular employee anymore. He was a consultant, so to speak; an on-call specialist and old friend. Featured on the Boss's short list, he got summoned half a dozen times a year. But his jobs were big ones, and he was paid better for his part-time work than most of the stooges who kept regular hours.

Charlie ate his pasta alfredo while the Boss chewed his veal parmesan. They drank house sangrias and talked about the Ravens and the Orioles, about their friends and relations. All the while, Charlie wondered what the job would be, how big, and how much. *Will it be enough to get out for good?* On the other hand, he didn't want it to be too big. He didn't care much for *those* jobs.

Most people in Fells Point who knew the Boss also knew the Boss's business, or they knew enough not to ask. But there were those innocents who did ask, not to catch him in the act, but out of sincere curiosity. For that reason, he'd acquired one of the Italian restaurants in neighboring Little Italy and a bar in Fells Point. He kept his home base at the Fells Point rowhouse, but with the new properties, he often preferred to meet people and do business in the offices of his more respectable establishments.

After dinner, they retired to the upstairs office. The Boss offered Charlie a Cuban and poured them each a snifter of French brandy, then took a seat in the leather high-back chair behind his large cherry desk. Charlie sat in one of the leather chairs on the opposite side of the desk.

The Boss leaned back and puffed on his cigar. Charlie followed suit. In the small attic office they soon found themselves in a musty cloud of their own making. The Boss got to the point. "You heard of Gene Silverman?"

"Yeah," Charlie said. "The fool who's saying everything should be legal. Trying to put the cops out of business."

The Boss studied the ash of his cigar. "Trying to put *us* out of business."

Charlie nodded. "I guess so."

"I *know* so," the Boss insisted. "Not that it'll ever happen. People been trying to legalize pot as long as I can remember and most states won't hear of it. But still, he's starting a regular grass-roots movement. He's got to be shut up."

"Want me to scare him? Disfigure his face or something?"

"I think a little more." His eyes caught Charlie's, making direct contact for the first time since they'd climbed the stairs. Charlie knew what the Boss found in his eyes: fear and regret, the reluctance of a tired man who no longer wanted the work. Regardless, the Boss continued. "Warning the bastard would just...well, warn him...alert him to us, put him on guard. He knows too much; that makes him dangerous. You know who he is?"

"Nope. Don't know his history."

"His history's with us." The lines of his face seemed deeper in the dim light of the stained-glass lamp. "Eugene Beckett."

Charlie searched his memory. "The computer geek?" He tried to remember the whiz kid, tried to picture him, before and after.

"The identity thief's gone and stolen himself an identity and didn't have the brains to keep it quiet. You'll silence him, but it'll take more than duct tape, I think."

"You know I've been trying to quit," Charlie said. "I'm getting too old for this sort of thing. Let's just beat him around a little. Scare him."

"Shit, Charlie. You're as good as they come. Too old my ass."

Charlie's cigar had died out. "That's just it. I've had my share of close calls with vengeful friends and clever cops. I'm getting Social Security, for Christ's sake, from the few legit jobs I paid taxes on. I don't want to spend the last decade of my life in jail. The stakes are too high. I don't want to lose these last few years I have left in me. I've been enjoying retirement too much."

The Boss stared Charlie down. "This is more than just a job. It's personal. Your retirement's at risk if you *don't* snuff him out."

Confused, Charlie asked, "How's that?"

"Think about who we're talking about here. Computer whiz, identity expert. Don't you think he took some insurance when he left?"

"I don't get you."

"Silverman's got our numbers. I'll bet he's got our Social Security numbers and all kinds of incriminating info on us. He had access to everything on our computers and I'll bet he still has it socked away. He goes to the cops, retirement's over."

The phone rang. The Boss picked up the black receiver and swiveled around so all Charlie could see of him was the back of the leather chair and the smoke rising from it. Charlie wanted out, but this Silverman issue was a delicate matter. How many times had he promised himself this would be the last man?

For the past few years, most of the jobs he'd been given were simple ones: he'd followed people, frightened them into paying, beaten them into submission. He'd broken a leg, flattened a nose, cracked a few ribs. He'd sliced a guy's little finger off with his cigar cutter. He didn't pretend they were good jobs, but they were better than death. He'd only taken one big job during the past year. He'd already killed enough men in his life. When he was young, death didn't bother him. Now it did.

The Boss turned around and put the phone back in the cradle, then refreshed their brandies. "Where were we?"

"You were just telling me that if I promise to do a good job on this one, it'll be the last time you ask." A tremor rang in Charlie's usually confident voice as he dared to speak so candidly to the Boss.

The Boss smiled. "You'll be paid well." He noticed Charlie's cigar was out and passed him the desk lighter. "Fifty thousand."

Charlie stalled. He flicked the lighter to life. "Since this will be my retirement bash, how about a little extra?" He puffed at his cigar until satisfied with the red-hot tip.

"Don't I always give you a bonus?"

Charlie nodded. "You do."

"I appreciate your work. You're one of the best, and I'll miss having you on call. But I understand. You've earned your retirement. You gonna get that place in the Keys?"

"Yeah," Charlie answered. "And I'll keep the place here, too, for the boy and his ma."

"You'll still stop by and see me when you're in town."

"No doubt about it."

The Boss nodded. A hush mixed with the smoke. The Boss finished his brandy. "You do a good job, untraceable, and your bonus'll be another fifty."

A hundred thousand! That would push his offshore account up to his goal of two mil, in just one job. Charlie grinned. "Hell, I'll kill his mother too."

The Boss laughed. "Not necessary," he said. "But as for Gene Silverman ..." He jabbed his cigar into the ashtray, twisting it until the smoke faded.

"Consider it done." Charlie put out his own, less dramatically.

The Boss picked up the brandy bottle, almost empty. "Let me hit you with this one last time." A shared drink was the only contract they'd ever required. They raised their glasses and sealed the deal.

Charlie wasn't born into organized crime; he'd sought it out. As the only child of a family living in a Little Italy rowhouse, he wasn't poor, but he'd had relatively humble beginnings that pointed to him becoming the manager of an ethnic grocery store or dry cleaner. His father was Italian and his mother was an immigrant from the Soviet Union. Some weeks they went to the Catholic church in town, other times they ventured out to the Ukrainian Orthodox church on Eastern Avenue. They were pretty much the same, as Charlie saw it. Some of the saints were different, but they taught him the same core values: it didn't matter who you were or what you did; one church or another, one line of work or another, one ethnicity or another, life was all pretty much what you made of it. He decided early on to make it big.

He started small. He got the idea when he was barely a teenager. Mid-summer days were long and pointless and even the promise of school seemed a welcome vacation from idleness. He spent his days roaming through the streets of Federal Hill—the other side of the Harbor, where people had money. On a telephone pole he saw a flyer with the picture of an ugly bulldog, contact information, and a reward amount: $100. Back then, that was a lot of money—more than Charlie'd ever seen. He spent the better part of the next few days playing pet detective, searching between rowhouses, in the parks, along the streets and in the alleyways. On the third day of his search, he surprised himself when, due more to luck than skill, he discovered the bulldog tied to a post outside one of the pubs along Charles Street. He unhitched it and ran to the first payphone he could find—the one in front of Cross Street Market.

"I found your dog," Charlie cried.

"Oh, you must have the wrong dog. We found Kooper day before yesterday."

Charlie was pissed. All the work with no payoff. He kicked the dog and it yelped. Then, he got the idea to keep the dog and hold it for ransom.

Sure enough, in a few days new flyers replaced the old, a picture he'd not have noticed was different, but certainly new contact information. And a new amount: $200. He called the number. "I found your dog."

"You found Regan? That's just great!" The woman at the other end of the line gave their address, just a few blocks over. The dog was exchanged for the money, and as easily as that, Charlie found himself richer than he'd ever been before.

He ate ice cream, took water taxis, stocked up on girlie magazines, and even conned himself some beer, whisky, and cigarettes. The money lasted him a luxurious couple weeks; then he schemed for more. He managed to coax a collie out of the park on the hill and led it out of sight, then fit it to the leash Charlie carried with him. A few days later, he exchanged the lost dog for $150. The rewards varied from a disappointing thank you and a piece of pie to an overwhelming half-grand. By the end of summer, he had more money stashed in his sock drawer than his parents had under their mattress.

Fells Point was only a short walk from Little Italy. There was a lot of action in Fells Point with all the pubs and clubs, the Broadway

Market, and the restaurants. He began hanging out in the area, when he wasn't stealing and saving rich people's pets. When the local drug dealers tried to sell to him, he offered to sell for them. His ambition met with success. Before he knew it, he was pushing more drugs at school than some of the adult dealers were selling on the street. At sixteen, Charlie became the youngest member of the local crime ring—not including some of the prostitutes—and he discovered there was a lot more money in dealing drugs than pets.

In those days, he learned to read people. He could spot an undercover cop by the cool, guarded caution. He could weed out a nark by the fearful twitch. He knew the users from the curious by how quickly they took their purchases. Sometimes, when he stood along Broadway and the adjoining streets and watched proud people strutting by, he wanted to beat the shit out of them. Sometimes he did. Once, after a college kid threatened to tell the cops that his friend had tried to sell him a joint, Charlie was so enraged that he took things a little too far. Fortunately for Charlie, it was in an unpopulated alley and no one saw who'd beaten the poor kid to death. Guilt nearly drove Charlie out of the business, but ambition overshadowed his guilt.

The Boss found out—his spies were everywhere—and summoned Charlie. "You have a real talent for clean dirty work." Most of the jobs the Boss gave him were just warnings: broken limbs, smashed faces, roughing up. But there were occasional hits. Charlie found it less difficult to deal with the second time around, and by his third kill, it came easily. He was sly, quick, and quiet about his work. He taught himself not to care, not to hear the pleas or cries. It wasn't long before he'd become the Boss's hit man of choice. Charlie didn't enjoy it, but he was good at it, and the money couldn't be beat.

Years later, he went his own way. He'd had enough of the violence and no longer wanted to be a full-time thug. He parted on good terms, still friends with the Boss. He parted with the understanding that he would still be called upon for favors—favors that, when done well, would be well compensated. And Charlie often came by when he wasn't relaxing in the Keys, just to say hi to the Boss, or to see whether he could do a job or two for some extra cash. Sometimes he just stopped by to share a cigar or a joint.

Charlie was smoking in the Fells Point rowhouse on Wolfe Street the day the computer geek showed up. He'd flown in for a couple weeks to spend some time with his son and had decided to drop in. They'd gone into the Boss's smoking chamber, the other office with lounge chairs and lava lamps instead of a desk and a computer. In the chamber, Charlie, the Boss, and a couple of other guys from the organization passed some joints around. Charlie found something special in being part of a dope ring with his Fells Point gang; there was something intimate about it. Aside from the feeling of a woman's body next to his, it didn't get much warmer than the feeling of a joint passed from one person to another.

"I gotta go," the Boss said. "Gotta check on the girls. They oughta be out by now. Streets are filling up."

"Aw, come on, Boss," Charlie said.

"Gotta check on that whiz kid out there too," the Boss said.

"Invite him in," one of the brotherhood said.

"I don't think it's his thing," the other said. They all laughed.

"Not yet, anyway," the Boss said.

"One last hit," Charlie offered, pushing the joint in their host's direction.

"The problem is, it's never the last hit," the Boss said. "It's always supposed to be the last one, but it never is unless you make it that way." He opened the door, letting out a puff of smoke that smelled even greener than it looked.

On the train, Charlie wanted to sleep, but he didn't allow it. Intuitively, he looked back at Silverman. The whiz kid had put away his paper and was snapping the latches of his briefcase securely shut. Then he stood and walked toward the front of the car. Charlie turned discreetly around and leaned back in his seat. He watched as Silverman passed him and exited the car.

Charlie stood and followed him. As he entered the next passenger car, Silverman was exiting. Charlie hung back so as not to be seen. In one car, he had to squeeze his bulk past the conductor who was making his rounds, validating new passengers after a recent stop. Finally, he watched his target enter the observation car. Charlie stalled, buffering their entries with time.

He took out a Basic, placing the cigarette between his lips as he glanced across the car at the faces in the crowd. A few mumbles and looks from the passengers reminded him: no smoking. He grumbled and placed the cigarette behind his ear.

Silverman didn't even notice as Charlie entered the observation car and took a seat in the opposite aisle. Charlie stared at the window. Beyond the picture window was a fantastic view of nature. They passed a small lake where a family was picnicking and a man showed his son how to cast a line. But in the glass, he could see the reflection of people in the aisle on the other side of the car. He could see the back of Silverman's head. It didn't take long before Silverman abandoned the observation car for the next one.

Charlie waited a moment, then entered the lounge car—more than half full already, and the day was young. On one of his better days, out in the Keys, Charlie wouldn't even be out of bed yet. Silverman sat toward the center of the car with a cup of hot tea and his yellow legal pad. For a moment, their eyes locked and Charlie feared the kid might actually have recognized him. *No. The few times we saw each other he was too scared to notice anyone but the Boss.* Charlie let the moment of eye contact slide away and scanned the room. He didn't care about these other people, but looked at each in turn in order to make his examination of Silverman seem indifferent.

He spotted a man about his age going through a leather-bound planner; a German couple drinking tea and beer; a young couple silently sipping bottled water; a soldier staring out the window, an old woman who looked like she had one foot in the grave.

Charlie ordered a black coffee, though he wanted a cigarette and a shot of bourbon. *Too early to get sloppy; coffee'll have to do.* He wanted to get off the train and smoke a cigarette at the next stop, but knew he had to stay with his target.

He'd wait awhile before striking. He'd wait for the rural flatlands of middle Indiana. Then he could get off in Chicago before anyone even found the body. One last hit, and that was it.

From his seat in the corner, offering him a view of the entire lounge car, Charlie continued studying people to pass the time. He watched the gray-haired man make notes in his planner, consider them, and make more notes, looking stressed. Another man came in, escorting a retarded guy. A young man parked himself to jot lines in a spiral notebook and a woman sat with tearful eyes, reading a paper she kept taking in and out of her purse. He wondered whether the red stones on her dragonfly broach had any value. A woman with a tattoo decorating her lower back looked just slutty enough to work for the Boss.

Charlie watched these people, all in their own little worlds, some intermingling, others completely isolated and unaware of his intruding eyes. Charlie wondered where they came from and where they were headed. Most people went through life clueless. They had no idea they were being watched and scrutinized, whether by a guy like him or a con man, a telemarketer or a boss. Most people were oblivious to the dangers all around them. But that wasn't Charlie's concern. Only one destiny concerned him: Silverman had to die before this train reached Chicago.

Reunion

The poem lay in her lap; Joan read it again. How many times had she read the piece in these past few days? How many days had it been? The poem, inked on parchment, both pained and comforted her.

She remembered the disoriented sensation she'd had back in college, the result of taking uppers and downers, and the neurotic sense induced by the drugs working against one another. Joan felt something like that now, only drugs weren't the cause, and the sensation was not one she would pay for or even accept for free. In fact, she'd be willing to pop a pill just to get rid of it.

The man seated next to her scribbled in a spiral notebook. He seemed consumed by his notes, but she didn't look at him for fear of being sucked into a conversation she was in no mood for. Once in a while she felt his gaze, but she didn't return it.

As she looked up from the parchment and out the window, the memory intruded. The sadness stuck there in her consciousness like the gum from the train's floor that was now affixed to the bottom of her shoe. Tears glided down her cheeks. She took a tissue from her purse.

When her younger brother called last week, she'd been a little surprised. He wasn't the calling type. He emailed her often and they visited each other at their parents' place during holidays and family reunions. Brad still lived in Baltimore, near Mom and Dad. He still went to Saturday Orioles games and Sunday dinners, still ran home for help and advice. Joan had relocated to Cincinnati years ago, where she'd taken a position as an office supervisor. Brad always joked that she really moved to Cincinnati because they put chocolate in their chili, but they both knew she had other reasons. She loved her parents, but she wouldn't be controlled by them. They were so good at planning out their own lives that they found it fitting to plan hers and Brad's as well. It was easier for her to live her own life when she lived beyond their reach. Joan and her brother often teased one another about her migration and his permanent place beneath parental wings. But he was in no joking mood when he called her in the middle of the night last week.

"Joan? Joan!"

"Brad?" she moaned. "What the hell? It's three in the morning."

Brad was thirty years old, but he spoke with the voice of a confused child. "Joan! It's Mom and Dad—car accident. They're at the hospital. Doesn't look good."

Joan sat up instantly, and woke almost as quickly. "What? Oh my God! How are they?"

"Doctors say it... doesn't look good." He spoke in spurts, finding places for words between moments of unconcealed crying. "You've gotta come!"

"Of course I'll come!" She turned on the bedside light. "They're okay, right? I mean, they're hurt, but they're gonna be okay?"

"Just hurry, Joan. It's bad."

Brad said it was bad, but he hadn't said how bad. She didn't know how long she'd need to stay: a few days, a month. Without taking time to consider the news, without putting down the receiver, she immediately called the airline and booked a one-way ticket.

She called work later, after the office opened. She told them of the tragedy from the airport, from her cell phone. Meetings would be missed, reports reassigned, projects postponed. When the time came, she turned off her cell, boarded the plane, and took off for home.

The hollow in the pit of her stomach ached as the plane ascended. She hadn't given any thought to breakfast. She ate the soy nuts the flight attendants distributed and drank the meager cup of orange juice.

That was last week. Now, on the train back to Cincinnati, she had less appetite, less thirst. Now she wanted to stay right where she was, lulled into a trance by her situation, by the motion of the train. She'd chosen the train because it was slower than the flight. She'd needed to leave Baltimore, but she was in no rush to get back to Cincinnati. Gliding along the tracks, Joan moved away from the source of her pain. But not away from the pain.

The plane ride to Baltimore had been one that she wished would go faster and take longer at the same time, like a commute to a business meeting she wanted to both avoid and be done with. She landed at BWI and found her way to baggage claim. She hadn't asked Brad to pick her up; she figured it was more important for him to stay at the hospital with Mom and Dad. Joan exited the airport and hailed a taxi. "St. Joseph's," she said to the driver. The yellow cab sped off and she wondered whether the foreign driver took the destination as permission to drive even faster than usual or whether this was his normal speed.

She made it to the hospital and raced to the reception desk for directions. In the frigid hallway, outside their parents' rooms, Brad sat hunched over, his face buried in his hands. "Brad," she called softly to him as she approached.

He looked up, his face scarlet, his eyes bloodshot. "It's terrible."

"It'll be okay, Brad."

"No, Joan. It won't."

"Think positive," she said, pretending to do so herself.

Brad shook his head. "They're gone."

She stood in stunned silence. She didn't ask him to repeat himself. But he did.

"They're gone, Joan." Brad sniffed and wiped his eyes with his sleeve. "Not more than an hour ago. They never regained consciousness after the accident."

Joan sat on the bench next to him. She put her arms around him, pulled him toward her. She cried with him. If tears could regenerate life, their parents would surely have gotten up and walked out to join them. But tears brought nothing, solved nothing, altered nothing. Still, Joan and Brad remained on the bench, shedding tears as though it could make a difference.

Brad looked into Joan's face. "Guess we ought to go to my place."

"No," Joan said. "We better go to Mom and Dad's."

Mom and Dad were more than control freaks; they were persistent planners. That made it easier for Joan and Brad. Their parents hadn't expected to die so soon, but they were prepared for it, knowing death could swoop down at any time along the course of a lifetime. The house Joan and Brad had grown up in was paid for and left to them. Mom and Dad had purchased the coffins, plots, and headstones. A foundation of flowers had already been provided through the funeral home, although it would be added to by most of the friends and loved ones coming to pay their final respects. Everything was clearly labeled in the folders of the library file cabinet. All Joan had to do was to make the calls to put everything in motion.

Joan was forty-six, though sometimes she still felt herself a child. She remembered wondering, as a teenager, how she could possibly survive in the bureaucratic world out there with all the paperwork, rules, and regulations. How would she keep up with the taxes and bills and legalities of life? She knew then she couldn't survive without her parents to help her.

But she *had* survived—survived and flourished. Even Brad had survived, she determined, and he was doing well. *Except for at the moment.*

Joan made the last of the difficult phone calls. She'd called her cousins first, and then moved on to friends. Finally, she searched Mom and Dad's planners, date books and calendars for contacts she and Brad didn't know. Joan tired of the *Oh no*s and *You're kidding*s and *Oh my God*s and *I'm so sorry to hear that*s that came with every call. She'd simply have sent an email if etiquette allowed.

Brad struggled with dinner, but Joan knew he'd prefer it to the task of making the calls. Joan came to the kitchen, the cordless phone turned off but still attached to her hand. "That's all of them."

Brad nodded. "Dinner's almost ready." He strained the water, leaving the steaming pasta in a white colander. He took the hot spaghetti sauce from the microwave, still in the jar.

Joan took two plates from the cabinet. It was a routine activity, setting the table in this house, something she'd done a hundred times before. "The wake's tomorrow evening, funeral the next day."

"What'll we do tomorrow?" Brad put the spaghetti and sauce on the kitchen table. "I mean, during the day?" He went to the fridge for the green cylinder of cheese and found that it wasn't there. "Guess we should go to the grocery store."

"No need to," Joan said. "People usually bring food."

"Bring food?" Brad asked. "That's weird."

"Just a way to help out. They know we're in no shape to cook." Joan spoke as though she were an authority on the subject. As though she had it together, even though she knew she didn't.

They ate. The ingredients had all come from Mom's kitchen, but the food did not taste right. What should he have added to it?

What was missing? Even Joan, who was used to cooking for herself, couldn't pinpoint the elusive ingredient.

Joan wasn't sure how she came to be in charge of the arrangements. She was the de facto go-to girl for all business matters revolving around the funeral and estate; she had even picked out the mums when the lilies were unavailable. It was fortunate that her parents had tried to make everything convenient for her, but emotionally, handling their final wishes was far from easy.

Most of the people at the wake and funeral were locals: friends, neighbors, co-workers, and their parents' church family. More than half the visitors were people Joan knew well; Brad knew about two thirds, still being a local.

One person in particular Joan remembered fondly. Jimmy used to play with Brad; they'd been best friends off and on during school years. Jimmy used to mow Mom and Dad's lawn and deliver their paper. Now, he worked at the local weekly, doing human interest stories on local anniversaries, unusual pets, and community events. He was one of the first to arrive at the funeral, and he shyly greeted Brad and Joan.

"Thanks for coming, Jimmy," Joan said. "It's been a long time."

Jimmy shifted the grass with his shoe. "Why is it that it takes tragedy to bring old friends together?"

Brad swallowed. "I don't know, Jimmy. But you're always welcome. You're like part of the family."

Every family member came. There were no aunts or uncles; Mom had been an only child and Dad's only brother had suffered a bitter divorce, followed by a fatal heart attack, a few years ago. The five cousins were all that remained of their extended family, now that the parents were gone. The remnants of a generation had vanished in the auto accident—an entire layer of the family reduced to pictures and memories.

Of the five cousins, two still lived in Baltimore and one resided in nearby Washington, DC. Sherry, John, and Kevin saw Brad often, every couple months or so. Once a year, Joan and Brad's parents had organized a family reunion that drew the other two cousins, Monica and Harry, from their homes in Philadelphia and upstate New York. For Joan, the years revolved around those family reunions. She weighed the importance of things that happened in her life by whether she would share them with her parents and brother and cousins at the family get-togethers. Reuniting with the family each December strung the moments of her life together and gave them a sense of order.

The funeral could be seen as their family's final reunion, Joan thought. Many of the guests came by Mom and Dad's house after the service, some bringing more flowers, others carrying casserole dishes. It was awkward, forcing conversation with these people, both the ones Joan knew and the ones she didn't. Long after most visitors parted, the cousins remained. They sat around the dining room table, a buffet of mismatched entrees—cold and unwanted—between them.

Monica took a doughnut to calm her jittery hands. She was the oldest of the five cousins, a year younger than Joan. "We're it, now."

The seven looked around the table at one another. "Hard to imagine," John said.

Tears began their practiced path down Brad's cheeks. "It's hard to put into words how hard it is."

Sherry sat next to him; she placed an arm around him. "We know, Brad. We understand. We've been through it."

Silence lingered above the table along with the colliding scents—chocolate cake, sauerkraut, chicken casserole, meatballs, baked beans. Kevin drank punch from a red plastic cup he'd been nursing for half an hour. "I don't know." Kevin eyed the cup, inched it around in his hands. "Life is never like it was before, after losing your parents, after losing someone you love. But it'll get better."

Sherry sighed, tightening her hold around Brad and looking across the table at Joan. "It's not easy. But you'll get through this." The line sounded too practiced to be comforting. "Life goes on and so will you."

Harry had been silent most of the day. He stirred in his chair and finally spoke. "We should stick together, you know."

"What do you mean?" Monica asked.

Harry looked at each of his cousins in turn, their unhappy faces staring back at him. "I mean, we're family. We need to stick together, now that we're the only ones left. It's up to us now, to keep the family together."

Kevin looked away from Harry, back to the punch cupped between his hands. "Hadn't thought of that." He took another drink. "You're right. We need to keep in touch."

"We'll have to do the annual reunion at Christmastime," John elaborated.

Monica swallowed her bite of doughnut. "Where?"

Harry looked at Joan. "Guess that's up you."

Joan felt the blood rush to her face, already reddened from crying. "What? Why me?"

"Well, you're the oldest," Harry said. "You're the head of the family now."

The other cousins considered the idea as though it hadn't occurred to them, then nodded. Once stated, it seemed an obvious truth.

Joan wiped a silent tear from her eye. "Oh." Her place in their family and the planning of a reunion were not responsibilities she wanted to think about now.

Monica put the remaining half of her doughnut on the plastic that covered the lace tablecloth. "Maybe we should go to Cincinnati this year. Make a few days out of it." She looked at Joan. "Then you won't have to come all the way here again."

Joan considered it for a moment, though thoughts of her parents made it hard to focus. "No, I'll probably come here. Everyone else is here."

Brad had stopped crying and was clinging to this new subject like a life preserver, something else to think about, something less painful.

Sherry folded her arms on the table. "We could do it at our house, Joan. It's not as spacious, but Tom and I can open our place up." Tom was Sherry's aloof husband, who had driven straight home from the funeral.

Joan was slow in responding. "We'll see. Maybe we'll do it here, like usual."

"Okay," Sherry said, leaning back in her chair. "But if it's too much trouble, our place is available."

John left the room and went into the kitchen. He returned with a hot pot of coffee. Styrofoam cups towered in a stack at the middle of the table. "Java?"

"Sure," some of them said. When the cups were filled and the pot put away, John returned to his chair. "So you're gonna keep the place?"

Joan looked at Brad, who didn't seem to care at the moment. But he would. "I don't know," she admitted. "Maybe we'll sell it. Or maybe we'll keep it. I just don't know yet. Either way, we'll probably still have it for several months. We can do the reunion here."

Kevin finished off his punch and continued staring at the empty plastic cup. "We should do it, wherever. I know friends whose families only get together for funerals. Like that's the only time important enough. I don't want that. We need to have happy reunions."

"Yes, we do," Brad said. He began sniffling again, which set Monica off. Joan lost the composure she'd fought so hard to keep. The three cried out loud; that left four to comfort them.

"It gets better," Kevin assured them.

"Yes," Sherry said, holding Brad tightly, just as Mom used to do.

Two days after the funeral, after the cousins had left and the driveway was empty, Jimmy stopped by the house. Joan answered his apprehensive knock. "Hi, Jimmy." She widened the door, momentarily allowing the sunlight in. "Brad's in the living room." She led the way and for a moment she became a teenage girl again, letting Jimmy in to play with Brad. But they were all adults now, and the mood was too sad for fantasy.

Once greetings were exchanged and condolences once again expressed, the three of them sat in the room where Mom and Dad had spent most of their time: Brad on the sofa, Joan in the recliner and Jimmy on the loveseat. "Thanks for the obituary," Joan said. "It was nice."

"I'm just sorry it had to be written," Jimmy said.

Joan and Brad always knew Jimmy would end up a writer. Sometimes it seemed he would make an English teacher of himself, perhaps even a college professor. Sometimes they'd pictured him as a novelist, reading and autographing his books at quaint shops. But the job at the community newspaper seemed to fit. Human interest stories, occasional front-page features—the sort of things more aligned with his shy personality than that of an aggressive reporter. Brad and Joan knew he still harbored dreams of writing a book. And once in a while, he fancied himself a poet.

Jimmy hesitated, pinching the outer ends of an ornamental envelope. "I wrote something else for them too. For you."

"What?" Joan leaned forward in the chair.

Jimmy got up and stood nervously between the two siblings. "An ode. I mean, a tribute."

"Oh, how thoughtful," Joan said, reaching out her hand. She took the envelope and opened it. The poem had been inked in fancy calligraphy on fine parchment. "Ode to a Mom and a Dad" headed the poem. She read it. Joan couldn't judge the poem, of course. There was no judging a poem so personal, so close to one so dear. Death sometimes brings out the best in a poet; it can also awaken the worst. But this poem said something and by the time she'd finished it, her eyes had welled with emotion. She revisited the part that touched her most.

Must be hard to swallow,
Losing the ones you follow.
To suddenly become the head
When they used to be the ones who led.
Mom and Dad, etched in stone,
Joan and Brad, left alone
Their love was firm.
For what it's worth,
Love still remains above the earth.

Joan looked up at Jimmy. The swift motion of her head sent the tears welled up in her lower lids streaming down her cheeks. "It's beautiful."

"I just felt like I needed to write it. I loved your parents too. And I know it's hard for you."

Brad reached over. "Let me see it." His eyes glistened as he scanned the lines.

Joan remembered when she was a senior in high school. A secret admirer used to leave love poems in her mailbox. She still had the poems, a dozen or so in a shoe box at the back of a closet shelf. She remembered that each one—with its mystery and promise— seemed a masterpiece. Years later, when she'd read them again, looking for some cheer and self-validation after a horrible break-up, she was surprised at how terrible they were. They had seemed so wonderful when fresh, but read as mediocre greeting cards after the connection had worn thin.

Looking up at Jimmy, Joan realized now for the first time who that secret admirer must have been. She wondered whether this poem was the same, seeming a fine tribute, the work of a master wordsmith, because of the sensitive subject matter and the intensity of the moment. *But what is poetry if not sensitive and intense and about the moment?* The poem touched her, and that made her certain that this was genuine poetry, not the greeting-card sludge of her shoe box.

Brad finished a second reading. He sniffed. "Thanks, Jimmy."

"Don't thank me," Jimmy said as he looked at Joan, then Brad. He had tears in his eyes too. "I needed to write it."

After the poem had been read and reread, the three of them sat awkwardly, like passengers forced together, trying to avoid getting sucked into conversation. It had been years since they'd really talked. Joan knew what that meant. Small talk is harder to ease into when there's a trunk full of experience between meetings. They'd opened the trunk, but this wasn't the time to unpack it. Jimmy left.

For dinner, Joan and Brad nibbled on the food brought by friends and neighbors. Joan toyed with a bowl of egg salad on lettuce; Brad nuked some gourmet lasagna and commented on it being inappropriate for the occasion.

"The occasion's over," Joan said. "We have to move on."

"The occasion will never be over. It's a part of us. It'll be there forever."

"A part of us, yes," Joan allowed. "But we don't have to dwell on it forever. Even you don't have to live by their rules anymore."

Their mouths, now emptied of words, were filled with food. Joan chewed on a rubbery chunk of egg as her brother peeled off another layer of lasagna. Brad swallowed and asked, "When do you have to go back?"

"Yesterday." Joan tried to smile. "But my staff's covering for me. I need to head back in a couple days."

"A couple days? Can't you stay a little longer?"

"There's a meeting I've got to head up." Joan shrugged. "Can't be postponed."

"What about the house? The stuff?" Brad peeled away another layer of lasagna. "What are we going to do?"

"Let's sleep on it," Joan suggested. "We can talk about it tomorrow."

They placed their dishes in the sink and retreated to their own rooms. Joan closed the door behind her and looked around her old bedroom. She came home a few times each year and had gotten used to her childhood room as a safe haven. But now, as she examined the floral pattern on the walls, the twin bed in the corner of the room, the chest of drawers in the far corner, she marveled that the room was still intact. As she made her way to stand before the dresser mirror, she half expected to see a little girl reflected back. But she was grown, with wavy brown hair, a shapely figure and heavy make-up—now a device to make her look younger instead of older, as it once had. Only the trappings of childhood remained around her in this nostalgic place.

Unlike her messy apartment in Cincinnati, with magazines, books and clothes cluttering each room, this shrine to childhood was immaculate. Even when she'd lived here, it was as though no one had. Everything was arranged according to the structure of the house. It would always be that way here.

Fresh out of college with an MBA from Johns Hopkins, Joan had been eager to move beyond these walls, beyond Baltimore and the east coast. When the job offer came from Cincinnati, she'd been thrilled. Mom and Dad were not.

"You could find as good a job here," Dad had said. "Probably a better one."

Her boyfriend at the time, Darin, had encouraged her. "Sounds like a great opportunity." He'd offered to move with her, to support her. After Joan began her new career and Darin enrolled at University of Cincinnati, Joan realized that despite all the emotional support he gave her, she was the one supporting him. But Darin knew how to convince her it would all work out in the end. His involvement in the college debate team only strengthened his arguments. Soon, Darin was the captain of UC's debate team. When she found out that another member of the debate team was giving intimate oration to Darin, Joan dumped him. He gave her just one more reason to go it alone.

In her childhood bedroom, Joan opened the closet door. The only clothes here were left-behinds she wouldn't wear. Her suitcase remained on the floor next to her bed, stuffed with her acceptable attire from Cincinnati. She rummaged through the closet until she found the old shoebox in a corner, buried under a pile of T-shirts. She took the shoebox to her bed and opened it.

Here were old letters and magazine clippings, even a few letters from Darin and her parents. She cast them aside. Then she found what she was looking for.

The old poems were penned in messy ink, blotched on pulpy stationery, tri-folded and tucked into envelopes addressed to her. A few of the fourteen poems she found had been written in calligraphy. She recognized the earlier, less-practiced handwriting.

She read through the poetry, taking in the sweet proclamations of love. There was no denying it: this was mediocre poetry at best. But Jimmy's essence lived in it and the words took on a new meaning now that she knew the author. She reminded herself that he'd been only a kid when he wrote them. How could she not be moved by poetry that sang her praises, that worshipped her? She chuckled as she read, but a deeper emotion stirred inside her.

Jimmy still lived in the apartment he'd moved into right out of college. Joan remembered driving Brad to Jimmy's place for movies and parties. This was the first time she'd visited alone. She paid the taxi driver, sent him on his way, then went to rap at Jimmy's door. Her heart thumped as she waited, his poetry still rhyming in her head.

Jimmy looked surprised when he opened the door and found Joan standing there. Still in his gray slacks and button-down shirt, he smiled nervously. "Joan! Hi. Is everything okay?"

"Under the circumstances." Joan offered a slight smile. "Can I come in?"

"Of course," he said, regaining his orientation. "Come in. Don't mind the mess. Never had your parents' knack for a tidy house."

"Who does?" Joan joked. She looked around. Magazines and comic books, most of them open, sprawled about on tables, chairs, sofas and the floor, along with folded newspapers and open books. DVDs and videos were stacked in shaky towers on and around the television. Movie posters and album advertisements cluttered his walls, as well as sticky notes and laminated poems in calligraphy. "Looks cozy."

"It's comfortable," Jimmy said. "Might not look like it, but I've got my own system. I can find anything in a heartbeat—books, stories, articles. If this is my own web, you can call me Google."

Joan walked to one of his posted notes and examined the handwriting on the wall. "I really appreciate the poetry."

"Oh, it's the least I could do. Your parents were like family."

She turned to face him. "I mean all of the poems."

Jimmy flushed. "Um, can I get you a drink?" He turned away from her and headed toward the kitchen. "Beer? Got a jug of wine around here somewhere. Water?"

"I never knew you felt that way." Joan slid out of her light jacket and tossed it into a chair where it blanketed a stack of cold books. She'd never considered she could feel this way about Jimmy.

He took a gulp from his can of beer. "I like to write poetry. Not that I'm any good at it. Better at human interest stories."

"I never made the connection until today."

Jimmy shrugged. "What can I say?"

"Do you still feel the same way?"

Jimmy stalled. "Yes."

Joan approached him with open arms and took him in, placed his head on her shoulder and pressed him against her. She whispered warmly in his ear, "I never knew it was you. I always loved those poems, but I never knew they were from you." She felt his desire fleshing out against her and knew this must be the climax to his childhood fantasies. She pulled back to face him and touched her lips to his.

Jimmy's love poems may have been mediocre, but his response to her kiss was anything but. She replayed his adoring lines in her head. Their mouths remained together as they explored one another from the inside. As they tasted and felt one another, she inched him back to the sofa and guided him downward. She began to unbutton her blouse.

Jimmy pulled away. "Joan, what are you doing?"

"Isn't it obvious?"

Jimmy took her hands in his. "No, we can't."

"Don't you want me?"

He let out an uncomfortable sigh of laughter. "Want you? Of course I do. But not like this."

"Not like what?"

"I can't take advantage of you. Not in your time of grief."

Joan hadn't forgotten. But she longed to lose herself in love. "I'm not grieving at this very moment." To prove it, she pressed her lips against his.

Jimmy gently pushed her away. "No. Not like this."

Joan looked at Jimmy and suddenly became aware of herself. "Oh God, what am I doing?" She fell onto the sofa and began to cry.

"Don't worry." Jimmy's face looked ready to explode with tension as he sat beside her and put an arm tightly around her. "Joan, I love you."

She didn't know what to say. Romance, lust, and passion she'd expected. But not this. "How can you love me? You don't even know me anymore."

"No, really. I do." Jimmy wiped the tears from beneath her eyes.

Silence lingered. Then, her desire found words where she hadn't. "Show me you love me." She leaned in toward him, their faces only inches apart. She could feel his nervous breath. When Jimmy didn't respond, she leaned closer, pushed him back and continued their passion play. This time he didn't object when she took off her blouse. She felt his excitement as she gently unbuttoned his shirt, stroking and kissing all the while. On the sofa, she brushed her breasts against him and drew his hands up to cup them. She had to lead, but he was a willing student, if a reluctant lover. She realized for an instant the good intention behind his hesitation, but the thought flashed away as his poetry resonated in her mind and his warm hands began to caress her body of their own free will. She stood and guided him up with her to discard the last of their clothing. She remained in control, but a wild animal emerged where the follower had been. She led him to the bedroom, led him to his bed, led him all the while as they made love.

When they'd finished, she remained in bed with him, his head resting upon her chest. She stared at the ceiling, numbness creeping in with a tinge of regret. She'd just buried her parents and already she'd seduced her brother's childhood friend. This could only end in disaster. The longer she examined the ceiling, the more she wanted to leave. When his breath fell heavy on her breast and she thought he was asleep, she began to inch out from under him, but the movement stirred him. He held her in a tight embrace, their nakedness pressed together. "I really do love you," he whispered.

She put her arms around him, gave him a quick squeeze, and pulled away. She couldn't tell him she loved him. Not even just to make it easier.

"Are you leaving?" he asked. "I mean, for Cincinnati?"

"Yes. Day after tomorrow."

He moved his head to face her. "I bet you could find a good job here in Baltimore, or DC."

Joan sat up. "No, I've found my place in Cincinnati. I like it there." She wanted to dress, but her clothes remained in the living room.

Jimmy sat up beside her and placed his hand on her inner thigh. "Maybe I could come. I mean, in a few months."

"What?" Joan took his hand from her body and stood. "Are you crazy?"

"For you I am." When he said this, Joan smiled, as though it were a joke. She walked through the open doorway into the living room to begin retrieving her clothes as he continued to speak. "Let me go with you. I can get a job as good as the one I've got here. I want to be with you."

Half dressed, Joan walked back to the bedroom door. "Jimmy, you can't. It would never work. You're Jimmy: Brad's friend, the paper boy, the kid who mowed the lawn. I mean, I love you, you're like part of the family." She smiled sweetly. "But you're Jimmy."

"You can call me Jim."

Joan smiled sadly. "No, Jimmy, I can't. I've got another life out there. This stays here."

Jimmy sighed. "For you, maybe. But I live here. It stays with me."

"I'm sorry, Jimmy. I shouldn't have come." She finished buttoning her blouse, then tucked it in. "It was wrong. I don't know what I was thinking."

Joan stood in the living room, fully clothed. In his briefs, Jimmy walked over to stand next to her. "Maybe I could visit. Just for a few days."

Joan looked sadly into his eyes, then gave him a tight hug. After a moment of holding him, she took her jacket from the books on the chair, and left.

The poem lay in Joan's lap now, on the train. She hadn't asked her brother if he wanted it. She'd just tucked it in her black leather purse and taken it with her, as though it were hers alone.

The train stopped to pick up new passengers and let off old ones. Joan ignored the inner shuffling and stared outside at a lake in the distance. The surrounding trees remained still. Moments before, they'd blown in the wind, but the wind had drifted away and was gone. The lake too, remained still and alone, segregated from the trees. Even the grass seemed to have crept away from it, only the messiness of mud and jagged rocks touching the edges of the water. The scene was suddenly veiled by black smoke from the train's engine. As the train began a slow motion forward, the lake, like the wind, drifted away and was gone.

As the train picked up speed, Joan's eyes glided along the lines of poetry. The ink was spotted in places, diluted by tears.

"Where are you headed?" Joan heard the stock question posed to another passenger, and was vaguely aware that this conductor had asked her the same thing only an hour or two ago. What had she answered? She couldn't even remember.

Joan wanted someone else to take control for a change. Independent as she'd become, her parents had always been there, just a phone call away, to give her advice, to guide her with knowledge and experience, whether she wanted it or not. Beneath her self-reliance, there'd always been the safety net, the fact that she wasn't alone. She didn't want to be head of the family. She just wanted to be the little girl in the dresser mirror.

Joan and Brad had discussed the arrangements. They would keep the house. They didn't want to lose all of the memories stored there. Brad would get rid of his apartment and live in that house full of sorrow. Joan would always have a room there, a shrine to girlhood. She would organize the family reunions. She might even invite Jimmy; he was practically family.

Joan felt someone's eyes on her and noticed that the man in the seat next to her no longer wrote in his notebook. The passenger peered over at the parchment in her lap. Joan pretended she didn't notice, but she folded the parchment. These words weren't for just any stranger's eyes.

"I'm a poet too," the man said. She pretended not to hear him, not wanting to be sucked into conversation. She saw his reflection in the window as he looked at her and then returned to his notebook. She noticed for the first time how much he looked like Jimmy. She reached up and touched the dragonfly broach Jimmy had given her when he showed up, unexpected, at the train station.

"I bought it for a girl a few years ago," he'd said. "But it never worked out. Your mom helped me pick it out. I think you should have it." She'd taken it reluctantly. But she had taken it.

She peeked down at the broach now, the red crystal eyes reflecting the train's reading light. For an instant, she entertained the notion of looking for a job in Baltimore. But after being away from home when her parents had lived there, it seemed wrong to move back now that they'd left.

Her cousins and brother thought she had it together, but she knew better. She'd been put in control, was now the head of the family, but she didn't know how to steer. Joan was just another passenger on the train, and she no longer knew where she was headed.

A Good Beer Needs a Good Stein

Fritz and Mary sat side-by-side in the train's lounge car. Sunlight poured through the window, warming them and making them thirsty.

The lounge car served beer. That was good; as far as Fritz was concerned, it didn't get much better than a good beer. He placed his order.

"It's a little early to start drinking, Fritz." Mary considered alcohol a vice that should be restricted to the night. It was just past noon. "Maybe we should have some iced tea for now."

"No, I'd like a beer," Fritz said, careful but confident. "What better way to start our vacation off on the right track?"

Mary got that look on her face, like she'd just bitten into a lemon wedge. "What better way to make a wreck of a good vacation?" she muttered.

"How's that, Mary?"

"It's too early to start drinking. Remember what happened last time you got drunk?"

"I'm just having a beer."

"I wouldn't drink beer before happy hour."

"I prefer to make my own hours happy." When his beer came, he took an animated gulp.

It had been six years since they'd really gotten away, their last several vacations devoted to working on the house or helping their grown kids move from home to home. This vacation to the Windy City was for themselves...and for their son, daughter-in-law, and their grandchild-to-be who all resided in Chicago.

Mary stirred the sugar at the bottom of her iced tea. The individual grains did not dissolve; instead, the pieces danced around in a circle with the spoon's movement.

Some weeks ago, Fritz experienced what he considered to be an exceptional day. Fridays normally made for better days at the office. He didn't have any meetings, which meant he didn't need to spend half his day wasting time listening to other people talk about things, half of which they'd never actually accomplish anyway. No brainstorms that usually resulted in nothing more than a flood of mediocre ideas and a quick flushing of any aspirations down the drain. No pep talks about teamwork, motivation, or leadership. On that particular day, Fritz had been left alone to enjoy the solace of his cubicle, his headphones tuned to easy listening, his bag of chips within easy reach. Without the interruption of the meetings, he could actually work. He didn't enjoy his work all that much—updating technical manuals as federal regulations and various laws changed—but he did like having the work done.

Fritz was so pleased with his day that he wore a genuine smile on his face as he left the office. An impulse overtook him; he wanted to do something spontaneous. On the way home from work he stopped in at the local liquor store.

German beer was his favorite. The Beck's beckoned to him, but St. Pauli Girl was cheaper. He took a twelve-pack of the dark label and walked to the counter.

"Will that be all?" asked the boy at the register. He didn't look old enough to sell alcohol, but Fritz had often talked with Mary about that interesting fact: the older you got, the younger young people looked. Back when he was a kid himself, thirteen-year-old girls had turned him on—he vividly remembered his first girlfriend in middle school. Now, even the college graduates looked like kids.

Fritz looked behind the boy and contemplated his answer as he scanned the shelved bottles. Scotch, bourbon, cognac, brandy. It all looked good. But beer was enough. "This'll do for now."

The boy rang him up. Fritz watched him—*Dan*, his nametag said—operate the cash register. He could be twelve just as well as twenty-one by Fritz's judgment. "Have a good night," Dan said in a voice that lacked sincerity.

"You too," said Fritz as he walked out the door. He put the beer in the trunk of his eleven-year-old Volkswagen Golf and slid into the driver's seat. Fifteen minutes later, he parked on the street in front of his suburban home.

Fritz unlocked the front door and struggled to open it, his briefcase in one hand and the box of beer hoisted up in his other arm. He managed to get inside and put everything on the floor just long enough to remove his shoes and put on his slippers. "I'm home," he called.

"In the kitchen, Fritz."

Fritz took the beer and followed his wife's voice toward the scent of corned beef and cabbage. He pecked her on the cheek as she continued to work on a salad at the counter. "How was your day?"

She sighed. "Oh, you know. Another day, another reason to consider early retirement." She chopped a carrot into slices. "Yours?"

"Good day," he said. "And I got us a little something." He showed her the St. Pauli Girl Dark.

Mary frowned at the image on the box, a large-breasted woman offering pleasure to onlookers, heady beers in her hands. "Oh, Fritz, you know I can't stand that dark stuff. I have a hard enough time with light beer." She turned to begin slicing a second carrot.

"You could water it down."

"There's some vegetable juice in the fridge," she said. "I'll have that."

"Suit yourself," Fritz said. "Smells good."

"Doesn't it?" She moved from carrots to radishes. "Got a nice cut of meat at the market." She looked back at the box of beer he'd placed on the counter. "Oh, I don't think there'll be room for all that in the fridge. I went to the store today."

Fritz opened the door. "I'll make room." He rummaged through the milk, juices, iced tea, vegetables, yogurts, leftovers, and everything else that always seemed to fill whatever size refrigerator they had. A few years back they'd bought this bigger one for more space; he'd never expected they'd actually fill it. By the time Mary finished preparing the salad, Fritz had found a place for all eleven bottles. He kept the twelfth out. "I think I'll begin. Sure you won't have one?"

"I'm sure." She turned off the roast.

"More for me." He found the bottle opener in the drawer. The bottle hissed. A visible mist circled the inside of the neck like a cloud and he sniffed it.

He left the bottle on the kitchen counter and went to the living room. There, in the display case, were just a few of the many things they never used, souvenirs they'd collected over the years of their marriage. The handsome ceramic beer stein sat on a glass shelf. He opened the door and felt the rim, then fingered the handle. He lifted it from the shelf. He hadn't touched the stein in years and had used it only once, fourteen years ago, just after their return from Germany. Mary had kept it safely away in the case since then.

"What're you doing, Fritz?" Mary called from the kitchen.

"Just thinking about using the stein."

Mary quickly abandoned the kitchen and went to the stein's aid. "Oh, Fritz, you know that's just for display. We don't want to damage it."

"I suppose not," Fritz sighed. "But it *is* a beer stein. Using it once in a while wouldn't..."

Mary pried the stein from his hands. They both admired it. The handle resembled intertwined branches, wide and easy on the hand. Around the stein were textured scenes of joy and decadence: a group of men sat at a table, one of them with a woman on his lap, another playing a guitar. In another scene a man and woman danced while men played cards and maids served beer. The scenes jumped right off the stein and touched the real world. But Fritz's world wasn't as carefree. He longed to touch theirs.

Mary smiled at Fritz. "I remember when we bought this." It was the first truly happy smile he'd seen on her lips in days. He remembered their German vacation, how well they had blended in as natives, the youthful passion between them back when they'd been newlyweds. He wanted to kiss Mary now, but the stein was between them, along with the years that had passed since those days of carefree bliss. "I wouldn't want you to ruin our only souvenir of that special time." She put the stein back in the case and closed the door.

Fritz gave in. "No, of course not."

They returned to the kitchen. She resumed preparing dinner and he took his beer. It was still cold, ready to drink. He opened the cabinet door and reached for a glass.

Though her back was to him, Mary spoke. "Good that you got bottles. You don't even have to dirty a glass."

Fritz froze. "Yes," he said, removing his hand from the glass and closing the cabinet door. "Quite right."

Mary never let him use the good stein. After that one lousy drink, Mary had put the thing away to be seen and not touched, admired but not used. Fritz understood her desire to keep things neat and tidy, to preserve things by non-use. But as he drove to work the following Monday morning, he stewed. *She just takes it too far. What's the point in having the stuff if we can't ever use it?*

It wasn't just the stein. Mary guarded everything that way. The cuckoo clock only ticked and the grandfather clock only tocked when they had company or on special occasions. They seldom used their good china or crystal—maybe once or twice a year. Last Christmas, she'd even suggested they use special decorative paper plates for their formal holiday dinner, something that had embarrassed him in front of their guests. Their home featured a beautiful formal dining room with an expensive table, china hutch and buffet, but they didn't use that room any more than the china and crystal itself.

"Come on, damn it, I'm late!" Fritz pressed his horn and immediately felt sorry for having done so. The light had only been green for a few seconds, but those seconds seemed to expand during the morning commute.

Then there was the living room. When the kids still lived at home, no one was even allowed to set foot in the living room. Now that they were empty nesters, Fritz would walk wherever the hell he damn well pleased. But he still bowed to most of his wife's wishes. She had set herself up as the master of the house by being the keeper of the house, and as far as she was concerned, the formal living room was not for living in—it was for use only when special guests visited, people so important they came only once or twice a year: out of town guests, old schoolmates and teachers, bosses and managers, the Tupperware ladies.

When the important company in need of impressing wasn't around, the room remained enshrined: the curtains, drawn; the sofa and chair, covered with plastic; the piano that no one played, covered with a shroud-like sheet, the kids gone and the lessons long forgotten.

Books that had never been cracked open lined the shelves of the study: *Get it at the public library so you won't damage our copy.* Fine stationery, aged and yellowing, hid in desk drawers: *Special stationery should be reserved for special occasions.* Old clothes, so out of style that their mere existence was unjustified, hung in the spare closets: *Everything comes back into style.* Newer clothing couldn't always be worn either: *When you have an outfit this nice you don't want to wear it out.* Their pantry held discolored chocolates gone bad: *These are fine chocolates and there's no expiration date.* And in the cellar, wine had turned to vinegar: *Corked wine in a nice bottle always improves with age.*

Fritz understood Mary. They'd been together for a long time. He'd gone along with her when it started, agreeing that some limitations should be set for the children, that they should abide by house rules. But since the kids were gone, her insistence on never using the nice things grew increasingly irritating, like the traffic that got heavier with every new housing development. The traffic and the job and Mary's house restrictions got worse with each passing year, but still he continued to run circles around the issues of contention instead of making a straight line to the center of his discontent.

Fritz was a few-drinks-now-and-then kind of guy. But it was Friday again, a few weeks after his last visit to the liquor store, and he'd experienced another exceptional day in his office cube. His wife had greeted him at home with a kiss and a delicious meal; the scent of sausage and sauerkraut filled the air and the food filled his belly. Even straight from the bottle, the dark St. Pauli Girl tasted good. Well after dinner, he was up to bottle number four when that disapproving scowl appeared on Mary's face.

"Don't you think you've had enough, Fritz?" She knitted because she needed something to do with her hands. Sometimes she thumbed through a book or magazine, but this week she was working on an afghan for their first grandchild, due in a few months.

"I don't think so. To tell you the truth, I feel pretty good."

"That's what I mean." She said with a smirk. "You're already drunk, why drink more?"

He looked at the afghan, then at his beer. The bottle was still fairly full. He took a hearty drink. "You know, this really would taste better in a stein."

Mary chuckled. "No, it would taste exactly the same in a stein."

"There's more to taste than the *sense* of taste."

"Now you're not making sense."

"There's the feel of the bottle or glass or ... stein ... in your hand, the weight of it, the feel of it against your lips. There's the surroundings. Like, for example, this beer would taste different in the family room, in the dining room, or out on the patio. It would taste better in a stein."

"It would taste exactly the same in a stein."

"Why don't I try it and find out?"

She hardened. "It's a display piece, Fritz."

"A good beer needs a good stein."

"A good beer doesn't need anything to doctor it up."

"Mary, if you had a taste for beer, you'd understand." He stood with his near-empty bottle and went to the kitchen. He swigged down the last of it in front of the recycling bin, then tossed the bottle in. From the fridge, he took another. He held the bottle in one hand and fumbled with the bottle opener in the other. As he tried to remove the cap, the bottle flipped out of his hand and shattered on the ceramic tile floor, sending shards of glass and a wave of dark beer all around him.

"Oh no, Fritz, what happened?" Before he could answer, Mary stood in the kitchen doorway in shock. "Oh, what a mess." She sighed and inched closer. "Get out of the way, Fritz. Get out of those clothes. Put them straight in the washer; they'll stink up the hamper."

"Just go back to your knitting, Mary." He tried to regain some dignity. "I'll take care of this."

Mary wouldn't allow it. "Just get out of the way. Get those clothes in the washer. I think you've had enough."

"I'm fine, Mary! It just slipped."

"Just slipped?" She sank to her hands and knees with the trash next to her, picking up the shards of glass. Next would be the towel, sopping up the beer. Then the brush broom. Finally, she would mop the entire kitchen, just to be sure no hidden slivers waited to creep into the flesh of their feet the next morning. "Just slipped," she muttered. Fritz stood there, watching her, still in his wet clothes. "This is exactly why I don't want you using the stein or the good crystal."

As Mary lectured, more to the floor than to him, Fritz slowly descended to the basement washroom. He removed his clothes and tried to strip himself of his humiliation.

Mr. Abbot stood at the head of the conference table and shouted. "A leader isn't just someone who leads people. A leader is someone who lives what he believes, lives by his convictions, and uses the example of his own life to motivate other people to want to follow him." He'd begun the meeting seated at the head. But, as usual, he'd motivated himself out of the chair within a few minutes. Monday meetings were the worst. What the hell did Fritz care about leadership theories? Who, exactly, was he supposed to be leading in his six by six cube? He was barely leading his own life.

It's my house as much as hers! It's my stein—I picked it out!

Abbot paced the floor. "You can't just bark orders and call that leadership. A leader has to be a team player. You have to show the other person you appreciate them, and encourage them to do the thing you want them to, not because you told them to do it but because they really want to do it." The other twenty or so people at the table appeared to be paying Mr. Abbot the same amount of attention as Fritz was, blankly nodding as Abbot strutted circles around them.

I ought to drink out of one of those fifty-dollar wine flutes she's got. Service for eight... I'll bet some of them have never known human lips, after all these years sitting up in that hutch.

Abbot placed a hand on Fritz's shoulder. "So don't go out there and do the great work you do day in and day out just because I tell you to! Do it because you know it makes a difference, because you know it's important, and it brings you pride!"

Unease washed over Fritz as the eyes of everyone at the table rested on him. He smiled up at Abbot and was glad when the guru moved on and allowed him to go back to his thoughts. *Embarrass me like that. Like I was drunk or something! I had a little buzz, but I wasn't drunk. It just slipped. Could've happened just as easily with a bottle of mineral water. Like she's never dropped anything.*

"So get out there and make yourselves proud!" Abbot concluded, and the workers herded themselves out of the conference room and into their cubes. In half an hour, many of them would flock to the coffee station and water cooler to mock what bits of the meeting they'd actually heard. Some of them were happy to have jobs, some were grateful for their work, but few of them actually took pride in their paperwork and even fewer believed it made any kind of difference to anyone but their own manager and the bureaucrats above him.

Morning lingered. Fritz returned to the coffee station with his favorite mug—an olive green ceramic piece from Mexico he'd managed to sneak out of the house four years ago. They had enough mugs at home, after all, for one to go unnoticed. He'd seen Mary inspecting the dark corners of the cabinet shortly after the Mexican piece disappeared, but she'd never questioned him outright, and he'd never offered to shed light on the subject.

In the office, he took the pot, half-full of viscous coffee, and swirled it to stir it a bit. He watched the black liquid spin around. He'd switch to water after lunch, but what he really wanted was a beer. And he wanted it in a stein. He was motivated; a bit of Abbot's ranting had gotten through after all.

Fritz pressed on the horn, but it did no good. The accident was a big one, bad enough to block the beltway longer than the usual traffic did. *Should've taken the back roads.* But it was too late to turn around. *I could be here two hours!* The drive usually took forty minutes; he remembered back when it had only taken fifteen. Without the traffic, he could circle the entire Baltimore beltway in less time than it took him to get home these days. How many times had he covered the beltway, going around and around and getting nowhere?

"That asshole sure knows how to manage," he said out loud to keep himself from yelling at the helpless car in front of him. Abbot had come by his cube late in the day to compliment him on his great work. At least, that was the pretense. Half an hour later he was back with the reward for work well done: more work. *Just when I get caught up—bam! Enough to keep me backed up for weeks.*

Fritz honked again, then slammed his back against the seat, sighing, knowing it was pointless. "Asshole Abbot," he said with a laugh. He'd share the nickname at the coffee station tomorrow. *If I don't call in sick. Sick and tired of all the bullshit.*

He stopped by the liquor store. It was Monday, but still a fine night for drinking. He could use a stiff drink, but he settled for beer again. The Beck's beckoned him once more, and this time it was on sale. St. Pauli Girl was still cute, flavorful and cheap, but he decided to live on the wild side for a change and get the beer he actually wanted.

Readers of *Esquire* had voted the St. Pauli Girl as the second sexiest woman in advertising, right behind Swiss Miss. That's what Bob had said at the water cooler a few days ago, his magazine in hand. Fritz could see why Swiss Miss got top billing; there was an attraction to the supposed innocence and a primal desire to corrupt it. But he'd take a St. Pauli Girl over a Swiss Miss any day. That's just the kind of guy Fritz was.

The girl behind the counter looked about as young as a Swiss Miss, but as experienced as a St. Pauli Girl. "Beck's, sweet," she crooned approvingly. The cashier flirted with him as he figured she probably flirted with most of the guys, whether antiques like him or the younger, barely legal studs. "Anything else with that?"

Fritz considered the selection of bottles behind her. The scotch and brandy looked good. But it was Monday. "No, that'll do for now."

"Mmkay." Fritz watched her—*Tilly*, her nametag said—operate the cash register. She was closer to fourteen than forty, by Fritz's judgment. "Have a good night," Tilly said in a voice that seemed to brim with promise, perhaps only because he desired it.

Fritz unlocked the front door and struggled to open it, his briefcase in one hand and the box of beer hoisted up in his other arm. Inside, he put it all down for a moment and took off his shoes, placing them in the comfortable nook Mary had set up. "I'm home," he called out, putting on his slippers.

"In the kitchen, Fritz." The scent of salmon filled their home, and he wondered whether she'd ever considered the effect such fishy air might have on their valuables.

"How was your day?" he asked as he entered the kitchen with the twelve-pack under his arm.

"Good," she said, looking genuinely happy. "Finally got the Henderson case off my desk. Feel like I can breathe again."

"Good for you," he said. He put the beer on the counter. "Got a little something to celebrate with."

"Oh, Fritz, again? You know I can't stand the dark stuff."

"I didn't get the dark, Mary. I got the Oktoberfest."

"Little early for Oktoberfest, isn't it?"

"Not by much," he said. "And it's never too early to celebrate."

"Oh, all right." She gave in. "I'll have one with dinner." She prepared their salad, chopping the iceberg lettuce. "I'm surprised you got another case already. You just swallowed one last week. On a binge, are you?"

He rummaged around in the fridge, fitting in the ten bottles. Two remained on the counter. "Just felt like a good beer."

Mary set the table, complete with two glasses apiece: one for beer, the other for water to counter it. Fritz acknowledged the effort and poured the beers into the glasses. *A step up from bottle-sucking.*

Their dinner included salmon loaf—Fritz's favorite—and fried potatoes, along with green beans and a fresh salad. "Mmm. This is a great meal," he said.

"I wanted to have a nice dinner," she said with a smile. "We both deserve it."

"Well, I appreciate it," Fritz said and raised his glass. "To your good day." The residue of his own bad day clung to him like the foam in the empty half of his glass.

After dinner, he helped her with the dishes. When they were finished, he took another Beck's from the fridge. "Want another?"

"Maybe one more," she said.

"Good," he said, taking a second. "Want a glass?"

"No, straight from the bottle. No need to dirty another glass when a nice drinking container's provided."

"Well, I'm going to use the stein," he said casually. He didn't wait to see her disapproving glare; he darted out of the kitchen and into the living room.

"Now Fritz..." she warned, following him. "We've been over this before."

Fritz stood before the display case, looking at Mary. "Over it? No. Around it? Yes. We've been around and around this a million times. And yes, I know how you feel about it. But do you know how I feel?" The words spewed out unfiltered. "Do you even give a damn?"

Mary looked more confused than angry. "Well Fritz, I'm sure you agree that this is a precious memory, a memento from Germany."

"What's so damn special about something you can't touch?" His casual tone was gone, replaced by one of anger. "What's the point of having the thing if we don't ever use it?"

"If I'd let you use the stein all these years, we probably wouldn't even have it any more." Mary put on her parental voice. "And what's the point of it then, not even having it to look at, to remember?"

"If you'd *let* me?" Fritz scoffed. "If I want to use my stein, I'll damn well use it!"

"Fritz, what's wrong with you? I think you should cut off your drinking for tonight. You're not in your right mind."

"I'll drink all I please, and I'll do it from my stein!" He opened the display case. She put her hand on his and tried to ease the door closed, but he was stronger.

"You'll break the collectibles," Mary warned. "Be careful!"

"They'll be fine if you quit pushing and shoving." He took the stein from its place and proceeded toward the kitchen.

Mary followed right behind. "You've managed all these years without dirtying our stein. Why do you have to use it now?"

"Because I *want* to. Because I have the *right* to use my stein! I have a right to eat on our china, to drink from our crystal, to pound out a tune on the piano, to take supper in our dining room, to relax in our formal living room. I want to use my stein, and that's what I'm going to do!" He blew into the stein to loosen the dust.

Mary watched as he rinsed out the stein and poured in the beer. He opened a second bottle to complete the fill. A white head crowned the stein, crowned his achievement. "In fact," he added calmly, "I think I'll retire to our formal living room."

"Fine!" she said, glaring at him with angry eyes. "Just spoil my day! I have the first half-decent day at work in a long time and you have to go and act like this! I go all out and fix a nice dinner and what thanks do I get?"

"*Here's* the thanks you got," Fritz yelled back. "I said thank you, remember? I said it was a good meal and I thanked you for it! I helped pay for the food. I helped pay for the house we ate it in, the plates we ate it on, the silverware we ate it with! I brought beer home for us to drink! I helped with the dishes! And if you want, I'll eat out tomorrow!"

"That's great, eat out! What do you need me for? To clean, cook and copulate! Is that it?"

"You know better than that!"

"And now you don't even need that! No cooking—you're eating out! No cleaning—looks like you plan to dirty the place up, ruin everything! And if all you have me around for is sex, you can forget it mister!"

"Don't flatter yourself!" He turned his back to her and walked through their family room to the formal living room. He turned on the light, chasing away the darkness that lived there. He set his stein on the cocktail table, pulled the plastic covering from a high-back chair, picked up the beer and fell back into a comfort he had seldom known.

"Ahh," he sighed. He took a long drink, beer dribbling from his mouth to his shirt. It was the nicest room of the house. It deserved to be protected, preserved. But it also deserved to be used, enjoyed. He enjoyed it now.

The walls were papered in a textured gray that gave the impression of stone. The carpeted floor radiated an immaculate white. The mahogany molding, chair rail, and trim capped the rich appearance. Two high-back chairs and a couch surrounded a large mahogany cocktail table. He took in a deep breath and finished his beer. He was ready for another.

Mary knitted furiously in the family room. He smiled at her as he passed, but she offered only an enraged glare. He refilled his stein in the kitchen. On the way back, he raised his stein in salute, only infuriating her more. He took his place in the high-back chair.

He was so pleased with his victory that he continued drinking long past his limit. It was after midnight, beyond their bedtime, when he stumbled back into the formal room with another stein of beer. "This is the life," he cheered to the imagined crowd of conspirators, raising his stein high, beer sloshing out and splattering about. On the way down, it sloshed again, raining onto the plastic-covered sofa, beading on the cover like droplets on an umbrella.

Mary had wanted to go to bed hours ago, but she wouldn't leave her husband to ravage the house. She heard the commotion, the beer pelting plastic, and marched into the formal room.

"Fritz, that's enough! Stop it!" Her yell concealed her crying, but only for a moment. With the next plea, her tears emerged. "Please, stop! Look at this mess!"

"What mess?" He turned to look and fell over the cocktail table. The stein flew from his hand and they both watched it plunge into the air and down to the floor. The ceramic memento—their one souvenir from a time when Mary used to join Fritz in throwing care to the wind and partying into the late hours of the night—shattered. The German stein sent ceramic shrapnel throughout the room and splattered beer on the table, the exposed chair, the textured wall paper, the Venetian blinds. Fritz had more than spoiled her evening; he'd soiled their formal living room. He'd broken more than a stein.

German beer was best. There were a lot of things Fritz hated about his grandparents' homeland—the nation that had given birth to Nazis and caused a terrible war—but beer was not one of them. Beer, he believed, was one of the country's saving graces.

The lounge car attendant didn't have any German beer in stock, but American would do for now. It was watery, but water was cleansing.

Mary sipped her iced tea through a straw to draw in some of the bottom-dwelling sugar. She'd forgiven him. She'd yelled and screamed and cried at him, giving time for the stain and stench of German beer to saturate the good chair, the polished table, the textured wallpaper, the immaculate curtains, and cared-for carpet. Fritz didn't talk back, simply sinking into the couch and eventually passing out. Then, as he snored and slobbered on the couch between drowsy peeks, he saw her cleaning the living room. It took her more than two hours. It was after three in the morning when Mary finally made her way to bed, and she had to be at work at seven.

The next day, Fritz woke with a hangover. But regret slowed him down more than the beer's aftereffects. He got to the office late and barely dented his pile of new work. He didn't see Mary that morning. She'd left early.

He came home with a dozen pink roses and puppy-dog eyes that acknowledged he had taken things too far. "I'm sorry about the stein, and the room," he said. "And I'm sorry for the way I acted. I'll be more careful from now on."

Mary had reluctantly accepted the roses. He could tell it was a pardoning concession when she put them in a precious vase on the formal dining room table and served dinner there.

Now, in the lounge car, he sipped his beer slowly, savoring the taste. The train's conductor, an old man whose speech was faster than a locomotive, had already chatted with them a time or two and was now having words with the young couple across the car. They sipped bottled water, not yet old enough for beer. They must have been in their late teens, on their first romantic getaway. Young as they were, they looked old-fashioned. That's what the conductor was talking to them about now.

"Sure is nice to see young folks with old values. You've got everything straight. Everyone wants to drive in the fast lane. But you should focus on what's really important to you. If you dig each other and if being together's more important than having flashy cars and big ol' houses full of fancy stuff no one uses anyhow because it's too expensive..." The old man seemed to forget where he was going. "You're doing all right." He chuckled. "Don't know how many times I had people tell me to get off the train and retire, get an easy part-time job. Can you see me greeting people at a department store?" The couple laughed, and Fritz smiled too. The conductor shook his head. "Now, I don't mind talking to people, but they'd all be in a hurry to get past me and get to their shopping. Naw, give me a smooth train full of people like you two. That's worth waking up to."

The young couple nodded their heads, huge grins across their faces. They seemed to enjoy the company of an older person who was on their side. The kids reminded Fritz of himself and Mary back when they first started dating. He recalled their train ride in Germany, as he finished off his beer.

The attendant approached. "Would you like another?"

Fritz saw the hopeful look on Mary's face as she sipped her own respectable beverage. "No," he answered. "I'll have an iced tea." Mary's face brightened, making him smile. It was give and take, marriage, and even after twenty-some years this lesson continued to need relearning. The train curved around a bend.

They looked forward to a week in Chicago with the kids. They'd learned about a shop in Chicago that sold a variety of hand-crafted steins imported from Germany. He intended to buy two: one to display, one to use. After all, Fritz thought as they sipped their iced tea, he didn't want to damage a valued souvenir, but a good beer needs a good stein.

Mountain of Sand

Colin thumbed through the tattered notebook, pondering his quickly-jotted notes and inspired lines. The spiral-bound book was worn, but not well-used. That is, the lined pages were gorged with his writing, but none of it was very good. Sometimes he considered casting the pulp aside; it was worth more to a recycling bin than it was to his career as a poet.

Career as a poet. The words were absurd, nearly laughable. But that was the miracle he'd had. That's how he'd made his living during the early years. That was the bird he hoped to cage again: those days when it was nothing for him to spit out a quick page of poetry and make a killing with it. He'd been a unique animal, an icon in his genre. Now, he wasn't even a has-been; he was even more past tense than that—only a had-been.

Ooh, that's good! Write that down! He did. The lines came out sloppier than usual due to the movement of the train. He read them back to himself. Like most of his recent inspirations, it no longer seemed any good a moment after writing it. He wondered, was it his talent that had dwindled, or just his popularity? Had he ever really been any good, or just lucky?

Colin had been a poetic prince, coasting along the tracks of success without much effort. He liked to think he had been rewarded for his talent, not his hard work. That's the way it had been. *Had been.* He looked to make sure he'd already written the phrase down.

He had been a creative writing major in college and had earned his MFA at Marshall University in Huntington, West Virginia. He'd been drawn to the college because it was in his hometown, but was reassured when he learned that one of the world's most prominent Poe scholars taught there. Since childhood, Colin had been spellbound by Poe's rhyme-driven lines.

Colin got his first poem published in a literary journal early in his college years. His professor knew the editor and put in a good word for him. By the time he was in grad school, the literary journals were approaching him. His first collection of poems was published by a small house when Colin was in his early twenties. It was an instant success.

The critics weren't all on board; one called his work "pulp poetry" and another described it as "sloppy writing in slick packaging." One review went so far as to praise the hyped marketing copy on the back cover as superior to anything inside the book. But other critics had good things to say, declaring him an "unofficial poet laureate for the masses" and "a poet for the average Joe." Thanks in part to the publisher's creative marketing team and a boost from his alma mater, buyers bought into his rhyming lines. Contrary to all he'd heard from his professors and fellow writers—that there was no money in poetry—he'd accumulated a small fortune and a sizable fan base before reaching twenty-three. By the time those digits had inverted to thirty-two, his success had dwindled. And now, at thirty-six, it was a distant memory.

"You're one lucky bastard," a jealous writer had once told him at a book signing.

"It's talent, not luck," the next person in line, a middle-aged woman, had corrected. But even then, Colin knew the resentful writer probably had it right. He wouldn't consciously admit it, but he knew it.

When his early words found a place in the hip new poetry movement, he'd simply hitched along for the ride. Before he knew what had hit him or where he was going, he found himself on a national book tour. Audiences came by the dozens to bookstores for autographed copies; they came in droves to hear him read from his poetry, accompanied by a cellist, drummer, and guitarist. Book sales, poetry grants, workshop presentations, and lecture fees provided a lavish life. He was the rock star of poetry, and he loved it.

Now, as he sat on the train with his spiral notebook and the weathered stub of a pencil, he wished he could regain the love people had once poured out to him. Not the love from the women who threw themselves at him, but the love in a room where he read, the feeling of an audience really listening to his words, asking for more, celebrating his catchy phrases and newly-crafted clichés with a sea of snapping fingers. It was one thing to *use* a cliché; creating fresh phrases that *became* cliché was entirely different.

Back in college, a friend and fellow poet used to call him Wordsworth. At the time, he took it as a compliment to be compared to the Romantic master. Now, he understood what Allen had been predicting by comparing him to a poet whose talent flourished in his early years, then faltered later in life.

Because Colin's success had come easily and unexpectedly, he hadn't given any thought to the preservation of it. He'd simply allowed the breeze of popularity to carry him along like a fresh green leaf pulled from a tree, airborne.

Now it was autumn. His fifteen minutes were up; he was a dry, crumbling leaf people stepped on and each passing gust of wind was less likely to lift him. *Write that down*. His dull, yellow pencil scrawled across the page.

Colin had never made a decision to give up writing poetry. He'd taken breaks now and again, six months here, a few months there, during which he wasn't actively writing. But most of the time he had a notebook with him and constantly jotted down phrases and ideas. His teachers and fellow writers used to marvel at his speed.

"How do you do it?" one of his professors, a gray-haired woman, had once asked when he turned in a poem moments after she had assigned it.

"It's like I piss the stuff out," he'd answered. The students laughed; the professor did not. She cringed at his crude imagery but couldn't help but melt as she read his work.

Back then, Colin regularly consumed countless cocktails, so he had urine in ample supply. And it was true that his poetry came just as easily and nearly as frequently. He wrote with the expectation that he'd have to go back and refine the ideas he was throwing down on paper. The fact was, when he returned to a poem a few days later, he'd often find that any tinkering only tampered with the original intent. His poetry used to come from a place beyond his consciousness, and its essence shone pure in its conception, not to be altered.

Once in a while, he would hit writer's block. He learned to stop writing during those times of desolation. When assignments were due during such blockages, he simply retreated to his arsenal of unused poems. What made it effortless for Colin in the early days was that he knew when to write and when to refrain. When he forced uninspired lines, it showed. Back then, he wrote only when something was struggling to escape his mind.

The more successful he became, the less he actually wrote. During those busy days, he still jotted notes and ideas in his Moleskine journals with his Monte Blanc, but he became consumed by the machine: reading, talking about his writing, signing books, and wooing women and wannabe writers. He was too busy enjoying the trappings of success to produce original work. After refraining from the craft too long, it was as though he'd lost his connection with the source.

On the train, he broke his reverie and looked down at his notes.

As a child I was a star, the wind blew me along.
Now I'm ... stuck inside a jar ... ?
a drunk on a stool inside a bar ... ?
a baby strapped in the seat of a car ... ?
a rock star without a guitar ... ?
A bird without a song.

He looked at the lines in his notebook, determining which phrase to use. *Yuck.* He turned the page.

Nowadays, he wrote even when inspiration was not there (which was most of the time), out of fear that the words would dry up forever. The notebook on his lap was filled with words and phrases with which to seed new masterworks. But what he tried to produce with these adequate ingredients was inevitably useless. *Or if it is any good, no one recognizes it.*

Sometimes he thought his poetry was the same as it had always been, just not as fresh. Like a fourth or fifth sequel, it was difficult for one voice to continue piece after piece and remain new to the critics. Sure, his fifth book had sounded much the same as his fourth and his third, but that was because it *was* the same voice— his voice. He wondered whether the problem wasn't so much his work as the changing culture, the attention deficit of his readers who came quickly to his work but moved nearly as quickly away from it to new things. Perhaps, he considered, it was time to stop rhyming, to truncate his trademark.

A dried up leaf in the air, crumbling pieces scattered,
My reflection—long face, short hair—broken, shattered.

The words still came, they just didn't jive. Perhaps he'd rhymed all the good lines he had in him.

When he'd first submitted his assignments in rhyming verse, his teachers had advised him against it. His literary friends had echoed the sentiment. "Free verse is where it's at."

Colin was quick to respond to such opinions with his own. "Free verse is nothing more than prose in a pretty package. It's got to rhyme to transcend time."

Of course, Colin studied John Lennon as much as John Keats. He was more a student of Green Day than Ginsberg and knew more Billy Idol than Billy Collins. When others asked which poets he admired, he answered, "Bob Dylan and Neil Young." Colin's strong opinions about poetry were unfounded on any real knowledge of the craft. He just knew what he liked and went with the flow.

The train's movement sent his open notebook sliding from his knee. He scrambled to collect it from the floor. He lost his place in the pages and found himself looking at faded scratches from months ago.

So this is despair:
no light at night
no comfort at home
no money in the bank
no food in the cupboard
no inspiration worth sharing
and no one to share the nothingness with

One of his few attempts to write free verse, to ditch his rhyming style. He realized now, looking back, that his insistence on rhyming was not out of a respect for the form. Differentiating quality poetry from pulp prose was work; finding words that rhymed and crafting a poem around them came easy. Once success validated his stumbled-upon form, he'd latched on.

The woman sitting in the seat beside him turned toward the window and wiped tears from her face. Colin focused on his words. *So this is despair,* he read again, before turning to a blank page.

He'd spent most of the past couple years living off what was left in his accounts. He'd only recently learned to live sober, and within his means. Even after the money began to go out faster than it came in, Colin had continued his extravagant lifestyle of excessive drugs, drinking and parties. He could no longer afford to do that; he needed income. That's why he was on the train from Huntington to Chicago. He had a reading in Chicago—his first bookstore event in months—and that meant a little bit of cash.

The phone didn't ring as it once had. Years ago, he'd hired a secretary to take care of all the requests. Bookstores, cafés, coffee houses, pubs, even private homes were graced with the sound of his reading. In those days, Colin could count on free accommodations, a reading fee, applauding fans, book sales, and an evening of hot sex with a poetry junkie. Now, they'd all become hard to get.

One thing he could still count on was his alma mater. They touted him as one of the successes of their English department and he was invited to read on campus once a year.

A few years ago, before he was aware that his days in the spotlight were numbered, Colin had just finished a reading at Marshall University when fans and students flocked to greet him at the podium with longing gazes and books to sign. Colin reached into his pocket, picked the fountain pen to fit his mood—a candy-apple red Schaffer with black ink—and took inventory of the women in line to determine which one merited a private reading. Possessing a magnetic voice and knowing how to dish out charm consistently closed the deal with a hot fan after such readings; he'd become accustomed to leaving with a poetry lover in tow.

"You're the reason I worship poetry," Danielle had said as Colin signed her well-worn copy of his second book.

"So you enjoyed the reading?"

"I adored it! But then, you could read anything and it would sound good." She played with a lock of her kinky blonde hair. Her eyes and body language spoke volumes.

"I could read you more. Over a drink?"

Danielle gazed down at his inscription in her book and back into his eyes. "I'd like that."

As he led her to his on-campus lodgings, he saw her as nothing more than another groupie. But after he read to her from his notebook, after they'd consumed two bottles of chardonnay, after they'd exhausted foreplay and made the sort of love poetry is made for, she hadn't relented. They remained beneath the white sheets, each smoking a cigarette, when she introduced herself and her intention.

"I'm a poet too."

"Are you now?" Colin looked at the smoke above them. He'd heard this one a hundred times before.

"Yes," she said, uncovering herself in hopes of regaining his attention. She reached for her purse at the side of the bed and took out some folded pages. "I already got one published in a college journal."

"That's a good start." He scanned her body.

"Look," she said, thrusting the pages at him.

Colin let out a heavy sigh and sat up, dropping his cigarette in his wine glass. He took the papers from her and skimmed them. "They don't rhyme."

"They're not supposed to."

"They're better when they do."

"Well, for free verse, what do you think?"

"Pretty good, for a student." He latched on to her wrists and fell back in bed, pulling her on top of him. "The whole package is pretty good, for a student."

Being a local, Colin saw Danielle from time to time. Encounters with her became as regular as his visits to college campuses. She followed him, turning up at local readings and craft lectures and tumbling into his bed afterwards. After a couple of years, she vanished. Even when he gave his annual reading at Marhsall University last year, she wasn't there. He wondered what had become of her. Then she turned up ... in *The Kenyon Review*. Then a poem in the pages of *Ploughshares*. But it was the free verse he found in *Snake Nation Review* that sent shivers up his spine. Her poem "Shallow" described loving a seasoned artist only to outgrow and outshine him.

The fact was, he'd recently submitted poetry to all three publications only to be politely rejected and asked to send something more substantial—something fresh, like his early work. Looking back, he considered Danielle's poem the first crossing signal that perhaps he was losing his place on the poetic peak.

Once in a while, Colin still got gigs. He placed the calls himself, to the cafés and pubs and bookstores where he'd started. Some of them wanted nothing to do with him; once he'd made it big, he'd been caught up in the excitement and had forgotten them. Some of his old cohorts were happy to hear from him and offered him a few bucks and the opportunity to sell books at a reading. For the past few months, he'd had a regular gig every Wednesday at a pub where he read poetry to haggard drunks and college students, a sax and a conga backing him up. Sometimes it seemed that *he* was backing up the musicians, the drunks tapping to the beat instead of listening to his words. *Drunks on stools inside a bar.* He looked in his notebook. Yes, he'd already written that line, or something close enough.

Given the state of things, the phone call he'd received a few weeks ago had come as a surprise. Colin had been sitting in his home office, thumbing through his notebooks, mining for gems in the muck. "Colin! It's Birk!"

Birk had been one of the guys he'd partied with back when he was on top. Birk had always known where the most "extreme" night clubs were, where to find the cleanest and dirtiest call girls, and which dealers had the best coke. Now his distant friend owned a bohemian bookstore.

"Haven't heard much from you lately, Colin. What's going on?"

"Nothing much. Just pissing out poetry."

"Tell me about it," Birk said. "I got a buyout of cheap books. Guess who hit the dollar list?" Colin didn't answer, so Birk did it for him. "You! That last one, *Saved by Damnation*. Got a hundred copies of the damned thing! Get it? Damned thing?"

"Lucky you," Colin said. *Unlucky me.*

"You take the prize in the luck department, my friend," Birk teased.

Half joking, Colin said, "Luck had nothing to do with anything."

Birk laughed. "Don't beat yourself up for not keeping up, man. No way a person could live up to that first ride, one-hit-wonder or not."

"I poured my heart and soul into my work," Colin said.

"We all put our heart and soul into something. Hey, I'm not telling you anything you don't already know. Sure, you knew how to put a few rhymes together, you had talent. But you won the lottery with those first couple books, man."

As in his efforts to write, Colin found himself at a loss for words.

Birk was full of them. "Listen, I'd like to turn you a trick here. How 'bout you come to my bookstore, do a reading and signing. I'll get the word out. We'll sell the books at face value, split the dif."

Colin considered. "I don't know, Birk. I'd end up spending most of it on travel."

"You can crash at my pad. And I can get you a free train ticket. Got a lady—a customer—who always pays transportation for the chance to have dinner with the writer of the month."

"Why the train?"

"Her old man works for Amtrak. Gets a discount." After a pause, Birk asked, "So how 'bout it, Colin?"

"I don't know." Humiliation was nearly as strong as desperation.

"Come on, Colin. You let me ride along when your stock was up. I'm sitting pretty here, so let me give you this gig."

"Why the hell not?" Colin said, and a laugh escaped along with the tension.

A train. It seemed old-fashioned. Maybe it would provide some old-time inspiration. At his paper-cluttered desk back home, he began writing train lines.

The train moves along the track
The pain tells me I want you back...
The iron horse, the steel breeze,
Your cold remorse, your gift of tease...

Colin shuddered. Maybe the romantic notion of a train in motion wasn't enough to inspire well-written lines. Maybe he was at the end of his.

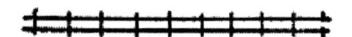

Colin was beginning to wonder why he continued to write. Early in his career, it wasn't so much that critics and fellow poets loved him as that they couldn't ignore him—the masses wouldn't let them. His rhythmic rhymes had struck a nerve with the young and youthful. Having a devoted fan start an indie rock band and include a verse of his poetry in a hit song hadn't hurt sales any, either.

Colin had convinced himself that his poetry was more than a passing fad. He was a Poet with a capital *P*. But a couple of books ago, he started his slide down the slope of the mountain. Even the locals lost interest. Gone were the adoring fans, applause, and accolades. It was like they'd all been standing around Colin's mountain when it imploded, leaving yesterday's Poet in the pit of a canyon. When he learned that Danielle had won the Whiting Award, it seemed that the pit's floor was made of quicksand. For all his former fame, he'd never received such an honor.

At least when Danielle's book came out, her name was in a small font. Colin was the Stephen King of poetry, his name always taking up half a book's cover. The only thing more important than one of his poems was its title, and the only thing more important than the title was his byline.

It was only days before leaving for Chicago that he ran into his old college buddy at the library. Allen was checking out some novels in the new fiction section; Colin had come to take a look at a directory of publishers seeking poetry submissions.

"Hey, Wordsworth!"

"Allen?" Colin barely recognized the old hippie. He'd gone yuppie, it appeared, his long hair cut short, his T-shirt and jeans traded in for a button down and dress slacks. Allen sported glasses now, along with a collection of new wrinkles around his eyes. Allen was twelve years Colin's senior.

"My God, look at you!" Allen sized him up. "You've aged, dude."

Colin let out what he'd politely held back. "You too, Allen. You look more...distinguished."

Allen shook his head in disbelief. "God, Colin! Do you realize you're as old now as I was back in college? Can you believe it?"

Colin could not, but he did the math and realized Allen wasn't far off. It came as a shock to Colin, since Allen had always been identified as the "older" student, the "non-traditional" partier. Allen had been popular back in college in part because, at his age, he'd done pretty much everything there was to do. He happened to be one of the campus drug dealers. He always knew where to get the sweetest bud; he also had weed that could leave a person tripping for hours. What you got depended on where you stood with him. Colin had always gotten the good stuff until the last few months of college. As Colin's poetry got better, Allen's weed got worse, until it got to the point where Colin didn't buy Allen's pot and Allen didn't read Colin's poetry.

Allen was a poet too, and had always marveled out loud at Colin's ability to "spew out a quick line that smelled like a bouquet from an April flower garden."

Now, in the library, the jealousy Colin remembered in Allen's face was gone. "Am I that old?" Colin asked. "It has been a while."

"So what happened to you, man?" Allen already knew what had happened, Colin suspected, and he realized he deserved to have his nose rubbed in it. When he and Allen had critiqued one another's poetry during college, they'd always been candid with one another. They agreed that the only way to improve was to knock one another down. Allen often took Colin's advice, but Colin was too in love with his own words. When Colin succeeded, he forgot to throw bones to his friends and fellow poets. Instead, he threw parties in his own honor, invited his friends and fellow poets to his readings and events—free admission—and showed his care for them not by helping them with their careers or their writing, but by flaunting his own.

At the start of Colin's heyday, Allen had said, "This is great for you, Wordsworth, but you know it won't last forever. You've got to expand, do something different, stretch your literary muscles. Try some free verse, haiku. And for God's sake, you've got to pace yourself. Don't go so fast. Save some talent for later."

Colin had laughed off the advice. "I won't have to worry about later." But he'd been wrong. He did have to worry about later. Later was now.

In the library, Colin considered his answer. "Oh, you know. I've just been pissing out poetry." The phrase was starting to sound stupid, even to him.

"Right," Allen said wryly. "Haven't seen much of it lately. Got a new book coming out, or are you hitting the journals?"

"Journals and mags for now," Colin said. "Plan to have a book together sometime in the next couple years."

"Is that so?" Allen shifted the two hardcover novels from one arm to the other. "I'll keep an eye out for it."

Colin put his hands in his pockets. "What do you do these days?" His notebook and pencil remained on the round table next to a writer's marketplace directory listing hundreds of places open to submissions with stockpiles of rejection slips ready to post.

"I've settled down a bit," Allen said. "I'm married and have a kid. Two years old. I write PR stuff for the college." The deviant smile Colin remembered came onto Allen's lips. "Keeps me in touch with the youth."

A librarian between bookshelves took an interest in their conversation. Colin followed Allen's gaze her way and the librarian smiled as though she'd just placed his face. "Didn't you used to hang out with Danielle?" she asked. "The poet?"

"Yes," Colin admitted reluctantly.

"I adore her work," the librarian said, and went back to shelving books. An awkward silence slipped between Colin and Allen.

"Well..." Colin offered his hand. "It was nice to run into you."

Allen gazed at Colin, as though searching for something that wasn't there. "You used to have this thing..."

"What?"

"I don't know. A sort of spark in your eye, like you were wiser than your years. You had this energy all around you. I never thought you'd lose it. But it looks like the years have caught up with you. Reality's caught up with you."

"Well, I *am* older," Colin said.

Allen shook his head. "It's like your body's caught up with your soul. So now you're just another guy. Nothing exceptional, like before." Allen smiled. They exchanged goodbyes and Allen walked away.

The lounge car hummed with conversation and the rhythm of the train. Colin got a glass of zin and looked around. A young couple sat in the corner, each drinking a bottled water. The blonde girl peered out the window, as though in deep thought. The rusty-headed boy had his face in a paperback of Poe's works. That drew Colin to them. "Poe's a master, isn't he?"

They both looked up at him. The boy said, "Ahead of his time."

"Too bad he died so young," Colin said. "Only forty. I'm sure his work would have gotten even better."

"How'd he die?" the girl asked.

"No one knows, exactly," Colin said. "He was found delirious on the streets of Baltimore and never recovered. Died in the hospital a few days later. Could have been foul play, maybe a drug or alcohol overdose. *Congestion of the brain* was what the newspapers reported. I make it a point to visit his grave whenever I'm in Baltimore. In fact, once I recited his poetry there on Halloween night—right over his grave."

"Cool," the boy said over the girl's "creepy." They introduced themselves as Malcolm and Tina.

Colin realized he was beginning to sound like a teacher. "Anyway, Poe's the reason I became a poet."

"I'm more into his short stories," Malcolm said.

"You write poetry?" Tina asked.

"Yes. I'm Colin White."

They both looked blankly at him. "Don't read much poetry," Malcolm said.

"You've probably heard of some of my books." He named them.

"Nope," Malcolm said. Tina looked like she wanted to know, but shook her head.

Colin sighed. "You know that song, "U Fill Me" by Scrambled Legs?" They searched their memories, then Colin hummed a bit of it.

"Oh, that one," Tina said, beginning to hum along.

Malcolm remembered it too. "That wasn't a bad song, except for that stupid rap at the end. Why?"

Tina instantly shot Malcolm a *do you realize what you just said, stupid?* glance. They both looked back to Colin and smiled politely.

Colin felt like a fool. It reminded him of the time he was teaching a poetry workshop and a student asked him, "What's the best way to get your chapbook to sell?"

When Colin had answered that there was no surefire way, the smartass in the back row said, "Sure there is. Just get an indie rock band to put one of your poems to music, and your books will sell like hotcakes. Right Mr. White?" Colin had laughed off the comment, but now he wondered whether getting Scrambled Legs to feature his poetry in one of their songs, giving his work radio play, wasn't the reason his books used to soar off the shelves.

Colin smiled politely back at Tina and Malcolm. "Well, enjoy your Poe," he said, and turned to walk away.

"We'll be sure to look for one of your books next time we're at The Book Thing," Tina called after him.

Colin pretended not to hear her. *Injury to insult*, he thought. The Book Thing, which gave away free books, and all of the countless places that sold used books weren't doing his sales any good. A used book didn't make him a penny. He shook off the thought and refocused on his zin.

The conductor was working the room, talking with everyone about whatever he thought was good for them. The black man in the blue uniform didn't strike Colin as a writer, but he could easily be a bard, words flowing from him naturally.

"We all got uniforms to wear. We all got to do what we got to do," the conductor said to an army kid in full uniform. "You do it, and get out of there. Make those parents of yours proud. Serve your country, do your duty, then get home safe. You're gonna be just fine."

The conductor left his conversation with the soldier and approached—*her*.

Colin nearly fell over when he saw her. The woman looked exactly like Danielle! At first he thought it *was* her, considered whether to approach her or duck out unseen. But a second glance at her mannerisms as she spoke to the conductor confirmed it was merely an uncanny resemblance. He took a gulp of his wine. She and the conductor were talking about her ex. *An appropriate subject for Danielle's ghost.*

"No, I dumped the bastard," she said to the conductor. She took a sip of white wine.

"Well, now, maybe he's not so bad. Maybe he just didn't know how to react when you hit him with the news. Maybe he didn't feel comfortable with his woman climbing the ladder faster than him. Makes a man feel less of a man."

"It's not that. He'll always wear the pants—he's a power lawyer. It was his ego. It always had to be his way. Even when he gave me things, the gifts were for me, but it was all about him."

"That just how you saw it, or how it really is?"

The woman caught Colin's stare; he looked away. "How it really is," she confirmed. When Colin looked back, she was fixed on the conductor again. "Key to his apartment. Tickets to concerts of his choice. Books that he liked. He even tried to write his own Hallmark once, but it was more about him and the things he'd do for me than it was about me."

"Did he do those things? The things he wrote?"

"No. He wouldn't know how to climb a mountain or cross a sea, even if there was a beer and cigar and ninety-nine virgins waiting for him there."

"Well then, maybe it was right, you leaving him. When it's him talking, it should be all about you." The conductor glanced Colin's way. Fearing he may be next, Colin killed his wine and left the lounge.

On the way back to his seat, he remembered when he'd purchased Danielle's book, used, from Amazon. He'd placed her book on his desk and surrounded it by his own books. He'd gawked at her tiny name in the lower right corner compared to each of his books, his name screaming in block letters. The truth was, it hit him now, she'd probably requested the small font, had probably wanted to be what he wasn't. She'd had her fill of flashy names when she'd been in the shadow of his.

It was all about him, Colin imagined Danielle saying.

Colin sat on the train and examined his notebook. There had to be *something* worthwhile in there. If not, he needed to put it there. If he came up with something good, maybe he could read it at Birk's after a few selections from his failed book. Already, he dreaded the sight of a hundred copies of the damned thing staring at him from the shelf, a hundred names bearing down on him.

The soul beneath my eyes, the spring beneath my step,
They're going, by and by. I've got to accept
that this life comes in stages; some low and some high.
The price of our wages: life passes us by...?
life allows us to try...?
we must reach for the sky...?
we must laugh more than cry...?
we must always ask why...?

Colin held his pencil over the page and sighed. *Why bother? What's the point?*

The woman in the seat next to him shifted. She was probably about his age. She'd greeted him when he boarded the train in Huntington, but after their initial hellos, she'd turned from him and peered out the window. She seemed upset. *Probably a lost boyfriend or something. Loss is something we all find.* He repeated his last phrase—*loss, find*—and quickly wrote it down.

In her lap, the woman had a piece of antique parchment. Colin strained to see what it was without being obvious. "Ode to a Mom and a Dad." Colin managed to read the calligraphy.

Must be hard to swallow,
losing the ones you follow.
To suddenly become the head
when they used to be the ones who led.

Now *that* was bad poetry. And yet, he noted the effect it had on this woman. The poem touched her, made a difference. He could read it in her face and her body language, in the way she clutched the parchment. The words meant so much to her that she'd carried them with her on this train and wouldn't let them go. Colin considered the subject matter. Words began to string together in his mind. *Some stops are happy ones, others bring sorrow.*

Colin snuck another peek and, without realizing it, began openly studying the poem in her lap. So the woman had lost her parents. He considered how it must feel. As his eyes scanned the lines again, she caught him looking and folded the poem from his view. She turned away and peered out the window.

"I'm a poet too," he said. Her attention was elsewhere. He looked at the window, but got the impression she saw his reflection, so he turned away. A blank page of his notebook called to him.

He'd gotten lucky. Then he'd gotten stupid and lazy. Now it was time to rein himself in and get serious. He oftentimes felt as though trying to make a living writing poetry was like trying to climb a mountain of sand. The harder you try, the more you slip. He looked around the train. The car was filled with young, old, and middle-aged couples. A mentally-impaired man with what looked like an older relative. A young soldier—barely an adult—wore his army uniform like a cancerous tumor. He certainly had many tales to tell, and buddies to share them with. Didn't everyone in war bond with their brothers-in-arms? He glanced back at the woman beside him. *Maybe that's what's lacking.* He considered. *I'm missing my muse.* He looked into the face reflected in the window, then back at the blank page in front of him.

He'd never needed anyone before, not even Danielle. Maybe pleasing Danielle would have been smarter than pleasing the masses after all. *Better to be someone to one person than nobody to the world.* He wrote the thought down. Then he added, *Better to be someone to one person than a celebrity to the world.* The line was liberating.

It wasn't too late. He reached deep within and searched for the soul that had once guided him. He searched for his center, for the source.

The woman next to him stared longingly at the parchment. Her mouth twitched into a slight smile, and she returned to the window again. She deserved more than bad poetry. His muse didn't have to be in the form of a permanent soul mate. It could just as well be a fellow passenger on a train.

Sorrow is a stranger on a train
Her only baggage, tears and pain

The lines came naturally, smoothly. It wasn't as easy as pissing and they didn't have that April-flower-garden scent, but this was something. This was the fragrance of a single bud yearning to bloom.

one station, joy; the next, grief
the soul pulled along
by the hope for peace
at the next junction.

Colin wrote hurriedly, barely able to keep up with his thoughts. He wasn't writing for himself and he wasn't writing for the world. He wasn't trying to fit a mold or a style. He didn't draft this poem for flair or fame or fortune. He didn't even want a byline. He just wanted to touch this stranger on the train.

It was all about him, Danielle had said in his imagination. He'd been self-centered all his life, a prodigy gone rotten. He needed to reach deeper. *It should be about the poetry.*

He looked at the woman beside him, then back to his tattered notebook. Perhaps the peak of a sand mountain wasn't the best place to balance a life. *It's more important to touch a person with poetry than to make a career out of it.*

He'd scratch out a decent poem—he hoped—and give it to this mourning woman, perhaps slip it into her black leather purse or the pocket of her overcoat. It wouldn't be his greatest, but it would be something. He wouldn't bother to copy it over for himself. This poem would be hers alone.

Cold Bars

Murdock loosened his tie and scratched at the irritated ring left by his stiff collar. The last cleaner had over-starched his shirt. He had little choice but to wear it, though, stuck on the train, swept into this series of cars that clunked along through life the way he did. He considered changing clothes in the little box of a bathroom, but he'd done that on a previous trip and found the maneuver more uncomfortable than a starchy shirt. He finally settled for the sloppy look of a loosened tie and an open collar. *Who around here gives a damn anyway?*

He hated the train, though trains had become his home, his life. He knew the rails of the land like the veins of his wrists. He spent more time on locomotives than he did in his own neglected room back home. He'd given up his two-bedroom apartment for the cheaper studio because he was never there to live in it. There was no life back home, no more than he found on the tracks or in the strange towns where he made his money. A smaller apartment meant less room to store his discontent.

Trains were the best way to get around. They beat the helplessness of being in a plane hundreds of feet above ground. And they beat the roads, with the unpredictable danger that lurked at every red light and each crossroads between too-festive parties and late-night bars at closing time. The idea of sitting behind the wheel of a car sent cold chills up his back. Trains were easy and safe, and there was always a designated driver. Murdock hated trains like he hated his work and his life, but they were all he had. The railway allowed him to remain on the move yet off the road and out of the air.

A traveling salesman had to get around, after all, and that's what Murdock was: a train-traveling salesman. Dyer was the next town he would hit—Dyer, Indiana. At one time or another, he'd hit just about every stop between Boston and Washington, DC on the Acela Express and all those between DC and Chicago on the Cardinal. Next, he planned to spend a week or two—however long it took—in Dyer and then move on to the suburbs of Chicago. There were plenty of businesses around Chicago he hadn't hit yet; the area was ripe with potential customers. He would taxi from business to business, or walk when proximity allowed. Then, he'd skip town and head west into new territory, into towns, cities and suburbs he hadn't worked in years.

Even as a self-employed salesman, Murdock remained bound to a strict schedule. It was the only way to get the quick sales, the easy cash—the only way to keep himself going. He swooped in and out of a town quickly, leaving with the money before minds could be changed or regrets realized.

Looking outside his window, into the rural countryside, he spied the back of an old farm house. In the yard, wet clothes hung on the line, drying in the setting sun. He saw white fabric blowing on the clothesline—was it a sheet or a robe?—and the sight of it sent a shiver up his spine. It reminded him of the women in his life, the ones he would always be connected to but no longer knew. He reached back and rubbed his raw neck.

He couldn't get comfortable in his seat. The only thrill of the ride so far had been when a hot young woman strolling down the aisle had fallen into his lap as the train jerked around a bend. He'd run into her again during a visit to the lounge car and had listened to her complain about the boyfriend she'd left behind in Baltimore. But before he'd been able to charm her, another man had spoiled the girl's mood by telling her she should go back to her man. Murdock didn't believe in karma, but he hoped the asshole would run into some bad luck for interfering with his potential squeeze.

Murdock stood. He slid his briefcase beneath the seat, smoothed out the wrinkles in his light blue blazer and staggered toward the lounge car over the bumpy rhythm of the train. Again he rubbed the reddened rash around his neck. He'd already popped a painkiller to calm his aching back but it didn't seem to be doing the job. He decided to drink the discomfort away. *I'll have a few greyhounds.*

Murdock began his career in sales right out of high school, thirty-some years ago. He answered an advertisement that claimed he could be making as much as $1,000 a week just by selling something that people already wanted, taking orders, door-to-door. It sounded like a quick and easy path, so Murdock jumped on it.

"You don't need a fancy education or investment capital to make yourself into a somebody," Mr. Valentine had taught him and thirty other people during the two-week training course. "You just need common sense, determination, a dream, and something to sell! My friends, I've got something to sell."

Mr. Valentine explained that he'd dropped out of high school to start his book business. He started by going door-to-door selling single books with some success, but soon realized the books that sold best were the sets nobody actually read: the beautiful, cloth-covered, gold-edged, stitch-bound beauties in the fifty-volume set *Classics of the Western World: Apollonius of Perga, Huygens, Lavoisier* and the like. Mr. Valentine had met with even more success when he moved up to encyclopedias. Within a few years, he had twenty people selling encyclopedias for him and was able to keep himself tucked away in a well-furnished office. Twenty years later, Mr. Valentine had hundreds of people selling encyclopedias door to door, making money for him.

Murdock was fired up in the beginning, ready to prove himself. His determined eyes fixed on Mr. Valentine. "I'm ready to go out and sell some knowledge," he pledged.

"That's the spirit," Mr. Valentine encouraged him. "With an attitude like that, you'll be sitting in my office one day!"

Murdock thrived on the enthusiasm churning within him when he sat in the classroom or in Mr. Valentine's office. But he found that the motivation mellowed as doors opened to his knocking. He remembered his spiel, the memorized lines about how he wasn't selling them anything; he wanted to offer them a *free* set of encyclopedias *just for subscribing* to the information supplements payable in *four easy installments* of $250 upon signing the contract. But somehow what rang true in the classroom and office clanged false as he tried to convince ordinary people in their living rooms and at their kitchen tables, people who were immediately turned off by the announcement that he wanted to give them something they didn't want for buying something they wanted even less.

Knock, knock, knock. It got to the point where Murdock actually willed the people not to answer their doors; he dreaded speaking to them. When the doors did open, he was forced to fake sincerity about something he knew was a lie. "Hello, sir! Good afternoon! Have I got a deal for you!"

His were hard knocks. After a month of failed attempts—Mr. Valentine egging him on, telling him that if he kept knocking, people would keep answering and eventually he'd make a sale that would wipe away weeks of no commission—Murdock gave up the spiel all together.

Knock, knock, knock. "Hi. I'm selling encyclopedias. You don't have an interest in buying a set, do you?"

Murdock went about his job not expecting to sell any, but making himself go through the motions he hated because it made him feel productive. One time out of ten, a bored housewife would let him in to give the entire half-hour sales pitch, or a young couple would sit him down in their living room for the entertainment of his song and dance. But even when people showed a little interest, even when he impressed them with the urgency of the deal that wouldn't last, Murdock never believed he was really going to make a sale. Being "on the draw" meant he didn't really have to. As long as Mr. Valentine thought he'd sell a set or two in time, he'd continue to get his meager pay.

As much as Murdock hated the work, some excitement did come with the job. The time he caught a pretty housewife fresh from the shower still came to Murdock's middle-aged mind often, the way a game-winning touchdown comes to the memory of an aged athlete. The twenty-something came down, still wet in her thin white robe, and he drank in the curves of her breasts and hips as the cloth clung to her flesh. She reluctantly invited him in and he stuttered through the sales routine, hoping his rising excitement didn't show and yet wishing she would see it and take the bait. He didn't sell any encyclopedias, but he did watch her as she adjusted and readjusted in her chair. Then, he watched indiscreetly as she crawled around the floor where he'd spread out the brochures. "Let me see," she said, as she searched for the pictures that interested her most, her robe creeping open.

"Take your time," Murdock encouraged, echoing her own words in his mind as he ran his eyes over her body. She caught his stare, smiled self-consciously, and tightened her robe, pretending to read one of the brochures.

The desire was thick between them, but neither had the confidence to pursue it. So she said she'd think about his offer and he promised to return.

The next time Murdock called, her husband was home and none too happy to see him. After ignoring the warning not to return with a third visit, Murdock got his face punched in and spent the rest of the workday making excuses for his ugly injury.

Two weeks later, however, he returned again on a Wednesday morning when the driveway was empty. He trembled with fear on the inside, but didn't show it as he swallowed his doubt and put on his self-assured sales face.

The door opened to him. She wore her white robe tightly around her body and let him in to share his wares. Weeks of pondering the possibilities had boosted their curiosity. "The bookshelf is upstairs." She invited him up to the guest bedroom and he followed her as though pulled along by a rope. In the room, the bookshelf stood cluttered with paperback romance novels and science fiction pulp.

"So what's your name, anyway?" Only he could read the nervousness hiding beneath his voice. She was dressed in white, but he was the inexperienced one.

"That's not important," she answered in a whispered tone that quivered with excitement. "Maybe you can look and see how the encyclopedias would fit." Her eyes looked down to Murdock's chest, then back up to the half-filled shelves. "Could you fill in the empty spaces?"

"Sure. I mean, I can try." Murdock stood behind her and reached up to the books on the shelves, his other hand rested on her covered shoulder as though for support. He allowed his hand to slip, pulling the robe from her shoulder. She drew a quick breath through her slightly parted lips. He placed his mouth on her pink shoulder and let his lips hover there. Awkwardly, he touched her warmth with his tongue. He hid his nervousness in her flesh as he kissed and sucked and smelled her shoulder, then her neck, her face, her mouth. The robe slid off with their combined wills. A moment later, his clothes joined hers on the floor. Beside the bookshelf, on the guest bed, he slid into her.

Sex and sales were much the same, Murdock considered. Outward appearance meant everything; what hid beneath the surface made little difference. After he had closed the deal, she turned away from him and sat at the edge of the guest bed. She stared blankly at the half-empty bookshelf.

With renewed confidence, Murdock placed his hands on her bare shoulders and massaged. "You don't really want any encyclopedias, do you?"

"You can stick your encyclopedias up your ass." Her voice had grown angry.

"I had to ask. Just doing my job."

"You've done a hell of job all right." Regret replaced anger. "It's done. I'm officially a slut. Thanks for your input."

"But I thought... I mean... you wanted—"

"Don't make it worse. Just get out."

Murdock's satisfaction fell, joining his clothes on the floor. He collected his clothing and re-dressed himself, but his confidence no longer fit. "I could... come back and... you know... check on you. See how you're doing."

"Don't come back," she insisted. But he couldn't help himself. A week later he returned and she invited him up to the spare bedroom. She seemed to have shelved away her regret, rather than encyclopedias. The more comfortable he became with each passing visit, the more Murdock fell in love with this white-robed housewife whose name he didn't know, and the more she insisted he stay away, during the bedside moments after they'd made love. His infatuation swelled and life seemed to revolve around their afternoon visits.

When she stopped answering the door—even though he heard her movement inside and imagined the white robe hugging her— he took the hint and reluctantly scratched her house number off his list of potential clients. As a salesman, he was used to people standing quietly on the other sides of doors—many numbers had been scratched off his list—but none of them stung the way this one did. The housewife's closed robe behind the closed door opened him to a new idea: don't get too attached to a woman. The only worthwhile relationship was one short-lived, uncommitted.

Mr. Valentine continued to encourage Murdock as the weeks sped past. "Even if you don't make any sales at first, you'll get lots of invaluable on-the-job experience." Indeed, with the woman in the white robe, Murdock had experienced his first full helping of sex. Before her, there had been heavy high-school petting at the end of dates and awkward tumbles in the back seat of his father's car, but never anything as fulfilling as the woman in white.

Murdock knew he couldn't sponge off his parents and friends much longer. He'd already gotten his own car and apartment, although he'd borrowed money to do it. The job selling encyclopedias didn't offer much money, but it continued to fulfill Valentine's promise of on-the-job experience. It gave Murdock his first taste of alcohol.

Knock, knock, knock. Murdock stood at a door with his packet of encyclopedia brochures in hand one late afternoon. The door opened to a party: loud heavy metal blared from the dining room, along with smoke and the smell of beer and bourbon.

"Yeah?" The young man's face was nearly concealed by his round Lennon glasses, bushy Dylan hair and thick Morrison beard.

"Um, do you need a set of encyclopedias? Because I'm selling them."

The young man at the door laughed. "No, dude." He yelled into the house. "Hey! Anyone want to buy some encyclopedias? We got a regular door-to-door salesman here!"

Laughter came from the other room. "Let him in," slurred a voice.

"We ain't gonna buy any," the man at the door said. "But if you want a drink, come on in."

Murdock stalled. He wasn't of drinking age. But drinking sounded better than trying to sell something nobody wanted, something he'd never buy himself. "Okay," he said, knowing this would be more of Mr. Valentine's promised on-the-job experience, if not the sort he'd had in mind.

Inside, four men in their mid-twenties sat around a table playing poker. Cigarette smoke filled the room. A bottle of Early Times Kentucky bourbon sat on the table and small pools of the amber liquid rested at the bottom of their emptied shot glasses. Silver beer cans, at various stages of emptiness, littered the table as well.

"Here," the man who'd answered the door said. He tossed Murdock a beer. "So you sell encyclopedias? For real? Suckers actually buy the damned things?"

"Not very many," Murdock admitted. He popped open the can and gulped the beer. The taste was unusual, not as pleasant as he'd expected, but the tingle of the alcohol and the illegality of it appealed to him. "They're good encyclopedias. But who's gonna read a whole volume? You can always go to the library."

"You're not a very good salesman," one of the players said. "You're supposed to convince us!"

"I don't know," Murdock said. "I guess I don't want to screw anyone over. I mean, they're good if you need them or want them. It's a good deal. But there're probably better ways to spend a thousand bucks."

"Like on whisky and beer!" A clean shot glass was found and they included Murdock in a round. "To an honest salesman!"

"Maybe the last in the world," one of them said.

Another griped, "We could use more like you. Especially for used cars. I always get stuck with lemons!"

Murdock shot back the bourbon and coughed from the lingering vapors. The beer tasted suddenly sweet and refreshing after the harshness of the whisky. A few hours later, Murdock thanked them and left, feeling very good. Not only had he gotten his first buzz on, but he'd sold his first set of encyclopedias.

The four men agreed to chip in and buy the set together, only $250 per person. They'd been drunk; Murdock was sure they wouldn't have bought them otherwise. But since they were shouldering the price four ways, he didn't feel bad about them spending their beer fund. In fact, once he'd tried it, he'd found it was easy to screw people out of their money. He'd gained their trust in those few hours. But he suspected he'd never drink with them again, just as he never again returned to the exciting comforts beneath the white robe.

It was the first and last set of encyclopedias Murdock would ever sell. He decided it wasn't his game. But the experience had taught him many things that would stay with him for the rest of his life. Encyclopedias taught him to love alcohol and gave him the taste for drunkenness that would stay with him, altering his path in ways he'd never anticipated. Encyclopedias taught him to love the excitement of sexual encounters with women he knew couldn't be his for the keeping—a valuable lesson for a restless drifter. The job had jumpstarted his career track, had taught him that in sales, there were ups and downs, but one good sale could make up for weeks of failure.

The first thing he did after getting his commission was to go to a bar and celebrate. He strutted in so proud and cocky that they didn't even card him. He didn't have many friends—no good ones—but he discovered that when he sat on a barstool, friends didn't matter. Murdock had never cracked open one of the encyclopedias he peddled, but he'd learned a lot from them. He'd learned to become a salesman.

In the train's lounge car, the grapefruit and gin tasted good. Murdock liked greyhounds—the drinks, not the buses. Buses, like automobiles, put you in harm's way. The roads were unsafe, filled with the threats of carelessness, speeding, old drivers no longer fit for the road, teenagers not yet capable of the responsibility, cellphone junkies better fit for phone booths. Not to mention the main offenders: drunk drivers who belonged either in bars or behind them. Murdock avoided the roads the way he avoided towns where he'd recently sold ads or bars where he'd already scored a piece of ass. But the drinks he could get comfortable with—greyhounds or just about any others.

Being a loner was a part of being a traveling salesman. There were other people here in the moving lounge car, but he didn't pay them any more attention than they paid him. The man with the planner still sat in the car, now sipping whisky instead of beer. It reminded Murdock of his first taste of the stuff, his first sale. He raced through the rest of his greyhound, ordered a whisky on the rocks, and relived the formidable memory of his first taste. With whisky and women, it had never gotten better than the first taste.

Last week's gig went well, he reminded himself. He'd sold twenty-three advertisements in one little town. He'd swooped in and gotten out within a week. The placemats were already laid out and at the printers. The cafés would have them in another week. He already had the money.

Years ago, after telling Mr. Valentine he no longer wanted to sell encyclopedias, he'd moved on to a regular job as an office clerk. He'd found that, as much as he hated selling books, it was in selling himself and his ideas to management that he made money, in the form of bonuses. Soon, his talent was recognized and he was promoted to in-office sales representative. As difficult as selling was, it was something he did well.

For two troubled years he'd tried to live the good life. He worked out of his metal desk under crisp, fluorescent lights, making sales calls and taking orders by phone. He schmoozed through cocktail hours with the boss and his co-workers. He tried the steady girlfriend with aspirations of upgrading to marriage, a two-bedroom house, and a mailbox with a little red flag. But the longest-lived relationship he could manage was the eight months he spent with a nightclub pick-up. She grew on him and he found himself imagining a future with her. They spent most of their quality time together in bars or in bed. She tried, unsuccessfully, to lure him to fancy restaurants, museums, and movies. That relationship ended when she tired of his commitment to booze.

"My drinking does *not* interfere with my work or my feelings for you!" he'd yelled at her when he came home drunk one night to find her packing. But she'd closed the door to his noise before he'd even realized she was leaving.

It was tough, but drinks dulled the pain. It wasn't nearly as hard as when his high school sweetheart had left him for college, dumping him for not wanting to continue his own education. But hardest of all was the vision imprinted in his mind of the housewife's white robe clinging to her moistened skin behind her locked door, no longer open to him.

Murdock couldn't stand the static office any more than he could stay in one place or in one relationship. Restlessness drove him back to the road. He got out of the windowless office and back into quick sales, roaming from one town to another. That was back when he still drove a car and loved the thrill of traveling. Before the accident.

On the train, Murdock took another sip of the stiff whisky. It connected him with that boy of years ago. Over the past thirty years, Murdock had sold everything from soap to spices, magazine subscriptions to magazine advertisements, vacuum cleaners to frozen foods. For the past eight years, he'd worked for himself. He regretted that it took him so long to realize that when he sold a thousand dollars of a product, he only got a hundred; after costs, most of the profits went to the companies that employed him. It was after he began selling advertisements that he got the idea: *Sell for myself and I'll keep the dough.*

It had been in Xenia, Ohio that he'd made the transition. He worked for Cal-Central Marketing, a company that he believed offered a valuable service when he started with them. But over the years, he came to realize just how over-inflated and worthless the service was. Cal-Central Marketing published television guides filled with more advertising than information. As an account rep, it was Murdock's job to sell the ads. It didn't matter how much they sold for, as long as he got his $55 per book in ad sales. He sold the ads as "by the week," with the assumption that people would refer to them daily. But the truth was, a one-year contract was required, the guides were printed only once a month, and few people who got the newspaper or *TV Guide* really used the flimsy product. The little guides were distributed free at each town's Rite-Aid store, which gave Murdock the right to say he was working in conjunction with the local manager. Each town had the same guide, but each Rite-Aid distributed a guide with different ads.

"Hi, this is Mr. Murdock," he'd say over the phone or with a handshake in the back office of a small business. "I'm working with Chad, at the local Rite-Aid. You know Chad? Hell of a guy." They usually knew the local drug store manager because they were expected to, even though these were cold sales calls—businesses found in phone books and other forms of advertisement in the community. "Anyway, we're putting together a community TV guide with cable listings—you're gonna love it."

Murdock learned how to distract potential buyers with flashy samples of glossy past editions that looked better than average. "Chad thinks highly of your establishment. You're an asset to the community. We'd like to offer you an ad on the front page. But only if you act today. I've got a dozen other companies dying to get on the cover." More times than not, Murdock had never even met the manager of the local Rite-Aid—he'd simply gotten the name from a store clerk and left a message that he'd be working the town.

One especially gullible real estate agent in Xenia decided she wanted to be the star feature of the guide, to be *the* woman of the community who brought people their television selections. So she purchased every single advertisement in the guide. Noting her eagerness, Murdock offered the ads at an inflated cost of $82 per week. He'd broken a company record with this one person buying so many ads. He'd sold $4,264 in advertising in one afternoon to one person. He excitedly did the math. At fifteen percent and with a hundred dollar bonus, his commission would be $649.60. He'd probably get another extra hundred for breaking a company record. *Not bad! But they're gonna make $3,000 or better after costs and commission.*

After reporting the sale to his boss over the phone, he went to a tavern to celebrate. He sat at a booth with his beer and emptied shot glass, waiting for his steak to arrive. As he waited, he looked around him, reading the table-side drink menus, studying the coasters advertising beer, looking at the posters on the wall. The waiter put a basket of sourdough bread on his table. Murdock buttered a piece and took a bite. An idea began to rise in his mind. *I could make a lot of dough. It just might work.*

The waiter brought his steak and baked potato. Murdock chewed his food as he fleshed out a plan. He ate excitedly, filling himself. He'd eaten half of his T-bone when his waiter returned. "How's the food?"

"Good." Murdock washed down his meat with a hearty gulp of beer. "Hey, is the manager here?"

"Yes sir," he answered. "Is there a problem?"

"No, but I need to see him. Business proposition."

The familiar self-doubt built in Murdock's chest as he waited, but he swallowed it down with beer. His sales persona knew no rival. Whether in sales or late-night pick-ups, presentation was everything. People judged books by their covers; Murdock's was pristine.

When the manager greeted him a moment later, Murdock flashed a smile. "If I gave you a year's supply of paper placemats for free, would you use them?"

The manager considered for a moment. "What's the catch?"

Murdock provided his card and TV guides to prove his expertise. "Your placemats will have information about Xenia and advertisements from respectable businesses in the area. The ads would pay for them. Would you use them?"

The manager looked at the dimly-lit fixture on the wall as though for guidance. "Sure," he agreed, looking back at Murdock. "I think we would."

After finishing dinner and another beer, Murdock took a risk. With the liquid courage still in him, he returned to the real estate agent's office.

"I was thinking," he said hurriedly. "What do people do when they're at a restaurant waiting for their food?"

The agent considered the questioner as much as the question. "I don't quite know. Talk? Drink? What do you do?"

"I read the stuff all around me. I don't just glance at something for quick reference, the way I would a TV guide—I look for something to read. And you know what I'd read first?"

"The menu?"

"No, after that." She didn't have an answer, but he did. "The placemat!" He grinned and expected to see understanding in her face. Instead she stared blankly at him. "Not a blank placemat," he elaborated. "One with information on it. You've seen them in other communities while you're on vacation, I'll bet. In the middle is a little information and along the edges are boxes offering services."

"Yes," she remembered. "I have seen them, now that you mention it."

"TV guides are good, but people *really* read placemats. It's a captive audience. People waiting for their food with nothing to do. And I'd like to make you the star of Xenia's placemat! A year's worth of reading material for customers at local diners and taverns. For the same price as the TV guide, you could be in front of everyone in the community who eats out, in front of the people who get off their duffs and go out and spend money."

"For the same price?" She considered for several moments, her face contorting as though a thought were trying to get out. "Who do I make the check out to?"

Just like that, Murdock had gone into business for himself and increased his own profits of the day by $3,000. Back at the bar next to his motel, he celebrated. "Three thousand dollars in one day!" he said out loud as he held up a shot of Hennessy. "In one hour, even!" He had to say it out loud to make himself believe it. "Not a bad profit!"

As with any sales job, Murdock still had ups and downs working for himself. He went days—sometimes weeks—without a sale. Then, one good day made up all the difference and filled him with excitement. When he'd sold enough ads to fill a placemat, he would go to the library, spend a day researching and writing a paragraph about the town he was in and then lay out the placemat with a template on his laptop. He always visited the local printers to see if one would print the placemats in exchange for an ad. Sometimes they would, or would give him a good enough discount. When that wasn't the case, he just emailed the file to a printer he'd found in Goshen, Ohio with low rates. The printer sent the placemats directly to the restaurants that had agreed to distribute them.

Murdock still hated sales. He couldn't stand his boss, even though he worked for himself. How could he love himself, a pathetic lout who conned small businesses out of their revenue for a living? But it was a good way to make money and one of the few things he knew how to do; he'd become a master of quick sales.

The one thing that kept him going was knowing that he'd be able to quit soon. Another few years of traveling from town to town by train and he'd be ready to retire to a second career of full-time drinking and lounging. He could forget sales and devote his life to scoring hard drinks and easy women.

The train screeched as it hugged a bend, the wheels gripping the rails. The attendant asked Murdock whether he wanted another drink. He *needed* another drink.

Murdock knew there were worse things than selling people stuff they didn't need or want. There was the frigidness of metal against skin and the callousness of the less comfortable sorts of bars. Like his lessons in love and consumption, this more traumatic lesson had come fast, in the dark moments of a winter night some thirteen years ago.

That night, cold metal rubbed his wrists raw, even after he'd stopped struggling to free himself. *Handcuffs.* Murdock cursed. *Should be called wrist rippers!* They hadn't even given him a sobriety test, didn't ask him to walk the line, recite the alphabet backward, or take the breathalyzer test. Or at least, if they had, he didn't remember. It was as though they didn't care whether he was drunk. They just cuffed him and threw him in the back of the police car, reading him his rights. Another set of flashing lights came in the form of an ambulance. They put the other driver on a stretcher, covered her with a white sheet and shoved her motionless body into the back of the ambulance. It rushed off, its lights and sirens more alive than the woman it escorted. The police car's lights and sirens blared, and off it went to the police station with Murdock in the back.

If the police asked him any questions, Murdock didn't remember. He staggered into the jail cell, already in the prison of his own drunken stupor. He remained disoriented, but he knew what had just happened. The feel of the wheel as he lost control. The blurry road, the appearance of a bright yellow sports car in the crossroad—or were there two of them?—the blinding brightness of headlights. The blaring of car horns, the sound of tires against asphalt, metal colliding against metal, windshields shattering into shards. He glimpsed the woman in the other car.

Then the scene disappeared in a flash as air bags erupted, concealing his view. Her image projected onto the white airbag like a light he'd stared at for too long: crimson highlights in her long, blond hair, her eyes opened and unblinking, red drenching her white blouse and covering her shoulders like a scarlet housecoat. Yes, Murdock knew what had happened. He'd killed a woman with the only weapon he'd ever owned: himself, intoxicated, behind the wheel of a speeding car.

Murdock awoke to find himself in the fetal position, tucked in a corner of the jail cell. He awoke as though from a bad dream, not fully believing what had happened in the fogginess of the night, not sure that he really sat where he appeared to be. The cement beneath him sent chills up his back.

The uniformed guard came to the icy cell, his keys jangling. "Murdock? Mike Murdock?"

"Yes." Murdock stood, and as he did, pressure squeezed his head like a vise. *A vice,* he thought beneath a pounding headache.

"You're one lucky son of a bitch," the policeman said.

"She's alive." Murdock gripped the bars between them. Their metal was colder than he'd anticipated. "Thank God."

"Don't thank God so fast," the policeman said. "She's dead all right—dead as a doornail. She was dead when they pulled her out of the car. But she was drunker than a skunk. Drunker than you." The guard unlocked the cell and let him out. "The accident was her fault. She's at fault, so you're free to go." In the office, Murdock was given paperwork to sign and a court date. "We're keeping your license. You can call for a ride." The police pointed to the phone.

"I don't know anyone in the area."

"Call a cab."

Murdock went to the phone and dialed the number of a cab service advertised on the wall. As he waited for the call to go through, the policeman continued. "You're one lucky son of a bitch. You'll fly with nothing but a DUI."

But it wasn't true. Murdock attended his day in court and accepted his DUI. He went one year without a license, one year without driving privileges. He retrained himself to ride a bike, to take the bus, metro, and public transportation. He discovered Greyhound and Amtrak, the only ways to continue his work as a traveling salesman. But his punishment consisted of more than that. Although the law had laid the blame on the woman's drunkenness, he knew he had made the same mistake. Without his drunkenness and his speeding car, she would still be alive.

Perhaps she would have hit another car or a tree if her death was meant to be, he reassured himself from time to time. He imagined her sweet voice calling to him, telling him that accidents happen and all was okay. But he knew that he was responsible for her death. It was something he wasn't sure he could live with.

There was more than mental pain alone. The accident had put his back out and given him whiplash; he'd been taking painkillers regularly ever since. He hadn't admitted to himself that he was addicted to the pills, but he knew it was probably true. He popped a couple every day.

Guilt and painkillers did not extinguish his thirst for alcohol. If anything, it increased his desire, a desire he happily quenched. After a year, his driving privileges were reinstated by civil law, but his own sense of justice still kept him off the road.

He couldn't bring himself to drive his car. He took his keys from the junk drawer and unlocked the beat-up Dodge Shadow parked in the lot of his apartment complex. He plopped behind the driver's seat and sank the key into the ignition. Then he stared at the wheel and imagined himself driving. The thought of being on the road brought the icy chill of the jail's cold bars up his back and neck. After murdering a woman, how could he allow himself behind the wheel of a car again? It was giving a weapon to a murderer.

He stepped out of his black Shadow and retreated to the safety of the sidewalk. With his feet on black asphalt, he sat on the brighter gray of the cement. Beside him, the gutter gurgled. Soapy residue slid atop a steady stream of water from a resident washing his car at the far end of the lot. Murdock looked at the gutter and dropped his car keys in after the dirty suds. He listened to the keys splash deep beneath him and sat there a long while. The water had finished trickling into the gutter by the time he stood and returned to his apartment, but the pavement remained wet.

He eventually came to his senses and had a locksmith come out. Once he had a new set of keys, selling the car was easy. The familiar feeling of cheating someone out of their money returned as he collected more than the blue-book value from a young woman. He felt like a sleazy, used-car salesman offloading an accident-prone lemon.

Sometimes, during his short stints back home from selling placemat advertisements in strange towns, Murdock sat on the sidewalk beside the gutter where he imagined his keys had sunk deep into the sludge. Sometimes he wanted to throw himself in after them, but he and his guilt were too large to fit through the bars.

Not only did Murdock not allow himself to drive, he avoided the roads as best he could. There were thousands of other jerks just like him out there, others who had already had their drunken collisions and some who had not yet been smacked with the reality of their deeds. *I deserved to die as much as she did*, Murdock convinced himself over warming drinks in lonely bars. *It could've been me.*

Could've soon became *should've* and *should've* soon became *will*. He convinced himself that he would eventually take his own life. The only thing that kept him alive was his job, selling things not because people needed them but because he needed their money.

That, and the joy he found in bottles and dimly-lit bars, the pleasure he got out of a quick score with a homely woman in a cheap motel. It wasn't much to keep him moving forward along the tracks from one railroad station to another or taxiing from one potential sale to the next. He often considered throwing himself in front of a moving train or buying a gun and shooting himself in the mouth or temple. He knew the veins in his wrist, how to cut them down instead of across, how to do it right. He considered the sturdy ropes at Home Depot and Ace and Lowe's. Ever since the accident, he got headaches and neck pain that shot down his spine. He always had his bottle of prescription painkillers with him. He imagined going peacefully in a doped-up sleep. *Wouldn't that be the way to go, to drift numbly away?*

There were many ways to die. He figured he could meet the woman he'd killed—white sheet and all—by taking his own life. They could have a warm reunion in Hell. *Was she all that different from the housewife in the white robe?* Surely drunk driving and adultery landed a person in the same place. Maybe they could all hook up in Hell.

Suicide was more than a passing thought; in the years since the accident, the idea of taking his life had become an obsession. But each time he considered death, he chose life. Each time, for that time only, he chose to board the train. There would always be the next stop, the next station, the next chance to kill himself, always the possibility of something worth living for around the bend, always another tunnel of darkness to pierce with the promise of light on the other side. The woman in white would be in Hell for all eternity; she could wait for him.

Standing in the lounge car, Murdock imagined that his rope remained wrapped in a tight loop, still in the New Carrollton motel room. Perhaps a maid had found it tucked under the bed, or maybe it had been left there, unnoticed, ready to invite another depressed traveler to contemplate the same end.

Last night the rope had felt strong, firm, and rough in his hands as he sat on the edge of the bed and massaged it. He knew he was pathetic, but if he was going to kill himself, he was going to do it right. He deserved to be punished for his sins, and a rope was more fitting than the euphoria of drugs. He'd imagined the rope rubbing off a ring of flesh before actually snapping his neck. Had he not been fearful of a painful failure, he might be hanging in the motel now.

I'll buy another rope in the next town, he decided. He'd be sure to use it by the end of the line. Or there was always the easy way out. He rattled the orange-brown bottle of pills in his pocket. There were enough to do the job. All he needed was a walk to the bathroom. *Just add water.*

He'd grown too tired, riding these rails in and out of stations and towns that had become too familiar. The newness he'd once thrived on had grown stale and bored him. Now, sometimes even drinking didn't make him forget his discontent. He took a swig of whisky. The ice in his glass had melted and diluted his drink. Even his whisky tasted empty.

But again, Murdock chose to swallow his regret instead of the bottle of pills, to ride on. He chose to travel to the next town on his list, sell overpriced advertisements, consume some more drinks, and drown out the death of the woman, the motionless, white sheet covering her as she slid into the back of the ambulance, then into a morgue drawer.

Maybe all he needed to make life worth its weight was a whole woman instead of just a piece of ass. Someone like the white-robed housewife, before she'd grown tired of the novelty of their affair and locked the door. He'd gotten to know her so well since then, in his own imagination. He imagined how his life may have turned out had he managed to sell her on the idea of them as a couple.

He considered again how the dead woman in the white sheet reminded him of the living housewife in the white robe. It could've been the same woman, for all he knew. Time and alcohol and painkillers had clouded his memory; in his mind, they were now as much figments of his imagination as they were real women. He wondered whether he'd even recognize either of them, sans the white attire, if they were to cross paths with him in the aisle of the train.

As he downed his watery whisky, he convinced himself that she *was* the same woman, that he'd killed the first woman he'd loved, the woman he imagined every time he bedded a one-night stand. He'd not only taken the housewife's faithfulness, he'd taken her life. Murdock decided he deserved to imagine a corpse draped beneath a white robe every time he tried to love a woman.

He ordered another whisky, neat. He took it to a section of empty seats and sank into one, rubbing his itchy neck.

He wanted a white-robed woman now, alive. Out of habit, he scanned the lounge for a prospect. The girl with the boyfriend in Baltimore was nowhere to be seen. A stout man in a leather jacket drank coffee in the corner and stared at a thin man with silver hair. A kid in uniform—no older than he'd been when he started selling encyclopedias—glared out the window, his face heavy with trouble. The conductor chatted with a couple of teenagers.

Then Murdock spotted a target and honed in. She'd been seated, but now she proceeded toward the attendant, empty plastic glass in hand. The tattoo jumped out at him from across the car. He noticed the intricate design before paying any attention to her face. The marking resembled a sort of open book, long wings spreading out from a spine that pointed directly to her shapely behind. He stared at the tattoo, at the tanned skin all around it, then down at the low-slung, tight-fitting jeans. After gazing openly at the tattoo and her backside, he looked up at the person and noticed her brown eyes looking back at him. Murdock looked away. *Hell, I don't deserve it. Don't even deserve to live.*

But here he sat, on the train, moving forward into the dark tunnels and through them to the light on the other side. The time would come when he'd no longer have to take trains. Another few years of this weariness and he'd have enough to retire. He could settle down and make a career of everyday drinking and one-night stands. Perhaps he'd find a woman who could accept him and overlook the fact that he'd killed the first woman he'd loved.

He drowned his feelings of unworthiness and brought to the surface his confident cover. He refocused on the tattooed woman. Her body language, her cognac eyes, the silver barbell in her navel—it was all tempting. Murdock imagined her dressed in a white robe. She became even more desirable. Standing at the bar, she smiled back at him, then turned away, sipping her red wine. *An invitation.* He decided to step up and make his pitch.

So there was something to live for, he considered as a smile crossed his lips. There was this, at least: the rush of the race, the cheap thrill of the ride, the instant gratification of quick sales, stiff drinks, and casual sex. Perhaps life was a choice Murdock didn't deserve to make; it was a choice the woman in white had not been allowed to make. But for now, he'd made it.

Murdock rubbed the raw skin around his neck, wanting to rip off his itchy shirt. He imagined a noose couldn't irritate his flesh much worse. He sipped his whisky, then headed for the tattoo as the train carried him further along the tracks.

The Deed's Doorstep

Charlie watched carefully as Silverman stood and stretched. Silverman had been here in the lounge car all night, staring at his note cards, looking dully out the window, scribbling on his yellow legal pad. *Coming up with more bullshit,* Charlie figured.

A pink shade painted the clear Indiana sky. It was east of midnight, early in the morning but still dark, the sun preparing to make another round.

Silverman shuffled to the lounge car door with a black bag, but left his locked briefcase next to his seat, indicating his intention to return. *The crapper,* Charlie guessed. It was as good a place as any to do the job as long as no one else was waiting behind him. Needing to use the restroom would be Charlie's excuse for standing outside the bathroom door when Silverman came back out, should anyone pass by. The time had come. Once the sun was up, the passengers would be too.

Charlie stood to leave the lounge car. As he did, he realized Silverman wasn't headed back to the bathroom stalls in the passenger cars. Instead, he walked in the opposite direction, into a sleeper car. Charlie waited a moment, then followed after him. Silverman went from one car to another until, a few cars later, he vanished.

At first it disoriented Charlie when he entered the sleeper car to find the corridor empty. Silverman couldn't have cleared the car's distance so quickly unless he'd broken into a sprint. Then Charlie heard the locking of the washroom door. *Guess he has to doll himself up for his next song and dance.* Charlie chuckled as he waited outside the door. *He doesn't realize he needn't bother.*

Silverman's desire for privacy—walking to this far sleeper car instead of the one closest to the lounge—served Charlie's purpose. The hall in the sleeper car was empty in the morning darkness.

Charlie looked to his left, then his right. From the side pockets of his ragged bomber jacket, he took two brown leather gloves and slipped them on. It was not particularly cold on the train, but there were those on board who slept under blankets and jackets, so there was nothing suspicious about sheathing his fingers. He unzipped the inside pocket of his jacket and pulled out his weapon. He checked the gun and placed it quickly in his outer jacket pocket on the right side—his gun-hand side. From the outside, Charlie's worn jacket appeared unscarred; inside, there was a purposeful rip in the lining. Charlie fit the tip of the suppresser through the hole and slipped into his assigned role.

Becoming the assassin was essential. Outside this role, he was just another man: a lover, a father, a fisherman, a friend. These quick jobs had to be easily discarded. Assuming the role, forgetting himself, was the only way to cope, the only way to be successful in this business and still have a place outside it.

As he waited for Silverman, he scoped out the car. He silently tried the first few sleeping compartment doors to find them locked, until he reached one, toward the middle of the car, that wasn't. He slipped it slowly open and peered in. A man and woman—that drunk and the tattoo lady—slept sloppily in the bunk. But he noted with satisfaction that the window was large enough for his purposes. He closed the door and went to the next, only to find it locked.

At the end of the hall, he came upon another unlocked door—only this one was empty, with the same big window. *Perfect.* He closed the door and stepped back into the dark hallway. A makeshift, handwritten sign was posted on the door to the next car: *Restricted — Do Not Enter.* Out of curiosity, he peeked in.

Inside, a dozen or so men slept in their seats—and in chains—wearing orange jumpsuits. Two men in blue uniforms watched over them. *Cops!* Charlie panicked and considered aborting the mission. Being right next to a prison car couldn't be a good omen. *Get a grip, Charlie—be professional.* He reminded himself that he couldn't hear anything from the other cars, so they couldn't hear him either. That was one advantage to the noise of a train. He returned to stand outside the washroom.

Charlie could hear the running water of Silverman's shower. He was supposed to be in character already, but he'd slipped back into himself. *Just this one last time.* He hesitated. It wasn't just the nearby cops and prison car; something else nagged at him. Why couldn't he let go? This was just one more in a long succession of successful hits he'd done over a lifetime. After this, he planned to set up residence in the Keys, keep the Baltimore rowhouse for the kid and his ma, and have a hell of a time living it up, without the nightmares. Maybe he could even get his teenage son to spend the summer with him, take him fishing, camping, hunting.

Silverman continued his business, taking his time. Charlie cleared his mind. *Stop dreaming,* he ordered himself. A hit man needed to be a doer, not a dreamer.

But he couldn't clear his mind as he normally did when assuming the role. Charlie thought of Gene Silverman as he stood outside the bathroom door waiting to kill him. He remembered when the target had been a geeky kid named Eugene Beckett. But

Beckett had vanished long ago; Silverman proved to be a different beast altogether, an animal worthy of hunting.

Yesterday had been a long one, but patience had kept Charlie focused. He'd watched Silverman with the concentration of a practiced yogi in deep meditation. Since the moment his target arrived on the train, he'd followed him from passenger seating to observation car to lounge car to diner car, then back to the lounge—with bathroom breaks in between. And he did all of it without raising suspicion.

When evening had come, the lounge car began to empty. The man with the planner had left earlier. He seemed to be on business; he probably had the luxury of a sleeper car. The sexy woman with the tattoo had left in the late hours of the night with an older man—*Murdock*, he'd said—both drunk. The army man had reassigned himself to another car. The young man with the tattered notebook scribbled away with his stub of a pencil late into the night, apparently inspired by this night train. The old conductor remained in the lounge, talking with the older woman. It seemed she needed to be here, among people, just as the conductor did. Charlie laughed to himself. So many people going in the same direction yet all headed for different places.

He'd gotten the shakes as he waited in the lounge. He usually felt some apprehension in the hours before a hit. He'd ordered a bourbon to calm his nerves. As he drank, he craved a cigarette. He pulled his Basic from behind his ear and then, remembering the no-smoking rule, began to put it back. *I'm about to kill a man and I'm afraid to break a no-smoking rule.* He laughed at the absurdity and placed the cigarette between his lips. He lit it.

"No, sir! You can't light that on the train!" The conductor darted his way, leaving the old lady's side. "No smoking on the train!"

"There's no one here who cares. This is the lounge car, ain't it? I'm trying to lounge!" Charlie frowned, but complied, dropping his cigarette to the floor and stomping it out. *Doesn't that old man ever give it a rest?*

The conductor made an annoyed face and cleaned up the flattened cigarette, disposing of it. Charlie scoffed. He'd have a cigarette soon enough, and not a Basic, either—a Nat Sherman or Davidoff or some other fancy smoke. As soon as this business was over, he'd get to Chicago and smoke as many cigarettes as he wanted. Then he'd get himself a room at a nice hotel and amble into the bar. He'd have a bottle of the best aged scotch they had in stock. And he'd relax knowing that, after being paid for this job, he'd have enough in the bank to retire comfortably on.

Don't spend the money until you've got it, he reminded himself.

When the eastern sky began to light, Charlie knew the time to strike was at hand. He'd wait for rural Indiana to do the deed. But he needed the lounge to clear completely, or for Silverman to step out. Then he could do his job peacefully.

Crime *could* be a relatively peaceful business, after all. His first kill had been accidental, an overly-ambitious beating gone bad. It all depended on a person's frame of mind. Charlie understood that for a law-abiding citizen, his line of work might seem complicated, perhaps even immoral. What such people didn't understand was that a person doesn't jump into such a profession. Such work is gradually eased into until it begins to feel normal. A criminal starts small and works his way up, the same way a reckless driver might get comfortable with ten miles over the speed limit before rushing into the one-hundred-miles-per-hour offenses.

Stealing people's pets and turning them in for reward money had been innocent enough. Threatening and beating people hadn't been much more intense than beating the stolen dogs into submission. Once he'd beaten a few people half to death, the second half hadn't been nearly as difficult to cross. Perhaps the kid trading stolen dogs for cash wouldn't have agreed to kill a person. But maneuvering slowly from one crime to another had made it easy to slide guilt-free into the more violent jobs. Most of the people Charlie knocked off deserved to be killed anyway.

The noise of the shower ceased. Charlie heard the hum of an electric razor. He let out a sigh and shifted on his feet.

So what's eating at me now? There was no need to ask the question; the answer was clear enough. He knew exactly why he wanted out of the business. In fact, he couldn't clear his mind of it.

Charlie's reputation as a thug was as intimidating as his bulky frame. Even back when he was new to the biz, he'd quickly become the Boss's top choice. Since going freelance, others had hired him. As long as it didn't conflict with the Boss and the pay was good, he was game. Charlie knew his stuff.

Normally, a hit went easily enough. It became easy because Charlie wasn't mentally there. Beneath bridges and in dark alleys, smoky pub bathrooms and harbor-side boats, taking a person's life was easy as long as you didn't keep it for yourself—as long as you killed for someone else, then let it go. A professional didn't keep notches on his belt.

The last job, however, hadn't gone so well. He'd been summoned to DC, where a wealthy collector resided. The former mogul had made millions in real estate; now he protected and cultivated his fortune with rare gems. When Charlie met the man in his Georgetown home, he appeared average enough, the three hundred pounds of him in a poolside lounge chair. But the man grew angry as they got to the heart of the matter.

"The scoundrel double-crossed me. He's got to pay."

"How'd he double-cross you?" Charlie always needed to understand the reason for the killing. As a hit man, he maintained his own code of ethics.

"He's a thief. He claimed to have a buyer for one of my diamonds. The price was right. It wasn't the first time I used Danny as a middle man. But this time, he robbed me blind! Took the stone and came back with nothing."

"He came back?"

"Bastard thought he was going to move another stone for me. Told me he lost it!"

"Just a diamond?" Charlie looked at the two carat stone on his own ring finger. "Couldn't he work it off?"

The man chuckled. "There's not that much work in the guy. The diamond he took was a natural pink, worth half a million."

Charlie whistled. "Some rock." He didn't ask about the shady dealings or why the stone hadn't been offered to an auction house. Stolen gems were valuable, but not as easy to place on the open market. Plus, there were tax considerations.

"This man steals from me, word gets around, and others will do the same. I need him taken care of. In his apartment, where his body will be found and identified."

"Not a problem." Charlie took the name—Danny Alderman—and agreed to do the job for twenty-five thousand.

"And another ten if you recover the diamond."

Charlie considered. "Say I found a stone worth half a million bucks. Why would I turn it over for ten thousand?"

The rich man's belly rippled as he laughed. "Because you don't have the know-how to move a stone like this one. And because hunters can be hunted too." He stood; Charlie followed suit. When the man shook Charlie's hand, he smiled and added, "And because after I find a buyer for the stone, I'll give you an extra twenty five from the proceeds." Charlie nodded his appreciation and left.

Charlie had an address and a name, but no photo to work from. He did have a picture of the pink diamond, a picture that wouldn't leave his mind. He imagined finding the rare gem and holding it for several years before cashing it in. Half a million dollars plus appreciation was worth a little research, worth learning the market and how to sell. The Boss could probably help, for a cut.

When Charlie entered the Silver Spring apartment complex and located the number he needed, he slipped into his alter ego, a knife in one pocket, a rope in another. But the diamond remained on the hit man's mind, where he'd normally have the target's face. Perhaps that's why shock blinded him when Danny became a person instead of the idea of one.

Charlie didn't bother knocking. He kicked in the flimsy apartment door and stormed in. The kid sat alert, on guard, in a second-hand recliner, his hands still attached to a video game controller. Fear assaulted his face.

"You Danny Alderman?"

The boy stiffened. "Who are you?"

That answered the question. Charlie looked around the studio apartment. Fast-food containers decorated the furniture, open Chinese take-out boxes and chopsticks on the television. Posters from old '80s slasher flicks covered the white walls—Jason, Freddie, Chucky. In the middle of it all, this kid couldn't have been much older than his own boy, not more than eighteen. "You alone?"

"Why?" The boy jittered. "What do you want?"

"I'm looking for something," Charlie said. Normally he'd just get the job done. But normally he wasn't on a treasure hunt. "Ice."

"Got some ice in the freezer," Danny said. "Want a drink? Got some beer, peach schnapps."

"Pink ice."

Understanding shone on Danny's worried face like a diamond catching light. "Oh shit! Listen, man, I swear I lost it! I didn't sell it! I don't have it! I told him that!"

"He doesn't buy it." Charlie moved slowly toward him. "Neither do I."

"I swear, man! Would I be living in this shithole if I had it?"

"Where is it?" Charlie took out the sturdy rope and began to uncurl it.

"Listen, man, you can take everything I've got in this place! I swear, I don't have it! I lost it, man!"

"I only intend to take one thing: the diamond or your life." It was okay to lie in his profession. Lying was hardly a sin, next to killing.

The boy began sobbing. "No! Please! I swear, I didn't steal it!"

Charlie stunned himself when he realized he actually believed the boy. But he wasn't paid to believe. Whether the kid knew where the stone was or not, he wasn't going to tell. The assassin moved in.

"God, no!"

He decided to make it neat. He kept his knife in his pocket and coiled the rope around the boy's neck. Danny tried to scream, but the rope was too tight around his windpipe. The boy hoarsely pleaded for mercy, but mercy was a word the professional didn't know.

Charlie knew he didn't have much time; it was good practice to leave the crime scene as soon as possible. So he moved quickly, searching with his gloved hands in the drawers and cabinets for signs of valuables, dumping out sugar and rice canisters, rummaging through underwear and sock drawers. No diamond. The boy wasn't a thief. Charlie had expected a hardened, old criminal and instead had found a kid, somebody's son. It may as well have been his own.

Charlie heard the electric razor power down. After some rummaging and the sound of the sink water running, a brushing sound came from the bathroom. Silverman was brushing his teeth. *Knowing this guy, that'll probably take him another ten minutes.*

A couple weeks after that last hit, Charlie had called his son. Chuck lived in Baltimore with his mother. When the kid had been younger, he had been thrilled with the two or three visits a year from Daddy. But now he wanted nothing to do with Charlie. Charlie considered it ironic how quickly the roles had reversed. His next job, after Silverman, was to convince Chuck to spend the summer with him in the Keys where they could go swimming and boating, where father and son could bond. His son was nearly an adult; Charlie wanted to make sure Chuck didn't become the kind of adult he had.

Silverman was spitting, the water running again. *Time to focus.* He shook off his thoughts as he listened to Silverman shake off his toothbrush.

Someone entered the hallway. It was that army guy, walking hastily along in his uniform. Someone who did legal killing and got medals for murder. Charlie nodded a good morning to him and the soldier grunted one back as he passed, double-time, to the end of the car. When the soldier saw he couldn't proceed, he turned, passed again, and went out the way he'd come.

Charlie shook off the interruption and refocused as he stood, alone again, in the darkened hall. To the soldier, to anyone on the train, Charlie was just a guy in a leather jacket, hands in his pockets, waiting to use the occupied washroom. Beneath the surface of the jacket, however, hid the professional assassin. Yes, he wanted out of the business, but right now he *was* the business. Whatever reluctance he had when taking the job had been necessarily silenced. Now there was only determination. The assassin was methodical, calculated, driven. He knew his business, he knew the tools of his trade, and he used them well.

The tool in his pocket was a Walther P22 with a TAC 65 suppressor. During his last visit to the bathroom, he'd threaded the suppressor to the gun. The .22's serial number and ballistic signatures—laser-etched—had been removed. It had been purchased years ago by someone he didn't know, someone in the Boss's employ, but removed three times even from the Boss. There was no connecting the gun to Charlie or the Boss, no connecting it even to the state of Maryland. The only connection was the current physical one, his gloved hand clasped around the handle, his finger on the trigger, all concealed inside his pocket.

Charlie never used the same weapon for two jobs; he knew he had to dispose of the evidence immediately. But he also got to know his gun before using it. He'd had a taste of this virgin .22, had practiced with it. He knew it inside and out, had used this gun and others like it before. He knew the Walther P22 as the gun to use for a fast, clean, quiet job. The TAC 65 suppressor silenced the sound of death; the loudest part of the shot would be the sound of the action clanking against itself and ejecting the shell casing. Charlie had even taken action to keep this minor detail silenced: a bit of felt buffered the point of impact to muffle the slight metallic sound, a sound not unlike that of the train clanging along the tracks. The gun would remain in his pocket to further muffle any sound. And with any luck, the shell would remain in the confines of his pocket and never hit the floor.

Charlie had never botched a job, and wouldn't start now. He'd done this enough times to know what to expect. Silverman would get the picture, would see the shape of the gun poking through his pocket, would place his hands on his head, offer him money to spare his life. Charlie would instruct Silverman to turn around. He'd enter the wash room and close the door behind him. He'd place the gun to the back of Silverman's head. One shot would do it; one second was all it would take. When the coast was clear, he'd drag the body to the empty sleeper car. He'd wait for a bend in the tracks. As the train veered, he'd tap his windshield hammer to the window and dispose of the body, push it out into rural Indiana where no one would find it for a day or more. It was still dark enough that no one would see. He'd dispose of the gun and hammer. Then, before the morning sun filled the sky, he'd dispose of the whole damn business.

Stop dreaming. Charlie checked himself. *Don't dream at the deed's doorstep.*

Charlie looked left, then right. He could hear Silverman fumbling with the washroom door. The assassin tightened his grip on the handle and pointed his pocketed piece. The sign switched from *Occupied* to *Vacant*.

Seconds

It still haunted her. Six months later, and the mishap still troubled her when she was alone and had quiet time to think about it. Not that this particular moment qualified as quiet time; the *ka-chunk, ka-chunk, ka-chunk* of the train unsettled her, even as she rested in her own private room. She'd given up smoking years ago, but she wanted a cigarette now.

Demi looked in her purse. No cigarettes. *Of course there aren't any, dumb ass, you quit!* Such things didn't materialize out of nowhere, and if there did happen to be a few cigs in a forgotten pack roaming around the nether regions of her oversized purse, they would be stale. *At least six months old. We smoked the last one together.* The vivid memory rushed in: Kurt crumbling the soft pack and cellophane and tossing it across the hotel room into the plastic wastebasket. "Two points," he'd cheered, although she remembered thinking she'd thrown him the whole game. But now, alone in her train bunk, she wished she'd called a foul. Regardless, Kurt was out of the game. She tried to clear her mind and think of something else.

Her gig in Culpepper had gone well. They'd bought all her samples and wanted her to send more. Demi was a pottery sculptor. In her hands, clay turned into the most attractive things—abstract ashtrays, cups, paperweights, and unique sculptures. She'd never made much of a living at it, but her husband didn't mind that.

Harold was just glad that she had something to be passionate about, something more than a job as a secretary or clerk; something outside the business offices that seemed to stiffen her like an overstarched shirt. He called her a free spirit, and she enjoyed the freedom of her work. *More play than work.* She made what she wanted, when she wanted. She was her own boss. The only orders she took were the ones she wanted to take, and they were all by word of mouth.

Mr. Johansson had been a friend of a friend she'd mailed a catalog to. She never expected a response from such cold mailings, but sometimes that lack of expectation seemed to bring it about. He'd called Demi two months after receiving the catalog and asked to meet with her at his expense. He wanted to see three-dimensional samples.

"I'll probably have to come by train, if you want me to bring samples," she'd advised him. Twice, she'd flown with her cargo and regretted it. The first time, her pottery had arrived late, after the scheduled meeting, and she'd lost the sale as a result. The second time, her art had arrived in pieces. She trusted trains more than planes. She could keep her luggage with her and didn't have to worry about uncaring handlers tossing it about. Besides, she had time to spare, and a train ride was a nice way to spend it.

She traveled light now, as she headed home to Chicago. Mr. Johansson had bought all twelve samples she'd brought with her. The four-foot abstract sculpture he most admired looked something like a Picasso-inspired tiger. Selling the samples was well worth the trip, not to mention that she'd longed for some alone time on the train. The true success of the trip, however, was that the samples were only that; Mr. Johansson had given her the largest order she'd had in years. He wanted sculptures in every office of the corporate building and asked for larger ones—in the five to eight foot range—for the lobbies and conference rooms. She could barely contain her excitement.

She'd celebrated with a few drinks in the lounge car after boarding the train earlier in the day. Then the indiscreet glances of the men around her made her uncomfortable. One balding man practically drooled as he pointed and talked out loud about her as though she hadn't been there. She was used to ogling, but she wasn't in the mood. The men were enough to put a damper on her celebration, so she'd retreated to her private room on the sleeper car.

The train chugged alongside the mighty Ohio River. She watched the rushing water outside and wished she could be out in it, allowing the cool force to wash her clean. But the rushing water couldn't wash away the past. Some filth remained a part of a person forever. Her cell phone spit out a rendition of Beethoven's Fifth; she flipped it open.

"Hi, Harold. How are things at home?"

"Good," he said. "I got your voicemail. Great news on the order! You'll be busy for the next few months!"

"At least! I may have to hire some help," Demi said through a smile, her happiness resurfacing.

"Sure, we'll get a maid and a chef so you can focus on your pottery."

Demi laughed. Maybe he was serious, but she doubted it. Harold was an accountant, and he hated to see the accounts tilt the wrong way. "I could call Alice," Demi suggested. "She'll cook for us and do some light cleaning for a third of what I'm getting."

"That's fine," Harold said. "Or I could lend an extra hand in the kitchen."

She laughed. "No, let's just get Alice's help."

"What? Like I never cook anything?"

"You try."

"Okay, call Alice." He chuckled. "How's the ride?"

"Nice," she said, looking out at the river. "Lots of nice scenery. We should do it together sometime." But he was always too busy and they seldom had time to get away from the constraints of everyday life.

"We will," he said. "As soon as things calm down a bit." But they never did. How many years had it been with the *when we have time* line? She'd lost count. But she didn't need to get away. She wanted to get back home to the comfort of her husband's embrace. She counted the seconds until she could be with him.

Most days, Demi had more time on her hands than clay. The orders didn't flow as consistently as the Ohio River alongside the train. Her business more resembled the stillness of the Chicago canals where she lived. Some months she kept busy replicating pottery from her catalog or filling custom requests. When the orders didn't keep her busy, she tried to come up with new pieces, both trendy and traditional. But most months, even that didn't fill her time. There was the housework, the cooking, the dishes, and the laundry. But Demi and Harold were a neat, childless couple, so even the housework didn't suck away the last grains of sand in the day's hourglass.

So Demi did other things—fun things that filled the seconds of the day and fulfilled her free spirit in the same way her art did; things Harold considered a little over the top. The three piercings in each ear had been "out there" but the barbell in her navel had thrown him off guard. He admitted to being turned on by the adornments, but wasn't sure these were the sorts of markings he'd want to show off to the world.

The marking she decided to show off to the world was of another sort. Her best friend, Courtney, had talked her into getting the tattoo. But even Courtney was shocked at the one Demi chose.

The tattoo took longer than she'd expected, in part because the hairy tattoo artist needling it onto her flesh took his time, enjoying the view. Demi lay with her trim tummy on the table, her shirt pulled high, her pants pulled low, the smooth skin of her firm buttocks exposed to him. "I have the best can*vass*," he'd said, breathing heavily. The real focus was above her hind quarters, but that didn't stop the scratcher from openly admiring her flesh.

"I can't believe you're doing this," Courtney admitted at Demi's side.

"You're the one who talked me into it."

"I was thinking a butterfly on the ankle or a rose on the breast."

"Too conventional," said Demi dismissively. "Old ladies playing bridge have those boring things. If I'm getting one, I'm really getting one!"

The tattoo spanned the entire width of her lower back. It was an intricate design of intertwining lines, resembling something like a bat, the wings making up most of the form. The tattoo's body—the center—ran along six inches of her spine and pointed like an arrow down to the crack between her cheeks.

"What's Harold going to say?" Courtney asked.

"God, I don't know." Demi laughed. "He'll freak out. But I think he'll come around. Deep down, he likes this sort of thing."

"Guys do," Courtney said as though she had them all figured out, as though this knowledge was the benefit of her in-depth field research.

It was more painful than Demi had expected and halfway through the procedure she wished she'd gone with a rose of Jericho, a dragonfly, or a cut of ivy. But when it was finished, scabbed over, and finally healed—when she looked at her naked backside in the mirror—the sight pleased her. The intricate design was as abstract and artistic as one of her sculptures. She'd chosen the right tattoo for her. That's why the decision had come so easily.

Harold did not warm up to the tattoo. Demi's husband had been disgusted by the scabby mutilation. It was enormous, taking up her entire lower back. He'd been so repulsed that he didn't even respond to her advances that week. It was later, when the scar had healed into its beautiful design—like an ugly cocoon into a beautiful butterfly—that Harold followed the arrow. He still adored her, of course. "But I don't think I'll ever get used to that monstrosity on your back."

Other men liked it, though. Demi supposed it was the sort of thing men liked on other women, not their own. It was bold, hot, gritty. It dared people to look, challenged them to comment. Demi had never had a problem attracting men's glances, but with the tattoo she seemed to tap double the drool from men around her. And the looks came with less discretion. Such a bold tattoo asked for it.

The ink was a part of her now, and she showed it off during the spring and summer months, when the weather allowed her to wear a shirt cut above her low-ride pants. Not half a minute passed as she walked along the edge of the water on Chicago's Lake Shore Drive before at least one man stared at her tattoo.

One such spring afternoon, after selling thirteen glazed vases, she popped into a restaurant just off Lake Shore to celebrate. At the bar she had a corned beef sandwich and chips with a Cosmopolitan. She was teasing a second Cosmo when Kurt approached. "Demi?"

Demi turned on her stool. "Kurt! Oh my God! How are you?"

"Doing great," he said. "I didn't recognize you at first. Check out that wild tattoo! Sweet!"

"Oh, yeah," Demi said and let out a soft laugh. "I like it. It's me!"

"I like it too!" He took a seat beside her. "Hey, it's great to run into you." He saw that her pink refreshment needed refilling. He called the bartender. "Another Cosmopolitan for the lady and a dry martini for me." He offered her a cigarette.

"No thanks. I quit a while back."

"Good for you," he said, lighting up. "But not for me. I need my vices, you know."

She knew. They'd gone to high school together. He'd been the guy who always got into trouble, but it was that very trouble that made him the envy of the student body. He did the forbidden drugs, drank the fashionable drinks, and did all the hip things kids weren't allowed to do. She'd wanted him then, wanted to lose herself to him, but he was too busy with other girls—the cheerleaders and wannabe models. He'd always been kind to her in the classroom and hallways, but not kind enough to ask her out. Throughout high school, she longed to be logged in his black book. "What do you do these days?" she asked, taking the first sip from her new drink.

"I'm an actor—can you believe it?" He lifted his glass to her. "To getting all we want," he proposed. She agreed with the clink of her glass, and they drank. "Mostly industrial films and corporate stuff," he continued. "But I did a commercial for Viagra. You can only see the back of my head. But still, I think it'll firm up my resumé."

"I'll bet." She told him about her work and that she too, was doing what she loved.

"I'd rather be acting for Spielberg or Tarantino," he said. "But I can't complain. I'm not waiting tables."

She figured they were more alike now than they had been in high school—both content with their work but hungry for something more. "To doing what we love," she proposed. He drank enthusiastically to that.

After another drink she accepted his offer of a cigarette. They were giggling, hanging on one another, impulsive. She knew how to flirt; there was excitement in the art. He fingered the tattoo on her back. "Man, that's one hell of a marking! Do you have any more?"

"There's more." She smiled playfully. "But no more tattoos."

His finger followed the design to her crack and lingered there just above her jeans. "I'd like to see more." She stopped laughing and he kissed her. For a second, she resisted, pulling away, but she slipped and fell into her desire. Kurt looked at the light reflecting off the silver piercing in her navel. "There's a nice place across the street," he said. "I could get a fresh pack of cigarettes, a bottle of wine... and a room."

She couldn't find the words to refuse. This wasn't a time for thinking. If she gave in to rational thought, she'd tell herself this—her wildest high school dream—was wrong. She followed, uncertain of the force pulling her along.

Kurt still had enough style to keep the popular girls around. He wore a knotty, long-sleeved shirt and brown wool pants, right off the racks of stores too hip to be named. Or rather, he didn't wear them. He piled his clothes in the corner chair of their hotel room in the sky. His boxer briefs revealed his rising excitement as Demi stood at the window and looked down at the bar across the street where they'd met. The solid, black Hancock Tower stood in the distance, towering above the Chicago skyline. Then she felt Kurt behind her, tracing her tattoo and then peeling off her shirt, her pants, her everything.

Demi's breath loitered low, soft. "Kurt, I don't know..."

"You don't have to know. Just feel." He followed his own advice, placing his hands all over her. He kissed her deeply, gently moistened the flesh of her neck, her breasts, her navel, and beyond.

She hesitated, suggested they keep it limited to heavy petting, but he tamed her wild streak by feeding it. After making love, Kurt offered her another cigarette. She sat at the edge of the bed and looked out at the Chicago skyline, the Hancock Tower in full view. She'd once sold a few sculptures to an executive in the Hancock. She remembered how repulsive it had been when the businessman insisted they close the deal with a kiss. That's how badly she'd wanted her sculptures to sell—she'd actually kissed the bastard, wiping away the old man's slimy saliva when he wasn't looking. The sight of the Hancock, coupled with what she'd just done with Kurt, made her feel sick. "I've gotta go."

"Are you sure?" Kurt asked.

"Yeah." She collected her clothing and dressed. It was six o'clock. Harold would be home soon, wondering where she was, fumbling around the kitchen in a pathetic attempt to create something edible. She would tell him she'd gone for a drink after closing a sale, and the evening would rest on the good news that she'd made a chunk of change with the deal of the day. But the hardness of the Hancock weighed down on her as she dressed.

Demi looked out the window of her compartment as the train continued alongside the Ohio River. Her husband called again. "You know, maybe I should call around for a maid. I'll bet I can haggle a better price for us."

"Poor Alice barely makes ends meet as it is," Demi said. "I'll call her from the train."

"All right," Harold agreed. "You take care of it then."

Another pause rested between them. Demi peered out the window, the yellow and orange leaves falling to the banks of the river. A craving stirred in her, between the barbell and the tattoo. "I can't wait to get back."

"It's only been a few days," Harold said.

"I still miss you. And want you."

"Me too." He stifled a laugh. "You know, I have a break in my schedule middle of next month. Maybe I'll take a couple weeks and we can do a train trip together. Or Paris. You still want to go to Paris, right?"

"I'd love to do Paris."

"Well, I'll get on the Internet and look for some deals. There was a great rate to Amst...or..."

"You're breaking up, Harold. Harold? I can't hear you." She figured the treed hills must be interfering. Either that, or the rural area with no satellites. Whatever the interference, it separated her from her husband, so she hung up.

Harold didn't know. Nobody knew about Kurt. It was such a dark secret—something she was so ashamed of—that she'd never revealed it to anyone. Sometimes the truth wasn't the right choice.

The weeks that followed her one-hour check-in with Kurt were the most miserable she'd known. But she was good at keeping her discontent to herself. When no one was around, the least things would set her off crying—a mistake in her wet clay, an overcooked casserole, a sensual cosmetics commercial—and she knew the real source of her grief was Kurt. The day she saw the Viagra commercial—she wouldn't have recognized the back of his head if he hadn't told her—she went back to bed and moped all day, only barely managing to dry her tears and make up her face in time to deceive Harold, surprising him with a dinner out to celebrate the completion of an especially difficult ceramic she'd really completed days before.

Harold's loving support, admiring eyes, emotional embraces, and tender lovemaking all comforted her. But some days, his love for her—and hers for him—only depressed her more because she'd violated it. No, he didn't know. But he didn't need to know. She knew.

Kurt called her a few weeks after their meeting. "Demi! I've been thinking about you a lot."

"I've been trying to forget about you." The tone of her voice begged to differ. "You really shouldn't call me here. How did you get my number anyway?"

"It's listed. Your husband's at work, right?"

"It was a mistake, Kurt." She sighed heavily, desire rising like an elevator. "A terribly wonderful mistake."

"Now you're talking. Come on, let's get together. Just because we have a little fun doesn't mean you love your man any less. Maybe I can teach you how to love him better."

"I've got things to do, Kurt. Bye." She folded her cell and placed it in her front pocket. It vibrated against her front, Kurt arousing her even while he was miles away. Before morning had given in to afternoon, she'd given in to him. It was so easy to give in to something so exciting and desirable, even if forbidden.

The second time with Kurt had been easier than the first. She'd expected to feel even worse after their second rendezvous, despite her desire. On the contrary, the second time seemed a smaller sin. It was easier to visit the forbidden garden once the wall had been torn down.

She didn't love Kurt. But Kurt enlivened her wild side in a way that Harold's genuine, gentlemanly love couldn't.

Now, on the train, Demi looked at her cell. *No Service.* She placed it in her front left pocket. Harold would call later and it would tickle her, just as Kurt had. She turned away from the Ohio River and exited her compartment.

She had a key for her private room, but she left her door unlocked. She always left doors unlocked—on the train, in her car, at home. The potential danger was just another way to put a little extra edge in her life, even if it never made a real difference. She didn't want anything to happen, but the possibility of danger around the bend exhilarated her. She passed through several sleeper cars on her way to the lounge.

Once there, she felt the pull of her tattoo on the men's eyes. She took her red wine and sat between two empty seats. She enjoyed the current of intertwined conversations around her, but she didn't feel like diving in.

Demi had been out of college a few years when she came to the conclusion that she needed to do what she loved instead of just what paid the bills. She quit her job as a secretary and devoted all her time to her art. She had aspirations of one day designing a sculpture to rival the Picasso downtown, but she started with more simple things: refrigerator magnets, flower vases, ash trays, and paperweights. Courtney's parents managed a restaurant not far from the Magnificent Mile and they let her put up a sidewalk booth during the week. Demi sat there for as long as ten hours a day with those little pieces of her clay and her soul. It took some time before she'd even made back the cost of her supplies and the used booth. She actually considered buying hotdogs and vending them alongside her wares, but that would've been biting the hand of the restaurant that fed her.

Demi met Harold one day as she sat behind her booth. He'd said hello when entering the restaurant for lunch; on the way out he said more. "So what's all this?"

"Oh, these are my own creations," Demi boasted with the lively movement of a game show showgirl. "Ashtray?"

"I don't smoke," he said with a humored smile.

"Vase, for your wife's flowers?"

Harold scoffed. "I don't even have a girlfriend!"

"How 'bout a paperweight?" The pens and pencils in his shirt pocket gave him away—his was an office job.

"Well, I do have paperwork."

"You won't find a better paperweight anywhere." Making a joke of her pitch made it easier. It told the world she was really an artist, not a salesperson.

He examined it out of kindness. She could tell he didn't want it. "Maybe next time." He offered her a gentlemanly smile and nothing more.

"Tightwad," she said under her breath as he left, but loud enough to put a pause in his step.

Harold was a regular at the restaurant. One lunch hour, she didn't even bother looking at him when he left the restaurant, and he seemed challenged by it. "Let me see that paperweight again," he said. She gave it to him. "I think I'll take it."

She brightened. "I didn't think this was your sort of thing." She wrapped it up for him. The next time he visited, she wrapped an ashtray for his boss and later a vase for his mother. He didn't buy her art every time he visited the restaurant, but he did admire it. He asked her about the carefree life of an artist and told her about his stable future at the firm. Then one day, he came with flowers and purchased another vase.

"No need to wrap it," he said. "The flowers are for you."

Demi beamed. "They're beautiful, Harold," she said, laughing. "And you have great taste in vases!"

"I better not see it for sale again. It's yours, from me."

"I'll put it in my bedroom," she said, cocking her head playfully to one side.

"How about dinner after you're done?"

She smelled the flowers. "Mmm. After a gift like this, how can I resist?"

She couldn't. And the more she got to know him, the more irresistible he became. He may not have been the hunk she'd always dreamed of, but he was gentle and kind, intelligent and loyal. She came to know substance where before she'd only played with boy-toys. Harold seemed more teddy bear than he-man, and she loved him for that. A year later, they were married. And nineteen years after that, she still loved her Harold. He was her anchor. Harold offered stability and safety, purpose and companionship. She didn't mind when he began to lose his hair and find extra pounds. The only thing she wished she could change was his devotion to work, his commitment to accounts. These days, Harold was too busy for vacations, too tired for fun. He got to work before she woke up and came home beat and disinterested in going out. She adored him, but her free spirit wanted to soar, needed excitement and adventure outside the margins of their life together.

Demi loved Harold. But she couldn't resist Kurt.

⊢⊣⊢⊣⊢⊣⊢⊣⊢⊣

Demi warmed up to Kurt in the spring, but by summer she was stifled by the heat. Since their first encounter, they'd met thirteen times. Thirteen daytime meetings of passion in twenty weeks' time, all the while satisfying her own husband's libido. It was like being back in college, only this time she was married.

She'd decided before their last meeting to break it off. But first, she permitted herself one last indulgence. She asked to meet at the same bar where they'd begun; she wanted to end it where it had started.

Fueled by Cosmos and martinis, they retired to a room and set one another ablaze—they rubbed and licked and nibbled one another like animals on the desk, the night stand, against the wall. They came together on the sweat-drenched bed.

After they cooled down, she sat at the edge of the moist mattress with a cigarette, looking at the tall black tower emerging from the cityscape horizon. It was time to douse the flame for good.

"Come back over here," Kurt insisted, her tattoo pointing to the direction of his attraction. He grabbed her, pressed himself against her back.

"I'm not going to see you anymore." She took a cigarette from his pack and placed it between her lips.

"What?" Kurt let go of her for a moment, but then held her harder, turning her to look him in the eyes. "What are you talking about?"

"Kurt, this isn't right." She lit up. "You know it and I know it."

"Little late for that, don't you think?" He lit a cigarette as well.

"Go ahead, rub it in!" Still naked, Demi walked to the window. "I'm not proud of this. Was it fun? Yes. Did I enjoy it? You bet. Would I do it again?" She paused. "I hope not. This isn't right."

"All I know is if it feels so good, it—"

"Don't even go there. Lots of wrong things feel good."

Kurt let out a large puff of smoke and she could feel his acceptance of the situation. "Why now?"

"I need to be true to Harold. It's not you, Kurt; I've enjoyed our little thing together."

"Little thing?"

"But I don't want to be someone who has an affair. I don't even know how this happened, how we got here. I don't want a secret life. I need to feel clean."

"Clean." Kurt scoffed, looking at the stained skin on her lower back. "Like you'll ever be clean. You're marked for life."

Demi lit another of his cigarettes and took a long, heavy draw. "We should never have gotten past the Cosmos and martinis."

Kurt remained silent. In a moment he said, "I'm glad we did."

Demi wiped away tears as she looked at the cityscape beyond their window. "Me too."

Once it was over, it was over. Sometimes Demi wished she hadn't called it off. Harold never knew, never would know. Her occasional desire to be with Kurt was just weakness seeping in; she remained strong enough to only meet Kurt in her memory, where there was no pleasure in it.

Now, on the train, the affair had been over as long as it had been on. She'd gotten a handle on her compulsion. Sure, she still flirted—it was her—but she drew the line there. She didn't feel anything was lacking now that she'd called it off, but she remembered her lunchtime affairs with delight and remorse.

Her flavor for danger was part of her. Before Kurt, there'd been the tattoo. Before that, the pierced navel, the barbell in her tongue. There were wild parties, outings with her girlfriends to clubs and, occasionally, strip joints. After big sales, she made a point of celebrating her successes in bars during happy hours while everyone else she knew worked. As she sipped her afternoon wine and cocktails, she imagined Harold in his office, getting excited about a ledger of numbers. She'd been barhopping alone for years and the figures she studied were of a more physical sort.

Kurt had been just a fluke, a moment of weakness, a return to younger years, free of care and full of promise. Harold was her stability. Sometimes marriage seemed both a life preserver and an anchor—her marriage was everything she wanted in a stable relationship, and yet it shackled her free spirit's desires. She'd never met a man she loved more, but her primal instinct was to prowl.

Demi stood from her seat, crossed the lounge, and asked the attendant for another merlot. This was her second, not including the ones she'd had earlier in the day. She was feeling good about things. She'd turned a new leaf. Autumn was a time to rake away decay, to prepare for a barren cleansing and await new life in the spring. It was a good time to be on the train, headed back home to Harold.

She turned and caught a handsome, middle-aged man checking out her lower back. He couldn't be blamed, really. The elaborate tattoo invited people to look, guided their eyes to her asset. As she watched the man watching her, he lifted his eyes from her lower parts and offered her a smile. Demi smiled back and looked away. She took a swallow of wine to hold down the excitement splashing in her chest. She walked to a corner of the lounge. A moment later, he was beside her.

"Nice ass," he said.

Demi didn't smile. "Takes one to know one." She looked him over: salt and pepper hair, medium build, crisp white shirt unbuttoned at the top, loosened red tie, blue blazer with gold buttons, casual dress slacks. Amber liquor, straight up. "Most people compliment the tattoo as a pretense."

"Guess I'm not that discreet." He looked at his drink, then back into her eyes, as though comparing them. "Why beat around the bush?"

"Sure, tell it like it is." She sipped her wine. "I don't like liars anyway. Most people say they're looking at the tattoo when I know damn well they're looking at my ass. Besides, I guess you were invited." She watched a red wave crash against the inner edge of her glass with the tide of the train. "I mean, with the attention-grabber...the tattoo." She could see that grabbing was the very thing on his mind.

"Name's Murdock," he said, offering his hand for a formal shake, an opportunity to touch skin against skin.

"Demi." She accepted his hand and allowed hers to linger inside it. Something sparked and she felt alive. Perhaps it was her lack of good judgment, the merlot, or a subconscious primal desire, but as they talked the moments away, she found herself increasingly attracted to this handsome loner—his suave gestures and sly charm that seemed to be hiding something deep inside. Something mysterious in him called to her. Suddenly, he swooped in to kiss her, but she turned her lips away and he smacked her cheek.

"I'm married," she said.

"I like married women. The best kind. Been married for long?"

"Twenty years next spring." She sipped her dry wine; her tongue tingled. "Twenty wonderful years."

"Wonderful, twenty years?" he asked. "Are you sure that's possible?"

"Why not? Aren't you married?"

"Nope. Married life's not for a guy like me."

"No? Why's that?"

"I'm a traveling salesman. Always on the move. No strings."

"How romantic," she quipped.

Murdock's hazel eyes drew hers in. "What's romantic is this: two strangers on a train, hooking up."

Demi stared into him for a moment. Then she released herself with a laugh. "Who said we're hooking up?"

"No one," Murdock allowed. "But even if we just sit here and talk, this is where it's at: the excitement, getting to know one another, feeling one another out."

"I see." Demi dipped a fingertip in her glass and touched it to her tongue. "Don't you have someone back home?"

"Nope," he responded quickly. "The train's my home."

"Must get lonely."

Murdock drank from his whisky. "Sometimes. But life's not always what we want it to be, is it? That's why we have to strike when we see something we want. There's a little perfection in life, but life's not perfect."

Demi nodded. Their eyes locked, and he moved in to kiss her. Again, she dodged his desire. Murdock sighed. "You're nearly perfect."

Demi laughed out loud. "Smooth salesman, aren't you?"

Murdock laughed along. "No, really, for me, this is about as perfect as it gets."

"No kidding?" Demi took a sip of wine and let it linger in her mouth a moment before swallowing.

"For a guy like me, meeting someone like you is everything," Murdock admitted. "Love for me is like my job. It's a thrill while it lasts, but by the next station, it's over."

Demi polished off her wine. "You can make choices, you know. You don't have to rationalize loneliness. You could try to change things if you wanted to."

"I keep saying it'll change. I'll stop. I'll get off and never reboard." He downed his whisky. "But when I'm honest with myself, I know it'll never stop. This is what I've become. This is who I am."

Demi found his honesty intriguing. "I'm in sales too. Sort of."

"Are you?"

"Well, I sell my own pottery. I'm an artist."

"A potter?" He smirked. "Must be good with your hands."

"I am." She played with her empty glass.

Murdock put his glass to his mouth and found it empty. "Like another?"

"Mmm-hmm," she sighed.

He pulled out a twenty. "I'll buy, you fly."

Demi stiffened. "What?"

"I mean, I'm asking because I'd like to watch you. Get another look at that magnificent tattoo."

She laughed. "You just want to check out my ass again." She offered him a playful smile as she took his money. "Whisky?"

"Cognac," he said, upgrading. "Like your eyes." Demi felt a rush as she stood, and walked to the attendant. Nearby, a burly man drank coffee and fumbled with an unlit cigarette. He cracked a smile when she looked at him; she looked away and placed her order. As she waited, she peeked behind her.

Murdock looked at her without discretion, sizing her up from her jet-black hair to her long neck to her curved back all the way down to her tattoo, pointing the way. She returned, handed him a Hennessy, and sat to take a sip of merlot. "Thanks," he said.

"Thank you," she responded, handing over his change. "So, are you headed for Chicago?"

"That's right. You too?"

"The Windy City's my home. Yours?"

"No, I'm from Baltimore."

"Business or pleasure?"

"Always business first," he said, looking into his glass. "But I hope for a little pleasure too." He looked into her face, leaned in, and this time managed to steal a kiss. Then he pushed further into her until it seemed more rape than robbery.

Demi pulled away. "It's late." She looked at the others around them: a silver-haired man reading notes, a young man in army attire, a middle-aged man writing furiously in a spiral notebook. Even the conductor was taking a rest, sitting alone with a canteen and staring out into the darkness. She'd never strayed until Kurt. Now that the garden gates had fallen, there seemed to be too many temptations and nothing to stop her from crossing the line. "I need to go."

"Let me walk you to your seat."

"I'm not that kind of girl," she whispered

He grinned slyly. "That's why I want to make sure you get back safely. Some guys may not have the best intentions."

"Like you?"

"I intend only the best." He shot back his cognac and let it soak his mouth a moment before swallowing it down. He stood and offered his hand to help her up.

Murdock walked her through the aisles, blue blazer folded in his left arm, her arm folded in his right. She opened the door to her compartment and stood at the opening. "It'll be nice to sleep this wine off," she said with a chuckle.

"I don't have a room," he said. "But the seats aren't too bad. Better than a plane." But she could tell he didn't want his seat, he wanted hers. He leaned in, pushing her gently back into her room. She'd planned to put up a little resistance, but the intoxicating sense of danger took hold of her as firmly as Murdock did. She latched on and pulled him in. He kissed her deeply; the taste of his cognac-cultured mouth pleased her. He closed the door with his foot, his arms around her waist, hers around his neck. His arms roamed until they had firm hold of her tattoo and its focus. He ripped off his white shirt and continued to push into her until he was above her on her bed. She couldn't escape his web; she didn't try to. She hadn't sought him out, she reminded herself as she took him in, but neither had she pushed him away.

With the darkness of early morning covering them, still half-dreaming, Demi sensed she wasn't alone—as though someone had entered her compartment, taken a look around, and left. Some moments later, she woke with a headache that throbbed with every *ka-chunk, ka-chunk, ka-chunk* of the train. That's when she realized why she'd felt another's presence. The hangover hovered, but it dulled next to the sting of seeing Murdock next to her in the cramped bunk. When she stirred to look at him, he woke. "Morning," he said.

"Oh my God!" she said and lied back down.

He traced the image on her back. "Hell of a tattoo. Glad you had it."

"Why?"

"Well, you're a great woman, beautiful, sexy…but it was the tattoo that broke the ice, got me checking you out."

"Nice," she grunted. *It's the tattoo's fault. With Murdock and with Kurt.* If she hadn't gotten the tattoo, these one-track-minded wolves wouldn't have attacked. "Got any cigarettes?"

"Nope," he said. "Don't smoke. Want me to go find some?"

"No," she responded, her back still to him, his finger still tracing the elaborate web of art. *That's just stupid. It's not the tattoo's fault—it's mine.* It was akin to what her mother used to say, back when Demi would scream at her stupid shoelaces that wouldn't tie right. *Shoelaces aren't stupid, Demi; they don't have brains—it's the person calling them stupid who's stupid.*

Now, Demi was annoyingly aware of Murdock's fingers on her tattoo, tickling the upper crack of her ass. Another moment and she felt his excitement rising. Then, he placed his mouth on her shoulder, her arm, and pulled himself above her to find her breasts. She began with some resistance, but he felt so good that she gave in to him a second time. There was no kidding herself—she was as much a part of the action as he was. She was taking him.

After another passionate round of lovemaking, Murdock spoke. "I'll be in Dyer for a week. Then I'll shoot through Chicago."

"Good for you."

"You're one wild woman. I think you put my back out! I'll be sucking down the painkillers today! But it sure was worth it."

She let a false laugh fall out.

He smiled. "When I'm in town, maybe we can see each other again. Can I get your number?"

She hesitated. "I don't think so."

Murdock nodded. "I understand." He began collecting his clothes. "Breakfast, then?"

"No thanks," she said. "I'd like to be alone." She smiled a *don't worry it's not your fault* smile.

"All right." He winced as he slipped into his white dress shirt and began to button it down. "Sure you don't want some cigarettes? I can get some. Bring them back."

"No, I'm sure," she said. "Don't come back. It's better if you don't."

Murdock nodded. He put the blue blazer over his white shirt and checked to make sure his red tie was wadded in his inside pocket. From an outer pocket, he pulled a business card and placed it on the table. "In case you change your mind."

In her bunk, she turned away and pulled the white sheet up over her. The sound of pills rattling in a bottle made her turn around. She watched him swallow a couple. "What are those?"

"Painkillers. Want one?"

"Will it get rid of my headache?" She sat up and held out her hand, ready for a remedy.

"It'll get rid of more than that." He knocked a couple pills into her hand. She popped one of the pills, placed the other on the table next to his card, and fell back to her bunk.

Standing above her, Murdock looked her over. She covered herself with the white sheet. He looked at her curves beneath the thin white linen and then stared at the orange-brown bottle in his hand. "I live for moments like last night. It's mornings like this that make me want to down the whole bottle. A handful would do the trick."

When he opened the door, she sat up and the sheet fell from her. "Murdock?" He turned in the open doorway and looked at her cognac eyes and the white sheet in her lap, then back to her eyes. She didn't know what to say.

Murdock put on a sarcastic smile. "Don't worry, this isn't pinned on you. You're just one of a hundred broads along the way."

The comment stung, but she persisted. "There's always something to live for."

Murdock nodded, looking her over. "But sometimes that something ain't enough."

She pulled the sheet over her naked body, holding it up to her chest. "You don't have to keep moving, you know. Bottles aren't the only way to relieve pain. You could settle down. Find a place you like and someone you love and stop roaming."

Murdock smiled and nodded. "Yeah. Not bad advice, there." He looked at her hand and she thought he wanted to reach out to hold it again. But instead he just stared at the gold ring on her finger. "Maybe you should follow it. Instead of guys like me." Murdock closed the door, leaving her alone.

Demi sobbed and it made the throbbing in her head swell. *Kurt, and now Murdock.* She'd given in again, to a second man. But it wasn't as hard to quit Murdock as it had been to quit Kurt.

Outside, in the hallway, she could hear the movements of other people. Morning was maturing; she imagined other passengers were making their ways to the showers.

She draped the white sheet over her shoulders and wore it like a cape, whiting out the black mark on her back, hiding the tattoo that seemed to initiate her infidelities. Beethoven's fifth sounded and she picked up her cell. "Hello?"

"Hi Honey," Harold said. "Where are you?"

Overjoyed, she said, "Harold, good morning!" She walked to the window in her open sheet. "I don't know, somewhere in Indiana, I guess."

"Great. Check it out: I found some great rates. We could go to Amsterdam, London, or Athens. I mean, we could go somewhere else too, but these are the best deals. What do you think? We can discuss it over dinner; maybe that little European bistro, to get us in the mood. I was thinking Amsterdam would be kind of wild."

A wild time with the accountant; something she'd not experienced in some time. Maybe Amsterdam with Harold would be enough to quench her wild side. Love and excitement in one package sounded better than the separate lives she'd resorted to. Her smile reflected back to her in the window. "That sounds wonderful," she said. She looked at her reflection: face, shoulders, breasts, pierced navel. "I miss you, Harold." She could count the seconds until she'd be home in his heartfelt embrace.

When she placed her cell phone back on the table, she noticed Murdock's pain pill and business card there. She realized her headache was gone. So was her heartache. She took the glossy card in her hand and read the raised black lettering. She ripped the card and threw it in the wastebasket.

Demi turned and examined her backside in the window. Her tattoo penetrated the thin white sheet; her own scarlet letter crossed over the blur of Indiana foliage.

The garden was open. Murdock would be in Chicago. The card was still in the waste basket. Seconds came easier.

Idle Chatter

Franklin still wore his Amtrak uniform, although he was officially off duty. He always wore it when he was on the train. He was never *really* off duty, because even when he was on break, he remained in view, on call, ready to assist the passengers, ready to make small talk. To everyone he met on the train, from the first punch of the ticket to the last farewell at the end of the line, he was *the conductor*. A mighty responsibility, but he'd been filling the shoes for decades. He knew how to make people comfortable with idle chatter. Being the conductor was more than just a job—it was who he was. That's the way it had been most of his life, and that's the way he liked it.

Now, after a long day of short talks, he sat in the lounge car—still available to anyone who wanted him—and looked into the darkness of the Indiana night as he drank from his canteen of water. It was black out, and he could barely see the shadowy trees waving in the distant wind. It had become quiet in the lounge car, but there were still people here: the young man who'd asked for a leaf of Amtrak stationery earlier in the day wrote hurriedly in a spiral notebook now; the guy with silver hair who looked like a preacher studied the notes to a speech; the gruff troublemaker toyed with his unlit cigarette and drank bourbon now instead of coffee. They all had stories. Everyone had a story to tell. Someday he'd write a book about it.

Franklin looked away from the people and back into the darkness. He took a gulp of water. The sun would rise soon, and then they'd all be pulling into Chicago.

He'd encountered the poet earlier in the day, back around Ashland, Kentucky. The guy had entered the lounge car in a fury, had stepped right up to the conductor. "Excuse me," he'd said excitedly.

"What can I do for you?" Franklin had asked with his usual customer service smile.

"Do you have a piece of paper I could borrow? Or have?"

Franklin looked at the guy's spiral notebook, opened to a page of chicken scratchings in dull pencil that looked like they were ready to rub right off the page. "Did you run out?"

"No, I need to write a letter. Something nicer than a page ripped out of this old thing. Maybe a blank piece of copy paper, or stationery."

Franklin reached a finger up beneath his cap and scratched the side of his head. "I think I can get you some Amtrak letterhead. Will a few sheets do?"

"That'd be great."

"What's your name, anyway?"

"Colin."

"I'll be back in a jiffy, Colin." He returned with a dozen pieces of Amtrak stationery and handed them to the young man. "What's this really for, son?"

Colin smiled sheepishly. "It's a poem for someone."

The conductor grinned. "Love poem, is it?"

"Not exactly." Colin tried to disguise the obvious. "Well, sort of."

"Don't you worry none. Writing poetry ain't nothing to be ashamed of. Might not be tough-guy talk, but a good poem's a fine thing. Ain't no shame in it."

"Well, no, there's not." Colin showed him his notebook. "I'm a poet by profession. Colin White."

Franklin whistled. "You don't say. That's something to be proud of. You get your poems published sometimes?"

"Some times more than others."

"Tell you what," Franklin confided, "I've written a love poem or two in my time. Especially when I was younger, when I was about your age. The women dig it."

"Well, sure. But that's not exactly the kind of poetry I write."

"What are you into, philosophy? Poems that ask questions or give answers?"

The poet shrugged. "I guess I just write what comes to me."

Franklin nodded. He could see that the wordsmith was in a hurry to spill out some words on the Amtrak letterhead he'd handed over, but the conductor had more to say. "Tell you what I learned a long time ago. Conversation is like poetry. You invite a person in with your words, hold them with a story or feeling or bit of information, and leave them with something they didn't have before. You can touch a person with small talk."

"Talk is poetry," the poet said, and he wrote the phrase in his notebook. "Touch with talk."

"You gonna write this nice love poem of yours with that poor excuse for a pencil?"

"Well, I guess I don't have much choice."

"Sure you do." Franklin grinned. "You can ask your conductor if he has a pen."

Colin tucked the pencil behind his ear. "Do you?"

"I'm one step ahead of you, boy." He pulled an Amtrak stick pen from his inside blazer pocket. "For you to keep. Write something about my train."

"I certainly will," the poet said. "You have my word."

Franklin had written a love poem or two in his time, but it had been a chore. He could talk, but talk was alive and in the air around him. Writing was different. With writing, he was confronted by the words on the page, challenged to make them more meaningful. Small talk, clichés, idle chatter—it was all meaningful when part of a living conversation, part of something bigger than himself. Without the interplay of others, his words fell flat.

He'd written a couple love poems for Latoya, ages ago. They'd really turned her on, but it was probably more the idea of having poetry written for her than the quality of the words on paper.

"You're a regular romantic," she'd teased.

"Only because you gave me a reason."

"I'm sure you've written a dozen poems for a dozen women."

"Nope. I've never had a reason to until you came along."

That had done the trick. She'd nuzzled into his chest and let out a warm sigh. "You sure know how to talk."

It was his talk, he imagined, that had attracted her to him. He was a decent looking fellow, nice trim physique, well-groomed. But so were a hundred other guys at the jazz clubs and blues joints. It was his turn of phrase, his knack for conversation that had brought them together. That's also what had driven them apart.

Earlier in the evening, the lounge car had rattled with activity, people walking in and out for their drinks and snacks or just to stretch. Mr. Silver-hair had his notes in his lap but was gazing out the window, looking like he could fall asleep at any moment. The coffee drinker who wanted to smoke looked like he never slept at any moment, alert as he watched the people in the car. The woman with the tattoo revealed on her lower back teased people as she passed through the lounge.

Then in came the two men, the retarded man and his escort. They'd been in the lounge car before, and he'd talked with them. They'd left quickly, the retarded guy seeming to be afraid of something he saw, a fly on one of the passengers or something. But they were back, this time for juice, and the guy looked worry-free. Franklin noticed the childlike man staring at him and his uniform in awe. Franklin decided to make the guy's day with a little small talk.

"Train's a wonderful way for a couple of guys to travel together."

"By God, it is," the man agreed with a laugh. "You bet it is!"

Franklin smiled. "No rushing, no distractions, just some quality time together as you survey America outside your window." He waved his hand toward the windows and the passing scenery. "Nothing like a train."

The older of the two traveling companions nodded. "Yep, Hubert sure loves trains."

Hubert laughed. "You got that right! But it sure takes a long time."

Franklin shifted his eyes from one man to the other. "Tell you what. That's part of the fun. You're probably so used to being in a hurry that you don't know how to relax. You don't need television or computers or video games to have a good time. Just sit back, talk with your family, watch the scenery, read a book."

"I like to read books!"

"That's good. That's real good."

"We're going to my new home in Chicago," he volunteered. "They have a library of books with pictures and lots of words. I'll get new friends there. And a job, if I want it. And there's gonna be lots of games and activities."

"Okay, that's fine," the older man said, placing a gentle hand on Hubert's arm. Then he looked at Franklin and explained. "We found a nice home for him, nearby."

Franklin nodded. "You can tell all your new friends about your adventure on the train."

"You got that right," Hubert agreed, and laughed again. "I'll tell them all about the train!"

Franklin smiled at Hubert's excitement. "You know, I have a few great nephews and nieces, still just kids. Know what they ask me every time I visit? 'Tell us a train story,' they say, 'tell us about the train.' And I can tell stories to them for hours on end about riding the rails. Make 'em feel like they're on the train themselves. One of these days I plan to bring the whole family on a train vacation across the country. You're lucky to be riding the rails."

"I'm lucky all right," Hubert said. But then his smile melted away and he stared into the distance. "Even though she's gone."

Franklin gave a quizzical look. The older man explained. "His mom passed."

That took Franklin by surprise. "Oh, I'm sorry to hear that." He didn't know what to say.

The older man looked uncomfortable, but seemed to be used to such awkward moments. "That's why he's moving to Chicago, to be near us," he said. "And Hubert wanted to take the train, because he knew it would be the most fun way to travel." He put on the sort of animated voice one might use with a young child. "The train's the best way to travel."

The thoughtful sorrow on Hubert's face disappeared as a new smile burst out. "It sure is! I have a toy train at home, but this one's even better! I wish I could live on a train!"

Saved by Hubert's quick mood shift, Franklin slid back into smooth conversation. "Why, next time I visit my nephew's family, I'll tell them a story about you. About the nice guy moving to his new home in Chicago and how much fun it was to take the train. That'll convince them to hop aboard for a trip."

"Why?" Hubert asked. "They don't want to get on the train?"

"Well, they just think it takes too long. They're always in a rush, would rather take the airplane or a van. Person needs patience to enjoy the train."

"How much longer until we're there?" Hubert asked.

Franklin grinned. Hubert wanted to live on the train, but was anxious to get off of it at the same time. Something that seemed common among the travelers he met on the train. "You ever sleep on a night train before?" Franklin asked.

"No," Hubert said. "Well, maybe once when I was a little kid, with Mom. But I don't remember if I slept or not."

"Well, there's nothing like it in the world. The way the train rocks and grinds, it lulls a person right to sleep."

"I got sleepy, a little, when I looked out the window at the buildings."

"Then you know what I mean. You'll sleep well tonight. And when you wake up, we'll be pulling into Chicago."

The older man placed a hand on Hubert's shoulder. "Well, guess it's about time for us to get back to our seats." He looked at the conductor. "Thank you."

"Thank you, sir. You two enjoy the ride, and have a nice sleep." He looked back from the older to the younger. "And good luck to both of you."

On the night train, Franklin left the lounge car to take a walk through general seating, just to check things out, make sure everyone was comfortable. He spotted the empty seat next to the poet. Colin was still there, snoring, his open notebook and a few pieces of the Amtrak stationery draped over the empty seat where the woman with the dragonfly pin had been. He remembered the pretty young thing with the broken heart. This cutie must have been the poet's muse, the reason he'd been in such a frantic hurry to get his poetry down. Franklin wondered whether it was her sadness or her good looks that had inspired him to write proclamations of love to her. Franklin once knew a girl with a broken heart. He still couldn't figure out what had broken it: his talking too much or not enough.

He remembered one night when they were driving home from a cocktail party sponsored by her work. Latoya was a secretary, but most of the people at the social came from a whole different society.

"From the other side of the tracks, you might say," he'd said to her boss with a sly wink. Franklin had filled the night with small talk about trains, people he'd met, trivia about Baltimore and America. He thought the party had gone well, that he'd made a good impression. Latoya didn't.

"Why you gotta be such an embarrassment?" They were driving to her place to spend the rest of the night alone, but she was applying another coat of lip gloss.

"What are you talking about? I think I did pretty good."

"Good at making a fool of yourself."

"Fool?" He gripped the steering wheel with both hands. "I'd say I held my own with those well-heeled big wheels. I was never at a loss for words."

"You got that right. You jabbered all night, but you didn't say a damn thing. Just a bunch of meaningless words."

"I said things. Everyone seemed interested in what I had to say."

"They acted interested because they're well-bred. No one gives a shit about your trains or the riff-raff that rides on them."

"People love trains. They like to hear about them. They tell me so."

"They tell you so because they're nice. I don't know nobody wants to hear about trains all night. How'd you like it if I started talking about my make-up for hours on end."

"I don't just talk about trains. Only when they seem interested. I talked about a lot of other things. I've got culture."

Latoya laughed.

In the car, Franklin had thought it odd that Latoya reapplied lip gloss and eye shadow, but at her place, he was glad she had. She looked sexy with the candlelight sparkling off her plump, red lips, a metallic sheen around her eyes. They sat quietly together on the loveseat, just looking at each other. Louis Armstrong and Ella Fitzgerald filled the living room with love songs. Latoya sipped blush wine and he drank a light beer. He sighed contentedly.

"You know the interesting thing about Armstrong and Fitzgerald?" he began in a whisper.

She huffed. "Would you drop it already?"

"Drop what?"

"Your auto-talk box!"

He looked at her, confused. "What's eating at you, baby?"

"Know what your problem is? You talk too much, but you don't got nothing to say."

"What're you talking about?"

"I mean, you chitter-chatter away with all this stuff, but you don't got no point. No one cares about "the thing" with dead jazz musicians, any more than they care about the state bird of Maryland, or that the state sport is jousting, or that the Ravens used to be the Colts, or the Browns, or whatever shit it is you're always blabbing about. You say so much stuff but you don't say nothing."

Franklin remained silent for a moment, watching the candle flicker in her wet eyes. "People do care, baby. I talk to people every day, and they like what I have to say. It's just small talk."

"I used to like your small talk too. But after a while, you need more than idle chatter. It's all superficial. What about you, your feelings, us? Who are you, anyway? You ain't got nothing inside. You got no soul."

Franklin felt tears welling in his eyes. "I . . . I don't know what to say, baby."

"That's my point. You gonna keep talking, you've gotta have something to say."

When Franklin got back to the lounge car, he found it nearly empty. The horizon was growing a light shade of pink in the east. For night owls, it was time to go to sleep. For early risers, it was time to start thinking about getting up. The army guy must have still been in military mode, because he was back in the car for a cup of coffee. The old woman, Helen, was still here, but she'd nodded off in her chair. He walked over to her and covered her with a blanket. She seemed to be doing all right now. She'd been scared out of her wits earlier, scared to death of trains. He'd spent some time talking with her to take her mind off it. Just idle chatter, the sort of thing strangers on a train could appreciate.

"I won't lie to you," he'd said to her late in the evening when she'd come back to the lounge car for another screwdriver to calm her, "I do like small talk. If you'd like to chat, I'm right here."

"I would like that," Helen had said.

"I could tell you a lot about trains and the sort of people who ride them. But I reckon you'd rather talk about something else."

"An easier subject, perhaps." She put a finger to her lips, then said, "Death, maybe?"

It startled Franklin, but then she laughed and he realized she was making light of her own fear of trains. "Won't be long now," he said, putting a hand on her arm. "We'll be in Chicago soon. Bet you have a nice family waiting for you at home."

"I was kidding. You *do* want to talk about death?" She gave him a smile to let him know it was more humor—a way to cope. "I've buried my husband, and we never had kids. I have people waiting for me. Neighbors, friends—they're my family."

"That's mighty fine, to have loved ones waiting for you, missing you."

"Yes, it is. What do we have in this life if we don't have other people? Who do you have waiting for you?"

"Oh, I've got a woman waiting for me in Baltimore."

"Married how long?"

Franklin scoffed. "No, not married. Each got our own place. I stay with her and she stays with me. But she has grown kids, you know. She spends her holidays with them and their families. I usually go to my nephew's place for Christmas and Easter and spend it with his family, his kids. So I've got family and a girl. Buddies. And the train. I meet so many good people on the train. Can't ask for much more than that."

"No, you can't." Helen smiled. "You love this woman, or she's just a girl?"

Franklin considered. "I love her. No need for us to dig deep and figure out why. She knows and I know. We're happy."

Helen nodded. "No one waiting in Chicago?"

Franklin frowned. "Oh, no, nothing like that. I'm true to my woman. I have friends in Chicago, but none I plan to call on. I'll be in town a day, then back on the train."

"You love the train as much as I hate it, don't you?"

Franklin nodded. "There's nothing quite like a train. Moments like this. Sometimes I feel like this is my home and my place is somewhere I visit. I plan to be working on the train until the day I die."

Helen smiled. "You must get tired of train food. Where do you like to eat when you're in Chicago?"

Franklin thought about it. "Tell you what I like best: a nice cut of steak at the Chop House. Or a Chicago-style deep-dish pizza. Or some hearty German sausage. Sometimes I like to hit the blues and jazz clubs at night for some drinks and conversation."

"Have you ever tasted homemade perogies? With potato vodka?"

"No, can't say that I've had either one."

"You should try them. Share a cab with me when we get to Chicago and I'll make perogies for lunch."

"Well, now, I don't want to impose."

"Who's imposing? I like talking with you. You're a good man with a day to kill. What would we have in this world without small talk?"

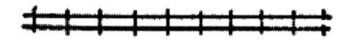

Franklin sat back down in the lounge car, not far from Helen, and looked out the window. The sky was still dark, the shadowy trees backlit by the increasingly pink horizon. The sun was about to begin another round. The train was about to end one.

Truth be told, there wasn't a woman he loved waiting for him in Baltimore. A woman, yes. They hooked up when he was in town, spent nights and days together. But they were lovers without the love. He had his nephew's family to spend the holidays with. But day in and day out, the only family he had was the transient one on the train.

He took a hearty gulp of water. The trains were the same, but they changed with each set of passengers. Every crowd brought the train alive with a new soul.

"Uncle Franklin, tell us train stories," his great nieces and nephews would beg at Thanksgiving. He contemplated what sort of tales he'd picked up from this trip. He looked over at the military man, drinking coffee in the corner. Couldn't tell whether he was happy or apprehensive about his destination. But Franklin imagined he'd be in a war zone soon, and there was little to be happy about there.

Franklin chuckled at his memory of the young poet, who seemed youthfully enthusiastic about scribbling love poems on Amtrak stationery. His smile faded as he considered the brokenhearted woman who'd gotten off in Cincinnati. He pictured Latoya in the candlelight.

Speaking of women, there was that sizzling woman with the tattoo everyone wanted a glimpse of. She'd left the car with that sly guy, the sleaze on the prowl. And then there was that poor young gal whose friend had the heart attack. She looked devastated when all her pumping and breathing couldn't bring the guy back to life. But last he saw her, she'd been sleeping peacefully in her reclined seat.

There were older couples who looked like the same person, young couples interlocking, families with parents and children, uncles and nephews. So many people. So many stories.

"Why, I ought to write a book about it," he said to his reflection in the dark window.

Franklin knew better. He didn't like to write, he liked to talk. His words were meaningless if not living in the air around him, connecting with the words of other people. He looked over at Helen, who slept peacefully as the train's vibration rattled her. He considered their conversation to come. Helen was asleep, but he spoke to her anyway. "Where in the world would we be without idle chatter?"

She's Gone

Hubert laughed out loud, the motion of the train amusing him. He'd been on a train before, years ago, with Mom. He was just a kid when he and Mom had gone to visit Granny and PapPap. Hubert was mesmerized by trains. He even had a train set at home that he played with from time to time. Real trains were more fun than make-believe ones. He looked over at Uncle Ned and grinned. Uncle Ned's straight face curved into a smile in response, but quickly straightened again, like a line of railroad track bending around a hill, then going as the crow flies once more.

"I like trains," Hubert said. He laughed excitedly. "By God, I do like trains!"

"Yes, Hubert, I know." Uncle Ned sighed. "Trains are nice."

Hubert relaxed his oversized smile, sensing Uncle Ned's irritation. He let out another, quieter laugh and mumbled, "You bet they are!" He looked out the window. Little houses decorated the distant hills, like the ones in the Monopoly game he and Mom sometimes played. Once, he'd even played with Mom, Uncle Ned, and Aunt Clara all at once—a big game that lasted a long time. Hubert hadn't won that time. When he and Mom played alone, they usually both won.

They didn't play Monopoly much anymore. Hubert had taken the little green houses and red hotels and put them around his train set. He wondered whether there would be a train set where he was going. "Maybe I can get mine," he said out loud. "I don't mind sharing mine, not one bit. That's how you make friends."

His reflection surrounded the houses on the hill, coming back to him in the window like a ghost in a movie with bad special effects. He was nearly bald now—it ran in the family—and he looked a lot like Dad had before Dad left him and Mom some thirty years ago. Hubert didn't know where Dad was now, but he remembered what Dad had looked like then, like the reflection in the window: shiny, bald head rimmed with a crown of reddish hair, drooping eyes, a plump nose, chubby cheeks, and a chin that hung beneath his head like the ball from the bottom of a train's bell.

Hubert's reflection disappeared as he returned his attention to the next set of hills. The leaves had fallen off the trees and the ground looked like it was covered with an orange-brown carpet. He could see the little houses with their smoking chimneys through the wooden skeletons the leaves had left behind.

He liked playing Monopoly with Mom. He wondered if she'd play with him at his new home. He refocused his attention from the distant hills to his own reflection and saw the joy vanishing from his face like the fading vibrations of a cartoon bell. He remembered, and his chin bobbed as he said, "She's gone."

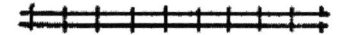

For as long as Hubert could remember, Mom had worried about him. "Don't worry, Mom," Hubert would say. "You don't got to worry about me. I'm fine."

"Of course you are," she'd said with a peaceful smile, but it was the kind of smile she used when she was saying one thing and meaning another.

Hubert was nineteen when his public school graduated him with a participation certificate. Hubert was proud to receive the certificate—and Mom was proud of him too. But one of the mean kids in school who always called him "retard" told him it was nothing more than a paper that said, yes, he had gone to special classes for mentally challenged children for the past twelve years and, no, they hadn't taught him to be an ordinary person, to hide his impairment, or to fit in with "normal" people.

The challenge for Mom after he finished school was to find work for him. For more than six months, Mom hunted while he waited. Filling his empty days with things to do—puzzles, games, learning activities—became increasingly difficult.

Living in a large city was a plus, Mom often said. Baltimore and nearby DC offered lots of options for people like Hubert. She'd finally found him a job at a workshop for adults with mental handicaps, making office supplies. Hubert went with Mom to the manager for an interview. Mom gave most of the information before Hubert even had a chance to say anything, but then the manager asked Hubert questions directly, like did he know how to use a pen, how they worked, could he match these colors, put these papers together in a binder and click the metal rings closed without pinching himself. Hubert passed the tests, and two weeks later they offered him a position.

"You'll like this job," Mom told him. "It'll be fun." Mom drove with Hubert seated next to her, his forehead chilled as it leaned on the cold window.

"I'll show them what I can do, by God," he said.

"That's right," Mom said. "You'll be a regular working man."

"You bet I will! Just like Dad!"

Mom coughed, even though it didn't sound like she needed to. "*Better* than him," she said with a big smile.

Mom walked Hubert into the warehouse. She stayed with him as he got to know the place. Hubert was led to a table where he sat with a pile of pen pieces. It was his job to assemble them: to put the little circular caps on one end and the regular pointy lids on the other end. Mom watched him as he went about his work. It reminded Hubert of when Mom watched him go after jigsaw puzzles, ready to help, but allowing him to show what he could do first. Halfway through the pile, he smiled at Mom. "I'm sure good at this, right?"

"You bet you are." Mom's smile beamed. Hubert could tell she felt better. She'd been worried he wouldn't make it here, wouldn't fit in. And if not here, then where? But he labored happily, doing something productive and feeling good about it. He showed her he could do it. There was a place in the world for people like Hubert. "You sure are good at this," Mom repeated.

Over the years, Hubert became one of the best employees at the workshop. He had a sturdy reputation and was even selected as the Employee of the Month once. He could assemble all sorts of pens: the kind that clicked, the kind that twisted, and—his favorite—the stick pens with pointy caps at one end and circular caps at the other. Those ones were like the wooden pegs of his toy tool bench; they fit neatly together.

"My favorites are the green ones," he'd told his manager once. "They're pretty. And they're like trees, or grass, or green beans."

"Well then, we'll be sure to give you all the green ones," Mrs. Dennison had promised. She hovered in the distance as Hubert worked, always in view, her short, stout body and feathery hair making Hubert think of a cartoon mother hen watching over her young. Sure enough, she made sure Hubert got all the green pens. He'd heard Mrs. Dennison tell Mom that the workshop was as much about helping challenged individuals, after all, as it was about making office supplies. She called Hubert their senior green pen expert.

But Hubert loathed the red ones. The first time Mrs. Dennison waddled over with a case of red pens to put together, Hubert stood and turned away from the sight of them.

"Got any green ones, Mrs. Dennison? I'm good at the green ones."

Mrs. Dennison appeared startled at his reaction, something she hadn't seen in him before. "No, Hubert. I'm afraid I don't. How about blue? I have some blue pens that need to be assembled."

"I can do blue ones too," Hubert said. "Not red ones." Those red circles on the butts of the pens frightened him. They reminded him of a dragonfly's eyes.

Mom didn't like Hubert to talk about Dad. But sometimes he forgot until he'd already mentioned him. He'd seen an old picture of Dad before, from the file box of photographs in the office. In the picture, Dad was younger and he had reddish-brown hair and red eyes. In real life, Hubert remembered Dad's bald head. But he couldn't remember the color of his eyes. Had they really been red, like a dragonfly's?

What he remembered most clearly about Dad was the day he'd left them. Hubert had been eight at the time.

"I just can't deal with it, by God!" Dad had yelled. "I just can't! That's all there is to it!"

"But Hughie, he's your son! He can't help it."

"I didn't say it was his fault, or yours. It is what it is. I'm just not gonna deal with it anymore. It's not in me."

"You can't just abandon us!" Mom had shrieked. "Abandon your son!"

Hubert had never seen a grown-up cry before. But in the entranceway, he watched Mom lose control. When Dad didn't say anything, Mom asked, "You'll send money? Child support?"

Dad had turned and smiled at Hubert. Had that been a red twinkle in his eye? Then he looked back at Mom. "You bet I will," he said. Then he left and never came back.

After Hubert started at the workshop, after he knew what it meant to be a working man, he asked Mom—again—whether Dad was ever coming back.

"Oh, Hubert," Mom said with a sigh. "I don't know." She seemed to be searching for the right answer. "I don't think so."

"Oh," Hubert responded.

"But I do know one thing," Mom said with spring in her voice.

"What?"

"I know that *I'll* never leave you. Not as long as I live." She gave him a big hug.

But now, on the train, she was as out of the picture as Dad. Mom was so much more a part of Hubert than the man he barely knew, but when he looked at his reflection in the train's window again, he saw Dad.

Uncle Ned touched Hubert's shoulder to draw him away from the window. "How about some juice?" he asked. "Let's go to the lounge car and get some juice."

"I like juice," Hubert confirmed. "But you know what? Soda pop's even better. I love pop."

Uncle Ned sighed. "All right, then." He smiled. "You can get a soda."

The two men stood and made their way to the lounge car. The lounge was full of people: an older man scratched notes in a planning calendar like the ones Hubert's workshop made; a man about Uncle Ned's age in a blue blazer and red tie was rubbing at his neck; an old couple drinking iced tea talked about their kids, and that made him think back to when he had both a Mom and Dad. And that made him remember again. "She's gone."

"Here's your soda," Uncle Ned said with a forced smile. "That is, if you still want it."

Instantly, Hubert bubbled back to an excited eagerness. "You bet I do," he said, taking the beverage. "I sure do like pop!"

"It's even better on a train ride, isn't it?" Uncle Ned asked in a sing-song voice.

Hubert giggled. "By God it is, Uncle Ned!" He took an excited gulp. "You bet it is!"

Uncle Ned was Mom's brother. He and Aunt Clara lived in Chicago. They'd flown to Baltimore for Mom's funeral. Aunt Clara had to work, so she'd returned after four days. Uncle Ned had work too, but he stayed behind to take care of things. Things like the house and Mom's stuff. Things like Hubert.

"Juice is pretty good on a train too," Uncle Ned said, putting the bottle to his lips. Uncle Ned used to be as bald as Hubert, but now he had a little bit of hair that a doctor had put there. Uncle Ned was bigger than Hubert—a little shorter, but a lot wider. He wore a button-down shirt, open at the collar, and a tan blazer that matched his Dockers. "And juice is good for you."

Regret pulled Hubert down as the bubbles fizzed out of his drink. "Pop's bad for you."

Uncle Ned smiled slightly. "It's all right to drink it once in a while. It sure does taste good. Especially on a train."

"You got that right, Uncle Ned!" Hubert laughed out loud and took another gulp.

Uncle Ned had been the nicest of his family members since Mom had died almost two weeks ago. He stayed with Hubert when everyone else went back to their own lives. Uncle Ned talked with Hubert, cried with him, hugged him. He took care of the house and the things, all the paperwork and business of the grown-up world that Hubert never could understand. Hubert could make the pens and planners that kept the world in motion, but he could not use them himself. He knew he was an important part of the system, but he didn't understand how the system worked or how he fit in.

He didn't have to tell Uncle Ned that he was afraid of airplanes or that he loved trains; his uncle already knew it and had arranged for their trip from Baltimore to Chicago. "He needs all the comfort he can get right now," Uncle Ned had told Aunt Clara on the phone when she began to gripe that the train took too long.

Hubert was comfortable now as he looked at the people around them in the lounge car. He spotted a pretty woman with a big tattoo on her back. "I like her tattoo," he said excitedly, pointing to it and smiling. Uncle Ned looked too.

The woman frowned at Hubert and Uncle Ned. Uncle Ned said in a soft voice, "I know it's pretty, but it's not nice to point."

Hubert gulped his soda. He looked around. He saw a man writing notes with a pencil in a spiral notebook and wondered if one of the pens he made at the workshop might be easier for the writer to use. Then he spotted something else of interest. "A really old lady," he said softly. Then he pointed and said in a loud voice, "Look! She got old!"

The woman looked startled, short of breath. Uncle Ned hushed Hubert. Hubert asked, "Why didn't Mom get old, like her?"

"Some people just live longer than others," Uncle Ned said, placing a hand on Hubert's shoulder. "It was Mom's time."

"But why?"

Uncle Ned looked uncomfortably at the old woman's back as she walked away. "Nobody can really explain it, Hubert. Your mom just had a different path."

Hubert and Ned stood quietly for a while, sipping their drinks. Hubert looked out the window and watched the fields of farmland flying by. Then he noticed another figure, seated near one of the windows. "Look, a soldier! Just like my army men!"

The young man in uniform looked over at them, his rigid face hardening.

Uncle Ned led Hubert to another part of the lounge car, away from the man in uniform, the woman with the tattoo and the woman who had been lucky enough to grow old.

The conductor, who'd punched their tickets earlier, was here. "Hello there," he said, greeting them with a cheery smile. He reminded Hubert of the conductor from *The Polar Express*, only he had black skin instead of white and no big, broom-like mustache.

"You have a nice train," Hubert said.

The conductor smiled. "You enjoying the ride?"

"You bet I am!" Hubert laughed out loud.

"Are you and your dad on vacation?"

Hubert looked around the car for Dad, confused.

"I'm his uncle," Uncle Ned explained.

Hubert looked at Uncle Ned, then back at the conductor. "Me and Uncle Ned are going to my new home."

The conductor smiled, but he looked like he needed to get away, like he was busy. "Well, that sounds great. You gentlemen have a nice trip." He left for another corner of the lounge to talk with the lady who was old.

Hubert spotted a lady sitting with a big, yellow-brown piece of paper. The woman looked up from the paper with teary eyes. Hubert offered her a big grin, wishing he could take her tears away. When she responded by turning and gazing out the window, Hubert noticed the decorative pin on her breast. Long and silver, the pin spread mother-of-pearl wings and peered out from her chest with red-hot eyes. It was a dragonfly. Its eyes stared into him, just like the ones on the lamp. He turned to face Uncle Ned.

"Can we go now?"

"Let's just finish our drinks first, all right?"

"No, I want to go now." He felt the redness brighten his face and neck. "Can we please go now?"

Uncle Ned sighed. "All right, Hubert, we'll go." They exited the lounge car, Hubert hurrying in front, and returned to their seats.

Back in his place, Hubert looked out the window at the autumn landscape but could not get the dragonflies to stop buzzing in his head. The dragonfly lamp was gone too. The lamp was gone, but the dragonflies remained in his mind and in the things that reminded him of them, just as his mother was with him even though she was in heaven. Mom still watched over him, but the dragonflies hovered there too.

Mom had a lot of unusual collectables in the house. She was a collector of odds and ends, "but mostly odds," Aunt Clara had once joked. Mom called her display pieces her own personal museum. The things she put on exhibit pleased her and caught the attention of visitors, but they sometimes scared Hubert.

There was the gray stone carving of elephants, four of them, each standing on the other's back. The elephants had netted skin and you could see a smaller elephant inside each one. The smaller elephants were caged inside the bigger ones; the bigger ones were carved open to display the smaller ones. Hubert couldn't decide who had it worse.

In the corner stood the wooden statue of men sitting one atop the other, elbows on knees and heads on hands. It had been as tall as Hubert when Mom had bought it, although he had grown and it had not.

The mask collection hung on one wall, more than a dozen masks from Africa, New Orleans, and Asia—Mom had them all labeled. The monkey figurines, the naked man and woman, the Native American tomahawk, headdress, and peace pipe—they didn't seem very peaceful to him. The devil carved from black wood reminded him of an ancient carving on an old *Brady Bunch* episode that put a curse on the family during their island vacation. The chest of coins from around the world reminded him of an old Saturday afternoon movie where people who dug up the treasure were haunted by a dead mummy wrapped in sheets. The Chinese statue reminded him of the smoky basement shop of a scary movie. These terrifying treasures stayed in the formal room—Mom's personal museum — and he stayed out.

When Mom first brought the lamp home and put it on the living room end table, it had appeared frightening enough. Then, she plugged it in and turned it on. It cast a twisted, shadowy light of dark blue with accents of blood red across her face. The glow of the lamp made Hubert shudder.

"I don't like it, Mom," he said. "Not one bit."

"Nonsense, Hubert," she said, admiring it. "It's a Tiffany lamp. And it's beautiful."

Two feet tall, the base was a blackened-silver metal, colorless dragonflies molded on the foot. Two balls hung on silver chains from the fixture. And on top of it all, the awful umbrella of stained glass. Uneven cuts of glass tainted the ugliest of colors pressed together in a metal web, oozing down from the pointed, metal cap. First, cuts of dull blue-green, then purple-brown, then amber. Jewels of green, red, purple, and yellow peeked out from the dripping shards. Along the bottom half of the stained-glass shade danced the dragonflies, their ivory wings touching one another like paper cut-out children holding hands. They had green bodies that ran up the center of the shade, cutting through the colored glass like knives. Worst of all, their beady scarlet eyes stared out in every direction. They peered into Hubert and they knew he was a slow learner. The dragonflies weren't fooled by his encouraging mother or his good job; they made him think of the kids in school who called him "Hubert the half-wit."

No matter where in the living room Hubert went, he could not escape their creepy eyes. He even began to hear them buzzing.

He feared they might fly right off the edge of the stained-glass shade and surround his own bald head in the same formation.

"Please, Mom!" A few minutes of staring at the lamp—of the dragonflies staring at him—had Hubert hysterical. "Please take it to the bad room! It scares me!"

"Hubert?" Mom's happy face grew sad when she turned from the lamp to see Hubert's fit. "Oh, Hubert." She hugged him, patted his back. "It's okay, Hubert. It's just a lamp."

"But I don't like them!"

Mom looked at the lamp and it seemed she saw the dragonflies for the first time. "We'll just move it to the museum room." She took his hands and held them tightly. "Why don't you go wash your face and I'll make you a nice bowl of tomato soup and a grilled cheese sandwich. Does that sound good?"

"Yes," he said, unsure. "But you're gonna move the lamp first, right?"

"Of course I will. You go on and wash up. The room will look a lot better when you come back down."

Hubert brightened. "You bet it will!" He went to the staircase. "Don't forget the pickle!"

"I won't," she said. She smiled at him and turned to unplug the lamp. When Hubert saw her coil the cord and lift the lamp, he felt relieved and bounded up the stairs.

A few weeks after Mom got the dragonfly lamp, Uncle Ned and Aunt Clara paid a visit. When they came, they always enjoyed a tour of Mom's museum room, expecting a new piece or two to be there.

"Oh, you finally got it!" Aunt Clara cheered when she saw the lamp on the table. "It's wonderful."

"It is a nice lamp," Uncle Ned agreed.

"Oh, I'd love one like this." Aunt Clara put her hands around it, feeling its heat. "It really looks good in here." Aunt Clara thought everything looked good in Mom and Hubert's house.

"Maybe someday," Uncle Ned said, feeling the web-like covering of the dragonfly wings. "When you give up your baskets and figurines."

"I'll never give up my Longabergers and Hummels." She looked around the room. "But I'd almost consider it to take up something eclectic like this."

Hubert had wished they would take the lamp back with them when they left. When Uncle Ned and Aunt Clara flew back to Chicago at the end of their visit, the dragonflies could fly right along with them. But the dragonflies stayed behind. After a week, Mom and Hubert drove Uncle Ned and Aunt Clara to the airport and bid their farewells until the next visit. When Mom and Hubert returned home in the dark, their guests were gone, but the dragonfly lamp remained on the museum room's end table, hot, red eyes burning.

Mom went for a run every morning. She always told Hubert, still in bed, that she was going and she'd be back in half an hour. She got back in time to help him get ready, have breakfast with him, and drive him to work on the way to her job at the American Visionary Art Museum. It was her job at the museum that started her collecting unusual pieces.

At first, Hubert didn't notice Mom had stopped running. After a couple weeks, when he saw her blue sneakers in the basement one afternoon, it occurred to him. "Did you get too tired?"

"Tired?" she asked, stirring curry in a pot.

"Too tired to run? You don't run anymore."

"Oh," she sighed. "Well, I just haven't felt like running lately." She looked tired, now that he noticed: bags under her eyes, a slouched posture, the wooden spoon heavy in her hand. "Yes, I guess I'm a little tired."

She was so tired, in fact, that after giving up running she gave up working too. Mrs. Dennison began picking up Hubert in the mornings and driving him home in the evenings. Mom remained in bed until the doctors said she needed to go to the hospital.

Uncle Ned and Aunt Clara came from Chicago to visit. They usually came a couple times a year, but this wasn't one of their regular visits. Aunt Clara said they were happy to see Hubert, but they looked awfully sad for happy people. They went into Mom's room while Hubert waited on a bench in the hospital's white hall. Soon, Aunt Clara came out and left Uncle Ned in the room with Mom.

"How are you doing, Hubert?" Aunt Clara asked, her eyes red from crying.

"I'm doing a-okay." He looked up at the ceiling, down at the floor, then around at the sterile walls. "I like hospitals," he said. "They're nice and clean and don't have so many decorations. And you don't need lamps 'cause all the lights are right in the ceiling." He laughed, but he sensed something was wrong. Aunt Clara said nothing, nodding but not really listening.

The door opened and Uncle Ned stepped out. "Hubert," he said. "Your mother wants to talk to you."

"Good! My turn!" Hubert jumped from his seat and laughed as though this were a sort of game. But he sensed that something was out of place—after all, hospitals were for sick people. He created his own cheer, wanting to make Mom feel less tired. He entered Mom's room and when he saw her with tubes in her nose and arm, he could feel the smile spill from his face.

"Come here, Hubert," she said. A nearby machine pinged.

"What's wrong, Mom?" Hubert asked. The room smelled funny, like the smell in a dentist's chair right before the sound of the drill.

"How are you, Hubert?"

"Okay, Mom, but what's wrong? What are they doing to you? Does it hurt?"

"No, Hubert. Don't worry. You know I love you."

"Yes." Hubert looked down the way he did when he was ashamed, but he didn't recognize the helpless feeling welling up inside him now. He wanted to scream and thrash his arms, but he wanted to roll up and be still at the same time. Confused, he simply looked at Mom.

Mom placed her hand on his. "Uncle Ned and Aunt Clara love you too."

He looked down at his lap, embarrassed again. "I know."

"They're going to take you to Chicago. There's a nice place there—like the workshop—where you can stay with new friends, people like you, where nice people will take care of you and help you."

Hubert looked up from his lap and into Mom's deep, blue eyes. "I don't want to go there! I want to stay here with you and work for Mrs. Dennison and make pens and stay with you. You can just sleep if you're tired. I'll work harder. I'll even try to do the red ones."

"It's a nice place, Hubert," Mom repeated. "You'll have your own apartment. And they'll fix nice meals for you. You'll have games and activities. And if you want, you can get a job like the one you have here. Or if you'd prefer they have things you can do, like games and field trips, movies and activities and—"

"Are you coming too?"

As the tears welled up in her crystal blue eyes, they shone like jewels. "No, Hubert. I'm going away."

"Where?"

"I'm going to a nice place too...to heaven."

"No, Mom! I want you to stay here. I want us to go back home! I like our home. By God, I do! Let's go home, Mom!"

Mom placed a shaky finger on Hubert's lips and hushed him. "Don't worry, Hubert. You'll like your new home. And I'll always be with you, even when I'm in heaven."

Hubert cried out loud. In time, his crying stopped and the two of them shared their final moments together. The tears would return, and leave again, and it would happen over and over until all that was left was the memory of her smile and her blue eyes.

Mom didn't want to die, but more than that, Hubert knew she didn't want to leave him alone in the world. "Don't worry, Mom," he said. "You don't got to worry about me. I'm gonna be fine."

But Mom wasn't worrying anymore. Her eyes were closed, her chest still, and a peaceful smile covered her lips. The machines around her began to make loud noises and the nurses and doctor rushed in and brushed Hubert aside. They put irons on her chest and made her jump, stuck big balloons on her face and squeezed them, but she didn't open her eyes. A nurse noticed Hubert still in the room, watching with wide, confused eyes; she put an arm around him and escorted him to the door.

"I don't want to leave," he yelled.

"I'm sorry," the nurse said. "You can wait with your family outside."

"I don't want to leave!" Hubert screamed and thrashed his arms. But the nurse sent him out and closed the door to Mom's room. When he saw Uncle Ned and Aunt Clara standing in the bright hall, Hubert lay on the floor, rolled up into a ball, and cried.

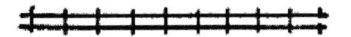

The day after the funeral, Uncle Ned and Aunt Clara went back to Hubert's home. There was lots of food from people—friends, neighbors, co-workers—and even more flowers. Uncle Ned sat on the couch in the living room while Aunt Clara went to the museum room and admired Mom's collection. Hubert brought his army men to the living room and played with them on the rug, one killing another and then bringing them back to life. He could bring the plastic men back to life, but not Mom.

Aunt Clara came to the living room with the dragonfly lamp and put it on the table.

"That doesn't go in here," Hubert insisted. "It goes in the museum room."

Aunt Clara smiled. "We'll just see how it looks in here." She plugged it in, turned it on, and sat next to Uncle Ned.

"But it goes in there!" Hubert pointed to the museum room.

Aunt Clara ignored him. "She sure built up a fine collection," she said, admiring the lamp. "Very nice legacy."

"Yes," Uncle Ned said, not really paying attention. "Everything belongs to Hubert now."

Army men still in hand, Hubert looked at him. "To me?"

"Yup," he said, staring blankly into space.

"We'll want to keep some of your mom's nicer things," Aunt Clara said. "To remember her by." From her seat, she put her hand on the dragonfly lamp.

Hubert stared directly at the lamp. The dragonflies stared back. They knew he was slow and weren't fooled by the fact that he owned them now or that he was moving to that nice place in Chicago. Hubert looked away from the lamp and back at Uncle Ned. "It's all mine now?"

"That's right," Uncle Ned answered. He remained somewhere else, distant.

"It's all mine now!" Hubert giggled. "I can do whatever I want with it now!"

Hubert's outburst woke Uncle Ned momentarily from his daze; Uncle Ned and Aunt Clara gave Hubert wide-awake looks in response to his reaction. So did the dragonflies. His army men were still in his hands.

"We'll sell the house," Uncle Ned said. "And most of her things. You can't take all this with you to Chicago. But the money's yours. It'll pay for your new home."

"And we'll keep some of your mom's collection at our place, so you can visit it." Aunt Clara reminded him.

"All mine now," he muttered. "I'll do whatever I want with it, by God!" He glared at the lamp.

Aunt Clara leaned into Uncle Ned on the sofa. "She had wonderful taste."

Hubert's action figures had finished their battle, killing one another off. He stood and dropped them to the floor. He walked to the end table and faced the blood-red eyes of the dragonflies. "I hate you." He started soft, then built into a yell, a confident scream. "I hate you, by God! I hate you!"

Uncle Ned looked as though he thought Hubert were talking about him. "It's okay to be angry, Hubert. It's not easy."

"You're mine now. You don't belong to Mom no more! You're all mine!" He grabbed the lamp by its base.

"Be careful, Hubert," Aunt Clara warned.

"It's mine!" he reminded her. He yanked the cord from the outlet and the two bulbs flickered out.

"Stop it!" Uncle Ned stood and put his hands on the base of the lamp. But Hubert held his ground, yanked the lamp from Uncle Ned, and ran out of his reach. Then, with all his strength, Hubert threw the Tiffany lamp across the living room and into the museum room where it belonged.

"Oh my God!" Aunt Clara gasped.

"Hubert, no!" Uncle Ned yelled. But it was too late. The lamp—dragonflies and all—crashed into the glass shelves that held so many of Mom's collectibles. The dragonfly lamp, the glass shelves and the collectibles crashed down to the hardwood floor. Hubert went to the heap and looked down at what he had done. He laughed at the jeweled eyes, no longer connected to the wings or the knife-like bodies. The dragonflies no longer belonged to Mom. Without her to protect them, he'd exterminated them.

Hubert went back to the living room as Uncle Ned and Aunt Clara went to pick through the remains. Hubert picked up his army men. They'd all killed one another, but he brought them back to life.

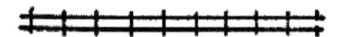

On the train, Hubert peered out the window. Cows grazed on a grassy hill. He turned to tell Mom—she loved to look at cows too, and to mimic their sounds with him—but when he saw Uncle Ned looking back at him, he remembered. "She's gone," he whispered, looking back to the window.

Uncle Ned put a hand on Hubert's knee. "You're really going to like your new home at the center. Your very own apartment. All kinds of foods you like: steak, mashed potatoes, green beans. And games, field trips, all kinds of activities."

"And a job if I want it," Hubert added.

"That's right. And, of course, Aunt Clara and I will visit you every week. And you can visit our house sometimes."

"And we'll go to the Brookfield Zoo." Hubert remembered promises, even though some of them were broken. *I know that I'll never leave you.* Mom's long-ago words echoed in his mind.

"That's right." Uncle Ned smiled. "We're close to the zoo."

Hubert turned back to the cows. "I wish I could have a cow," he said.

Uncle Ned laughed. "Cows are too big. Maybe a fish."

"Oh, yeah, a fish," he said excitedly. "A goldfish, by God! And I can take care of it—I had a goldfish once, before it died. But I won't let this one die, no way!"

"Maybe we'll get you a goldfish," Uncle Ned said, "after you're settled in. Amazing how much joy and excitement a quarter can still buy."

"And I'll name it Mom."

Uncle Ned looked confused. "That's...nice."

Hubert heard a buzzing in the window. He turned to see a horsefly there, hovering against the inside of the glass, trying to fly out through the transparent wall. The fly buzzed just the way he'd heard the dragonflies buzz—in a laughter that mocked him. Hubert saw the dragonflies in his head, staring at him. He'd killed the dragonflies on the lamp, but still they haunted him sometimes, in the things that reminded him of them. His mother had gone to heaven, but part of her remained in his heart and made him want to be strong, to be good. He thought of Mom's deep, comforting eyes and ignored the irritating buzz in the window. A moment later, the horsefly flew away.

New Course

Inside the train's washroom, Gene Silverman finished his shower. He didn't have a towel with him, so he slicked the water off with his hands and allowed himself to air dry as he went to the mirror. He plugged in his electric razor and shaved, then brushed his teeth. It was still dark out and he knew he had plenty of time before arriving in Chicago, but passengers would line up for the showers with the rising of the sun, so he decided to get ready for his speaking engagement early. As he dressed, the train swept through middle Indiana.

Gene eased open the washroom door and prepared to amble out, then stopped dead in his tracks. Instead of an empty hall, he found the gruff man who'd been watching everyone from the corner of the lounge car.

Watching me, Gene realized for the first time as he noted determination in the man's eyes. "Excuse me," Gene said casually, trying to pass.

"Afraid it's too late for excuses," the man mumbled. He poked a silver cylinder further through a hole in his jacket pocket. Gene knew at once it was a silencer—and where there was a silencer and a man like this, there was sure to be a gun connecting them. "You're staying in the shower."

Gene stared at the barrel poking through the leather. Panicked, he hoped for a reason besides the obvious and searched for an escape. He must have looked rich to the thief, silver briefcase and ring and his air of importance. "What do you want? Money?"

"Turn around," the man said.

"I've got a few hundred on me. You can have it."

"Turn around," he repeated, so close Gene could feel the spittle on his face.

"You, there!" A voice called from down the hall. It was the conductor, still wearing his Amtrak uniform, cap and all.

"It can wait," the armed man insisted. The employee didn't seem to be aware of the hidden gun.

"No, you, in the bathroom," the conductor persisted. "Is that your briefcase in the lounge car? The silver one? It's yours, isn't it?"

Gene looked nervously at the gunman, who nodded his permission. "Yes," Gene said weakly.

The conductor sighed. "Well, you know you really should let someone know when you leave something like that behind." He stood right next to both of them now. "It's easy to cause a scare these days. You know, explosives and terrorists and all."

The gunman looked shaken by the intrusion, but he kept his aim on Gene. "We'll be back to get it," he said. Whatever he had planned was getting mucked up; the conductor would be able to identify him.

The Amtrak man scratched at the five o'clock shadow that had grown on his face since leaving Baltimore. "Thought I ought to check," he said with a smile. "Can't be too safe, you know, these days. Don't want anyone getting hurt."

"Nobody's hurt," the thug said stiffly.

Gene saw an out. "Be a good man and bring it to me, would you? I'd really appreciate it."

The crook's eyes widened, his face stiffening, rock hard. "No. Don't."

The conductor considered them. "Well, I suppose I could fetch it for you." He looked at each of them in turn. The gunman inched closer to Gene, as though to block him from exiting the washroom.

The conductor examined them quizzically. "I'm sorry fellas, only one person in the shower at a time."

"Fine," the thug said, still looking at Gene. "He's not finished yet. I'll wait out here 'till he's done."

The conductor wasn't convinced. He stood directly next to the gruff man and placed a hand on his leathery arm. "There's two washrooms in each sleeper car."

"No," the thug insisted. "I want this one."

The conductor huffed. "I try to have a good thing to say to everyone, but you've been nothing but trouble this whole trip—with your cigarettes and stubbornness and I don't know what all. You're not even supposed to use the showers if you're in general seating."

Gene's mind raced as his adversary listened to the conductor. By now, he realized this was not an ordinary thief; had this been a robbery, the thug would've simply let them both go and moved on to an easier victim. No, this man was after *him* alone. A professional hit man stood before him. He couldn't believe he hadn't picked up on it right away, yesterday, when he'd first seen him on the train. All these years of paranoia had become such an internalized part of him that when the hit man finally struck, he didn't even notice it. There was only one person who would hire someone to do this... and Gene knew the Boss's killer of choice, even though they'd never met.

The hit man hardened as he responded to the conductor in a low voice. "If you know what's good for you, old man, you'll turn around and leave. Now." But Gene could see the job was already botched; the conductor would be able to tie him to any murder that took place on the train. Gene sighed at the relief of knowing he'd escaped by a stroke of luck. Or had it been intuition that made him leave his briefcase behind? Saving his seat may have saved his life.

"I'm not accustomed to being bossed around on my own train, mister."

Gene was tempted to point out the gun hidden in the leather jacket, the conductor still unaware of it. But if this was who Gene thought it was, that would probably just mean both of them being killed. In fact, Gene feared that was the direction this was going. Better to have the sole witness leave and come back than stay and get shot. Or maybe this was an opportunity to take his own leave. "I'd better go get that briefcase," Gene said, wondering whether it could be so easy.

The professional's temper nearly burst. "No, we've got unfinished business." He turned to the conductor. "Look, I'm sorry if I'm a little testy. He and I've got a private matter to work out. If you'll just go back and keep an eye on that briefcase, we'll be there to pick it up pronto. He and I work together. And there'll be a big tip in it for you, for your trouble."

The conductor took off his cap and rubbed his sweaty head with a red bandana. "Well, I've got no use for your tip. But I'll make sure the case isn't stolen." He capped himself and eyed the two of them suspiciously. Then he turned and left the car.

Gene's nerves shuddered when saw the silver tube poking through the leather again. The assassin glanced around, left, then right. Nobody else stood in the car. "Get back in the washroom."

"Charlie," Gene said, trying to sound confident as he trembled and peered into the cold, empty eyes.

"Name doesn't matter," Charlie said in his low, gravelly voice. "What matters is that you don't leave this train...alive."

Gene could feel his heart pumping too rapidly and he knew he looked as nervous as he felt. He took a deep breath to steady himself as they bounced along with the train's movement. "I'll pay you whatever he's paying," Gene pleaded, partly because he would, partly because it bought him time. All he needed was for another person to walk into the car, see the gun, see the murderer. His attempt to show strength faltered as his voice quaked. "Let me go, tell the Boss you got me, and you can collect from both of us. I'll lay low, leave the country, stop my speaking racket, get a new identity, start a new career. I'll be as good as dead to you and the Boss."

Firmly, the hit man spoke, his gun now in full view. "Good as dead ain't good enough. Shut up and turn around. Now."

Gene twisted around. Having his back to the killer was even more unnerving than facing him and his gun. He continued to grovel. "That conductor was already suspicious. He'll ID you."

"I said I'd give him a tip," he said, pressing the tip of his silencer into the back of Gene's head and making him cringe. "Now get in there."

"What if you can't get him alone? He's the conductor. Is it worth the risk?"

"Not your problem."

Gene stalled. "At your age, you'd be locked up for the rest of your life. No retirement years. No time with your family, your boy." Gene remembered the information file from his days with the Boss. "He's nearly an adult now, isn't he?"

Charlie pressed the gun into his neck, pushing him hard. "I can make this painful."

Reluctantly, Gene began to inch into the washroom. Before he made it all the way in, he heard one of the sleeping compartment doors open at the far end of the hall. Gene recognized the voice as it spoke into the room, still unaware of the murder about to take place. It was that drunk who'd picked up the tattooed girl—Murdock, he'd overheard in the lounge car last night. Gene tried to figure out a way to get Murdock to save his ass, but it was hard to think with a .22 to the back of his head. Charlie remained silent as they listened. Gene realized Charlie was just as disoriented as he, trying to figure out what to do now.

Gene could barely make out the woman's soft voice from the distant compartment. "There's always something to live for."

Murdock, still oblivious to them, spoke back into the room from the doorway. "But sometimes that something ain't enough."

Gene felt the gun move away from him. He peeked over his shoulder and sensed Charlie's quiet confusion. The gun was back in the pocket of his leather jacket. Exhausted, Gene released a heavy breath.

"Get in there," Charlie whispered, shoving him further into the shower. But Gene knew this was his only opportunity, so he took it. With the rocking of the train, he shoved back until both he and Charlie stood outside the washroom, in the center of the hallway's path.

Gene registered renewed anxiety on his attacker's face; they both looked over as Murdock closed the compartment door and turned to see them. After the initial surprise of spotting them, Murdock fell back into his uncaring expression and walked toward them nonchalantly. "Morning," he said, rattling an orange-brown pill bottle in his hand.

"There's another bathroom in the next car," Charlie grunted as Murdock closed the distance between them. The three men stood together now, in a tense triangle. Charlie looked edgy, having lost control of the situation yet again.

"I need a drink, not a bathroom." Murdock said.

"Shut up and leave us alone." The gravity in Charlie's voice sounded like it could crush them all. Gene looked at Murdock, trying to figure out how to turn this intrusion into an escape route.

Murdock pointed his head at the washroom. "Is there drinking water in there?" He spilled pills into his hand and began counting them.

Charlie hardened. "No. Go to the bar."

Hoping to prolong the intrusion, Gene jabbered. "There's tap water. No water fountain, just from the sink faucet. You could use that."

Murdock sighed. "I hate tap water."

"Sorry to disappoint you," Gene said.

"Disappointment." Murdock swallowed a pill dry. "Story of my life."

"Cut the bullshit," Charlie said, "and get out."

A thin strand of bravery appeared within Gene's fear. "You can't kill us both," he said in a last-ditch effort to throw Charlie off guard. "Shoot one of us, the other will overtake you."

"Kill? What are you talking about? We're just talking business." Charlie played innocent, but anger filled his brown eyes where the emptiness had been. Gene knew that Charlie had no question regarding his target. If only one person went down, it would be him.

Murdock didn't even flinch, unfazed by the mention of a gun. He pinched another pill from his hand and popped it into his mouth, swallowing hard. "The ones I took when I woke up already kicked in. These ones aren't far behind." He let the remaining pills drop from his palm back into the bottle and capped it. "Won't be feeling any pain today." He looked up at Charlie and Gene with a cloudy expression. "But I could use a drink." As casually as he'd come, he walked out of the car toward the lounge.

Coldness clouded Charlie's eyes again and they appeared empty, as though no soul lived behind them. "Where were we?"

Gene felt like he'd taken a handful of Murdock's drugs, adrenaline racing through him. He took a deep breath and resumed pleading for his life. "Charlie, you know you can't do me here on the train. Not now. Two witnesses put us together. If I'm found dead, you're found guilty."

For a moment, Gene was certain this was it, that the killer was so consumed by his mission and angered by the intrusions that he'd pull the trigger regardless of consequence. Then, a nervous twitch on the killer's face changed everything. There was the click of the safety being put in place. Charlie let go of the gun and left it in his pocket. Gene held back a reflexive smirk, barely believing he'd escaped.

Charlie's face tensed. "You think you're gonna walk? Better watch your back when you step off this train." His hand drew back and then pounded Gene's gut, knocking the wind out of him. Then Charlie slammed down with his fist on Gene's hunched over spine, knocking him to the floor. "See you in Chicago, whiz kid."

When Gene pulled himself back to his feet, Charlie was gone. *Now what?* He considered calling the cops, having them ready at the station when the train arrived. Charlie had the gun on him and there were witnesses who could verify their struggle.

No. He couldn't tell the authorities what had happened. Even if it got rid of Charlie, there would be someone to take his place. Gene remembered the vast database on the Boss's computer. And there would be too many questions about his own connections to a past life he knew he'd be wiser to forget. *Better to leave well enough alone.* He was well enough, after all.

The sun was on the rise, but shadows lurked in the hallway of the sleeper car. He returned to the lounge and retrieved his silver briefcase. After thanking the annoyed conductor for keeping an eye on it, he left the lounge and found his seat in the passenger car. He tried to get comfortable, but could not. He twitched and felt his heart pounding irregularly in his chest. There was no sign of Charlie, but he knew the hit man was watching.

They were due to arrive in Chicago in another twenty minutes. Gene's lively nerves buzzed. He couldn't wait to get off the train, but he feared what he might find when he did.

All of these years, Gene had feared exactly this, but had convinced himself he was only being paranoid. How did that Nirvana song go? *Just because you're paranoid doesn't mean they're not after you.* Gene had every reason to worry now, every motive to flee the country, shed his identity, and begin a quieter, simpler life. If he was able to give Charlie the slip now, he still had a price on his head, and it was sure to get more expensive. He'd been warned.

Now he wished he had met with the feds when they'd called him all those years ago. Perhaps it wasn't too late. He looked out the window at the urban sprawl. Maybe instead of fleeing the country he should call the FBI, work out a deal, come clean. Betray the Boss and redeem himself, earn his silver. He'd never before considered that betrayal and redemption could be one and the same.

It would be easy to make the call. But he thought about how difficult one little call could make the months that followed. Was that what it would take to allow him to face forward and stop looking behind him?

Gene had learned early in life how to wipe a computer clean; then he'd learned how to wipe his own slate clean. He'd restarted so many times, he couldn't keep track. *Resetting a life can be as easy as resetting a computer.*

Any moment now, the Cardinal would pull into Chicago's Union Station. Gene breathed more easily at the thought of slipping slyly off the train. It wouldn't be as simple to slither out of this dangerous existence into a new, secure one—but he'd give it a shot. Better than getting shot, which he'd just barely escaped.

Gene imagined what new life he could conjure and where it might be. Chicago was as good a place as any to start out, just for a week or so, until he decided which country to inhabit. Chicago was large and diverse—an easy place to get lost.

He would get a new Social Security number, new credit cards, driver's license, passport. A new name, of course. Perhaps a little face work to go along with a new hair color. A long vacation to the European countryside wasn't a bad idea. He had enough stashed away.

His gut still ached from Charlie's fist and his back was killing him. He could use an adjustment. He visualized himself leaving the bustling station, inching farther away from the train and the struggle with Charlie. He imagined the distance between his old life and his new one expanding until he managed to escape the train station and Charlie and Gene Silverman altogether.

He'd stayed at the nearby Hotel Monaco before. He couldn't remember who had recommended it to him years ago. He'd check in under a fake name, say he'd lost his wallet, and pay cash up front. That would ensure his privacy. He'd stay put a week or so, his only companion the hotel's signature goldfish in his room, while he worked on sorting out his new identity. Once Gene Silverman was dead, he and his new name could slip away on a ship to Europe via Canada where he could lay low and map a new course. He contemplated which country to settle into. The world was a big place, after all, and the possibilities were infinite.

The passengers stood and collected their baggage. The conductor had already begun saying his goodbyes to people as they prepared to leave the train. Gene looked behind him. No sign of Charlie anywhere. Looking back was only slowing him down. He took a deep breath and faced forward.

Late Lunch

The morning sun lit up the cars of the train as Franklin walked through them. A few passengers still snoozed in their seats, but most of them were wide awake, ready to enter the new day in a new city. They were only minutes from Chicago, the Cardinal's final destination. For the sake of the sleepers, he made the announcement—just a part of his job as *the conductor*.

"We'll be blowing into the Windy City momentarily, folks. Please make sure you collect all your belongings. Don't want you leaving anything behind."

Rustling, muttering, some stretches and yawns; Franklin was used to the sounds of dawn on the train.

He saw Christi, the thirty-something businesswoman, sitting impatiently in her seat and raring to go make a splash in a new place. He couldn't blame her for wanting to get off this train, after she'd tried to save a fellow passenger's life and failed. *That's two men she lost.* She looked anxious, excited—but a tinge of sadness remained in her eyes, as though a piece of her remained in Baltimore. *She left everything behind for this.*

He placed a hand on her shoulder. "Best of luck to you at your new job. Why, I remember when I was fresh on the train. Whole life ahead of me. You may be a little unsure now going in, but there's nothing like the excitement of starting a new job and going to new places."

She looked up and smiled. "Thanks. I'm sure I'll do fine at work. It's finding people that might be a challenge."

"People are everywhere," Franklin said with a wink. "Pretty girl like you? Won't have any trouble finding friends in Chicago." He gave her shoulder a squeeze, and walked on. He believed what he said. She was a bright woman and would fit in well. But he knew what she was feeling. It was nothing unusual in this day and age to be surrounded by millions of people and still be the loneliest person in the world.

The young lovers directly behind Christi twittered with excitement, like hummingbirds who'd found a new feeder filled with syrup. The boy's book had been stashed away and the two of them giggled and pointed out the window at the urban landscape passing by.

"First visit to Chicago," Franklin said, more an observation than a question. The youngsters looked at him with wound-up grins.

"First time anywhere this far from home," Tina said. Malcolm put his arm around her and squeezed.

"You'll have a lot of fun in the Windy City," Franklin said.

Tina took a deep breath. "There's so much to do. Our friends are going to show us around. The Field Museum, art museum, planetarium, Magnificent Mile, Navy Pier, Grant Park..."

Malcolm interjected. "Ed Debevic's for lunch today, Hard Rock for dinner, Michael Jordan's place for lunch tomorrow—and the Bulls and the Bears..."

Franklin interrupted them with his laughter. "Don't you kids try to get too much in on your first visit. Might wear yourselves out!"

"We've got it all planned," Tina said.

"Well, you two have a fun time, and hop back on the train sometime." He smiled and left them to their excited planning, walking on and remembering when he was just a kid full of dreams and excitement. He'd fulfilled his dream on the train, always meeting new people and having interesting conversations, but never being forced to get too intimate. On again and off again, none of them latched on for a lifetime.

Mr. Silver Hair was back in general seating, his briefcase in his lap. Franklin wondered what was in the case that was so important. Silver Hair and Leather Jacket were really having it out, not more than two hours ago. He'd expected a full-out fight, and was afraid he was going to have to break it up as best he could. Seemed it all had something to do with that briefcase. Franklin imagined the case to be filled with money or drugs or jewelry. After spotting them in the hall, he saw this silver-haired guy come to pick up the case in the lounge car moments later, but he hadn't spotted the tough guy again. The trouble maker was probably sneaking a cigarette in one of the bathrooms.

The two men and that silver briefcase made Franklin suspicious. Almost suspicious enough to call the cops. But the last time he'd let his suspicion get the best of him, the one who'd been taken to the station was him.

"What's a man like you doing getting involved with a little girl like that?" the cop had asked before escorting him to the cruiser and taking him to the station to "answer a few questions."

The fact was, he'd been looking out for the little girl. Hilary had been her name, and the girl had come to the lounge car to escape the grown man she traveled with.

"I hate him," Hilary had said.

"That's a pretty strong statement," Franklin had said to try and calm her. "Especially to say about your daddy."

"Daddy dearest, maybe," she'd responded. Then she proceeded to show the bruises on her twelve-year-old legs and arms. "He's so inappropriate." Franklin didn't know that they were the sort of bruises most kids her age wore as badges of play.

"Does he hurt you?" Franklin asked, getting more involved than he felt he should.

"Every chance the perv gets," she said with a snort. Franklin got the girl a soda and the two talked for more than an hour. She was a cute little girl, but seemed to know more than a girl her age should about certain things. Franklin began to doubt the guy was even her father, remembering that *Lolita* movie he'd seen years ago.

The father stormed into the lounge car just as the little girl was starting to fall asleep in the booth beside Franklin. "There you are, you little brat," he yelled. "What the hell's going on here?" he demanded of the conductor. Franklin didn't know what to say. Before they arrived at the train's destination, Franklin called the police, wanting to save the abused girl. But when the passenger's story checked out—he was her father and he was on his way to take Hilary back to her mother after a summer visit—the father told the police about finding her sleeping with the conductor.

Franklin liked people and he enjoyed helping them. But he'd learned the hard way that sometimes you had to leave people to their own problems and not get involved. He didn't know what was going to happen between Silver Hair and Leather Jacket. But it was none of his business, and he didn't want it to be. Aside from a little small talk, it was best to leave people alone.

The lounge was practically empty now—most people had returned to their seats or compartments, getting their things ready to leave the train. Fritz and Mary stood from their seats. Fritz had traded yesterday's beer for a morning cup of hot tea. The couple finished their drinks and walked toward the exit.

"You gonna hit that German restaurant today?" Franklin asked them.

"Probably tomorrow," Fritz said. "I expect our family will have lunch waiting for us at their place today."

"The Berghoff is just a couple blocks from the Art Institute," Franklin reminded them. "Adams and Quincy."

"Thanks," Mary and Fritz both said.

"Enjoy your visit," said Franklin. He watched them exit the lounge and wondered what it was like to be so effortlessly in love with someone for so many years. It was a marvel, really, two people joined together as one for the majority of a lifetime. To still have that much to say to one another. He'd never been able to last more than a few years. The only way to make a relationship last, he figured, was to keep everything on the surface.

Still in the lounge, Helen awoke in her seat, looking around in confusion. For a moment, panic overtook her, but she quickly realized where she was and regained her composure. She spotted Franklin, stood, and approached him. "Hi there," she said

"Good morning," he greeted.

"No offense, but it's going to be a relief to get off this train."

"So we still haven't won you over with our superior service?"

Helen frowned and smiled at the same time. "Nothing's ever going to make me like a train. Not even *your* sweet talk." She began to leave the lounge car for her seat, but turned back. "I'm looking forward to lunch. I'll look for you on the way off. We can share that cab."

"Now I don't want to be any trouble. Maybe I could just buy you a cup of coffee at the station."

"No trouble at all," Helen insisted. "I promised to give you a taste of homemade perogies and Polish potato vodka, and that's what I have my heart set on. You're not going to break an old woman's heart, now, are you?"

"Last thing in the world I'd want to do, ma'am," he said. He'd enjoyed talking with her on the train. Lunch would be nice.

The truth was, Franklin was more of a coffee break kind of guy. Getting a cup of coffee was the safest date you could make, because it could be cut off easily. If the conversation was flowing and living in the air around them, they could have a refill, a piece of pie, a pastry. If the conversation was really sparking, they could move on to lunch or dinner or a walk in the park. But if the conversation began to grow stilted or forced or awkward, a cup of coffee could be consumed quickly, and the date could be discarded. Not that this was a date by any stretch of the imagination. She was at least ten years his senior, barely capable of taking the train on her own. But the sort of conversational intercourse they were having was the most exciting type of intercourse there was, when you really got down to it. Conversation, when it was good, was as good as it got. But the escape route of a potentially short coffee break was vital to making it relaxed, keeping it unforced.

Long lunches were more likely to go bad. You never knew where lunch was going to go or how it was going to end. Especially a lunch at someone's home, a hostess preparing and serving the meal herself. When placed in a situation like that, a person had to expect to devote hours to one conversation. Idle chatter was obliged to evolve into something more, into meaningful, soul-deep discourse. That could be unpleasant.

The last time Franklin had gone to lunch with a passenger from the train, it hadn't ended so well. Unlike Helen, the woman had been nearly twenty years his junior, and he had an interest in getting to know her inside and out. Jamie was a hippie, and her conversational riffs seemed to ride on the waves of an ocean—which was where she kept saying she wanted to settle down and become a beach bum. Looking back, Franklin realized she reminded him a little of the tattoo lady on the train now, only from what Jamie told him, her tattoo was in a place only a lucky few were allowed to glimpse, not shouting from the open skin of her back for the world to see.

Jamie's dizzy conversation topics on the train should have been Franklin's first warning, and the drug paraphernalia in her messy studio apartment was the second hint that Jamie was not your typical nine-to-five working girl. She had a job as a waitress at a diner and used her tip money for drugs first, basic needs second. After a late lunch of hot dogs and canned beans, she lit up the main course.

Franklin hadn't gotten high since he was a kid—sometime in his twenties—and he didn't exactly remember it doing much for him then. But the prospect of Jamie doing something for him made the joint that much more enticing. He drew on the hand-rolled cigarette and held the smoke in his lungs.

What had started on the train and on the bus and in her apartment as a vivid and energetic conversation about everything from politics and music to UFOs and life in distant galaxies, began to slow as the remains of the joint smoldered in the fish-shaped ashtray on the floor before them. Usually so full of words, he couldn't think of anything witty to say. When he did think of something, he ran the phrase through his head backwards and forwards, examining it under a microscope until he knew he had it right. Then when he said it, the words came out all wrong. When Jamie laughed at something he said, he didn't know whether she was laughing at his clever witticisms, or at him for saying something so stupid. Everything he said seemed ridiculous and irrelevant. He became so paranoid, he wondered who he was, what he was all about. He remembered Latoya, his old girlfriend, who had first put the idea in his head—an idea that still haunted him to this day: "You gonna keep talking, you've gotta have something to say."

Sitting on the dirty plaid couch with Jamie, Franklin didn't know what to say. So under the influence of paranoia, he stopped talking altogether. He was silent when he slipped away from her, leaving her on the couch alone. He was quiet as he made his way out of her apartment, onto the bus, and back to the station. He didn't say another word until he was on the train and surrounded by a new round of passengers. By then, his paranoia had worn off, and he was hungry for small talk again.

Franklin spotted the tough guy, an unlit cigarette between his lips. He stood at the back of the car, his only carry-on a Zippo lighter, which he flicked and closed, flicked and closed, as though he were ready to jump off and smoke himself silly the moment the train came to a stop. "I'll have to ask you not to light that until you're off the train," Franklin said.

"Relax, old man," he said, although he must have been close to retirement age himself. "It's unlit. See?" He pointed to the cigarette in his mouth.

"I mean the lighter," Franklin said. "Please save your flame for outside."

"You're lucky we're almost there," the man said in a gravelly voice. "I've just about had my fill of you."

"Here we are," Franklin said as the train slowly began to pull into Union Station. He had no doubt this guy would meet up with Mr. Silver Hair outside and work out his frustration. He just hoped it didn't get too violent. In his opinion, most matters could be solved without violence or anger or hatred if people would only try to see from the other passenger's seat.

The train hadn't even come to a complete stop, but passengers were already out of their seats and crowding into the aisle, in a hurry to file off the train. There was a subtle, unspoken language being communicated here, the push and pull of people out of their places and into the aisle, away from the person behind them and into the person before them. Franklin would never pretend to know anything about science or theology, but he imagined the passengers who made up the soul of a train were much like the cells of a person. Every single one had a place in making up the whole, but every one was an individual. And when they all left this train, they would go off to form other matter. The soul bringing life to this train would never live again. Franklin peered out the window.

Outside, people waited for the doors to open and release their visitors. Some bored and impatient, others excited and already jumping and waving to the train as though the cars themselves were the ones being welcomed. Franklin liked that idea.

He spotted Murdock inside the train, a heavy suitcase in one hand and an oversized briefcase in the other. Both of them pulled him down, hunching him over. He'd readjusted the red tie around his neck and it looked too snug for comfort. Not that this miserable man had ever looked comfortable, even when he'd been drunk. It didn't seem to be the luggage alone that weighed him down.

The doors opened. Franklin bid farewell to the passengers as they got off the train. He smiled at the sight of people reuniting outside. The army kid was embracing his mother and father, the parents obviously proud of their son and relieved to see him back from harm's way. Hubert, the mentally impaired guy, and his Uncle Ned were having their own pleasant reunion with a charming woman, all hugs and smiles.

The woman with the tattoo stood in front of Franklin, waiting in line to get off the train, her expression troubled and relieved. "Have a nice day," Franklin said to her, not knowing what else to say.

The beautiful woman smiled. "The train's like Vegas, right?"

"How's that?"

"What happens on the train stays on the train?"

Franklin nodded. "If that's the way you'd like it, that's the way it can be." When she got off the train, she embraced a balding, middle-aged man. The man held her tightly, lovingly, and then began chattering away at her about his busy schedule and limited vacation window. For a moment, Franklin found himself longing for someone to be waiting for him at the station.

"You coming?" It was Helen, standing directly next to him.

"Oh," Franklin said, at a loss. "Well, I have to finish up on the train. It'll probably be another hour or two."

"I can wait," Helen said. "No reason to take two cabs when we can share one."

"Tell you what. I have some errands to run in the city," he said. "Maybe I should just take the address down and I'll come when I get done."

"You're not skipping out on me?" She took a pen and a used envelope from her purse and began writing.

"No siree," he assured her. "You've got my mouth watering for some perogies."

"The potato vodka's nothing to sneeze at either," Helen said, ripping off the back flap of the envelope and handing it to the conductor.

"Not to mention the savory conversation," he added with a wink. He took the flap of envelope, the glue on its back still a little sticky, and put it in the pocket of his Amtrak jacket.

"Does two or three sound good? It'll be a late lunch."

"Three sounds just fine," he said. "I can't wait." She took his hand to shake it and they embraced as though they were good friends saying goodbye forever.

"I still hate trains," she said as she stepped down to the platform.

"And I still love them," he called to her. He couldn't help but laugh as she waved him away like an annoying horsefly. She walked off, alone, but she looked happier than she had when he first met her.

Many of the passengers got off the train alone and had no one waiting for them at the station. Colin was one of them. The poet had a spring in his step, a notebook in one hand, a backpack over his shoulder, and that little yellow joke of a pencil, bite marks and all, resting behind his ear. He looked like a man on a mission with somewhere he needed to be. The guy was putting himself there, wherever it was.

As people continued to file off the train, Franklin thought back to other passengers who had gotten off early. That sad woman with the black purse and overcoat who had been sitting next to the poet. She looked like she had been in mourning as she got off the train in Cincinnati, clutching a page of parchment in her hand. He remembered noticing her outside the window, on the platform, as she put the folded paper in her purse and discovered a piece of the Amtrak stationery he'd given Colin. As far as Franklin had seen, Colin and this girl hadn't said more than two words to one another on the train. He doubted they'd ever see each other again as long as they lived. But the sight of her finding that poem in her purse made him smile.

Franklin could write a poem or two—probably a book or two—about the people he'd met on trains. All of them alike, but none of them the same. Each person with his own story, each story complicated and exciting, with as many ups and downs as any story you'd find on the TV or in a movie theater. More exciting than the life he'd led himself. But then, that's why he marveled at the passengers on the train. What better entertainment was there than the drama of those around him every day as he engaged in idle chatter? Maybe he'd never actually write them down—he knew he was better at talking than at writing—but he certainly had a book or two in his head about all these rides.

"Tell us a train story," his great nephews and nieces back home would ask him next time he visited. That would be Thanksgiving. He was thankful that he had his train stories to tell them.

Some stories were sadder than others. He remembered the nice old man with the calendar book, his nose stuck in it for the better part of his ride. Poor guy had suffered a heart attack right on the train. Christi had tried to save him with her CPR, but there was no saving the guy, being it was his time to go. Now that wasn't a sight you saw every day, even with all of the people filing on and off the train day in and day out. Franklin had noticed the wedding ring and imagined the guy's widow waiting back home, pictured her receiving the news. What things had been planned in that leather-bound book of his, left undone? He imagined getting the kind of news that this guy's wife must have woken to this morning—that the person you lived for no longer lived for you. Just another reason it was better to go through life surrounded by people to chat with and go home alone.

Franklin was practically alone now. The train was empty. There were other workers aboard, but none of the noise and energy that filled a train when the passengers were on board. The soul had dispossessed the train, just as it always did at the end of a line. Outside, he caught a glimpse of the silver briefcase, but the man carrying it moved so swiftly out of view that Franklin couldn't tell whether it was Silver Hair or Leather Jacket. Truth be told, it didn't matter much.

There was plenty to keep Franklin busy in Chicago, but he really had nothing to do. He imagined lunch with Helen, a pleasant afternoon of homemade cuisine. And better still, the lovely conversation they could continue. On the surface, they'd had a wonderful time chatting on the train. Now he had the opportunity to deepen their friendship, to have a meaningful relationship with someone whose company he enjoyed.

He'd learned long ago that surface relationships were the best kind. People put their best foot forward, in many cases, because the other foot had something wrong with it. A person put up a good front, presented the better side for a photograph. That's why everyone was a pleasure to know when you were just getting to know them. It was only when you scratched that shiny surface that you began to notice the tarnished innards. The deeper you dug, the more rot you would find there. The more you scrutinized, the more damage became apparent. Deep, meaningful conversation could be a drag. Small talk was almost always a pleasure.

Franklin took the envelope flap from his pocket and read the address in its blue ink script. The still-sticky glue clung to his finger. Lunch and conversation in the suburbs wasn't going to kill him, he told himself. Maybe he would take the plunge and go. He didn't want to disappoint her after putting her through all the work of making lunch from scratch. That last late lunch had been years ago, and it was with an aimless loser. Helen didn't seem like the type who would judge him or put him in an uncomfortable situation. She was a reasonable woman, someone he could really talk with.

The conductor had come to the end of another line. He put the paper back in the pocket of his blue uniform jacket. All of the passengers were long gone, nowhere to be seen. It was time to get off the train, remove his uniform, and get ready for a late lunch. But already, he found himself longing to put the uniform back on, wondering what sort of soul would greet him on the train back to Baltimore.

Acknowledgements

As an author, I may be the engineer. But it takes a good number of people to operate a passenger train. I would like to thank those who have helped me stay on track:

Christine Stewart, Nitin Jagdish, Lauren Beth Eisenberg, Gregg Wilhelm, Bathsheba Monk, Sherry Audette Morrow, Fernando Quijano III, Caryn Coyle, Nancy O. Greene, Paul Lagasse, Kristin Groulx, Manisha Gadia Bewtra, Rick Connor, Holly Morse-Ellington, Harvey Stanbrough, Barbara Friedland, Ally E. Peltier, Stephanie Senyak, Janet Knee, Mark Mirabello, Aaron Henkin, Sunshine O'Donnell, Rafael Alvarez, Judy Turner, Jen Michalski, Manzar, Susan Muaddi-Darraj, and Nataliya Goodman.

Thanks to the literary groups and organizations that have helped put steam into my writing: the CityLit Project, Maryland Writer's Association, Write Here Write Now, Creative Alliance, Writers' Center, Baltimore Book Festival, Lit & Art Reading Series, Watermark Gallery, and Baltimore's NPR station, WYPR (88.1 FM).

Finally, thank you to those who believed in this book enough to steer it toward publication: my agent, Doris S. Michaels; her creative staff, Delia Berrigan Fakis, Maranda L. Ward, Lianne Schmidt, and Georgia Mierswa; and my publisher, Dan Cafaro of Atticus Books.

About the Author

Eric D. Goodman has been writing fiction since he was in the third grade, when a story assignment turned him on to the craft more than a quarter century ago. He regularly reads his fiction on Baltimore's NPR station, WYPR, and at book festivals and literary events. His work has appeared in a number of publications, including *The Baltimore Review*, *The Pedestal Magazine*, *Writers Weekly*, *The Potomac*, *Grub Street*, *Scribble Magazine*, *The Arabesques Review*, *JMWW*, *Barrelhouse*, *Slow Trains*, and *New Lines from the Old Line State: An Anthology of Maryland Writers*. Eric is the author of *Flightless Goose*, a storybook for children (www.RunGoose.com). Learn more about Eric and his writing at www.Writeful.blogspot.com or www.EricDGoodman.com.